Augustus H.F. Duke of Grafton

Autobiography and Political Correspondence

From hitherto unpublished documents in the possession of his family

Augustus H.F. Duke of Grafton

Autobiography and Political Correspondence
From hitherto unpublished documents in the possession of his family

ISBN/EAN: 9783337011987

Printed in Europe, USA, Canada, Australia, Japan

Cover: Foto ©Raphael Reischuk / pixelio.de

More available books at **www.hansebooks.com**

AUTOBIOGRAPHY
AND POLITICAL CORRESPONDENCE

OF

AUGUSTUS HENRY
THIRD DUKE OF GRAFTON
K.G.

FROM HITHERTO UNPUBLISHED DOCUMENTS IN THE
POSSESSION OF HIS FAMILY

EDITED BY

SIR WILLIAM R. ANSON, Bart., D.C.L.
WARDEN OF ALL SOULS COLLEGE, OXFORD

WITH PORTRAITS

LONDON
JOHN MURRAY, ALBEMARLE STREET
1898

CONTENTS

CONTENTS

LIST OF ILLUSTRATIONS

INTRODUCTION

AUGUSTUS HENRY FITZ-ROY, the third Duke of Grafton, has received somewhat hard measure in the histories of the eighteenth century. The bitterest invective of Junius has assailed his character, and has thrown contempt on his political capacity: the solemn denunciations of the Whig historians have marked his departure, albeit in the company of Chatham and Camden, from the true Whig faith: his own record of his political career has been ransacked by writers of history and editors of memoirs, but of these scarcely one has been impelled by gratitude to present an adequate picture of the statesman who has contributed to their knowledge of his times.

At least the Duke should be allowed to tell his own story. It is the story of a man whom no biographer's enthusiasm could describe as a statesman of the first rank, and yet it sets before us a character not very common in the eighteenth century.

For the Duke of Grafton was a nobleman with a high sense of public duty, with a real desire to use his powers and his position for the good of his country, and very ready to recognize virtue and ability in others. If his instinct was not sufficiently sure, nor his confidence in himself strong enough to save him from grave error at critical points in his career, he was led astray by no sordid or self-seeking motive; he did not seek or retain office to satisfy personal ambition, or the greed of hungry followers.

For the work of that ill-assorted Ministry which was formed

by Chatham, and recruited, after the effacement of Chatham, from the least promising of the political groups, Grafton cannot escape responsibility. Perhaps his own narrative is his best defence. It is written, as it should be read, with perfect candour. The history of the reign of George III has too often been written in the style of a political pamphlet. The modern Liberal idealizes the Rockingham Whigs, the modern Tory takes a kindly view of the king's friends, and the narrative is coloured by the sympathies of the writer. But the men of that time are entitled to be judged on their merits, and their merits determined by the circumstances in which they lived, the difficulties with which they had to contend, and the spirit in which they met them.

I propose to preface the Autobiography with a short account of the Duke's career in relation to the history of parties during his time. As the Autobiography becomes fuller, my introductory statement will become slighter: nor is it necessary to follow the Duke beyond the period during which he took part in political life.

The Autobiography was commenced in October, 1804, and was resumed after a brief interval in February, 1805. It is worked up, in the more important parts, from journals or memoranda made at the time of the events recorded. There are, or were, three copies of this memoir: a 'foul copy,' a copy written out clean in thirteen books, examined and revised by the Duke, and a copy of this last, made for the use of the late Lord Carlingford, who at one time had contemplated an edition of the Autobiography. Of the 'foul copy' some books have been lost. This is unfortunate, for these contained notes indicating in one or two places the points at which the Duke began and ended the use of contemporary memoranda. The third copy, however, contains some notes by Lord Carlingford referring to these lost portions, and supplying to some extent the information which they contained.

The third Duke of Grafton was descended in the third generation from Henry Fitz-Roy, the son of Charles II, by Barbara Villiers, Duchess of Cleveland. This Henry, the first Duke, was a man of courage and ability beyond the other sons of Charles II. He served with credit, first in the navy and then in the army, and was killed at the siege of Cork in 1690. He was married, at the age of nine, to Isabella Bennett, daughter and heiress of the Earl of Arlington, who was then five years of age. Charles, the second Duke, born in 1683, was the only child of this marriage. He was Lord-Lieutenant of Ireland from 1721 to 1724, and held the office of Lord Chamberlain for the thirty years before his death in 1757. He was a great favourite with George II[1]. He married, in 1713, Lady Henrietta Somerset, daughter of the Marquis of Worcester, and by her had five sons, all of whom died in his lifetime, and all but one childless. The third son, Lord Augustus Fitz-Roy, was a naval officer of some promise, who died of fever, at Jamaica, in 1741. By his wife Elizabeth, daughter of Colonel Cosby, he left two sons, Augustus Henry, the third Duke, and Charles, afterwards Lord Southampton.

Augustus Henry was born on October 9, 1735. Of his early years there is little to say. He was educated at Hackney School and at Peterhouse College, Cambridge, and as a boy he received kindly attention from Mr. Pitt when staying at Stowe[2]. Evidently he was brought up in Whig circles, and instructed in Whig doctrines, basing his political studies on 'the sound system of Mr. Locke'; and evidently too he read seriously and with a view to political life.

At the end of his time at Cambridge he went the tour of Europe, and not long after his return he married Anne Liddell, the only child of Lord Ravensworth.

In the same year (1756) he was returned for the two boroughs of Bury St. Edmunds and Boroughbridge. He

---

[1] See Autobiography, p. 10.   [2] Ibid., p. 52.

chose to sit for the former, but his career in the House of
Commons was short. His grandfather died in May, 1757,
and he took his seat in the House of Lords.

At this very moment was being formed the great Coalition
Ministry which stilled political turmoil by the combination of
all sections of the Whig party, and by a series of unexampled
triumphs in the war with France. I will not dwell here on
the process by which this Ministry was formed [1], but it may
not be out of place to consider the political situation as it was
when George III came to the throne, and the action which he
took almost immediately upon his accession.

We read, not infrequently, in these Memoirs and elsewhere,
of the principles of the Revolution, and of the departure from
these principles of George III and the group of politicians
which formed itself around him. It is reasonable to ask what
these principles were, and in what respect George III departed
from them.

So far as the Constitution of the eighteenth century is
discoverable, it must be sought in the Bill of Rights and the
Act of Settlement, and the course or conventions of Government which grew up on the basis of these enactments.

The king is a part of the Constitution of the realm : if he
fail in his duty he has no divine immunity from resistance by
his injured subjects. He may not make, suspend, or dispense
with the law ; nor tamper with the interpretation of the law by
removing the judges at his pleasure ; nor raise money without
consent of Parliament. Speaking and voting in Parliament
should be free, not merely from direct interference by king or
minister, but from the more subtle influence which might be
exercised by the presence of placemen or pensioners in the
House of Commons. When to all this was added the
control assumed by the Commons over the grant of supplies,
and the maintenance of a standing army, it is plain that the

[1] See Autobiography, pp. 8, 9.

king and his ministers were constrained to work in harmony with the House of Commons, and that the king's choice of ministers must be determined by the willingness of the House of Commons to support them.

In the main these rules and principles were observed, but they were marred in their operation by a serious flaw. While every care had been taken to make the king's ministers responsible to the House of Commons, no provision had been made for securing that the members of that House should be responsible to any one but to themselves, or to the proprietors of the boroughs which they professed to represent. The counties excepted, the constitue cies were for the most part small, listless, or subject to some influence which made their choice of members no real expression of their political opinion.

The same sort of influence affected their representatives. The statesmen of the reign of William and Anne had diminished, but not very seriously, the number of places held of the Crown which were compatible with a seat in the House of Commons. Their successors supplemented these sources of influence by a system of pecuniary bribes.

The principles of the Revolution did not involve the withdrawal of the king from all control over the policy of the country. The personal inclinations of William and Anne had weight in the choice of ministers, and the conduct of business: but the Hanoverian kings allowed these matters to slip out of their grasp, and when once a system of Parliamentary influence had grown up, and the distribution of places and bribes had passed into the hands of ministers, it was not easy for a king who knew little of the Constitution or the language of his subjects to obtain a control of machinery which every one else was interested in keeping out of sight.

Thus the minister who knew the processes of corruption held strings by which he could make the House of Commons dance to any tune he pleased ; while the man who despised or neglected the arts of Parliamentary management might, like Pitt, be the idol of the nation, or, like Carteret, stand first in the regard of the king, but he could not command a majority in the House of Commons, and without this his tenure of office would be transient.

The statesmen of the Revolution were impressed, and we cannot blame them for it, with the paramount necessity for controlling the power of the Crown. They did not realize that a House of Commons which professed to represent the people might be so manipulated as to become subservient to the objects of a king or an oligarchy. There is less excuse for the Whig opposition to George III, to whom politics were merely a contest for power between themselves and the Crown, and who never saw that to obtain a sure footing they must rest their power upon public approval, indicated by the votes of a House of Commons which had something of a representative character. Even under the conditions of the eighteenth century the nation might be so vehemently stirred by indignation against one minister, or admiration for another, as to produce some effect on political combinations. Ill represented as it was, an angry people could not be gainsaid. Thus Walpole fell in 1741 and Newcastle in 1756, and thus was Pitt called to office in 1756 and 1757.

The strength of the Coalition Government of Pitt and Newcastle lay in this; that Newcastle, awed by the popularity of Pitt, placed at the disposal of the Ministry all his resources for gaining and keeping a majority. Pitt, in quiet times, was helpless without Newcastle: Newcastle, in times of national anxiety, could not sleep secure unless shielded by the character and reputation of Pitt.

Such was the combination when Grafton entered the House of Lords, and its success left little opening for a young peer to take part in debate. Parliament met to vote congratulations and subsidies ; and Grafton, in 1761, went abroad for his wife's health, and did not return to England for more than a year.

George III had succeeded his grandfather before Grafton left England, but the changes which thereupon ensued had not then become apparent. The new king was young and popular. His father, who died in 1751, left the impression of a character at once frivolous and unamiable ; but his mother, the Princess of Wales, a clever woman with the autocratic notions of German royalty, trained her son, in a narrow practical way, to try to govern as well as to reign. In these instructions she was seconded by Lord Bute, who had served in the household of Frederick Prince of Wales and had been recalled to act as Groom of the Stole when an establishment was formed for the young prince in 1757.

Bute was unused to Parliamentary or public life, but he seems to have known what the young king wanted, and to have been able to obtain it for him.

The Autobiography[1] mentions three points in which the new king departed, in Grafton's opinion, from sound and constitutional policy :—in the exclusion of the Whig families ; in the assumption of personal control in the choice and support of his ministers ; and in his want of loyalty to those who were his ministers for the time being.

The first two of these charges mean no more than this, that the king intended to be his own master, and was determined that if Parliament was to be corrupted—and he had no objection to its corruption—it should be corrupted to serve his purposes, and not those of his ministers. His political morality was the morality of the day.

The third charge goes deeper. It was an unamiable as well as an unconstitutional habit of George III, to regard every minister as a mere instrument, not only to be used or

[1] pp. 13, 14.

cast aside at pleasure, but to be used while he was in the act of negotiating with others, or intriguing with the little group of his personal adherents, the 'king's friends,' to supplant the men whom he was treating with apparent confidence and goodwill.

When we consider that George III managed his Parliaments, chose his ministers, and never allowed an independent minister to feel secure in his employment, or a subservient minister to leave office if he could possibly be retained, we may realize what risks the country ran under the rule of this king. For the capacity of George III did not extend beyond the arts of obtaining power ; our history can hardly produce a sovereign less capable of governing an empire.

George III would have found it hard to put his policy into action, to break up the Whig party, and to seize the strings of Parliamentary management, without the aid of a minister who was entirely in his confidence. Such a minister was Bute. Within less than a week from the death of George II he was made a member of the Privy Council and of the Cabinet, and he very shortly afterwards became Secretary of State in the place of Lord Holdernesse. Thus situated he could interfere in many matters of detail in a way that would have been impossible for the king.

His first object was to bring about a peace ; for it was impossible to break up and humiliate a party which was in the midst of conducting a glorious and successful war. Events favoured him. Pitt had commenced negotiations for peace with France, when he became aware of the projected alliance between France and Spain. Anxious to strike the first blow, he urged upon his colleagues an immediate declaration of war with Spain. With the exception of Temple, his colleagues declined to support him, and, with Temple, he retired from office in October, 1761. The sequel justified his policy. War with Spain broke out very shortly, and was prosecuted with such success that our victories seemed likely to postpone for a time the possibility of peace.

Newcastle would have done well to resign with Pitt. He now found himself subjected to constant slights, inflicted with the obvious intention of driving him from office. Matters came to an issue over the subsidy hitherto paid annually to the king of Prussia during the war. Newcastle found that the king and Bute were determined against the continuance of this subsidy, and he resigned in May, 1762, not without undignified lamentations.

Bute took his place as First Lord of the Treasury, and became in name and substance Prime Minister, so far as we may apply a term with a recognized modern meaning to the leading spirit in an eighteenth century Administration.

As Grafton passed through Paris on his way home [1], he found that the Duke of Bedford was expected there, and that the Duc de Nivernois was starting thence, to negotiate for peace ; before the autumn was far advanced the preliminaries were signed. On the merits of the Peace of Paris historians have long ago pronounced, or provided materials for pronouncing. The war was costly ; the peace was not unwelcome, and, such as it was, it was practically assured when Grafton returned to England. He came at a stirring time, and his political career may now be said to commence.

Political feeling was running high as the new scheme of government began to assume a clear outline. The resignation of Pitt deprived the old *régime* of popularity ; the removal of Newcastle placed the machinery of party management in the hands of the king's friends. But it was necessary to find some one who would work this machinery boldly and without scruple. When Bute stepped into Newcastle's place as First Lord of the Treasury, George Grenville succeeded Bute as Secretary of State. He was also what we now call the

[1] Autobiography, p. 19.

'Leader,' but what in those days was called the '*Manager*[1]' of the House of Commons. He was now required to give place to Fox, who entered the Cabinet with no higher office than the lucrative post, which he had enjoyed since 1757, of Paymaster of the Forces. Under these circumstances Fox could not lead the House when a Secretary of State was present, so Grenville was bidden, much to his annoyance, to change places with Lord Halifax, and to become First Lord of the Admiralty.

Fox now led the House: the machine of corruption was set going, and the king was in a position to show the Whig families that he meant to be master. His treatment of the Duke of Devonshire is described in the Autobiography[2]; and thus was war openly declared against the great Whig connexion. But Fox and the secret service money had done their work efficiently, and the preliminaries of the peace were approved in both Houses.

In the House of Lords Grafton made his first appearance as a speaker ; he says of his speech that it was too declamatory, but it created a very favourable impression. Nevertheless, the opponents of the peace did not venture to divide the House. The king had triumphed, and the next step was to make the vanquished realize the consequences of defeat. Grafton, Newcastle and Rockingham were removed from the Lieutenancies of their respective counties. The Duke of Devonshire only escaped a similar affront by a timely resignation. Then followed a proscription of the friends of the late ministers. ' I believe,' said Rigby, 'that there will be a general *déroute*, from the Duke of Grafton's Lieutenancy of Suffolk to the underlings of the Custom House[3].'

An organized Opposition was now formed, and among the Whig peers of whom it consisted, Grafton held a promi-

---

[1] *Walpole, Letters,* iv. 36.   [2] p. 21.
[3] *Bedford Correspondence,* iii. 171.

nent place. From the first he took the view which guided his policy and conduct for some years to come, that no Ministry could be strong or lasting without Pitt. When therefore the Opposition tried to secure the leadership of Pitt, Grafton was sent to Hayes to offer any terms which Pitt might be pleased to accept[1]. But these overtures were fruitless; the Opposition remained a group of great nobles and landowners, respectable in character, moderate in abilities, and helpless in their attempts to subvert the new system of government.

The Ministry too was weak, especially in the Commons. Fox had done his work and claimed his peerage; Grenville was tedious and pedantic; Sir Francis Dashwood was a singularly incompetent Chancellor of the Exchequer. Yet Bute thought that his following might hold its own, and would be stronger if it were relieved from the load of unpopularity which attached to his name. He resigned early in April, 1763.

There is no need to look far for an explanation of the retirement of Bute. He had neither interest nor experience in the business of administration; his nationality and his supposed relations with the Princess of Wales made him exceedingly unpopular; and the objects for which he had entered upon office were attained.

From some points of view, Bute's short political career was one of remarkable success. He found the Whig families in full possession of political power, and, with the aid of Pitt, waging a war of unexampled popularity and triumph. In little more than two years the Whig leaders were dissociated from Pitt, the war on which their popularity rested was at an end, and not only were they driven from place and power, but the proscription of January, 1763, had taught the crowd

---

[1] *Bedford Correspondence*, iii. 186.

of office-seekers that favour must be sought elsewhere than from Newcastle and his friends.

The adversaries of Bute, no doubt, played into his hands ; the imperious courage of George III, and the unscrupulous management of Fox, were essential elements in the success of the new policy. But in truth the Whig system of government had no sure foundation ; otherwise the long domination of the Whig families would hardly have collapsed before a young king new to affairs, a bold party-manager, and a pompous amateur, like Bute, who had neither eloquence, experience, nor business capacity.

Bute had made arrangements for his successors in office without much reference to their personal wishes. Grenville became First Lord of the Treasury, with Egremont and Halifax as Secretaries of State. Bute would have preferred Shelburne to Halifax, but in this instance alone was Grenville allowed to have a voice in the formation of the Ministry of which he was the nominal head [1]. Bedford who had returned from Paris was invited to become President of the Council, but he treated the whole arrangement as ephemeral and suggested a resort to such of the Whig Opposition as were least disagreeable to the king, mentioning Grafton among others [2]. Bute was not prepared to ask the Whigs to return to the place from which he had so lately ousted them, and so the Ministry of George Grenville started on its ill-starred career.

Inasmuch as the most important, at any rate the most conspicuous, part of Grafton's career was determined by the influence exercised over him by Pitt, it is well to consider for a moment the position of Pitt in relation to the political groups of this period.

All dealings with Pitt were at this time beset by three serious difficulties. The first of these was his health, which was never good, and which now, after the strain of several

[1] *Grenville Papers*, ii. 32-39.   [2] *Bedford Correspondence*, iii. 228.

anxious years of office, made him really unfit for continuous active work. The second was his temperament. Pitt no doubt possessed genius, but genius is not always the best companion for every-day life. For great occasions he was the greatest of living Englishmen; for ordinary business he was too often pompous, affected, intractable[1]. The third was his relationship to Temple and the Grenville family. Of all the political cliques of the time the Grenvilles, though not the least capable, are certainly the least attractive; the pretentious vanity of Temple, and his determination to resist any political combination which did not give to himself and his family the importance which he conceived them to deserve, make one deplore that at a critical period in the history of the country Pitt allowed his conduct to be influenced by this mischievous connexion.

To the recognized Whig leaders Pitt was a disturbing element in party combinations. To these men such combinations were an end in themselves: a Ministry was a success if an adequate number of persons, whom it was important to satisfy, were satisfied with the offices conferred upon them, and the business of the country was somehow carried on. To Pitt a Ministry was an instrument for carrying into effect a great imperial policy, for furthering colonial enterprise, and for ensuring to us the command of the sea. So long as these ends were served he did not care how the various offices were distributed, or whether the friends of Newcastle or of Bedford were most gratified by the distribution.

The attitude of the older Whigs towards Pitt was not that of Grafton, nor, after the first years of his public life, of Shelburne. Grafton in particular was convinced that no

---

[1] The two essays of Macaulay on Pitt seem to give an admirably just portrait of the man, well balanced between the fustian of Carlyle and the ill-natured reminiscences of Shelburne.

Ministry could be of service to the country unless Pitt were at its head. His Autobiography tells us how strenuous and unremitting were his efforts from the beginning of 1763 to induce Pitt once more to take the lead. These efforts culminated in his unwilling acceptance, in 1766, of an office to which he felt himself unequal—an office which he only accepted because Pitt told him that otherwise his projected Ministry would fall to the ground [1].

To George III, and to Bute, Pitt was invaluable as a solvent of party combinations. In the course of the war a coldness had arisen between Bute and Pitt, but it was always possible for the king, with or without the recommendation of Bute, to unsettle any Ministry by opening negotiations with Pitt.

Grafton then, though a member of the Whig Opposition, differed from the followers of Newcastle, of Bedford, and of Rockingham in this that he was prepared to waive all personal considerations which might stand in the way of Pitt's return to power. He was at this time in frequent communication with Pitt, and realized sooner than others—sooner than Pitt himself—what an obstacle the impracticable disposition of Temple might prove to the formation of a strong Ministry.

On the first occasion that recourse was had to Pitt the failure of the negotiations was not due to Temple. Grenville had not been in office many months when Egremont, one of the Secretaries of State, died suddenly. Bute, without consulting Grenville, advised the king to send for Pitt. On August 27, 1763 (a Saturday), Pitt had a long interview with the king, and stated the conditions under which he thought a strong Ministry might be formed. It was to include the Whig leaders, and, of the younger men, Grafton was to have a place in the Cabinet. The interview was to be resumed on the Monday, but meantime Bute seems to have taken

[1] Autobiography, p. 90.

alarm. In the course of Sunday he advised the king to withdraw from the negotiation, and simultaneously advised Pitt to moderate his terms. This Pitt was not prepared to do, and on the Monday the scheme broke down [1].

But the negotiation had two results. It exasperated Grenville against Bute, who had certainly treated the Ministry as puppets to be removed at his pleasure. And it procured for Grenville unexpected support. For the king talked freely of his conversation with Pitt [2], and as the narrative grew in repetition those whom Pitt had proposed to exclude were greatly irritated. Among them was Bedford, whom Pitt considered to be responsible for the Peace of Paris, and therefore proscribed. Bedford, in consequence, with his following, joined Grenville, and with this accession of strength the Ministry held on.

The measures of the Grenville Ministry do not specially concern us here. During the remainder of their term of office Grafton was, as he tells us in the Autobiography, negligent of his political duties.

It was at this time that he formed the connexion which Junius has made historical. Nancy Parsons has been immortalized by Gainsborough, and the refined beauty of her face furnishes the only excuse that can be offered for the conduct which at once involved Grafton in domestic troubles and lowered his public character. He was separated from his wife in December, 1764. They parted on terms of mutual civility, but as their friends feared at the time, they were never reconciled. In 1769 they were divorced, and each married again.

The Autobiography from the conclusion of the Peace in

---

[1] *Grenville Papers*, ii. 95, 96.

[2] This practice of George III is mentioned more than once in the memoirs of the time. He would induce public men to talk freely of their colleagues or rivals, and would then betray their confidence for his own ends.

1763, to the negotiations which preceded the fall of the Grenville Ministry, is slight and in some places not free from confusion, but from the middle of May, 1765, it is evidently taken from contemporary memoranda. In the spring of 1765 the Grenville Ministry managed at once to offend the king, and to lower themselves in public esteem by their mismanagement of the Regency Bill. Grenville himself, in his dealings with the king, was dull, plain-spoken, and intolerably lengthy, and George determined to have recourse to Pitt. The Duke of Cumberland was asked to intervene, and though broken in health and retired from public life he did his best to help his nephew. He sent Lord Albemarle to see Pitt, and summoned Temple and Grafton to London. Pitt's language was obscure, though not altogether discouraging: but when Temple appeared on the scene difficulties at once arose. Lord Northumberland had been suggested as First Lord of the Treasury, and Northumberland was Bute's son-in-law. This objection, though not made at the time, was dwelt upon afterwards. In vain Albemarle went twice to Hayes, and Cumberland once. Pitt, at the instance of Temple, refused to come forward. The true ground of Temple's conduct appeared a little later: he had become reconciled to his brother George, and formed visions of a Ministry in which the Grenville family should be supreme.

For a moment the ministers triumphed, but they pushed their success too far; they endeavoured to put slights not only upon Bute and his friends but upon the Duke of Cumberland, and they drove the king to despair. In June a second application was made to Pitt. This time Pitt, as well as the king, seemed to be in earnest. Temple was to be First Lord of the Treasury, Grafton and Pitt Secretaries of State. Again did Temple interpose, and refuse to take the place assigned to him, or any other. Pitt sorrowfully withdrew, and thus ended a fair prospect of a strong Ministry.

The king asked the Duke of Cumberland to find him a Ministry of some sort, and the Duke turned to the Whig leaders. They met, and agreed to take office. Rockingham became First Lord of the Treasury, Grafton and Conway Secretaries of State, Newcastle Privy Seal, with the church patronage thrown in, Northington remained Chancellor, and Chief Justice Pratt, the life-long friend of Grafton, became a peer, with the title of Lord Camden.

We must give to Lord Rockingham and his followers all the credit that is due to public spirit and good intentions; but it must be admitted that they were fortunate in securing Burke as a dependant, and, in their later career, Fox as an ally. Still more fortunate have they been in their literary history, since Macaulay has treated them as the direct ancestors of the Whigs of 1832. Most fortunate of all in the incapacity of the ministers, or the incoherence of the Ministries, to whom they found themselves opposed between 1765 and 1783.

So far as they could be said to have a policy when they entered office, their policy was to recover for the Whig families the position which they had lost in 1762. Here Grafton stood apart from his colleagues, and it is here that he has come under the censure of the Whig historians. He did not regard the supremacy of the Whig families as an end in itself. In fact, he ventured to think that Pitt was more essential to the service of the country than Rockingham, with all the Cavendishes at his back. This difference of opinion made itself felt later on.

The Ministry was perfectly frank in the admission of its helplessness. For the first few weeks of its existence the meetings of the Cabinet Council were attended, with the king's approbation, by the Duke of Cumberland, and it is clear from the *Rockingham Memoirs* that the Duke's advice was asked on all questions of importance. But the Duke died early in October, and the ministers were left to their own resources.

Meanwhile, the American policy of George Grenville had borne fruit in disturbance and disaffection throughout the New England colonies and Virginia, and the ministers knew not whether to propose repressive or conciliatory measures. They sent Mr. T. Townshend to consult Pitt, but Pitt would give no counsel. The Session opened before Christmas, but no serious discussion took place until the House reassembled after the Christmas recess, when a debate ensued on the address in answer to a second speech from the throne. Then Pitt declared for the repeal of the Stamp Act, and the policy of the Ministry was determined.

Against the will of the king, and in spite of the open hostility of the king's friends, the Ministry carried the repeal of the Stamp Act. The accompanying Act, which declared the right of Parliament to tax the colonies, if it so pleased, did not satisfy the king, while it discounted in great measure the attempt to conciliate the colonists.

On this Declaratory Act Pitt and the Ministry were at variance. Yet a serious effort was made, with the king's sanction, so soon as ministers had announced their American policy, to secure the accession of Pitt. Pitt and Temple now differed widely on the American question, and from Grafton's account of the negotiations[1], it would seem that Pitt might have been induced to join the Ministry but for the determination of Rockingham to retain the Treasury. Later, in February, Rockingham sent messages to Pitt, through Shelburne[2], and through Nuthall[3], the Solicitor to the Treasury, intimating a willingness to accept him as leader, but always with a view to 'preventing the breaking up of the present Administration.' Pitt replied, very reasonably, that he

---

[1] Autobiography, p. 65; *Rockingham Memoirs*, i. 312.

[2] *Chatham Correspondence*, iii. 7.

[3] *Ibid.* ii. 399.

could only confer on such a subject with His Majesty's commands.

Thus all attempts to obtain the help of Pitt failed, and Grafton discovered that, whereas he desired Pitt to enter the Ministry as a leader, Rockingham wanted the assistance of Pitt as an ally to support the Whig families against the king. At the end of April Grafton resigned. It was not easy to find a successor, but eventually the Duke of Richmond took the seals, and the Ministry struggled on until July, when Northington, seeing that his colleagues were helpless and doomed, brought matters to an issue by tendering his resignation. Rockingham did not realize his own weakness, and was beginning to look about for a new Chancellor, when he and his colleagues were informed, on July 9, that Pitt had been sent for, and that their services were no longer required.

Now comes the most important part of Grafton's career. Pitt came to town on July 11, 1766, and received full powers from the king to form a Ministry. He at once addressed himself to Conway, whom he asked to retain the seals of Secretary of State, and to lead the House of Commons, a request ominous of the part which he intended to play in his Ministry. Temple was summoned as a matter of course. It is difficult to see how Temple, associated as he now was with his brother George, and differing from Pitt on the vital question of our American policy, could possibly have acted with Pitt or with Pitt's allies. But the brothers-in-law quarrelled, not on the policy to be adopted, but on the distribution of patronage and power. Temple proposed to deal with Pitt as an equal, Pitt made it clear to Temple that he might, if he pleased, be First Lord of the Treasury, but that was all[1].

Then Pitt sent for Grafton, who, after much misgiving, accepted the post which Temple had rejected, and, unhappily

---

[1] It is curious that the Autobiography says nothing of the quarrel between Pitt and Temple, though there is an allusion to it in a letter from Camden.

for the Empire, prevailed on Pitt to appoint Charles Townshend as his Chancellor of the Exchequer. For a time the
process of forming a Ministry went on smoothly. Pitt was
resolved to depend on no group or family connexion. He
brought into office only four followers of his own, Grafton,
Shelburne, Camden, and Bristol. Of these the first two were,
as his correspondence shows, devoted lieutenants, and Camden
was a creditable and popular Chancellor. There was no
desire to displace the main body of the former Ministry, but
Rockingham and his following chose to consider themselves
aggrieved by their supersession. Rockingham treated Pitt
with marked rudeness[1]. Dowdeswell declined the place
which was offered to him. Egmont, Lord John Cavendish
and some others resigned. Then Pitt, to the dismay of his
colleagues, became Earl of Chatham, and lost thereby the
devotion of his countrymen, as well as the control of the
House of Commons.

Two great sources of weakness soon became apparent in
the Ministry.

It was extraordinarily deficient for purposes of management and debate in the House of Commons. Conway, who led
the House, was honourable and amiable, a hero of romance
on the battle-field, in the political arena timid and vacillating,
and yet opinionated. But the virtuous incapacity of Conway
was wisdom itself compared to the Puck-like vagaries of the
Chancellor of the Exchequer. To Charles Townshend the
emoluments of office were the only serious part of politics.
Where these were concerned he was anxious and oppressed:
apart from these, such matters as the character of his colleagues, the finances of the kingdom, the loyalty of our
colonial dependencies, were trifles with which he dealt more
as though he were an actor in a charade than a statesman
responsible for the well-being of an empire.

[1] See Autobiography, 95, and note.

But a more serious source of weakness was the difficulty which Pitt experienced in dealing with men and attending to the details necessary for making and working a Ministry. As a great war minister he had been a dictator in large matters of policy. The business of management for everyday purposes of government had been taken off his hands. In those days too men of experience were about him : Newcastle and Hardwicke were 'old Parliamentary hands,' and knew how the necessary jobs should be done : Legge was an efficient and tried financier. Now he had to deal with a set of recruits, for Grafton and Shelburne, though capable and devoted to their leader, had little experience, nor was Camden of much account in politics. Grafton tells us that Pitt was in the habit of forming grandiose designs, and expecting that every one would assist him to carry them out, but he did not take the trouble to conciliate those whom he relied upon to help him. Thus he was led into a series of blunders, not the least of which was the alienation of such of the Rockingham Whigs as had retained office under him. Even Conway, the leader of the Commons, received little of his confidence, and was with difficulty induced to continue at his post.

After the Autumn Session of 1766 Chatham returned to Bath, and from that time forth he ceased to take any part in the affairs of his Ministry. The disastrous malady which befell him must leave it for ever doubtful whether he could have succeeded, by the force of his genius and the splendour of his name, in controlling the diverse elements of which his Ministry was compacted.

The Autobiography tells in simple language the story of Chatham's deserted followers. In the first months of 1767 king and ministers continued to urge the Prime Minister to communicate, in some form or other, some hints for the guidance of his colleagues. The answers were all of the same tenour. Chatham could offer neither advice nor consolation. The painful interview which Grafton obtained after much solicitation, at the end of May, resulted only in entreaties to him to retain office, and suggestions that aid might be sought from the Duke of Bedford and his following.

In June the Ministry seemed on the point of breaking up. Conway, ill-suited to his office, and distracted between Horace Walpole, who wanted him to hold on, and the Cavendishes, who pressed him to resign, had informed the king that he must retire. Northington's health was breaking. Townshend asked for some evidence of the stability of the Ministry, and Grafton could furnish none [1].

In June negotiations were commenced with the Rockingham party, and Rockingham endeavoured to form a junction of all the Whig families. Bedford and his following were prepared to come into the arrangement, but they had renewed their connexion with Temple and George Grenville, and this proved fatal to the scheme of reunion. The Bedford and Rockingham parties held a great meeting at the house of the Duke of Newcastle on July 20, where Bedford spoke for the Grenvilles, who were absent.

Bedford, on behalf of the Grenvilles, called on Rockingham for a declaration of his American policy. This Rockingham denounced as 'a trap [2].' Then Bedford claimed the leadership of the House of Commons for Grenville; Rockingham desired to retain Conway. So the meeting broke up without issue.

Rockingham and Bedford met on the following day, but the question of the leadership again proved fatal. Bedford offered

---

[1] The king to Chatham (*Chatham Correspondence*, iii. 275).

[2] *Bedford Correspondence*, iii. 383, 384; *Rockingham Memoirs*, ii. 51. Considering the importance of the American question at this time, Rock-ingham's objection seems absurd, but he was evidently, for all his honesty, a very dull man, with no conception of a general policy beyond the restoration of the Whig families as a check on royal power.

to accept Dowdeswell as leader, but Rockingham, who was in communication with the king through the agency of Grafton and Conway, must have felt that he could hardly displace both; that Conway might resent the substitution of Dowdeswell for himself, and that, if the Grenvilles and Bedford held together and the union of the Whig families was to be effected, George Grenville must inevitably lead the House. On this point the negotiation failed.

Then Charles Townshend died, and Lord North, succeeding to his place, displayed an unexpected power of managing the House of Commons, and an unhappy readiness to adapt his opinions to those of the king. At the end of the year arrangements were concluded with the Bedford party, and though the Duke took no office, his followers were admitted to places. No more unfortunate alliance could have been made. The residue of Chatham's Ministry had, at any rate, some notion of the mode in which Chatham had proposed to treat Indian, American, and Irish affairs: the Rockingham party, incompetent as they were, desired honestly to govern well; the Grenvilles had a definite, though probably a mistaken policy of colonial government; but the followers of Bedford had no political opinions except that office was desirable, and together with North, they were ready to do as the king wished. Possibly this very indeterminateness of political opinion may have commended them to Chatham, who liked his following to be servants or disciples. To Grafton, whose fault was infirmity of purpose, the admission of these men to office brought the failure and the discredit which is associated, and rightly, with what was henceforth the Grafton Ministry.

The rest of the story of that Ministry is told in the Autobiography; there is no need to follow in detail the history of the gradual strengthening of royal power and influence, which for the next fifteen years was to prove so fruitful in disaster to the country.

The Ministry is known mainly by the incidents of the Middlesex election, by the taxation of the American colonies, and by the invectives of Junius.

The affair of the Middlesex election was allowed by the weakness of the Ministry and the rancorous obstinacy of the king to grow, from a matter which merely concerned the privileges of the House of Commons, into a serious attack on electoral rights. The vacillations of Camden afford some excuse for Grafton, so far as the legal aspect of the case is concerned. But he ought to have seen that when members or supporters of the Ministry moved the resolutions by which Wilkes was expelled and the votes of the Middlesex electors set aside, the Ministry itself became responsible for the action of the House of Commons.

The account given by Grafton of the way in which he was outvoted on the question of the duties imposed on the colonies, reads strangely at the present day. But the conception of a Prime Minister, as we understand the term, is barely a hundred years old, and may be said to date from the time of the younger Pitt. It is clear that Grafton never regarded himself as Prime Minister in the sense that he was responsible for the policy of the Ministry. He held the most important office in the Government, one which was supposed to carry with it the first place in the king's confidence, and the responsibility for seeing that there was a Ministry of some sort to carry on the business of the country: but this was all. The idea of resigning because he was outvoted in his own Cabinet on a question to which he attached great importance, does not seem to have occurred to him. And indeed it is rare, throughout the last century, that a minister should resign because he could not agree with his colleagues on a definite political issue. Ministers waited to be turned out, or resigned from personal reasons because their friends were turned out ; or because, in the language of the time, they 'found the ground insecure.' The retirement of Pitt and Temple in 1761, on the question of the Spanish war, stands out as a rare instance of a political opinion held strongly enough to compensate for the loss of office. The American war produced a few such resignations, Grafton's (in 1775) among the number; but in 1769 precedents would have been hard to find.

It is remarkable that, throughout the Autobiography, no allusion is made to the letters of Junius: indeed, from one end to another of the memoir there is not an ill-natured word said of any contemporary. Whether this was due to a natural careless magnanimity of temper which led Grafton to disregard all personal attacks, or whether to the deep religious feeling which came over him during the last twenty-five years of his life; it is in keeping with his strange silence concerning the savage attacks of the unknown writer.

It is now commonly assumed that Sir Philip Francis, who was at this time a clerk in the War Office, was the author of the letters. Macaulay was sure of it, for five reasons. Sir George Trevelyan is sure of it, probably because Macaulay was sure. A biography of Francis has been composed by Messrs. Parkes and Merivale, of which the first volume is mainly composed of assumptions and of arguments founded on assumptions, to the effect that Francis wrote the letters of Junius and a good deal else besides. The handwriting of Francis has been compared with that of the letters, and Francis has been convicted on the evidence of experts.

And yet it is impossible to read these letters and not to feel that they suggest an intimacy with the higher walks of political life, and a knowledge of the persons concerned, which could hardly have been acquired or affected by a clerk in the War Office, living, as Francis evidently lived, in commonplace if not vulgar surroundings. Nor does anything in the career of Francis explain the savage ferocity of the attacks made by Junius upon the Dukes of Grafton and Bedford.

The extraordinary superficial resemblance between the delicate and characteristic handwriting of Lady Temple and that of the Junian MSS. may perhaps be disregarded in deference to the evidence of experts[1]. But if, besides the letters of Junius, the mass of pre-Junian controversial literature is considered, including the *Candor* and *Anti Sejanus* papers, attributed by Messrs. Parkes and Merivale to Junius and therefore to Francis, it will be observed that there is a curious correspondence between the tone taken towards Pitt, both before and after his acceptance of a peerage, and the varying relations of Temple to his distinguished brother-in-law.

I will not disturb the ashes of the Junius controversy except to express a conviction that whatever part Francis may have played in the composition of these letters, Temple directed their policy, supplied much of their information, and may conceivably have polished their invective. And it is the invective and nothing else that has made the letters famous. Of political wisdom there is little, if any; where the writer is maintaining a political opinion or a constitutional right, he seldom rises above the level of a clever advocate; but when character is to be assailed, the polish of his weapon shines forth and its cruel edge; and the sentences rise to the splendour of rhythm and balance, which have made Junius an English classic. And thus Grafton appears to all time as depicted in the tremendous apostrophe: ' Sullen and severe without religion, profligate without gaiety, you may live like Charles II, without being an amiable companion, and for aught I know may die as his father did, without the reputation of a martyr.'

If we suppose that Temple was the guiding spirit of Junius, the excessive animosity to Grafton is explained. Grafton,

---

[1] *The handwriting of Junius professionally investigated.* By W. C. Chabot. With preface and collateral evidence. By the Hon. E. Twisleton.

and Conway whom Grafton brought into Parliament, had been the mainstay of the weak Rockingham Ministry which ousted George Grenville at the moment that Temple had become reconciled to his brother. When the Rockingham Ministry collapsed, and Pitt was requested to form a Ministry, he invited Temple to become First Lord of the Treasury. Temple thinking that Pitt, as on previous occasions, would be unable to do without him, demanded a larger share in the arrangement of offices than Pitt was willing to grant. Pitt broke with Temple and turned to Grafton. When Grafton hesitated, Pitt said that if the Duke failed him his Ministry was at an end: the acceptance of Grafton made it possible for Pitt to take office without Temple.

Bedford, too, had been closely associated with Temple in the negotiations for a re-union of the Whig families, which took place in the summer of 1767. This was natural since Bedford had been a prominent figure in the Ministry of George Grenville. And so, when Bedford allowed his followers to reinforce the tottering Grafton Ministry in the winter of 1767–8, the bitter jealous spirit of Temple might well regard this not only as a disappointment, but as a betrayal.

There was no conceivable reason why a clerk in the War Office should have regarded either Grafton or Bedford with peculiar malignity, nor is there anything in the relations of Francis with the politics of the time to explain the calculated malevolence of the letters addressed to these men. To strike at them as Junius struck, needed a motive; Temple, whose life was passed in political intrigue, had a motive; and had, moreover, the sort of temper which would not be gainsaid by considerations of charity or even of decency.

We may dismiss Junius with a regret that the Duke of Grafton should not have thought it worth while to hazard a surmise as to the identity of his libeller. In truth the blows directed at Grafton were not well aimed. If Junius had possessed real insight he might have laid his finger on the sources of Grafton's weakness as a Prime Minister.

There can be no doubt that Grafton allowed hunting and racing to occupy more of his time than was suitable or convenient in his high office. We read of a Cabinet meeting specially summoned by the Prime Minister and then not attended by him, in consequence of some engrossing interest at Newmarket. No doubt, too, his domestic affairs were somewhat distracting at a critical period, during the first six months of 1769. But the secret of his ill-success lies somewhat deeper.

Shelburne, difficult as he was to work with, was a man of great ability, and an acute, though not always an accurate, student of character. He had a good opportunity of taking the measure of Grafton, and in a phrase he has touched precisely the weakness of his colleague's political character.

Talking to Fox, at, or soon after, the time that Fox seceded from his Ministry, Shelburne said to him, ' It was very provoking, I must own, for you to see Lord Camden and the Duke of Grafton come down *with their lounging opinions*, to outvote you in the Cabinet [1].'

The words express very happily the quality of the Duke's political convictions ; they were, as we can see from his autobiography, those of an advanced liberal, more suited in many respects to a follower of Cobden than to a disciple of Chatham, far removed certainly from those of the aristocratic Whigs, of Rockingham, and the Cavendishes. But, either these opinions were not formulated so as to be fit for expression in action, or, if so formulated, the Duke shrank from putting them into force when the moment for action came.

The most conspicuous illustration of this infirmity of purpose is afforded by his policy in respect to the American colonies. Here he had not only the force of strong personal conviction

---

[1] *Memorials of C. J. Fox*, i. 454.

to move him to decided action, but the knowledge that Chatham, who had formed the Ministry of which Grafton was left in charge, was profoundly opposed to the taxation of the colonies. He must have known also that if he had announced to his colleagues that he would resign unless his opinion was allowed to prevail, the majority must almost inevitably have given way. It was not want of conviction, but weakness of will, that made him accept with a grudging assent the adverse decision of a majority of one.

The same features mark his subsequent career. He accepted office under Lord North in 1771, in the hope that his influence might be of use in obtaining concessions on behalf of the colonies. But though he held a Cabinet office he begged to be excused from attendance at Cabinet meetings, and, as a matter of course, a man who declined responsibility could not expect to exercise influence. His 'lounging opinions' had little effect on his colleagues, and absolutely none upon the king.

It was unfortunate that North did not offer him, in the beginning of 1771, the post which he would undoubtedly have accepted—that of First Lord of the Admiralty. He was interested in the navy; his father had been a promising naval officer, and he had some definite views[1] as to the management of the Admiralty. But George III disliked having Lord Sandwich about him as Secretary of State, and so, when Hawke retired, Sandwich was moved to the Admiralty; the comparative fitness of one man or another for a great administrative post was a matter of indifference to a king who desired to manage everything himself. Thus Grafton lost the chance of showing what he could do as an administrator. It was unfortunate for him, and also for the country. The hopeless mismanagement of the Admiralty under Sandwich is only one instance of the administrative incapacity of the

---

[1] Autobiography, p. 259.

Government of Lord North, but it was the chief cause of our failure in the unhappy war in which we had to face, not only our American colonies, but the combined powers of Europe. The change which came over the fortunes of the war when, after the fall of North, Keppel succeeded Sandwich at the Admiralty, is a significant comment on the previous conduct of affairs.

As it was, Grafton held the office of Lord Privy Seal for nearly four years, until it was forced upon him that good advice and sound opinions are of little value when offered to those who are unwilling to receive them, and cannot be made to attend to them. He resigned in 1775, and at once took an active and useful part in opposition.

When the Whigs returned to office in 1782, Grafton became, once more, Lord Privy Seal in the Rockingham Ministry. The disunion of this Ministry is often attributed to the insincerity of Shelburne, and to his attempts to secure and use the favour of the king at the expense of his colleagues : but the Ministry was, in truth, a coalition of the Chathamite and Rockingham Whigs, and contained various elements of discord. It was the nature of Shelburne to distrust his associates and to play for his own hand, and the exaggerated politeness of manner, which ill concealed the low opinion he formed of his colleagues, was not calculated to smooth over differences or win confidence. Fox, as his father's son, had an hereditary grudge against Shelburne, and the methods and dispositions of the two men were so dissimilar that they were not likely to work together.

But the two sections of the party differed in this, that the reduction of the king's power and influence was the end and aim of the Rockingham Whigs. While they thought that George III exercised any control in the choice of his ministers, or had any voice in the determination of policy, they were uneasy in their places.

Shelburne, who, with Grafton, Camden and Dunning, represented the following of Chatham, were disposed to allow to the king some place in the working of the Constitution. George III was quick to see the rift in the apparently united Whig Government, and he took full advantage of the differences of its members. From the first he gave his confidence, or appeared to give his confidence, to Shelburne, though Rockingham was ostensibly Prime Minister, and with Thurlow, the Tory Chancellor, in the Cabinet, business never was allowed to work easily.

It must be confessed that Grafton did not help to smooth the difficulties of the Ministry. He had come to adopt the attitude, so unsatisfactory in a colleague, of the critic who finds fault with everything, and yet suggests nothing at all, or nothing to the point. Fox, who seems to have been really attached to him, complains of this in the discussions in the Cabinet on Burke's bill, saying that 'he was rather hostile, *though professing right principles in the strongest terms*, but full of little projects of his own, and troublesome in the extreme.'

When Rockingham died, and many of his adherents, in company with Fox, broke away from Shelburne, Grafton retained his office, and gave Shelburne his support. But the support was given grudgingly, and it is unsatisfactory to see how little sense of the relative importance of things is shown in the Duke's complaints of his leader.

The proposed cession of Gibraltar to Spain was one of the matters in which he was opposed to Shelburne, but the admission of the Duke of Rutland to the Cabinet, without the previous assent of the other Cabinet ministers, seems to him to be a more serious ground of complaint, and most serious of all was the refusal of Shelburne to promote Bishop Hinchcliffe to the See of Salisbury. It was characteristic of his temper that, though always on the point of resigning, he held office until the Coalition Government of Fox and North was actually formed. Of that coalition he takes a reasonable view, which comes out in his conversation with Fox [1], that in the existing state of parties, and with the American question practically disposed of, some combination with the followers of North was inevitable, and that the serious objection to the junction of Fox and North was the personal discredit which it brought upon the two leaders.

His political career was now at an end; the half-hearted offers made to him by Pitt mark its close. Pitt may well have thought that Grafton would bring no great accession of strength to his Ministry, and that in securing Camden he had secured the Parliamentary support of Grafton. This was not invariably the case, as appeared when Pitt brought us to the verge of war with Russia: but Grafton's attitude to politics had by this time become that of a bystander. Country pursuits had always possessed a strong attraction for him, and for the last five-and-twenty years of his life theological interests engrossed him: from his own sketch of his political career, it seems tolerably clear that he had no liking at any time for the practical work of politics, and that a sense of duty alone brought him from his hounds and his farms to office or to the House of Lords.

This want of genuine interest in politics, coupled with his want of clearness in forming, and firmness in enforcing, his convictions, combine to make him the ineffectual figure which he appears in our history. So he is represented in Walpole's *Memoirs*, vehement in the purpose of the moment, and yet unstable, wanting to get business done, and to get away into the country; trying this man and that, without much thought of their capacities or power of working together, if somehow he could patch up a Ministry. So, too, he appears in later memoirs, and in his own account of himself, with right prin-

[1] *Autobiography*, p. 375.

ciples of a very general character, and captious doubts and hesitations to which he could give as little effect as to his larger views.

But though we may point out easily enough his shortcomings as a statesman, it is only fair to the Duke of Grafton that, looking back on his political career as a whole, we should recognize the honesty of purpose and the sense of public duty with which it was inspired. He did not enjoy the business of office, and he did not care for its emoluments; he had no ambition to make a great figure in history, nor any sordid purpose of finding places or fortunes for his family and friends, yet he was prepared to play his part in office or in opposition for the service of his country and, according to his lights, for the maintenance of certain principles of government which he believed to be sound and right. Such characters were not common in the eighteenth century. Nor can we say that at any period of history is it easy to find the generous treatment of contemporaries which the Duke of Grafton, buffeted and maligned as he was by storms of adverse criticism, shows when, in the autumn of life, he wrote down his recollections of his career. Chatham, in the last interview which he accorded to Grafton before the cloud of illness wholly overshadowed him, exhorted the Duke to retain office, and counselled an alliance with the Bedford Whigs. In both matters the advice was taken, but when Chatham recovered he denounced the Duke, in language wholly unjustified by anything that had passed, as a traitor to himself and to the liberties of his country : yet Grafton only expresses surprise and regret, and a cordial satisfaction when, near the close of Chatham's life, their friendly relations were restored. Camden held office with Grafton until Chatham re-appeared on the scene, and then, with an undignified self-abasement, which must have made his desertion doubly irritating, expressed in public his regret for the share he had taken in the policy of his colleagues.

Yet Grafton welcomed the first signs of returning friendship on the part of Camden, and seemed hardly to think that there was anything to forgive. The two men had much in common. Their political principles were admirable, but each needed a leader; they found one in Chatham, but from the time of his disappearance from the political scene they seem to have leaned on one another. Grafton was the younger, and perhaps the more vigorous in action; Camden had the more cultivated intelligence. There is something pathetic in the life-long friendship of these two forlorn disciples of Chatham.

In his later years Grafton drifted away from his first faith under the influence of another master-spirit. Fox and Grafton had always lived in friendship, though they had not always agreed in politics, but towards the close of the century Grafton's deepening sense of the horrors of war, and his strong dislike to the repressive measures at home, which were thought to be a necessary safeguard against the revolutionary propaganda of France, brought him more closely into accord with the policy of Fox. And thus, by a strange revolution of feeling and opinion, Grafton, who opened his political career as an opponent of the peace of Paris, a devoted supporter of the bold Imperialism of the elder Pitt, ends his autobiography with regrets that public feeling cannot be brought round to the anti-national, peace-at-any-price policy of Fox, and that the younger Pitt is still encouraged in his resistance to France, and his efforts on behalf of the freedom of England and of Europe.

The religious inquiries which seem to have engrossed him after his retirement in 1783, and determined him in the acceptance of the Unitarian creed and form of worship may to some extent account for some characteristics of his reminiscences. But the reader of history who knows the Duke of Grafton mainly through the *Letters of Junius* or the *Memoirs* of Horace Walpole, may well be surprised at the liberality of opinion, the sombre gravity of treatment, and the kindliness in the estimate of others which mark the Autobiography.

For the division of the Autobiography into chapters I am responsible, and also for the selection of the letters which are inserted at the close of some of the chapters.

W. R. A.

ALL SOULS COLLEGE,
August, 1898.

Autobiography and Correspondence

of

AUGUSTUS HENRY, DUKE OF GRAFTON

———•———

CHAPTER I

AUTOBIOGRAPHY. 1735–1765

Octr. 9th, 1804.

MY DEAR EUSTON,

The interest you appeared to take, and the earnestness with which you perused the political letters and papers, which I put into your hands last winter, have convinced me, that I ought, long since, to have arranged all the important papers on public transactions and concerns, that are in my possession, into some connected order. With this object in view, and with a desire that, after my death, they should come under public inspection, I have undertaken the work which I hope will not be unwelcome to you now, as forming a kind of memoir of my life ; and hereafter possibly gratify the curiosity of an historian by a relation of those occurrences, which came within the circle of those years, in which I was most concerned : I foresee, that I shall have perpetually to insert whole letters, as well as other authentic documents : these alone are calculated to render such a memoir acceptable ; and as I trust, will not bring reproach on a parent, whose character, I well know, in every instance, you would rejoice to support.

The weight on my spirits, caused by the late melancholy

B

losses of members of our family[1], the recollection of whose long sufferings is constantly reverting to my mind in spite of every effort to draw comfort from reflection, has furnished an additional incitement to me to sit down to some serious task: Not knowing where to attain this object better, I adopted this, hoping to derive relief and probably some satisfaction from the occupation.

If I am led to say more of myself, than appears to be becoming; let it be remembered, that it is unavoidable in a narrative of this nature: for it is founded, in its most interesting periods, on the relation of transactions where I was necessarily a principal actor.

The too good opinion also of my friends, discovered in their letters,—friends, some of whom were of the best and greatest characters, must naturally be very flattering: but let me not be reckoned so vain as to imagine that I was entitled to what their kind partiality inclined them to express.

It is always most pleasing to read what we know to be true: and without further and unnecessary profession, allow me to add only that, at the proper day, when the public eye may be called to the examination of every circumstance herein contained, I feel a pleasure in foreseeing that justice will be done to the memoir on this head. Adhering to this declaration, and considering the importance and authenticity of the materials furnished for the building, I trust that I have not gone too far, when I say, that these alone, however unably they may be handled, may possibly produce a work not unacceptable to the accurate and curious historian.

Entering this day into the seventieth year of my life, I am more particularly led to offer up my unfeigned thanks to the great and merciful Author of my being, the benevolent Governor of the universe, that I am allowed to apply to this undertaking under as few of the infirmities of age as fall to the lot of most men. May I ever be truly grateful for all

---

[1] The Duke had recently lost two daughters — Lady Caroline Fitz-Roy, died May 28, 1803; Lady Harriott Fitz-Roy, April 14, 1804.

the blessings which I am still permitted by a kind Providence to enjoy! May I never, *dum spiritus hos regit artus*, be deprived of that greatest of comforts which I have in seeing yourself, and so many of my amiable and excellent young people about me!

The early loss of my own father, Lord Augustus Fitz Roy [1], who commanding the Orford at the Siege of Carthagena 1741 was attacked there by the malignant fever, of which he died, naturally turned my brother and myself over to the care of my grand-father; and deprived us of the great advantages we might have derived from the presence, advice, and example of a parent, who, had he lived, would probably have been as distinguished a character in the civil, as he had shown that he was in the military line.

The education, however, that I received was liberal, under the worthy Mr. Newcome [2], at Hackney School; and afterwards at Peter-house, Cambridge, where M[r]. Stonhewer [3] was my private tutor. Here commenced my knowledge of this gentleman, whom you all with great reason respect and love; and who stands in no want of the voice of any advocate to sound his praise: for to his merits the world universally subscribe. But it is pleasing to reflect that he and I have lived for fifty-three years in the most uninterrupted attachment, confidence, and friendship for each other.

Leaving this seat of learning 1753, with the reputation of a fair progress for my age, I set out for the Continent, accompanied by Monsr. Alléon, a Genevois, a real gentleman, and a man of great honor, with much knowledge of the world; but who was more fitted to form the polite man than to assist, or encourage any progress in literary pursuits.

---

[1] Lord Augustus Fitz-Roy, born Oct. 1716, a promising naval officer, who had commanded several ships of war between 1735 and 1741. He married Elizabeth, daughter of Colonel Cosby, in 1734. At the time of his death he was M.P. for Thetford.

[2] Hackney School flourished for more than eighty years of the last century, under three generations of Newcomes.

[3] Stonhewer, the friend of Gray, Mason, and of Horace Walpole, in whose correspondence his name frequently appears. He was afterwards private secretary to the Duke of Grafton.

However, I by no means neglected the little I had attained :
and a natural inclination leading me to history, and to study
those principles of government which were ever present to
my mind from the time I first read the sound system of
M^r. Locke, I lost no opportunity of improving myself in that
science, on which the most essential interests of mankind in
this world depend.

In this tour, we stretched down as far as Naples, and
passing through the South of France, making a second stay
at Geneva, we visited Switzerland, a very small part of
Germany, and turned, through Holland, back by Flanders
to Paris, with the intention of making a longer abode in
that city, than we were afterwards enabled to accomplish.
Our stay at Paris, and Fontainbleau, however, was not less
than five months : and I had, thro' the means of L^d. Albemarle[1], our ambassador, in whose family I was intimate,
the opportunity of seeing the best company at Paris, which
I cultivated much to my satisfaction.

Before I left France, there was full reason to expect that
the disputes and jealousies then subsisting between the two
Courts regarding their boundaries on the back settlements
of the colonies and near the Ohio were increasing every day,
and likely to terminate in a rupture.

On my return to London, I found the various parties of
political men ambitiously struggling to advance their own
power and that of their friends, and appearing to be less
attentive to the state of the nation. From the late death of the
respectable M^r. Pelham[2] strong contentions had taken place
between those statesmen who were entitled to have the lead.

Notwithstanding this state of things the Duke of Newcastle

---

[1] William Anne, second Earl of
Albemarle, born 1702; died 1754;
married Lady Anne Lennox, daughter
of the first Duke of Richmond (see
Walpole, *Letters*, iii. 320).

[2] Henry Pelham, died on March 6,
1754. Whigs of all sections of the
party had combined to serve quietly

under him. He knew the details of
parliamentary management, was a good
man of business, and 'without being
an orator, or having the finest parts,
no man in the House of Commons
argued with more weight, or was heard
with more attention' (Waldegrave,
Memoirs, 18).

was still the Minister : because he was supported by the body of Whigs [1] ; and he secured this preference by the confidence they had in the sincerity of his principles, and the disinterestedness of his character.   Obligations for favors past bound some, but the power actually placed with him enticed more, to declare for the Government under his Ministry.   The confidence, however, which had been shewn by the city of London in the administration of the two brothers was by no means the same, when the Duke of Newcastle had patched up a weak Cabinet including neither of the two most distinguished statesmen of the time [2].   M[r]. William Pitt and Mr. Henry Fox were both men of considerable penetration, sound judgement, manly understanding, and great ability. Fox derived the influence he possessed not only from the favor of the Duke of Cumberland, but also from the weight he had with many of the first and most powerful families in the kingdom : the Dukes of Bedford, Marlborough, Richmond, Bridgwater, the Marquis of Hartington, with all the Cavendishes, Lords Gower, Sandwich, Weymouth, and many others, were reckoned to be of this number.   On the side of M[r]. Pitt,

[1] ' They (the Whigs) have not always been united in one body, under one general, like a regular and well-disciplined army: but may more aptly be compared to an alliance of different clans, fighting in the same cause, professing the · same principles, but influenced and guided by their different chieftains (Waldegrave, *Memoirs*, 20).

[2] Newcastle was Secretary of State at the time of Pelham's death, and he and Lord Hardwicke who acted in close concert were evidently anxious lest Fox should succeed Pelham as First Lord of the Treasury, and in this position control the springs of parliamentary influence (Hardwicke,*Life*,vol.ii.512). The Cabinet was induced to impress upon the king the importance of placing Newcastle at the Treasury, and treating him as Prime Minister, and to this the king assented. But the death of Pelham left the House of Commons without a leader, and Newcastle could not bear to entrust to any one the powers which his brother had exercised. Fox was invited to become Secretary of State, and to manage the business of Government in the House of Commons. This he was ready to do without the control of the Secret Service money, but he asked that he might be informed how it was spent, so far as ' to enable him to speak to the members without appearing ridiculous.'   Newcastle refused this, nor would he confide to Fox any of the ordinary details of parliamentary management (Walpole, *Memoirs*, i. 382). So the negotiation broke off, and Sir Thomas Robinson became Secretary of State, and the butt of Pitt's denunciation and Fox's raillery. The House of Commons was left to manage itself.

his followers were few, nor did he pay court to any; but his pretensions stood on higher grounds, namely, the voice of the nation, from a full persuasion of his eminent ability, as well as his unbiassed attachment to the welfare of his country. By a letter of the Duke of Newcastle to my grandfather I have reason to think, that they both inclined to wish M^r. Pitt to be the man received into the Ministry, together with his friends, in preference to his rival [1].

Whether the Duke of Newcastle could have carried this point or not I will not take upon me to assert; but the power of M^r. Fox prevailed [2], and he was entrusted to uphold that Administration which S^r. George Lyttleton [3] and S^r. Thos. Robinson were not able to defend [4].

[1] It is difficult to say in what direction the jealous and vacillating temper of Newcastle might not have veered from day to day. Fox would be more ready to give way to him on matters of general policy than Pitt: on the other hand Fox would be more likely to interfere with the business of patronage and corruption. In April, 1754, Newcastle and Hardwicke assured Pitt that the king's aversion was the reason for not offering him high office; but serious negotiations with him did not begin until August, 1755, when he and Legge had entered into friendly relations with Lord Bute and the party of the Princess of Wales and the heir to the throne.

In the meantime, in April, 1755, Fox was admitted to the Cabinet, and places were found for some of his friends. Although this took place after friendly communications between Fox and Pitt (*Chatham Correspondence*, i. 124 et sq.) it caused a breach between the two, and Pitt renounced further connexion with Fox (Dodington's *Diary*, 319; Walpole, *Memoirs*, ii. 37). Although Newcastle had secured Fox and disunited him from Pitt, the events of the summer of 1755 made him anxious to secure the aid of Pitt.

[2] The friendly relations established between Pitt and the party of the Princess and the young Prince of Wales; the commencement of war with France in July; the unpopularity of the subsidies paid to foreign powers for the protection of the King's Hanoverian dominions, all these things combined to induce Newcastle to make another effort to gain Pitt. In August, 1755, negotiations were re-opened through Hardwicke, but Pitt declined to support the subsidies (Hardwicke's *Life*, iii. 28). In September, Newcastle and Pitt met, but with no better results; Pitt objected not only to the subsidies but to the Duke's method of conducting the business of Government, he demanded to be 'not a secretary merely to write letters according to order, or to talk like a lawyer from a brief, but to be really a minister' (Waldegrave, p. 45). So in November, 1755, Pitt was dismissed from his office of Paymaster. Fox became Secretary of State, and Sir Thomas Robinson retired on a pension of £2,000 a year for thirty-one years (Walpole, *Memoirs*, ii. 45).

[3] George, the first Lord Lyttelton (1709–1773), *vide infra*, p. 47.

[4] Thomas Robinson, the first Lord

However, this arrangement, tho' supported by M^r. Fox's talents as Secretary, did not enable the Duke of Newcastle to stand his ground. The account of disasters and ill success poured in from different quarters; and in particular the ill-planned, and worse conducted enterprize under Braddock who fell himself in the action near Crown Point, a victim to his own rashness, together with the feeble attempt of Admiral Byng to relieve St. Philip's Castle in Minorca, raised loudly the public cry against the Ministry, and encreased their unpopularity to such a degree that they retired from office in consequence, Nov^r., 1756 [1].

The Duke of Newcastle was succeeded by the Duke of Devonshire, who had an able Chancellor of the Exchequer in M^r. Legge [2]; and M^r. James Grenville [3] was also of this Board of Treasury. Lord Temple became First Lord of the Admiralty in the room of Lord Anson, and M^r. Pitt was Secretary of State. This Ministry was also of short duration ; and, though composed of men much respected and approved by the public, they were not equally fortunate in rendering themselves acceptable in the closet. It was even said, and I believe with much truth, that the old king could never be brought to treat Lord Temple with common civility. The engaging manners of M^r. Pitt, on the other hand, softened much those prejudices his Majesty had conceived against him [4].

Grantham. He held various diplomatic appointments between 1723-1749, when he returned to England and entered Parliament. He was raised to the peerage 1761, and died in 1770.

[1] Fox found that Newcastle did not trust him with the management of the House of Commons, and that the king regarded him with ill-concealed dislike. He began to fear that he might be made the scape-goat of an incompetent Ministry, and he asked leave to resign in October, 1756.

Newcastle searched in vain for a Leader of the House of Commons. Pitt refused to act with him; Egmont wanted to be a peer of Great Britain. He applied for aid to Lord Granville, who said he ' would be hung before he became responsible for the Duke's measures rather than after.' Finally he resigned with Hardwicke, Anson, and Fox in November, 1756.

[2] Henry Bilson Legge (1708-1764) sat for various constituencies from 1740 until his death, and enjoyed a high reputation as a financier.

[3] James Grenville (1715-1783) was fourth son of Richard Grenville, and brother of Lord Temple and George Grenville.

[4] Pitt seems to have bored the king

The strongest debates of the Session of 1756 (the first in which I sat in Parliament[1]) were on the inquiry into the loss of Minorca[2]. My vote was given with M[r]. Pitt, and with a respectable minority; but the defence of the last Cabinet was espoused by the Court, as well as by the First Lord of the Treasury, with all his friends. M[r]. Pitt, Lord Temple, &c., soon after resigned their offices, and the nation was left a considerable time under what was *then* styled an *inter-regnum*. Indeed there was no minister, although the moment called for the ablest. At length the impatient expectation of the public was satisfied by the coalition[3] that took place; which was so comprehensive as to leave no room for dis-content to be attended to in any quarter; and the nation

without offending him, but Temple was always pompous, prolix, and impertinent. The Ministry however failed, not because the king disliked its members, but because it had no interest in the boroughs, and no support in the House of Commons (see Walpole to Mason, *Letters*, iii. 44–48).

[1] Lord Euston was elected for Bury St. Edmunds in 1756, and sat for that borough until the death of his grand-father in May, 1757.

[2] The debates on the inquiry into the loss of Minorca did not begin till April 19, 1757. Temple had been dismissed on the 5th, and Pitt a day later with his immediate followers Legge, George Grenville, and Charles Townshend. The immediate cause of dismissal was the dislike of the Duke of Cumberland to take the command of the Electoral forces in Hanover while Pitt was Secretary of State.

The debates to which the Duke alludes ended a few days before the death of his grandfather and his succes-sion to the dukedom.

[3] On the dismissal of Pitt in April, 1757, the king requested Newcastle to form a Ministry, and he was empowered to treat with Pitt. Pitt, however, would not come to terms with Newcastle, and the Duke was ready once more to attempt to govern the country with only a nominal leader of the House of Commons (Walpole, *Letters*, iii. 78). Lord Chesterfield now intervened at the instance of Lord Bute and the party of the Princess of Wales. He persuaded Newcastle that it was to his interest to keep on good terms with Pitt, who in his turn had established friendly relations with the party which sur-rounded the heir to the throne. Thus Newcastle and Pitt were brought to-gether, but now the king resented this new combination and induced Lord Waldegrave to attempt the formation of a Ministry. This attempt was frustrated by Newcastle, who had many friends in and out of office bound to him by obligations or promises. These with one consent refused or resigned office, and Lord Waldegrave withdrew. Then the king gave way and entrusted, first, Lord Mansfield and then Lord Hardwicke with powers to negotiate with Pitt and Newcastle, stipulating only that he should see as little as possible of Temple, and that Fox should be Paymaster. Thus was formed the Ministry described in the text.

gave the new administration its fullest confidence. Indeed, that of the houses of Parliament was so strongly marked that every measure passed in houses much too thin.

M[r]. Pitt returned to the Seals of the Northern Department —the Duke of Newcastle, with M[r]. Legge Chancellor of the Exchequer, to the Treasury—Lord Temple became Privy Seal—Lord Anson took up his former post [1]—and the Duke of Devonshire [2], with a seat at the Cabinet, Lord Chamberlain : and I always understood, that the Earl of Hardwicke [3], though not in office, was called to the Cabinet. Lord Granville [4] presided at the head of the Council. If it be thought necessary to go farther, I should mention that M[r]. Pratt, afterwards Lord Camden, and M[r]. Chas. Yorke [5], were Attorney and Solicitor General. With such an Administration, backed by the good-will of the nation so decidedly in their favor, public affairs soon took a more successful turn.

Those persons who were not witnesses would hardly be brought to credit the degree of despondency which, from some time back till this moment, prevailed almost universally through all ranks of people. I can never forget it, nor the indignation with which I, as a young man, viewed an alarm so foreign to the just character of the country. ' The contention

---

[1] George Lord Anson, First Lord of the Admiralty 1751-1756, and 1757-1762.

[2] William, fourth Duke of Devonshire, Lord Lieutenant of Ireland 1755; First Lord of the Treasury 1756. The circumstances of his retirement from the post of Lord Chamberlain and from all other offices are told later, p. 21. He died in the forty-fourth year of his age, at Spa, in 1764.

[3] Lord Hardwicke seems to have occupied the peculiar position, possible during part of the last century, of a statesman holding cabinet rank, but not habitually attendant at cabinet meetings. After helping to arrange the Ministry he took no office, and retired from

regular political work. Nevertheless, he says, on Aug. 27, 1757, 'I attended a meeting of the king's servants;' and a little later, 'as I know there is to be a meeting of the king's servants, I have added my opinion' (Harris, *Life of Hardwicke*, iii. 153, 156).

[4] John, Lord Carteret, and Earl of Granville, who for a brief period after Walpole's fall was the ruling influence in the Ministry which succeeded to power; he died 1763.

[5] Charles Yorke (1722-1770), second son of the first Lord Hardwicke. His melancholy end is told later in the Memoir. There is an excellent account of his character in Trevelyan's *Early History of C. J. Fox* at p. 233.

with the power of France,' too many usually argued, ' was vain and hopeless,' and that, ' if we could fortuitously hold up against it for their own times, it would crown their highest expectations.' No less striking, nor less wonderful was the almost instantaneous turn from that dejection which the nation soon demonstrated. M^r. Pitt's spirit, vigour and perseverance seemed to instill itself into the hearts of every individual, as well as of those employed in both services, in a manner more than natural, and this in every quarter of the globe. The consequences were security at home, and as complete success by sea and land as Britain has to boast.

About this time, my grandfather[1], who had held for so many years the Staff of Lord Chamberlain, and who had long been the much honored friend of the late king, died in consequence of a fall from his horse a hunting. I shall not attempt to give you his full character, but I may say that few men have ever been more agreeable in society, or surpassed him in the knowledge of men, or in his brilliancy in company, which was equally coveted by the young as by the older of his numerous acquaintance.

The freedom with which he often delivered his opinions, and even advice, to the king, encreased his royal master's esteem. He would speak truths to His Majesty which others did not venture to risk; and the ministers were duly thankful for the effective support they thence received.

When I waited on His Majesty at Kensington, and was admitted into the closet, in order to deliver the ensigns of the Order of the Garter of my late grandfather, the king, after a few common questions, said, and with tears evidently

---

[1] Charles, second Duke of Grafton. ' He had been Lord Chamberlain during the whole reign, and had a particular manner of talking to his master on all subjects, and touching upon the most tender points which no other person ventured to imitate. . . . He usually turned politics into ridicule; had never applied himself to business, and as to books was totally illiterate: yet from long observation and natural sagacity he became the ablest courtier of his time; had the most perfect knowledge both of king and ministers, and more opportunities than any man of doing good or bad offices ' (Waldegrave, *Memoirs*, 114).

rising in his eyes, 'Duke of Grafton, I always honored, and loved your grandfather ; and lament his loss: I wish you may be like him : I hear you are a very good *boy*.'

This may be the proper place to mention that in the preceding autumn I had accepted the offer of being one of the Prince of Wales's Lords of the Bedchamber ; but it was not till after kissing his Royal Highness's hand that I was informed by himself, that he had failed in his endeavour to have me as his Master of the Horse[1] ; but that the Duke of Newcastle would not recede from his recommendation of Lord Huntingdon[2] to the king.   I retained, however, my place about the prince, with great kindness from himself, until, from the absence of some of my colleagues and from the illness of others, the duty was become so irksome and constant that I was really compelled to ask leave to resign this post, Lord Bute[3] not being able to give me any expectation of further relief.

It is not the business of this memoir to enter into a relation of any of the events which happened during the course of this war ; brilliant as they were in that light in which the world in general view these horrid scenes of endless calamities : and, having little further knowledge of all the transactions than what will be found in most of the accounts published of that period, I shall refer you for particulars to them. Suffice it for me to say, that the military success of Great Britain, both by sea and land, was uniformly striking.

Voltaire, if I mistake not, has at the head of one of the chapters of his *Histoire universelle* ' Les Anglois victorieux

---

[1] The bickerings which took place in settling the establishment of the Prince of Wales ; the insistence by the Princess and her son on the appointment of Lord Bute as Groom of the Stole, and the way in which Newcastle, after having made this concession, filled up other places about the Prince with his personal friends are described in Lord Waldegrave's *Memoirs*, 62-79.

[2] Francis, tenth Earl of Huntingdon, who carried the sword of state at the coronation of George III, and succeeded 'Lord Bute as Groom of the Stole.   On his death, in 1790, the earldom fell into abeyance until a title to it was established in 1819.

[3] John, third Earl of Bute (1713-1792), had been Lord of the Bedchamber to Frederick Prince of Wales, and was now Groom of the Stole in the household of his son.

dans les Quatre Parties du Monde[1].' He alluded particularly to the occurrences of 1759, when this nation was favored with so many victories as to redound everywhere to the honor of the country, and especially of those gallant officers whose skill and bravery were so instrumental to our success. The like spirit and consequences appeared in the subsequent years of the war, and had not the Duc de Choiseul succeeded in stirring up the Court of Spain to declare in favor of France[2], that kingdom would probably have been reduced to as low an ebb as it was under Lewis 14th, previously to the Peace of Utrecht.

However the hostile declaration of Spain did not take place till after the Accession of George the 3d. The disposition of that Court, did not escape the sagacious foresight of Mr. Pitt: but his counsels were over-ruled, though the event proved the superiority of his political wisdom.

During the life of the late king Mr. Pitt had as little opposition in the Cabinet to any of his measures as there was in Parliament: and he had gained so much the esteem of His Majesty by the brilliancy he had given to the setting years of his reign, and by his attention to those who were most in the king's favor, that I was assured by Lord Northington[3], as a fact which he well knew, that had the king lived,

---

[1] Walpole writes to Sir Horace Mann, Oct. 3, 1762, 'Voltaire is continuing his Universal History; he showed the Duke of Grafton a chapter, to which the title is Les Anglais vainqueurs dans les Quatre Parties du Monde' (Letters, vol. iv. p. 32).

[2] The overtures for an alliance would seem to have come from Spain, judging from the letters which passed between the Marquis Grimaldi and the Count de Fuentes, the Spanish ambassadors at the Courts of France and England. The French were anxious for peace; Grimaldi was equally anxious that a peace should not be concluded, which would leave Spain alone to settle her differences with England; and in February, 1761, he began 'working

to see if we can make some alliance with France which should protect us from those accidents we ought to fear' (Chatham Correspondence, vol. ii. pp. 91, 92, 95, 101). Grimaldi, by his influence with the French Court, seems to have forced the hand of de Choiseul and obtained the introduction of the Spanish difficulties with England, and their settlement, into the negotiations which were going on in London between Bussy, de Choiseul's agent, and Pitt. Stanley to Pitt, August 20, 1761 (Chatham Correspondence, ii. 139).

[3] Robert Henley, Earl of Northington was Keeper of the Great Seal 1757-1761, Lord Chancellor 1761-1766, President of the Council 1766-67, died 1772.

he would have placed the full power, as his minister, into the hands of M^r. Pitt.

The Administration, constituted as I have stated it to be, continued without the smallest change through the remainder of the life of George the 2^d, gaining every day more and more the confidence of the nation, as also weight and consideration from foreign states who admired and envied the prosperity of this country.

On the death of the old king a new scene appeared, though it was at first held out that the same system was to be maintained. Happy, indeed, would it have been for this nation had such a disposition been realized.

Few princes have ever ascended the throne under more advantages and auspicious circumstances: and the prudent and virtuous conduct of H.R.H. in his youth increased the public expectation.

Few kings, however, have lived to see, without any signal calamity, the condition of their subjects so wholly changed as no longer to afford to the enquiring eye the view of that once happy nation, enjoying almost every blessing that could be desired under a well-principled Government at home, and one which was admired courted and respected abroad. If it be asked whence such a downfall has taken place, I should not hesitate in saying, that it would be no difficult task to trace the cause of most of our misfortunes to fatal errors in the governing powers; though I cannot confine the blame to the executive alone. At the beginning of the reign, and probably some time before, notions were instilled into the mind of his present Majesty, that the late king had never been so far his own master as to have about him those ministers whom he would himself have chosen; and it was insinuated to the young king, that in order to secure himself from the like dilemma no measures would with equal certainty effect this object, until the body of the Whigs, whose influence from long possession of power had become formidable, was fairly broken asunder.

Other fatal principles and declarations were soon advanced

in every company that I frequented, namely, 'that there was no person so insignificant whom, through the power of the Crown, the king could not appoint and support as his minister.' It has also been said, and the event has too much justified the observation, that, through a dread of seeing a strong and powerful administration, His Majesty has discovered to most of the Ministers who have served him, that, as they rose in the esteem of the public and met with the support of Parliament, so were they to depend less on that which they might naturally expect from the Court. I am afraid that these pernicious ideas have led to great mischiefs, and that the Constitution itself has much suffered from the introduction of the violent measures these have produced [1].

But I will enter here on no discussions on government; where the relation of facts I have known and observations I have made are to be the main subjects for my purpose. Still, allow me to declare, in confirmation of some of my assertions, that at no period of my time have I ever known the situation of this country to be equally gloomy, and alarming as at this present, while I hold my pen. I pray to God to avert the blow [2]!

The Administration, though unaltered, soon perceived that their advice was not attended to with that deference which was shewn to that of others who were consulted in private; and it was considered to be wiser, and less dangerous, that Lord Bute [2] should himself hold a Cabinet office. It was soon arranged: and Lord Holdernesse [3] resigned the seals of Secretary of State, which were delivered to the Earl of Bute.

---

[1] In the Introduction, I have endeavoured to explain somewhat more fully the nature of this new system which the Duke has here briefly and graphically described.

[2] The year 1804, in which the Duke commenced his memoir, was one of general anxiety and dejection in England. The failure of the Addington Ministry, the impending outbreak of hostilities with France and Spain, the doubt as to the sufficiency of our resources, were not compensated by the return to power of Pitt with broken health and a weak following.

[3] Robert Darcy, fourth and last Earl of Holderness, died 1778.

It was immediately found that the old system was to exist no longer; and that all power was quickly hastening to the hands of Lord Bute, who was patronized by the Princess Mother, and supposed through H.R.H's. assistance to influence the young king.

The change of system did not escape the vigilance and penetration of Frederic of Prussia: and to the political principles and conduct of the favorite, which he had watched with suspicion from the commencement of the reign, he often imputed the disappointing termination of the Seven Years War; together with the breach of an alliance so well calculated to maintain and secure a just balance of power in Europe. The Duke of Newcastle and some other Whig members of the Cabinet had not the same discernment; and when they joined to over-rule M^r. Pitt in his conviction of the necessity of declaring war against Spain they had soon the mortification to see themselves placed also in a situation, where to retreat was the only honorable step left for them to take[1].

As a new state of things is now discovering itself here at home, before I enter on the subject, it will perhaps not be improper to mention that, on account of some domestic concerns[2], I set off in June 1761 for the benefit of a change of

---

[1] Pitt retired with Temple in October 1761, and Newcastle alone, in May, 1762. It was plain that if the king and Bute were to manage public business they must get rid of Newcastle, who worked the machinery of corruption. This was done by a series of insulting slights. He was left uninformed about important negotiations: his proposals for appointments and the filling up of boroughs were refused or criticized; finally, Bute interfered in the business of the Treasury, and as the Duke put it, 'engaged my colleagues and my secretary in open opposition to me' (*Rockingham Memoirs*, i. 110). On May 19 he resigned, and complains with some justice, 'the king did not drop one word of concern at my leaving him or even made me a polite compliment, after near fifty years service and devotion to the interest of his royal family' (*ibid*. i. 112).

[2] The cause of the journey was the health of the Duchess of Grafton. 'The Graftons go abroad for the Duchess' health, another climate may mend that.' (Walpole to Montagu, April 28, 1761.) Walpole's letters to Mann contain many allusions to the movements of the Duchess of Grafton, of whom he was a great admirer and a lifelong friend. As no allusion is made in the diary to the Duke of Grafton's first marriage, it may be well to state here that, as Lord Euston, he married, in 1756, Anne Liddell, daughter of the first Lord Ravensworth. They separated at the end of 1764, and were divorced in 1769,

climate. Your dear sister Georgiana [1] was with us. Through the interest of the Marquis Du Quesne, a prisoner on his parole at Northampton, I obtained a passport, which for years past had been refused to every Englishman. Mons[r]. Bussy was just arrived to treat with M[r]. Pitt on preliminaries for a general peace[2]; and when I reached Paris I found M[r]. Stanley negociating on our part, (though unsuccessfully), with Mons[r]. de Choiseul. Belle Isle was at this time attacked, and an account of its surrender to my old friend L[t]. General Hodgson was received before I left that city.

The attentive politeness with which the news was communicated to M[r]. Stanley was remarkable in words very complimentary on the success of the arms of the king his master. Mr. Stanley favored me with a sight of the note from the French Minister, and of his intended answer; in the conclusion of which he expressed the hope that it would be the last contest between two nations honoring and esteeming each other.

We received particular civilities from various quarters during our short stay at Paris. At the old and respectable Duke of Biron's [3] I dined with a numerous set of officers; and his reception of me was flattering. He had commanded the 'Gardes Françoises' ever since the battle of Fontenoy, and was adored by persons of every rank. I had lived a great deal with him at Lord Albemarle's, with whom he was intimate.

From Paris we passed through Dijon, and Pontarlier to

in which year the late Duchess married the Earl of Upper Ossory; and the Duke, as he mentions later, married the daughter of Sir Richard Wrottesley.

[1] Lady Georgiana Fitz Roy (1737–1799) married (1778) Mr. John Smyth.

[2] A congress to discuss the terms of a general peace was in contemplation, but separate negotiations were commenced in 1761 between France and England. M. de Bussy was sent to London, and Mr. Hans Stanley to Paris.

These negotiations lasted from June to September, 1761. The prospect of a Spanish alliance had by that time disinclined de Choiseul to make the concessions with which he might otherwise have satisfied Pitt. The resignation of Pitt shortly followed, on the refusal of his colleagues to anticipate Spain in a declaration of war. He retired on October 5, 1761.

[3] Louis Antoine, Duke de Biron (1701-1788).

Geneva, and to a good house I had hired at Chouilly, two leagues from that city. It was impossible for us to pass our time better than we did here. Our house was open to all our acquaintance, and was frequented by the best company. In the beginning of winter we passed the Mount Cénis, and stopped about six weeks at Turin.

It happened that the old King of Sardinia[1], soon after our arrival, was taken ill and confined to his room. This circumstance gave the Duke of Savoy[2] an opportunity of paying me a compliment which had been rarely, if ever, offered to any foreigner. I was invited to H.R.H.'s private dinner; where the company consisted of no other than the Duke, his lords and equerries, military men. At coffee I was much flattered and surprized on the Duke of Savoy's coming up and telling me that he should expect to see me in the same manner every hunting day, until his royal father's recovery. The conversation ran principally on general political, and military matters; sometimes on horses and hounds, with great affability and no restraint but such as became well-bred gentry. From my constant correspondance with my brother[3], who was then in Germany and aid-de-camp to Prince Ferdinand, I had the means of letting the Duke of Savoy know the exact operations of that army, which was gratifying to H.R.H. to a great degree. Another particular favor was offered to me, that of wearing the royal hunting uniform; which was looked up to as an uncommon distinction, and which I found would have been of great use, if I had had to travel much in Piedmont. Our next stop was at Milan, where I profited of my former acquaintance with the Comte de Firmian[4], whom I had known at Naples in my former tour. He was now the governor of the Austrian territories in Lombardy; and had contrived, by great attentions, management and impartiality,

[1] Charles Emmanuel III, reigned 1730–1773.

[2] Afterwards Victor Amadeus III, who died in 1796, before his kingdom, all but the island of Sardinia, was swept away by the arms of the French.

[3] Lord Charles FitzRoy, born 1737; created Lord Southampton, 1780.

[4] He was appointed Governor of Austrian Lombardy, 1759.

to draw unusual sums without complaint from individuals for the Empress Queen's war necessities. Comte Firmian received us with all the cordiality, and indeed friendship, that could be shewn, and more than I could have expected. But those who knew the amiable and friendly character of this nobleman will not be surprized at this courtesy from him: and we kept up ever afterwards a friendly intercourse. From Milan our course was along the Adriatic coast to Rome. Here we made a longer stay, and found a very pleasing society. Many of the English who were there were very agreeable young men; and we were particularly recommended by Comte Firmian to Monsignore Piccuolomeni [sic], governor of Rome, and by the Marquis de Breigle [sic] to his own son, who was ambassador from Malta to Rome. Lord Tavistock[1] lived much in our society: as did Mess[rs]. Crewe[2], Hinchcliffe[3], Crauford, James, and others.

The governor and the ambassador I have just mentioned were both of an amiable disposition; men of the world, and well informed. Piccuolomeni became cardinal afterwards. We were much gratified by the frequent opportunities we had, of enjoying their company, both at their houses and at ours.

Here my intimacy with Hinchcliffe, Bishop of Peterborough, began, and continued stedfastly till his death. It is not common to find a man of so pleasing and engaging manners, and whose affectionate gratitude to his friends could not be

---

[1] Francis, Marquis of Tavistock (1739–1767), eldest son of John, Duke of Bedford; was killed by a fall from his horse.

[2] John Crewe, afterwards the first Lord Crewe, was at this time making the grand tour with Hinchcliffe as his tutor. For many years he represented Cheshire in the House of Commons, and in 1782 brought in the bill which disqualified officers of the excise and customs from voting at parliamentary elections.

[3] Hinchcliffe was a Westminster scholar, and afterwards a Fellow of Trinity College, Cambridge. On his return to England he was made Headmaster of Westminster, but almost immediately resigned this post. His friendship with the Duke of Grafton procured for him, in rapid succession, the Rectory of Greenwich (1766), the Mastership of Trinity (1768), the Bishopric of Peterborough (1769). In 1788 he gave up the Mastership for the Deanery of Durham, but retained the Bishopric until his death.

surpassed: but no one has a better right to weigh his merits than you, who knew him so well and regarded him so much.

We passed two or three weeks at Florence; and a few days only to pay our court at Turin; then proceeded to Geneva, near which place we arrived at the beautiful villa I had hired of Mons[r]. Galatin. We passed our summer in a most agreeable manner, receiving all the best company at our house. La Duchesse d'Anville was also at Geneva, with her son; the Duc de la Rocheguin, afterwards Rochefocault, and here he probably imbibed those principles of government which, though they did him so much credit, yet brought him to his fatal and cruel end[1]. We had the pleasure of meeting them frequently in different houses; for a foolish etiquette prevented us from visiting directly each other, while our countries were at war; but we were not prevented from interchanging every possible attention and civility. With Voltaire there was not the same scruple; and we not only visited him frequently, but were treated one day after dinner with a representation of his own *Alzire*, himself, Mad[e]. Dennis, and Mad[lle]. Corneille[2] performing the principal parts, and in a small theatre within the Château de Ferney.

Leaving the neighbourhood of Geneva before the expiration of the summer, 1762, we found on our arrival at Paris that a fresh negociation for peace was expected to take place immediately, on which the French relied with much confidence and joy.

I must not omit here, that, by invitation from them, I met at Gravelines the Comte and Comtesse d'Herouville, with whom I passed a most pleasant day. He was a respectable officer, having the rank of Lieut.-General and the command in Flanders. Madame d'Herouville was of a disposition and figure to be beloved and admired by all her acquaintance; but her uncommon merit, and very superior

---

[1] The Duke was murdered at Gisors, in the presence of his wife and mother, on September 4, 1792.

[2] A great-niece of the poet, for whose benefit Voltaire was now engaged upon an edition of the works of Corneille (*Chatham Corresp.* ii. 132).

understanding were best known to those with whom she was more intimate.

On our arrival in London, I found a confirmation of the pacific dispositions of the two countries. The Duke of Bed-ford[1] was on his departure for Paris. The Duc de Nivernois at the same time, as ambassador from France, passed over to England[2]. The noted Madame d'Eon attended him; she was only known in those days as the gallant *Capitaine de Dragons*, and the intelligent and active *Secrétaire d'Ambassade*[3].

After a visit to Lord and Lady Ravensworth, at Erlington, and to yourself who was with them, I came up to London for the meeting of Parliament. The business of the preliminaries was soon to be discussed in both Houses; and the agitation arising from the unfeeling proscription which issued forth against every being, down to the lowest clerks in office, who owed their situations to the Pelhams was so universal as to draw down great reproach against the Ministry[4]. Whether it was a measure proposed at Court or chargeable to the ministers only did not appear; but the outcry against so cruel a proscription was general; and the hardships and distress it occasioned to numberless families were of a greater extent than could be at first imagined. However, when we came into office in 1765 we stipulated in the very first instance, that every person who was dismissed at this juncture should be restored his place or office. This mode of concluding the business will probably prevent the same harsh step from being ever resorted to henceforward. May every violent measure meet with a like disgraceful end!

[1] John, fourth Duke of Bedford (1710–1771). See Introduction.

[2] This was in September, 1762. There is a full account of the Duc de Nivernais in the *Rockingham Memoirs*, i. 119.

[3] The Chevalier d'Éon de Beaumont (1728–1810). On the return of the Duc de Nivernais he remained in England as *chargé d'affaires* and quarrelled violently with the succeeding ambassador, Count de Guerchey. In 1777 he was recalled to France, and received a pension on condition that he wore female dress. This he did until his death. The disputes as to his sex were settled by a *post mortem* examination, which proved him to be a man.

[4] This proscription is ante-dated by the Duke. It took place after the proceedings in Parliament upon the Preliminaries.

I have already mentioned that when Mr. Pitt found himself in a minority in the Cabinet and unable to persuade his colleagues of the unavoidable necessity of a war with Spain, he had retired in much disgust to a private station together with Lord Temple. The Duke of Newcastle and Lord Hardwicke were not aware, that, though thus delivered from the over-ruling genius and ability of Mr. Pitt, which they dreaded, their own fate was hastened by his retreat[1]. Every one expected such an event except those who were most personally interested in it. Even the Duke of Devonshire had not the foresight of the loss of all his court favor. He was at Bath for his health, and was summoned in a hurry up to assist at a Council on the consideration of the Preliminaries. The Duke did not obey the summons, but came up with a full determination, as Lord John Cavendish's letter now before me states, in the civilest manner possible to acquaint His Majesty, that he could not hold his place any longer, as he felt that he must decline in future attending the Cabinet.

The accounts of this resignation were variously reported: but, as Lord John[2] informed me that it was attended with some extraordinary circumstances, I shall deliver them in his own words:

'As soon as my brother came to town he went to Court, and sent in one of the pages to desire an audience: the page returned, and told him that the king *would* not see him. He desired him to go in again, and enquire in whose hands he should leave his staff. The king sent word back, that he would *send* him his orders. Upon this he went immediately to Lord Egremont's[3], and desired him to take the staff and key to the king, as he wanted to go out of town: and so left them in his lordship's hands. Lord Besborough[4] and George[5] were to resign the next day.'

---

[1] The retirement of Newcastle has been mentioned. It took place in May, 1762, and he was succeeded as First Lord of the Treasury by Lord Bute.

[2] Lord John Cavendish, third brother of the Duke of Devonshire, was the most active politician of the family. He figures prominently in the history of the Rockingham Whigs (*Rockingham Memoirs*, i. 226).

[3] See p. 26.

[4] William Ponsonby, Earl of Besborough, had married the Duke of Devonshire's sister, and was at this time Joint Postmaster-General.

[5] Lord George Cavendish, eldest brother of the Duke of Devonshire, was member for Derbyshire, and at this time Comptroller of the Household.

This transaction undoubtedly passed as related above, but infinite pains were taken to represent it as improperly conducted by the worthy Duke. It was industriously propagated that his Grace had left the staff of Lord Chamberlain with the page of the back stairs: which is peremptorily contradicted by Lord John's relation. But a blow was probably to be aimed at the Whig Party, and one of the heads of that description was to be disgraced; and the fall of this respected character was the first object destined to satisfy the expectations of those who wished about this time to be denominated *the King's Friends*[1]. At a Privy Council assembled on purpose, the Duke of Devonshire's name was struck out of the list of Counsellors, but this feeble stroke of vengeance carried no more edge in his Grace's instance, than did the similar proceeding against Mr. Charles Fox[2] in later days.

In a letter from the Duke of Devonshire to me, from Chatsworth, Novr. 6. 1762, he says:

'It is no small satisfaction to me to find you approve of my conduct; but, indeed, my lord, there was scarce any option left me. It seems as if they had a mind to get quit of me, and acted in such a manner as I must have been the lowest of mortals to have submitted to. There is some mystery in the great resentment that the king has shewed against me; what it is I am at a loss to guess.'

His Grace at the close of this letter writes:

'It is indeed a great pleasure to me to find our sentiments agree, and that we are likely to act together; for I fear parties will run high, and consequently friendship and connexions break: but believe me, my dear lord, whatever happens, my friendship and regard for your Grace will always be the same.'

Thus began this new system, where corruption and intimidation were prevalent features.

The war, though glorious and successful, could offer no

---

[1] The phrase 'King's Friends' appears in a letter of Bute to Grenville of March 25, 1763 (*Grenville Corresp.* ii. 33). The editor notes that the phrase is here used for the first time.

[2] Charles James Fox was sworn of the Privy Council in 1782, was struck out of the list of Councillors on May 9, 1798, and was re-admitted in 1806, when he became Secretary of State for Foreign Affairs.

moment more suitable for an advantageous peace than the present. The wishes of the nation were evidently for peace, and I have no doubt that the Preliminaries would have become quite popular, if the King of Prussia, our faithful and undaunted ally, had not been abandoned in a manner disgraceful to the honor of this country and unmerited by him, who had never swerved one instant in his steadiness to the alliance[1], even in the most formidable situations, in which he was more than once placed. After the defeat at Cunersdoff the similarity of situations might have brought the letter of Francis the first into the King of Prussia's head ; as he repeats the very words the French King used in his letter to the Queen after the Battle of Pavia : ' Tout, Madame, est perdu—hormis l'honneur ! ' No, his honor was never tarnished ; nor was his spirit ever subdued, even when he saw himself surrounded with threatening difficulties and the most formidable distresses.

Under these impressions the Preliminaries came to be considered in Parliament at the beginning of Decr. 1762 : and the public was sanguine enough to hope for an adequate resistance to a system which was generally condemned ; but they witnessed only the melancholy proof of the all-powerful influence of the Crown, though it had not then mounted to that height where we now behold it [2].

[1] Frederick of Prussia was doubtless ill-treated by us. Bute withdrew at short notice a subsidy of £2,000,000 which we had paid for some years; and he opened separate and secret negotiations for peace at Vienna. But the fidelity of Frederick to the alliance was, with him, a matter of self-interest. There is no reason to suppose that he would have remained our ally a moment longer than he found to be convenient.

[2] It must be doubted whether the influence of the Crown was so potent a factor in politics in 1804 as it had been in 1762. There was less corruption at the later date, and more party-loyalty. But the king's wishes had a weight due to the accident that George III was, at the later date, always on the verge of insanity. Very recently Pitt had been constrained by the pressure of this anxiety to abandon the idea of a Ministry in which Fox would have been Secretary of State and his followers in office. No doubt a king has a quite exceptional influence if he can intimate that unless his wishes are gratified he shall probably go mad, and throw the whole machinery of government out of gear.

Mr. Pitt came into the House suffering so much under an attack of gout as to be allowed permission to deliver great part of his speech as he sat. Speeches since that night have been as long, or longer ; but the length of this was in those days particular.

Though Mr. Pitt's indisposition rendered his manner of delivering his speech less spirited than usual, there was no defect in the matter of it. On the contrary, he displayed such an intimate knowledge of the interests of these kingdoms, as well as of the condition and views of foreign states, as justly excited the admiration of the whole House. After hearing a few speeches from the other side, he retired ; and, as it was given out that there would be no division, many of the Opposition left the House on that idea[1]. About sixty or seventy of those who remained did divide, and complained much that they were deserted by their friends. This misapprehension caused some ill-humour ; and the absentees came down the next day to divide on the Report against the Address.

In the House of Lords, on the division, the number of Peers who opposed the Address was short of the expectations we had formed ; but their consideration as to character and property was too weighty to be over-looked. Lords Suffolk[2] and Shelburne[3], moved and seconded the Address. I was the first who rose to condemn what appeared to be the disadvantageous parts of the Preliminaries under our consideration.

This my first speech was too declamatory, and directed chiefly against Lord Bute.—The violence of my language was

[1] For an account of the debate of December 9, 1762, see Walpole, *Memoirs*, i. 223.

[2] Henry, twelfth Earl of Suffolk, and fifth Earl of Berkshire, born May 10, 1739, died March 6, 1779, was Lord Privy Seal in 1771, and Secretary of State in the same year.

[3] William, eldest son of John Fitzmaurice, a younger son of the first Earl of Kerry. In 1751 John Fitzmaurice inherited the fortune and assumed the name of his uncle, Henry Petty, Earl of Shelburne. His eldest son William succeeded him as Earl of Shelburne in the peerage of Ireland, and Lord Wycombe in the peerage of England. He was created Marquis of Lansdowne in 1784. He was born in 1739 and died in 1805. See his life by Lord E. Fitzmaurice. (Macmillan & Co., 1875.)

easily excused in a young man speaking from his heart[1]: and it had one good effect at least, for it called up the Earl of Bute, who by his manner of speaking rather exposed himself than supported his cause.

The Opposition, however, soon began to get together[2], better to understand each other, and to act with more system. A considerable club[3] of the Whigs was formed, consisting of a very large number: many members of it dining or supping there every day. The spirit of the Whig party was much raised by these exertions: still it was the fix'd resolution to oppose only on points which bore the clearest sanction of rectitude and truth.

In spring 1763[4], Number 45 of the North Briton made its appearance. I shall not detail the particular steps taken against M[r]. Wilkes by the messengers under a *general* warrant, issued by Lord Hallifax[5], as Secretary of State, to apprehend the author, and all others concerned in the publication of the paper above mentioned, and to seize all his other papers.

The particulars of the whole transaction are well worthy of attention, but these will be found accurately stated in many different publications.

M[r]. Wilkes was apprehended under this *general* warrant; and his papers seized and tumbled about in a manner not warrantable, even had the seizure been less questionably legal. He was committed *close* prisoner to the Tower, under a fresh warrant. Of the close imprisonment, I, with many of his acquaintance, was witness; for we were denied admittance to him; Major Rainsford shewing us the warrant under which

---

[1] Walpole (*Letters*, iv. 52) writes: 'I received your letter for the Duchess of Grafton. . . Her Duke is appearing in a new light, and by the figure he makes will soon be at the head of the Opposition if it continues.'

[2] The Duke here deals with the principal topics of opposition during the years 1763, 1764, and then goes back, on p. 28, to the formation of the Gren-ville Ministry, against whom this opposition was directed.

[3] This was Wildman's in Albemarle Street. The club was called *The Coterie* (*Grenville Papers*, ii. 47).

[4] On April 23.

[5] George Dunk, third and last Earl of Halifax, was Secretary of State throughout the Grenville Ministry, and again from January to June, 1771, when he died.

he acted. In signing this, as well as the other subsequent warrants, Lord Egremont [1] was equally implicated with his colleague.

A writ of habeas corpus was moved for, and obtained as soon as could be by two of M[r]. Wilkes's friends, and when he was brought up to the bar of the Common Pleas, the case appeared so important that the Lord Chief Justice Pratt desired two days for the consideration of it ; and remanded M[r]. Wilkes back to the Tower, but expressly directing that he was not to be a *close* prisoner.

On the hearing on the 6th of May, M[r]. Wilkes was liberated ; the Lord Chief Justice declaring the unanimous opinion and decision of the Court, that publishing a libel did not come within the offences of treason, felony, or breach of the peace, which cases alone deprived a member from privilege of Parliament [2].

From this business arose some questions in both Houses : and M[r]. Pitt [3] joined heartily in the attempt to condemn these proceedings against the indisputable rights and privilege of Parliament.

Though the Opposition was foiled in a noble struggle, on a close division in a very full house, and after long debate, and was not able to bring the house directly to stigmatize the Secretary who had issued a *general* warrant, the nation had an extreme satisfaction in hearing from the mouth of the

---

[1] Charles, eldest son of Sir William Wyndham. He succeeded to the Earldom of Egremont on the death of his uncle, the ninth Duke of Somerset, on whom this peerage had been conferred, with a limitation to his nephew Charles Wyndham, in 1749. Lord Egremont was Secretary of State from October 9, 1761–August 21, 1763, when he died very suddenly. His sister, Elizabeth, married George Grenville.

[2] The ground of decision was that a seditious libel was not a breach of the peace, though it tended to a breach of the peace. As soon as Parliament re-assembled the two Houses resolved that 'privilege of Parliament does not extend to the case of writing or publishing seditious libels.' Chief Justice Pratt was technically right, but the resolutions of the Houses were needed to prevent parliamentary privilege from interfering with the course of the criminal law.

[3] Pitt strongly opposed the abandonment of this 'privilege,' and in the Lords Grafton joined in a protest against the resolution (*Parl. Hist.* xv. 1378).

same illustrious Lord Chief Justice the declaration that, except in cases of treason, a *general* warrant was *illegal*, oppressive, and unwarrantable; a victory in the cause of liberty thus obtained in a court of justice gave additional comfort[1].

The judges received the applause to which this proof of their spirit and independance had the fairest claim; and this weighty decision tended greatly to ennoble the constitutional lawyer who had so peculiarly distinguished himself, and the tenor of whose whole life was a constant testimony how well he was deserving of the honor to which he was afterwards called. Near the end of his days, another point Lord Camden also carried, and which he often mentioned to me with exultation that he had lived to see decided, and in the success of which he had been so instrumental; for his lordship and M[r]. Cha[s]. Fox had the principal honor in getting a bill through the two Houses which restored to juries that constitutional right, in cases of a libel, of judging of the law as well as of the fact[2].

It could not be expected that Lord Bute's Treasury[3], with S[r]. Francis Dashwood[4] as Chancellor of the Exchequer could long resist that torrent which appeared breaking in upon them.

---

[1] The two matters of this nature which came before Pratt were—

(*a*) The legality of a general warrant, i.e. a warrant issued by a Secretary of State to seize a person, not named in the warrant, as being concerned in a specified offence.

(*b*) The legality of a warrant, similarly issued, to enter premises and to seize and bring books and papers to be examined.

On the first of these points his ruling was questioned in a bill of exceptions, the case was taken to the King's Bench as a court of error, and went off on a bye-point after Lord Mansfield and the three puisne judges had left no doubt of their opinion as to the illegality of these warrants (Leach *v.* Money, 19 *State Trials*, 1001).

On the second of these points the decision of the Court of Common Pleas was not questioned (Entick *v.* Carrington, 19 *State Trials*, 1030).

[2] This is not quite accurate. By 32 Geo. III, c. 60, a jury in cases of libel may find a verdict on the general issue of libel or no libel, and is not confined to the question of publication.

[3] Here we go back to the beginning of 1763.

[4] Sir Francis Dashwood, afterwards Lord Despencer. Historians chiefly dwell on the profligacy of his private life and the incapacity which he displayed as Chancellor of the Exchequer, but he seems to have been a man of taste and ability, though not a financier. See Walpole, *Memoirs*, i. 172 *note*, by Sir Denis Le Marchant.

An injudicious and ill framed tax on cyder, giving formidable powers to the officers of excise, raised a ferment in the country; and nothing but its repeal could have allayed the out-cry. The nation, even where a tax on cyder was no grievance, caught the alarm from conceiving that the disposition of Government was to extend arbitrary and oppressive laws on the people. The dread of these exasperated the populace, and drove them to unwarrantable lengths, and Lord Bute, was, in consequence, assaulted by them in the most menacing manner[1]. Soon after, and suddenly, the Earl of Bute withdrew from the Treasury[2] and from the helm, to the management of which his talents were by no means equal; neither did he possess sufficient political fortitude, a quality so essential to a statesman in a high responsible situation, that every other would lose its proper effect for want of this.

M[r]. George Grenville[3] became First Lord and Chancellor of the Exchequer; and, as we understood, on the advice of Lord Bute to the king[4], though there may be good reason for believing, that his manners were never agreeable to His Majesty. I had not sufficient knowledge of M[r]. Grenville to venture to describe his character, though I believe he meant well for the public, in whose service he was certainly indefatigable; but many of his measures were undoubtedly most injudiciously chosen. On the resolution regarding general warrants, he was nearly pushed in the House of Commons[5], but on every other question he had from both houses the

---

[1] The assault upon Bute took place not in consequence of the Cyder Bill, but at the opening of Parliament, on November 25, 1762.

[2] The Cyder Bill received the royal assent on March 31, 1763. Bute resigned on April 8.

[3] George Grenville (1712 – 1770), second son of Richard Grenville and brother of the first Earl Temple.

[4] The entire Ministry was settled by Bute. The only point on which Grenville seems to have been allowed a voice was whether Shelburne or Halifax should be Secretary of State, and his opinion in favour of Halifax prevailed (*Grenville Papers*, 32–40).

[5] The Ministry were most closely pushed in a division on a motion for an adjournment of the debate on a resolution condemning general warrants as contrary to law. Their majority was reduced to 10. This was in the early morning of February 15, 1764. The House sat till 7.30 a.m. (*Grenville Papers*, ii. 263, 491).

fullest support. The particular measures to which I have alluded were the laws and regulations which put a stop to that trade between the Americans and the Spanish West India Islands and Main which had been so long winked at by every Government with advantage, because the British manufactures &c. were spread through the extent of these countries, and the return to a great proportion paid in bullion. With this assistance the American trader could take off and pay for large shares of the exports from Great Britain: the mother country thus deriving every essential commercial advantage from this most lucrative traffick. The sourness and discontents occasioned by these measures were great and general throughout the American colonies. Associations were entered into to promote their own manufactures of every description. But the minister's foresight did not reach such an event; nor did this angry resolution of our American brethren instruct him to relax from his threatened Stamp Act, the notorious source of still greater evils.

During the course of the summer many were the ministerial intrigues between the different parties to approach nearer to each other; but, as they all missed their object, I have not retained such a recollection of them as to wish to relate them; nor would they be interesting if I had. An attempt to bring the Ministry, namely, D. of Bedford, M^r. Grenville, and the two Secretaries, the Earls of Sandwich and Hallifax, to a more close and cordial connexion with Lord Bute[1] and his friends failed entirely.

Various overtures were also made to M^r. Pitt; but none of these did shew the ground sufficiently secure for him to venture into office. I was with him several times both at

---

[1] When Egremont died suddenly in August, 1763, Bute, without consulting Grenville, advised the king to send for Pitt. Pitt saw the king on Saturday, August 27, and Monday, August 29. The negotiation fell through, but the interference of Bute made Grenville intensely hostile to him, and the alleged proscription of Bedford by Pitt caused Bedford and his friends to join the Grenville Ministry. It is difficult therefore to see how any attempts could have been made with the faintest likelihood of success to bring Bute and the ministers together. (*Life of Hardwicke*, iii. 377–381).

Hayes and in Harley Street, and afterwards at his small
lodging in Bond Street; he always treated me with great
frankness; but all his conversations and observations, which
were long, constantly terminated with his firm opinion that
the ground was not secure. With Lord Temple I lived a
great deal, both in town and in the country. His lordship
was more backward than M[r]. Pitt in his hopes of seeing an
Administration again established that could give confidence
to the nation, and gain its support in return ; and this persuasion or determination in Lord Temple encreased so much, and
beyond the observation of M[r]. Pitt himself, that when, some
little time after[1], he had considered all things to be settled
with His Majesty, and had sent for his Lordship, he laughed
at my idea, when I declared that I believed he would not find
Lord Temple so accommodating as he might expect. However, on their first discussion of the business after Lord
Temple's arrival, M[r]. Pitt found that I had judged right; and
the want of Lord Temple's concurrence at that time was
given out as the cause of M[r]. Pitt's declining also. If that
arrangement had taken place, M[r]. Pitt intended that I should
have been one of the Secretaries of State [2].

But to return to M[r]. Grenville's Ministry, which had been
supported by great majorities, (except on the debate on
general warrants,) in both Houses; we can but remark that
the vexatious and impolitic acts that were passed in the year
1764, and at the beginning of 1765 under these mighty
majorities were rapidly working out the greatest distresses
and losses to the country.

The Administration met the Parliament in 1765 with great
confidence in their own strength ; and too little attention to
those steps by which they had ascended to their power. The
illness of the king during the session awakened the duty of

---

[1] In June, 1765, see *infra*, p. 53.

[2] Perhaps this is a confusion of Pitt's
intentions in August, 1763, and in June,
1765. In the first case, Pitt intended
that he and Charles Townshend should
be Secretaries of State, while Grafton
was to be of the Cabinet. At the later
date Grafton was offered the post of
Secretary of State (*Grenville Papers*,
ii. 199).

Parliament to bring forward a Regency Bill, which was early suggested by the king himself. The bill was accordingly brought into the House of Peers and there passed, though so drawn as to exclude the princess mother from being nominated regent. In the Commons this affront was taken off by the insertion of H. R. H.'s name, and by the amendment carried up and agreed to, by the Lords : when the ministers had the mortification of being obliged to submit to bear that affront which they had destined for others [1].

The evident intention of the king's principal servants in this business sealed their own overthrow; and as they had never been graciously considered in the closet, the consequences which would naturally follow were easily foreseen. Yet some were so blinded with ambition as not to be aware of the slippery ground on which the Ministry stood : and it was observed with surprize that M[r]. Cha[s]. Townshend [2] in particular, a short time after, accepted the part of Paymaster on the dismission of Lord Holland [3], who had, on the retreat of Lord Bute, given up the lead of the House of Commons to M[r]. George Grenville.

My friends very justly reproached me for idling my time away in the country during a great part of this Session, without attending sufficiently to that duty in Parliament which became my station and was expected from me. They, however,

---

[1] The ministers first proposed that the king should be empowered to nominate, as regent, the queen or any other member of the royal family usually resident in England. Then arose the question whether the Princess of Wales, the king's mother, was of the royal family. On this point the Lord Chancellor differed from Bedford and Halifax, who maintained that the royal family meant those who were in the succession. Ministers, by representing to the king that the princess' name if introduced would be struck out, persuaded him to agree to a form of words which definitely excluded her. Then came the insertion of the name of the princess as described in the text.

[2] Charles, second son of the third Viscount Townshend (1725-1767). His talent, his social charm, and his infirmity of purpose, make him a prominent figure in the memoirs of the time ; his disastrous American policy gives him a permanent and melancholy place in our history.

[3] Henry Fox, the first Lord Holland (1705-1774). The story of this dismission is most fully told in Fitzmaurice's *Life of Shelburne*, vol. i. ch. iii, 'The Pious Fraud.'

treated me with more attention than such conduct deserved ; for I was by them constantly acquainted with all that was passing in the political world, and the Opposition had so little expectation of being called upon to take a part in administration, unless under, and by the recommendation of M^r. Pitt, that even when the coolness between the king and his servants was apparent to all mankind, to act under M^r. Pitt became the general voice and was our principal wish.

It may not be amiss to insert Lord Rockingham's[1] letter, which brought me up to attend the Regency Bill, as it may serve to shew the light in which the marquis and his friends considered the Bill in its introduction ; and afterwards it will be proper to enter into some detail on many negociations and occurrences that followed.

April 24th, 1765.

MY DEAR LORD,

His Majesty came to the House to day to open the affair of the Regency Bill. I enclose to your Grace the speech. Our Address was only in general terms, to congratulate upon His Majesty's recovery, and to thank him for his care and foresight &c. in providing for the security of the country &c., and to promise that we will proceed in this matter with all expedition. Nothing was said in our House by any of our friends. Lord Temple and L^d. Lyttleton went away before the Address was moved. The Bill I expect will be brought in on Friday and read the first time, and it would not surprize me if a second reading and commitment should be pressed for that day or for Saturday.

Upon so great a point I cannot refrain expressing my earnest wish that your Grace should not be absent. Your Grace will observe by the speech that it is not intended that *the regent* shall be appointed by the Act ; but that it is left to the king by instrument to nominate either the queen or some *one of his royal family*. It is said that by this description a certain great lady is excluded : how far it is so, I am not certain. But supposing it was so, yet a fresh objection lies from the unusualness of the Regent not being nominally inserted. There are other parts expected in the Bill which will be liable to great objections, and I doubt not but that there will be some lords who can and will make their objections.

Lord Temple yesterday wished I would have sent an express to you for to-day : but the time was so short that your Grace would scarce have

---

[1] Charles Watson Wentworth, second Marquis of Rockingham, born March 19, 1730 ; died July 1, 1782. He was a direct descendant of the Earl of Strafford.

arrived in London before 3 °clock this evening, and indeed I doubted whether anything would have been entered upon in the House to day.

I have more expectation on what may pass on Friday, but even on that I have hesitated for some hours whether to send to you or no, as I would not willingly occasion you a long journey to little purpose. The very chance of a debate deserves your attention, and in that light I will hope to apologize for my venturing to do what I now do.

I am ever &c.
ROCKINGHAM.

GROSVENOR SQUARE,
   Wednesday night, 12 °clock.

LETTERS, 1761–1765 .

THE REV. JOHN YOUNG TO THE DUKE OF GRAFTON

MY DEAR LORD,

Tho' I make no doubt but your Grace has many who give you far better accounts of what is doing here, than I am able to do, I will not make that any longer my excuse lest your Grace think it a pretence to cover my laziness, and that I fail in my regard and respect to you, which would give me very great concern.

As I have not seen our new queen, I cannot give your Grace any account of her person on my own authority. They who have seen her, do not say much of her beauty. By what I hear, she is a little woman, not unlike Miss Pitt who refused Lord Buckingham. But whatever her person is the king is highly pleased with her, and very happy in his choice. The shew of cloth and jewels was very extravagant: the Court well conducted. L^d. Westmoreland[1] kneeled to Lady Sarah Lennox mistaking her for the queen, as she stood next to Her Majesty, being first bridemaid. It was observed that there is a fatality on the Chancellors of Oxford, always to mistake their kings and queens. George Selwyn says the lady in waiting should have told him that was the Pretender.

Lord Huntingdon has raised a flame in the bed-chamber, wh. will at last destroy him; tho he has less interest than any one in so high a post, he carries it higher than any of his predecessors, and has made all the

---

[1] Chancellor of the University of Oxford, 1758–1762.

lords his enemies, who seem agreed to dispute with him every point, and will at last drive him out of his place.

Your old friend the Abp. of York[1] is at last gone to his own home. The Bp. of London is dead too[2]. L[d]. Talbot[3] who is become a very great man, and an attentive hearer of sermons (I am not in jest) pushes Bp. Hayter for London. He made Hayter's peace for him at Leicester House in the late reign. The D. of Newcastle, who has never forgiven him the affair of the preceptorship, sets up Bp. Thomas of Lincoln against him, tho he never cared for Thomas, but he is L[d]. Granville's man, whose assistance I suppose his Grace expects, and that by their joint interest they may keep Hayter out of London. Bp. Drummond of Salisbury is talked of for Abp. of York, and L[d]. Talbot's brother and Dr. Newton of St. George's for the new bishops : but I believe nothing will be settled till after the coronation.

As to peace or war, what I hear is, that there were great divisions in the Cabinet. L[ds]. Granville, Temple, Bute, Halifax, Legonier[4] and Mr. Pitt were for continuing the war, L[d]. Chancellor, the Dukes of Devonshire, Bedford, and Newcastle, L[ds]. Hardwick and Mansfield for accepting the terms offered by France ; and it is surmised that L[d]. Bute came at last over to their opinion. There was some heat between the D. of Bedford and Mr. Pitt. The present negociation relates only to the separate interests of England and France ; whatever relates to the Allies on either side (and consequently the towns in Flanders) is to be referred to the Treaty of Augsburgh. The great dispute relates to the Newfoundland Fishery. By the Treaty of Utrecht the French have a right to build stages and dry their fish on Newfoundland from Cape Bonavista northwards; they demand Canso in Nova Scotia for their small craft to run into : we refuse it because it is on the continent, and offer them St. Pierre, a small island in the Gulf of St. Laurence instead of it, and are now in expectation of their answer. Mr. Pitt's friends affect to give out that they are not sincere in the negociation : I should think their distress a good pledge of their sincerity.

And now I think I have troubled y[r] Grace with a great deal. I wish you may not be tired with so long a letter, and so little worth y[r] knowledge. I beg my most humble respects to her Grace. What has she

---

[1] John Gilbert (1693-1761), he was succeeded by the Hon. R. H. Drummond.

[2] Thomas Sherlock, he was succeeded by Bishop Hayter.

[3] William, son of Lord Chancellor Talbot, he was Steward of the Household 1761-1782, and Lord High Steward at the coronation. He is described as a man of parts, but violent and eccentric.

[4] John, Earl Ligonier (1680-1770), he had fought in all Marlborough's battles, and served in our campaigns in Flanders and Germany 1742-1747. He was at this time Master-General of the Ordnance.

been about, that the world has not yet seen an ode from Voltaire on the Duchess of Grafton ? That was one of the first things I expected from her residence in his neighbourhood. I hope she is pleased with the Swiss, and happy there and wherever she goes. I am, my lord, with the sincerest wishes for your health and happiness,

Y^r Grace's most obliged and obedient ser.

JOHN YOUNG.

LONDON, *Sep^{ber}*. 11th, 1761.

LORD JOHN CAVENDISH TO THE DUKE OF GRAFTON

LONDON, Decr. 15th, 1761.

MY DEAR LORD,

I had the honour of yours on the 5th of this month, I believe it was very long in its journey. Considering the events which have happened here, I ought to have wrote to you without waiting for an answer, but everything is so perplex'd both in politicks and upon the turf, that I do not know how to give an account of them. It is difficult to assign any reason for Pitt's quitting, which does not make strongly against him. Whether he was averse to all peace, because he found that his importance, would diminish at the end of the war; or that finding the war grow too expensive, and its conduct too difficult, he chuse to get out of the scrape in time ; or whether he really had formed the magnificent project which is imputed to him, of crushing both branches of the house of Bourbon at once, none but himself can tell. His subsequent conduct has been weak ; the accepting the peerage and pension, at the same time that his brothers resigned their places, was absurd. His writing the letter was mean[1], but the going to dine at Guildhall in such a parade as almost to excite the mob to insult the king, was criminal. He conduct in the House of Commons has been calm and proper (his indecent inveteracy against G. Grenville excepted).. A few days ago Rigby as the Duke of Bedford's *mouth* made a violent and good speech against the German war, particularly against employing English troops there; after much speeching, Pitt spoke for an hour and a half in defence of the measure with great compliments to the late king and Prince Ferdinand, but no question was put upon it. The next day Pitt not being there, your knight of the shire Mr. Banbury stood up, and with a very theatrical tone and gesture made a flimzy kind of speech against the German war, and took the liberty of abusing Pitt heartily. Soon after L^d. George Sackville

---

[1] This must be Pitt's reply to Bute's letter asking him, by the king's direction, what mark of royal favour he would be disposed to accept. The letters are in the *Chatham Corresp*. ii. pp. 146-153.

D 2

spoke very well and moderately against the expence of it. He was heard as quietly and replied to as civilly by those who answered him, as if nothing had happened[1]; he has been up twice with equall success. Soon after, spoke a Col[l]. Barrè, an Irishman, brought in by L[d]. Shelburne (who is a great man now). He has served in America with reputation and is called clever; I only know him to be the most impudent man living. He said that during the late reign everything was made subservient to Hanoverian counsels and interests. That he believed this king had never looked on the map of Hanover. From the late king he proceeded to Pitt, whom he called the most profligate of men, and abused him for about ten minutes, and so finished. Our friend Townshend called him to order about the late king, but being wrong in his point of order was forced to let him proceed. The worthy gentlemen with great places were shamefully cool in vindicating their late master. At last Charles Yorke did it prodigiously well, he gave the history of the last seven years, and vindicated the conduct of the king and his ministers throughout. I think it was the best argumentative speech I ever heard, his manner could not be pleasing. The next day, Barrè having been told, as I imagine, that it was wrong to attack a man behind his back, fell upon Pitt in a more outrageous manner than before, and went on to the end with a torrent of Billinsgate, without the least appearance of talking to the question. He was interrupted four or five times, but nothing could shake his steady Irish countenance. Pitt only explained one point, did not answer, was quite calm. I suppose this to be a favourite, but I think he will do his friends more harm than good. Now for the more important point of the turf. I had a great deal of money upon Prospect, so never went below the turn of the lands. When I first saw Cassandra she was quite done, yet the colt she beat came in a tolerable good place. I know that L[d]. Rockingham thought Ottley's mare a good one, he had tried her a long course, and that kind of lameness from a bruise in the foot very often does not stop horses much after they are warm. Your mare is certainly no Tartar, but she need not be quite so bad as she appeared. I do not know what to think of your match with Dorimond. S[r] John Moore's Dan has made such improvement, that there is no reasoning about him. Panton certainly thought his grey horse an extraordinary one, but his being beat by Pangloss Fribble seems to prove the contrary. I am persuaded he did not race in his form the last day. Fortunatus's beating Prospect has compleated the confusion and proved that our stable knew nothing. I believe Dorimond is speedy and a great jade, but a son of Panton's Arabian ought not to make the play. Upon the whole I think it a *cross and pile*[2] match ; I should be glad he could be tried again if possible.

I am glad your Grace is grown so great a courtier; shall you come

---

[1] See p. 66 *n*.   [2] *Cross and pile* = heads and tails, a toss-up.

back as great a coxcomb as you did the last time. I must trouble your Grace to give my most respectful compliments to the Dutchess, and thank her for her goodness in remembering me. I take it for granted that Lady Georgiana grows very tall and jabbers French prodigiously, but pray do not lett her forget her English. I suppose you have heard that my brother George is made Comptroller ; it was done in the handsomest manner possible. I have been forced to stay generally in town, and have had very little hunting hitherto ; and London has been remarkably dull. Charles Fitzroy is grown very fat. I never saw him look so well.

I am yrs sincerely,

J. Cavendish.

Duke of Devonshire to the Duke of Grafton

Chatsworth, Novr. 6, 1762.

My dear Lord,

I shou'd have answered your Graces very kind letter immediately, but I was apprehensive that if I trusted it to the post that it wou'd go round by London and there undergo an inspection, which I was unwilling to indulge the Ministry with.

Your Graces friendship and goodness to me on this occasion has made me happy beyond measure. I do assure you no one can set a higher value upon it than I do, I only wish to have it in my power to shew my gratitude to your Grace, and to convince you that I think myself most infinitely oblig'd to you. It is no small satisfaction to me to find you approve of my conduct, but indeed, my lord, there was scarce any option left me, it seems as if they had a mind to get quit of me, and acted in such a manner as I must have been the lowest of mortals to have submitted to; there is some mistery in the great resentment that the king has show'd against me, what it is I am at a loss to guess. My brother deliver'd your message. The Whigs will certainly think themselves much oblig'd to you as it can not be in better hands ; as yet I am quite a stranger to what ought or can be done, we can not be too cautious how we set out, and whenever we attempt to show our strength, take care to do it upon a strong point, and in which we shall be well grounded, as yet there are no overt acts, and nothing to lay hold of but a favourite, and that always weighs sufficiently on the nation. What effect it will have in both Houses I can not pretend to determine. I take for granted you will be up at the meeting, every body will then be in town, and we must consult together and see what is proper to be done. It is indeed a great pleasure to me to find our sentiments agree, and that we are likely to act together, for I fear parties will run high, and consequently friendships and connections broke. But believe me, my dear lord, whatever happens,

my friendship and regard for your Grace will always be the same, and
you will ever find me

Your Graces

most faithfull friend

·   and obed^t. humble serv^t.

DEVONSHIRE.

May I beg my most respectfull compliments to the Dutchess and beg
leave to assure her Grace y^t I am her most humble serv^t.

GENERAL CONWAY [1] TO THE DUKE OF GRAFTON

Near WILLEMSDAHL, 25 *June*, 1762.

MY LORD,

As Fitz Roy is not with us I think it a duty I owe to your Grace's
goodness for me to acquaint you with any of our military events that are
deserving of your notice.   That of yesterday I really think so : and tho'
not a battle, as glorious an action for our commander as any that has
happen'd perhaps since the war began.

We were encamp'd since the 21st near the Dymmel ; the French near
Halle, about two leagues on the other side.   Our situation seem'd defen-
sive; but yesterday morning our Duke [2] executed his very noble design
of passing the Dymmel and attacking the two marshals in their camp.
Ld Granby with his corps march'd to their right flank and Gen^{ls}.   [3]
and   [3]   to their left, while the rest march'd to their front.   We
crossed the river about 4 o'clock in the morning and it's past all credi-
bility that at the distance we lay and in full daylight these gentlemen
shou'd let themselves be surpriz'd ; yet so it was, their tents were standing
till L^d. Granby was withing about half a mile of their flank : after the
attack began it was rather a flight than an action on their part throughout.   The chief stand they made was on their left, where L^d. Granby
attack'd with his usual spirit and where he must have been overpower'd
I think by their numbers if we had not mov'd up in the critical time to
disengage him, which indeed was H.S.H.'s plan.

The French did not stop till they came to Cassel.   They have lost
I reckon about 5,000 men, as we have 100 officers and above 3,000
prisoners, and I saw a great many kill'd and wounded.   Our loss

---

[1] General Conway was connected by
marriage with Grafton, whose aunt
Lady Arabella Fitzroy married Conway's elder brother, the first Marquis
of Hertford.

[2] Ferdinand of Brunswick (1721-
1792). He succeeded to the Duke of

Cumberland in the command of the
English forces in 1758.   This fight was
the beginning of a series of operations
which ended in the surrender of Cassel
by the French.

[3] These names are illegible in the
MS.

I imagine does not exceed a few hundred, and scarce an officer of note but poor Col. Harry Townshend, who I am afraid is mortally wounded, and Cap. Middleton of the Guards.

We have taken a good many colours and a few canon; but the Grenadiers I think also lost two or three of the latter.

The French officers whom I spoke to all talk of their commanders in terms of the highest contempt and of ours with the greatest admiration as he deserves.

I beg my best respects to the Duchess, I hope you have had all the agrément and satisfaction you cou'd wish for in your Italian journey, and am, my lord, with the greatest respect,

Your Grace's most obedient
and faithful servant
H. S. Conway.

CHAPTER II

AUTOBIOGRAPHY. 1765-1766

GRAFTON AS SECRETARY OF STATE IN THE ROCKINGHAM MINISTRY

[1] NOTWITHSTANDING there had been many reports of dissentions among His Majesty's ministers and servants during the course of the whole winter, and particularly towards the conclusion of the session, no authentic accounts ever reached me of them, nor of the king's displeasure at their conduct and behaviour to himself, till I received an express from the Duke of Cumberland. The letter written by H.R.H. was brought to me at Wakefield Lodge the 14th of May at night [2]. It contained an intimation of the king's intention of *changing his Administration,* of taking in their places those whom H.R.H. said, both *he* and *myself* had wished in power, and adding a desire of talking *public, as well as private affairs over with me.*

This summons was instantly obeyed, and I got to Cumberland House even before the Duke was called. He sent for me to come immediately into his bedchamber, and opened

---

[1] Here begins that portion of the autobiography which was composed from memoranda made at the time. It is unfortunate that the 'foul copy' in which this is noted should here be wanting. I rely for the statement as to the use of the memoranda upon a manuscript note of Lord Carlingford, who had the 'foul copy' before him in its entirety (see Introduction). The letter referred to, with others turning on these

negotiations, will be found at the end of the chapter.

[2] The account given by the Duke of Cumberland of these negotiations—set out in the *Rockingham Memoirs,* p. 193 et seq.—tallies in the most remarkable way with that given by the Duke of Grafton, only the Duke of Cumberland has made the whole transaction earlier by a week, than it really was.

the discourse by telling me, that, though he was only commanded by the king to intimate his present dispositions to
employ M^r. Pitt, and the Lords Rockingham and Temple, yet
he was confident that he should be forgiven, if he stretched
his commission by adding me to the number, saying at the
same time with his usual goodness, that he had that regard
and opinion of me, that he could not avoid wishing to hear
my thoughts and inclinations, as well for myself, as for my
friends on such an occasion. After expressions of this sort the
Duke told me that he had had some knowledge of His Majesty's
intentions before the Regency Bill was brought into our
house; but as he had endeavored to dissuade the king from
bringing it in, at so short a notice, and when so little time was
left to consider a matter of that importance, he had humbly
begged to decline giving His Majesty his opinion of men,
as he was sure those whom he might recommend would not
undertake that Bill so drawn and pressed at such a moment.

The behaviour of the ministers on that occasion, who wished
to exclude the princess dowager, was such, as neither answered
their own design, nor in any way turned to their honor, but
put the finishing stroke to the dislike the king had already
conceived against them. After Lord Hallifax had moved,
that the king might in that Bill be empowered to name
as regent any one of his royal family, descendant of
George 2^d, they thought their end was answered; but soon
saw the meanness to which they were obliged to bend by
assenting afterwards to the amendment, proposed and made
to it in the lower house, of allowing the princess dowager
by name to be added to those who might be regent. The
defeat of their design was not the only consequence of their
attempt, which was plainly seen through, and the princess
was naturally expected to resent this affront. Their servility
in submitting was sufficient to add in the king's mind a contempt of their characters to that disgust he already had for
men who had brought an odium on his Government and who
had not, as he expressed, served him with decency in the closet.

The king, in this situation and a few days before the intended prorogation of Parliament, sent for the Duke of Cumberland[1], and asked his advice in forming such an Administration as would please his kingdom, and carry weight and credit both at home and abroad; two points, of which he was sensible the country as well as the Crown stood in need. The Duke, penetrated with this mark of the king's favor, and more with the return of His Majesty's confidence, expressed his sensibility of both, but added that he was certain that the king would not, in any shape, mean that he should engage in an affair of such delicacy and real consequence in any manner derogatory to his honor. Give me leave, Sir, said the Duke, to observe that I should hurt that honor, as well as lose the esteem of the world, if I was forming an Administration in which Lord Bute should have either weight or power. After every assurance given by the king, on this head the Duke could no longer doubt of the sincerity of such a proposal. Much conversation then passed on the means of forming a new Administration, and the Duke left the king, commanded by him to think fully upon it.

His Majesty had intimated, however, his *wish* to have Lord Northumberland[2] at the head of the Treasury; a proposal, of which, in the hurry of so many and important matters, I sincerely think the Duke did not immediately weigh the consequence, but he soon afterwards saw it, and had the satisfaction also to find that the king himself abandoned it, when it was shewn to him to be inconsistent that so near a relation of Lord Bute's should hold so great a post of

---

[1] The Duke of Cumberland evidently left on Grafton's mind the impression that he had recently seen the king, and his own account of the negotiations, printed in the *Rockingham Memoirs*, reads as though he must have known more of the king's wishes than he could have learned at second-hand; but he does not there mention any interview with the king before Saturday, May 18, or, as he calls it, the 11th (*Rockingham Memoirs*, i. 200); except the one

described as having taken place on Easter Day, April 7 (*ibid.* 186), when the king seemed to wish to say something which he never said.

[2] Sir Hugh Smithson married the eldest daughter of the seventh Duke of Somerset, on whose death, in 1749, he succeeded to the earldom of Northumberland. A dukedom was conferred on him in 1766. His eldest son, Lord Warkworth, married Lord Bute's daughter.

business. For, let his professions have been ever so satisfactory to those, who were to act with him; the world would
still deem the Treasury in the hands of a lieutenant of Lord
Bute's, and would consider such a step incompatible with all
the former conduct and professions of those who were to form
the new Administration.

This was the Duke's account of what had passed: he
then sounded my own inclinations, and whether I wished
any thing in such a change for myself, or what for my
friends: he told me he both disapproved and much lamented
that I was so much retired from the world, and not giving,
in my rank, every assistance which my country had a right
to require of me. I answered H.R.H., with many thanks
for the favorable opinion he had of me, that I was very
sensible that my power of serving my country he rated
infinitely beyond my abilities, but that no one could in his
heart wish it better, nor would go further to serve it, and
that I did not mean to retire another year so much from
the world as I had done. I expressed next, that the small
experience I had early in my life of a Court had made me
take a resolution, which was every day strongly confirmed,
that no inducement could lead me to take a Court employment, but that I was ready to undertake any one of business,
provided I was satisfied that I could go through such an
office with credit to myself and without prejudice to my
country; that I owned my wish was to have my brother,
Col: Fitzroy, Scudamore, and some other friends who had
been sufferers on my account, replaced, which would
sufficiently shew my intentions, and to be left myself to
applaud and forwardly to support the measures, which I was
confident would be pursued by an *honorable Administration*[1].

---

[1] 'I proposed to him, if Secretary of
State should stagger him, that he would
be first Lord of Trade with the Cabinet
Council, as that would be reckoned in
the world to be short of what he had
shown himself fit for. It did not avail
me, as he was equally sanguine that the
affair in general must succeed: and that
there was no present need for him to
engage in business: yet that a place in
Court was what he could not endure,
from the attendance requisite. Therefore, fearing his stay in town might add
to the other suspicions the ministers

Indeed such appeared to me, and does still, the way in which I could have been of the most use. The lower parts of business were not fit for the rank I stood in, nor were the greater more fit for the total inexperience I had of any office. Whereas the support of a man, who was looked upon as steady in his conduct, and not famed for supporting all Administrations, would have given weight to a cause, if I could have been allowed to have served it without being in place.

The Duke was not satisfied with my answer, and proposed and pressed me to be at the head of the Board of Trade, which I begged to decline, looking upon it in a very different light from what I found H.R.H. did, as I really thought it as difficult a post as any whatever. As this transaction was not to transpire at that time, I asked the Duke's leave to return into the country again that very day, which I did. I should have mentioned before, that whilst I was with the Duke, he asked me this question, whether I thought an Administration could be formed (principally out of the minority) without M^r. Pitt ? On my assuring him that my opinion was, that nothing so formed could be stable, he said he hoped there was every reason to think he would engage, as Lord Albemarle[1] had been with him the day before, and that his Lordship thought he saw it in a favorable light. With these hopes I left London, and in a few days afterwards had the mortification to see them blasted, by receiving a fresh messenger from the Duke of Cumberland desiring my immediate attendance in London. A letter written by Lord Albemarle by the Duke's order, dated at night May 22^d: brought me this account in words to this effect, that the Duke had been five hours with M^r. Pitt at Hayes, without prevailing on him to take a part, that the king was the next morning to answer

---

would have, he would return directly into the country most heartily wishing us success.' Such is the Duke of Cumberland's account of the end of the interview (*Rockingham Memoirs*, i. 194). The correspondence of the two statements is creditable to both parties.

[1] George, third Earl of Albemarle (1724–1772), had been the Duke's aide-de-camp at Fontenoy and Culloden, and as commander of the land forces at the taking of the Havannah, had greatly distinguished himself. He was now a lord of the bedchamber to the Duke.

some *questions*, to be put to him by his present ministers, in one of which H.R.H. was personally concerned, and that the Duke desired my support on the occasion. Lord Albemarle also adds, that the king had been most insolently treated by his ministers, and shamefully abandoned by those who should have profitted by this occasion to serve their king and country[1].

On receiving this account, my first step was to go instantly to receive H.R.H.'s commands, whom I found just going to Court to know the king's determination. He told me, however, in a few words the advice he had given to the king the night before, and referred me to Lord Albemarle for the whole of what had passed since I last waited upon him, commanding me also to wait upon him on his return from St. James's, and to dine with him. Lord Albemarle's account tallied so exactly with what the Duke afterwards related to me, that it is needless to repeat both.

H.R.H. said, that finding L^d. Temple cooler on the subject than he expected, and that M^r. Pitt was also less forward since Lord Temple's arrival in London, he had explained to the king the absolute necessity there was of every object being removed that might prevent M^r. Pitt's taking a part, and hoping even to have His Majesty's assurance that many measures might be redressed, and some wholly broken through, to make it more satisfactory to M^r. Pitt on entering upon his Ministry. On the preceding Saturday the king had sent for H.R.H., and told him, in the kindest terms and most explicit words, that he put himself wholly, in this affair, into his hands, that he saw plainly the propriety of his advice. For which reason he ordered him to go the next morning to M^r. Pitt with full powers from him to treat with M^r. Pitt, and to come into the constitutional steps he had before mentioned, as essential to the country; as also that the king was not backward to lean to his foreign politics, if he (M^r. Pitt) should think it most beneficial, when he saw how affairs then stood. H.R.H. told me, that he had patience

[1] The letter is printed *infra*, p. 81.

to attend to very long discourses which M^r. Pitt held on the
subject, in which the Duke declared he could not always
follow him; as he was sometimes speaking of himself as
already the acting minister, and then would turn about by
showing how impossible it was for him ever to be in an
employment of such a nature, and always would end by
observing that if such and such measures were pursued, he
would *applaud* them loudly from whatever men they came.

M^r. Pitt also told H.R.H. that if an Administration went
in on such ground as he had laid down, he would *exhort* his
friends, nay his brothers, to accept, but that he doubted much
whether the latter (meaning L^d. Temple and James Grenville) would.   His plan abroad was for a close union with the
northern Courts of Germany together with Russia, to balance
the Bourbon alliance, to which the Duke gave the answer
I before mentioned, and that the king was ready to support
M^r. Pitt in any alliance that he should judge the most valid
to check any attempts that might arise from the family compact of the House of Bourbon.   At home M^r. Pitt lamented
(and in which the Duke most sincerely joined) the infringe-
ment on our Constitution in the affair of the warrants left still
undecided, though twice before Parliament; the army degraded, as well as our liberties struck at, by the dismission
of officers who had taken the part in Parliament which their
consciences prompted them to; so much to their honor, tho'
contrary to their interest; and in addition to these, should
be taken into consideration the propriety of rewarding the
uprightness of L^d. Chief Justice Pratt at such a crisis, by
giving him a peerage.   To M^r. Pitt's question to the Duke
whether the great seal was promised to M^r. Chas. Yorke?
H.R.H. could only answer, that he could not say how far
the king had engaged himself with that gentleman.

The Duke did not tell me what I afterwards heard from M^r.
Pitt; that the Duke had that day mentioned it to be the king's
wish to have L^d. Northumberland at the head of the Treasury.
If it was mentioned, it is very clear that it was almost as
soon dropped, and I am confident that it was not, that day,

CH. II] PITT'S FIRST REFUSAL 47

the Duke's desire, any more that that of M[r]. Pitt; in which case I think it was possible that it was named more to feel M[r]. Pitt's notion or affections to that quarter, or perhaps by a policy, very unnecessary with so great a man, thinking it might be a concession that would please, when he found that L[d]. Temple would be agreeable to the king in that office. H.R.H. often, as he told me, pressed M[r]. Pitt to chalk out to the king a list of such as he would wish to fill all the posts of business, which, the Duke answered for, the king would instantly adopt. This was to no purpose; and the Duke was obliged to return to Richmond with the unpleasant account of his ill-success. The day following[1], the Duke, by His Majesty's command, was employed in endeavoring to form an Administration without M[r]. Pitt, and to that end L[d]. Lyttleton[2] was sounded to be placed at the head of the Treasury, with M[r]. C. Townshend as the Chancellor of the Exchequer[3]. These gentlemen both thought the ground too weak to stand long upon and wished to decline it. The latter of them accepted the pay office two days after under the old Ministry[4]. Many different posts were thought of and proposed for me during this *arrangement*; but none of them ever came to my ears till my coming to London, as it was unnecessary I should know of them, till the greater posts were fixed on and accepted. The king, on the day following[5], disappointed of this plan also, with his present Ministry at the door of the closet ready to resign, was under a difficulty, and in such a situation that he knew not which way to turn.

---

[1] Monday, May 20.

[2] George, first Lord Lyttleton: he was first cousin to Temple and George Grenville. His father, Sir Thomas Lyttleton, married Christian, daughter of Sir Richard Temple: Richard Grenville, father of Temple and G. Grenville, married Esther, an elder daughter of Sir R. Temple. Lord Lyttleton was connected by marriage with Pitt, his sister having married Pitt's only brother.

[3] Walpole, *Memoirs*, ii. 170, says that Newcastle and the Cavendishes were anxious for such a Ministry. Conway was to have been Secretary at War, so Walpole probably heard all that was under discussion. He and Conway agreed, and with reason, that such a Ministry could not last. No one at this time seems to have thought of Rockingham.

[4] Charles Townshend kissed hands as Paymaster on Friday, May 24 (*Grenville Papers*, iii. 182).

[5] Tuesday, May 21.

The Duke's advice then was, as the lesser evil of the two, to call in his old Administration rather than to leave the country without ministers, while the town was in a tumult raised against the Duke of Bedford by the Weavers, and the House of Lords passing the most strange, as well as violent, resolutions [1]. On the Wednesday morning, M[r]. Grenville, in the name of the rest, acquainted the king that before they should again undertake his affairs, they must lay before him some questions to be answered by His Majesty, on which the king taking him up, said ' *Terms*, I suppose you mean Sir, what are they [2] ?' M[r]. Grenville answered that they should expect further assurance that Lord Bute should never meddle in State affairs of whatsoever sort : that M[r]. Mackenzie [3] (his brother) should be dismissed from his employment : that Lord Holland should also meet with the same treatment : that Lord Weymouth [4] should be named Lord Lieutenant to Ireland, and that Lord Granby should be appointed Commander-in-Chief. He then left the king, from whom they were to have their answer the next day. M[r]. G. Grenville on that day also took the lead in the name of the rest ; and the king, advised by the D. of Cumberland, except in that point relating to himself, told them that he would never give up the possibility of

---

[1] The House of Lords, at the instance of the Duke of Bedford, had thrown out a Bill for raising the duty on Italian silks. In a riot which arose from the disappointment of the Spitalfields weavers at the rejection of the Bill, the Duke of Bedford was assaulted and struck with a stone on his way to the House: two days later his residence was attacked, and blood was shed in dispersing the rioters. The House of Lords examined witnesses and passed resolutions for the maintenance of the peace, but the expressions 'strange and violent' seem uncalled for.

[2] The statement made here as to the terms imposed by Grenville upon the king is confirmed by various contemporary authorities (*Grenville Papers*, iii. 181, 182, 187 ; Walpole, *Memoirs*, ii. 174). *Bedford Correspondence*, iii. 284, where an extract from the diary of Sir Gilbert Elliott describes the not unnatural anger of George III.

[3] James Stuart Mackenzie, the only brother of Lord Bute. For an account of his dismissal, see Walpole, *Letters*, iv. 367. He held the Privy Seal of Scotland, and was reinstated in 1766.

[4] Thomas Thynne, third Viscount Weymouth (1734-1796). He was appointed Lord Lieutenant of Ireland in May, 1765, but never entered on the office ; was Secretary of State 1768-1770 and 1775-1779 ; was created Marquis of Bath 1789.

employing his uncle on an emergency; which he should do, if he put any one in the post of Commander-in-Chief; that he assented to the others, tho' against his opinion; and that he supposed they would not press him to break his word which he had given to M[r]. Mackenzie, but that he was ready to give up the management of the Scotch affairs, if they would leave him in as Privy Seal to that kingdom. On their still insisting on his total dismission, the king was obliged to assent; and then by their friends they were considered as much stronger than they ever had been [1].

This affair being thus concluded, after having paid my duty at the king's levee I returned again into the country, and soon waited upon H.R.H. at Windsor Lodge during the races.

[The Duke of Cumberland was over at Hayes the day after I went back to Wakefield Lodge; and M[r]. Pitt had two long conferences, in consequence, with the king; and in the latter on Saturday May 19th had expectation that a thorough change would have taken place, according to the fullest of our wishes. Our hopes however were strangely thwarted by the disinclination of Lord Temple, who made such use of the mention of the Earl of Northumberland for the Treasury, as to stagger M[r]. Pitt himself, as I conjectured. But the cause of the failure of this negociation was imputed differently according as the partialities and prejudices of political men led them to represent it; that no obstacle arose from His Majesty I am perfectly assured. Those with whom I chiefly consorted were much inclined to blame M[r]. Pitt, who, as they

---

[1] A confusion arises here from an interpolation made by the Duke of Grafton into the first draft of the MS. As that draft is lost I must rely upon Lord Carlingford's notes for an explanation.

I collect from these notes that in the first draft the memoir went without interruption from the words 'Stronger than they ever had been,' to the words on p. 52, 'It was not to be wondered at.' Into this draft two later introductions were made. First came the sentence beginning 'This affair being now concluded,' after which sentence came the words 'In the mean while' on p. 50, followed by the narrative and correspondence describing the interview of Colonel FitzRoy with Pitt.

Next came a later insertion of the words now included in brackets. They seem to import a confusion between the interviews which Lord Albemarle and the Duke of Cumberland had with Pitt in May, and the interviews between Pitt and the king in June. See p. 53.

said, had *carte blanche* from the king.   M^r. Pitt, on the other hand, would not allow that this was the case ; and he observed that the expression itself was unfit to be used on such an occasion; and M^r. James Grenville has assured my brother that M^r. Pitt was much hurt to find the latter offer, *to which he had acceded*, broken off before M^r. P. had returned his answer; and M^r. J. G. added, that the reconciliation with George Grenville did not regard the public.]

In the mean while, I received a letter from my brother, who mentioned a conversation with M^r. J. Grenville, in which that gentleman had declared his own thoughts on the late negociation; adding that M^r. Pitt desired much an opportunity of explaining the whole to me.   My brother pressed me strongly from himself, as well as from M^r. Meynell[1] and other of my friends, to see M^r. Pitt as soon as possible, in order that I might be able to clear up and put a stop to divisions that this whole affair had made among friends, eager to defend the part those to whom they were most attached had taken in it.   I returned for answer to my brother that I must have some plainer certainty of such a wish of M^r. Pitt's, and that I would desire him to go to Hayes to know whether the case was as represented, and to lay before him my thoughts of his conduct on the occasion, which, partial as I was to him, even to me appeared unfathomable, and to want great explanation.   I even offered, in case of any thing having been misunderstood, that I should be too happy to be thought worthy of being employed by him either to get explained or renewed a measure that appeared to me the only one by which our king and country could attain their ancient glory.   Immediately on the receipt of my letter, my brother went to Hayes, and having heard from M^r. Pitt the whole relation, he transmitted the chief purport to me that same evening in the following letters.

---

[1] Mr. Meynell is slightingly spoken of in Walpole's *Memoirs*, iii. 119, but he was a man of considerable position in his county (Staffordshire), and was member successively for Lichfield, Lymington, and Stafford.   He moved more in sporting than in political circles.

LONDON, Wednesday, *May* 29th.

DEAR BROTHER,

At the end of my conversation with Mr. Pitt, I asked if I should write word to you, that he was resolved not to renew the negociation; he said, *Resolved* was a *large* word, and desired I would express myself thus *'Mr. Pitt's determination was final, and the negociation is at an end.'* (These are his own words.) As to your coming, he shall be extreamly happy to have the honor of seeing you, but would be ashamed to bring you to town for so little an object; yet, if you should come to London, would not only be proud to see you at Hayes and talk things over, but, if he could walk on foot to London to pay his respects to you, he would do it. Having said this, at your own leisure, any time within a week or so, if you come to London, he should think himself happy to see you at Hayes.

I am &c.

CHARLES FITZROY.

DEAR BROTHER,

My other is a formal answer to my commission,—this is a private account of my conversation at Hayes, as near as I can recollect the different heads and shorten in substance Mr. Pitt's two hours incessant talking. It is quite private between us, I mean you and myself.—

1st. I found he had not been acquainted with James Grenville's conversation with me; upon my telling it to him *in part*, he said it might have come from Lord Temple, but that the different periods were not exactly stated. He then went through every part of what had passed, and made his remarks with several refinements upon *manner* and *words*; and often declared his unwillingness to engage again in office. He rested the whole objections of this negociation upon the transaction's opening with the king's wish to have Ld. Northumberland at the head of the Treasury: at the same time, he expressed that he, *Mr. Pitt,* did not desire Ld. Temple should be there; but that he thought the whole transaction a phantom, and could never have been intended serious. He declared it impossible for him and H. R. H. to talk a different language as to fact, but that nothing like carte blanche was ever hinted (N.B. he thinks that an improper phrase, as it sounds like capitulating). He talked much of revolution families *personally* from their weight, but unconnected and under no banner; for all *that* was factious. He mentioned the great popular points: restitution of officers, privilege, &c., &c., change of system of politics, both domestic and foreign: said everything you would like, and resolved nothing but retirement—I must add, the highest commendations of H. R. H., his judgment, abilities, integrity, &c., &c.—but said that 'no man in England but himself would have brought such terms, no, not even Ld. Bute.' He left me totally in the dark, further than I could easily distinguish, he thinks that it was not meant to have it his administration.

For God's sake see him; it must not be tomorrow, as he has his reconciling dinner with George Grenville; *this he told me*[1]. The D. of C. goes to the birthday, so you may come on Monday, if you will, to see M[r]. Pitt, and take the birthday on Tuesday, if you like it.

Adieu yours
C. F. R.

It was not to be wondered at if His Majesty, under these circumstances[2], was led to try every practical means by which he could form an Administration capable of relieving him from the irksome situation in which he stood with his present servants. Among others, I was myself commanded by the king, thro' the D. of Cumberland, to wait on M[r]. Pitt at Hayes, and to bear to him His Majesty's wishes to be informed what steps would be the fittest for His Majesty to take in order to constitute an Administration, of which M[r]. Pitt was to be the head, and which might, thro' a confidence of the principles and abilities of the other ministers, give satisfaction to his people. H.R.H. told me, that if I had any doubt as to the authority, I might receive it from the king himself. I was young and unsuspicious, and moreover perfectly relied on the honor of those who were then present at this conference at Windsor Great Lodge, when the king's commands were communicated to me; and I desired no other authority. Since that time, experience would probably have stopt me from undertaking a commission so critical and, I may add, so hazardous[3]; yet I received the satisfactory declaration from all parties, that I had discharged my commission faithfully. M[r]. Pitt received me with the usual kindness which I had constantly met with from him ever since he first knew me at Stowe, when I was a boy from school; indeed his obliging attention had been daily encreasing. He appeared to be much pleased with the subject of the

---

[1] This dinner took place at Hayes on Thursday, May 30 (*Grenville Papers*, iii. 191). The reconciliation occurred just when the first applications were being made to Pitt, and accounts in part for the conduct of Temple.

[2] This sentence, in the original draft, followed after the words 'stronger than they had ever been,' on p. 49.

[3] The Duke's anxieties on this head are expressed in a letter to Albemarle, p. 84.

message I brought. He talked over many weighty political considerations and situations in a very open manner; some of which were to be considered as going no further than my own breast; the rest I was desired to report. In a visit of more than 2 hours[1], he concluded that, with every sense of duty to His Majesty for his obliging condescension, he could not, but to the king himself, state his views, and what would be his advice for the king's dignity and the public welfare.

M[r]. Pitt did see the king in a day or two after this, and again on June 22[d]; but, alas! it will appear by the following letters, that he was much disappointed in the warm expectation he had formed.

MY LORD,   PALL MALL, Saturday, *June* 22[d], 1765.

Having had an audience again to-day of His Majesty at the queen's house, I find myself under a necessity of expressing my extreme desire to have the honor of a conversation with your Grace; did my shatter'd health permit I would have had the pleasure of being my own messenger to Wakefield Lodge; as it is, I trust your Grace will, in consideration of my sincere respect and attachment, pardon the great liberty I take in desiring that your Grace would take the trouble of a journey to town. I am going to sleep at Hayes, where I find it necessary for me to be, as much as may be, for the air; and shall be proud and happy to have the honor of waiting on your Grace at my return to London Monday night, in case you should be then arrived, or some time on Tuesday next. A letter would but ill convey what I have to impart, I therefore defer entering into matter till I have the satisfaction of meeting; and will only say, that I think the royal dispositions are most propitious to the wishes of the publick, with regard to *measures* most likely to spread satisfaction; when your Grace arrives, you will hear with your own ears and see with your own eyes, which will be better than any lights I can convey. I have the honor to be, with perfect truth and respect

Your Grace's most obed[t]. and most humble serv[t].

WILLIAM PITT.

HAYES, Tuesday Even[g].

MY LORD,

It is with extreme concern that I am to acquaint your Grace, that L[d]. Temple declines to take the Treasury. This unfortunate event wholly disables me from undertaking that part which my zeal, under all

---

[1] This visit of the Duke of Grafton to Hayes seems to have taken place on June 18 (*Grenville Papers*, iii. 197). He went on to Stowe to confer with Temple before the king had seen Pitt (*ibid.* 199).

the weight of infirmities, had determined me to attempt. As, in this crisis, I imagine your Grace will judge proper to come to town; I trust you will pardon the trouble of this line, and believe me with true respect and attachment, Your Grace's most faithful and most obed[t]. humble serv[t].

WILLIAM PITT.

Despairing of receiving M[r]. Pitt's assistance at our head, a new plan for establishing a Ministry was proposed to His Majesty by H.R.H., and accepted; several, with myself, understanding that it came forward with the full declaration of our desire to receive M[r]. Pitt at our head, *whenever* he should see the situation of affairs to be such as to allow him to take that part. My concern afterwards was great, when I found, before the conclusion of our first session, that this idea was already vanished from the minds of some of my colleagues. I always understood this to be the ground on which I engaged; and it will be seen that I adhered to my own resolution to the last.

When the principal line of ministerial departments was settled between His Majesty and H.R.H., a considerable number of the leading men in both Houses were invited to a great dinner, (at whose house[1] I do not exactly recollect); where the great officers were to be fix'd on, as much as possible to the general satisfaction of the meeting as to the person himself. A real difficulty, however, arose concerning the Treasury; for the delicacy of Lord Rockingham kept him back, for sometime, from accepting that post, to which the Duke of Newcastle was giving up the claim reluctantly, though most of his own friends felt that his advanced age rendered him inadequate to fill it. After long resistance the Marquis yielded; and the other officers were nearly agreed upon, as we kissed hands for them on the 10th of July[2].

---

[1] The meeting took place at the Duke of Newcastle's house, Claremont, on June 30. Grafton was not present, but Newcastle answered for his readiness to take part in an Administration. The list of those present, and an account of what took place, is given in the *Rockingham* *Memoirs*, i. 218, and some further details in Walpole, *Memoirs*, ii. 189.

[2] The Ministry was settled as follows:—

First Lord of the Treasury, Marquis of Rockingham.

From many visits to Hayes, I was fully persuaded that M[r]. Pitt would be glad to see a Ministry take place, which was formed of men whose principles were in a great degree congenial with his own, notwithstanding his disappointment, and although he could not allow the new formation to pass in the world as of his recommendation to the king. On this ground I embarked with confidence, and am convinced that M[r]. Pitt approved, though he would not allow it to be said in so many distinct words ; and when Admirals Saunders and Keppel [1] were in doubt whether they should come in as Lords of the Admiralty, they had the express sanction of M[r]. Pitt. To keep the Duke of Newcastle in good humour, the patronage of the Church was added to the Privy Seal. Lord Winchelsea [2] came to the Presidency of the Council, and Mr. Conway [3] Secretary for the Southern and myself for the Northern Department.

One of the first acts of our Administration was to obtain from His Majesty the honors of a peerage for the true patriot, Lord Chief Justice Pratt, which the king had the condescension to grant to our earnest entreaties, the news of which was received by the nation with much applause.

The Duke of Cumberland was present at all our councils, on a general request made to H.R.H., approved by the king. We proceeded in business with great zeal and perfect concord, and we had every reason to be satisfied with the conduct of our new friends Lords Northington and Egmont in all our meetings. May I be allowed to say, that our entry into the Ministry was pleasing to the nation, though it must be

Chancellor of the Exchequer, Mr. W. Dowdeswell.

Lord Chancellor, Lord Northington.

Lord Privy Seal, Duke of Newcastle.

President of the Council, Lord Winchelsea.

Secretaries of State, Duke of Grafton, and General Conway.

First Lord of the Admiralty, Lord Egmont. (See p. 93, note.)

[1] See p. 101, note.

[2] Daniel, seventh Earl of Winchelsea, was now in his seventy-seventh year. He had on two previous occasions, in 1741 and 1757, held the office of First Lord of the Admiralty for a few months on each occasion.

[3] Second son of Francis, Lord Conway, and brother to the first Marquis of Hertford. He was born in 1721 and died in 1795.

owned that the disappointment was great, particularly in the
city, when it was seen that M^r. Pitt was not the minister?
Men's minds were so worked up by their wishes, that those
who affirmed that the Administration had the approval of
M^r. Pitt, and those who maintained the reverse equally, in
their extremes, passed over the strict boundary of truth ; and
by these very altercations they contrived to add much to the
popular opinion of his consequence.

When we had been about a month in office, I received
the following letter from M^r. Hopkins [1], which occasioned
a letter of mine to M^r. Pitt, and his answer. These will
probably be the best means of shewing what were his sentiments and dispositions at that point of time.

OVING, *Augst*. 12th, 1765.

MY LORD,

I was exceedingly sorry, on my return home from M^r. Bridgeman's,
to find that your Grace had been in the country, and that I had been
deprived of the pleasure of waiting on you by the other engagement.
I wanted to have seen you, to have told you how industrious M^r. G. G——e
is among his country neighbours in assuring them how much M^r. Pitt
disapproves of the present Administration. He dined a few days since
at a neighboring baronet's, where he entertained the company with
a conversation which had passed at Hayes between you, and the master
of it, which, I believe, was not all of it exactly the truth, but which I am
prevented from repeating by being told it was private conversation and
therefore to go no further. As to the former part, viz. his *disapprobation*,
&c. I said it was one thing to say, he not approved, and another that
he disapproved ; that the former might be true, but that I did not believe
the latter. I was answered,—M^r. G. said over and over, that M^r. Pitt
had absolutely expressed his disapprobation of the Ministry to him very
strongly, and to such a positive assertion I had nothing to reply more
than that I did not believe it.

I shall not trouble you with any remarks of my own, nor make this
letter longer by apologizing for the trouble I am giving you, being happy
in every opportunity I can have, of assuring your Grace how much
I am &c. &c.

RICH^d. HOPKINS.

Having received this intelligence from M^r. Hopkins, I sent
the following letter to M^r. Pitt.

---

[1] Richard Hopkins was member for Dartmouth, 1766.

BOND ST., *Augst*. 20th, 1765.

DEAR SIR[1],

I have received the enclosed letter from a particular friend of mine, who is a neighbour of M^r. G. Grenville's in Buckinghamshire. If he has the honor to be known to you, I am confident that he is not without your good opinion. You will see by the language M^r. Hopkins held, that *he* was never told that you *approved* the present set of ministers ; but the having it reported to the other extreme, and even with a conversation between us at Hayes laid down as the inculcating proof, I own, hurts me in more than one light ; and in none so strongly, as that I should be construed to have engaged on any *political system* where you would have endeavored to have kept me back. What passed between us I never thought myself at liberty to reveal, except that part which I understood I was to mention by your desire ; the substance of which was not so flattering to us as to have made me eager to have divulged it, unless I had thought that, by concealing it, I should not act consistently with that sincerity and friendship which you have ever shewn me. To this intent I declared, (though much against my inclinations), that you had not allowed me to name even the post that was to be entrusted to myself, and that you would have it to be understood and known, that the whole was so far from being approved by you, that you would disavow the knowledge even of the *dramatis personæ* ; that, though you might have wished to see Admirals Saunders and Keppel at their Board, the difference was great between saying so much to them, and to recommend to the D. of G. a post to which it was probable he might be nominated on this occasion. Such were the words I repeated, and thought myself bound to do, since it was your express desire : but these were not sufficient to furnish argument for M^r. Grenville : this makes me imagine that gentleman to have been told by some *newsmonger or other* that which never had passed between us at Hayes.

The experience of every day shews me that the points on which you had the most apprehensions, and which are unfit to be mentioned by letter, are less and less to be feared ; and I only wish for that hour in which I could resign the Seals, and stand forth the loudest supporter of the measures of *you*, my successor. On foreign measures I must, from my situation, be silent, whatever may be my desire to the contrary ; but I must say, (reasoning from the conversations we have had together) that the almost only internal one which the recess of Parliament allows to come to light was done in the very manner you could yourself have recommended on that particular point.

Words of disapprobation, before any other steps appeared, can never

[1] This letter and Mr. Pitt's reply are printed in the *Chatham Correspondence*, ii. 318. See also Walpole's *Memoirs*, ii. 202.

come from one who thinks so candidly and so justly as I have always found that you did; I must therefore suppose that they were brought to M^r. Grenville from some improper quarter, and must beg to submit to you whether it should not be explained to M^r. Grenville, particularly as he brings me so *personally* into it.

I have the honor to be,

with every sentiment of the most unfeigned

esteem and respect &c. &c.

GRAFTON.

BURTON PYNSENT, *Augst*. 25th, 1765.

MY LORD,

I am extremely sorry that a report, from hand to hand, of discourse attributed to M^r. G. Grenville, in which I am mixt, should have given your Grace a moment's uneasiness, and occasioned you the trouble of the letter with which I am honored, and to which I am under no small impatience to return an answer. Upon matters of this nature, it is fit to be explicit; I assure your Grace, then, that I have seen M^r. G. Grenville but once since the present Ministry took effect, and then in the presence of others; that *I never said to him*, nor to any *man living*, that I blamed, or in the least disapproved, either the ministers or any individual for going into the king's service, nor that I ever had a wish to keep back the Duke of Grafton from taking the Seals. Let me now be as explicit, my lord, in declaring *what I have said*, as often as occasion offered, with regard to certain rumours industriously propagated, in which I could not acquiesce, namely, that the present Ministry was formed by my advice and approbation. To men under such impressions I have constantly averred, that this Ministry was not formed by my advice, but by the counsels of others; that, from experience of different ways of thinking and of acting, Claremont[1] could not be supposed an object to me of confidence and expectation of a solid system of measures, according to my notion of things; and, as an authority I wished to refer to upon

---

[1] The Duke of Newcastle's residence is used as a sort of impersonation of the Whig families, and the secret of Pitt's distrust and dislike of the Rockingham section of the Whig party is here indicated. It represented the men who refused to support Pitt's war policy in 1761, and assented to terms of peace which he regarded as a virtual censure on his action as Secretary of State. This comes out clearly in a letter from Pitt to Newcastle, of October, 1764:—

' I humbly and earnestly entreat that for the future the consideration of me may not weigh at all, in any answer your Grace may have to make to propositions of a political nature. Having seen the close of last session and the system of that great war in which my share of the Ministry was so largely arraigned, given up *by silence* in a full House I have little thought of beginning the world again upon a new centre of union' (*Chatham Corresp.* ii. 297).

these subjects, I have appealed, as I have every right to do, to the conversation I had the honour to hold with the Duke of Grafton at Hayes. The exact and candid manner in which your Grace has taken the trouble to collect the substance of that conversation is the best proof that I well knew where I might securely appeal. I trust your Grace will think I am sufficiently direct, upon a subject where it would be very painful to me to be misunderstood; and especially to be supposed by any man to entertain any sentiments towards the Duke of Grafton, but those of sincere respect, esteem, and friendship. After this state of the affair, I must submit to your Grace's judgment how far any explanation from me to M^r. G. Grenville would be proper, considering that names are not mentioned in the letter of intelligence to your Grace, and that some misapprehension, without intention, cannot but have had a share in this business. Give me leave now, my dear lord, to express how truly I feel the honor you do me in the continuation of your favourable sentiments and flattering wishes, upon the subject of one, who sees his zeal for the king and for the publick become every hour more and more unavailing; who despairs of being enabled to do any essential good, and would indeed be sorry to do hurt, as far as his lights carry him. Accept then, my lord, the best wishes of a Somersetshire bystander, that the affairs in your Grace's hands may turn out so fortunately and happily, as to make you as full of ardour for business as I am of disrelish for the political scene, for which I am, on so many accounts, very unfit. I have the honour to be, with

the truest sentiments of esteem and respect, your Grace's
most obed^t. and most humble serv^t.

WILLIAM PITT.

BURTON PYNSENT, *Sep^r*. 18th, 1765.

MY DEAR LORD,

I am honoured by a king's messenger, with your Grace's very obliging letter, accompanying one from the Hereditary Prince of Brunswick, and am extremely sensible of your Grace's kind attention upon the occasion, and of the honour of expressions so flattering to me. You will see, I have taken the liberty to enclose to your Grace a letter for H. S. H., which I beg may be conveyed to his hands. I will not add to your trouble and retard the messenger, *si longo sermone morer*; please to accept then, my dear lord, in one line, my best acknowledgments, and believe me to be with all the sentiments of the truest respect and esteem

Your Grace's most obed^t. and most humble serv^t.

WILLIAM PITT.

The declarations contained in my former letter, were intended for such proper use as your Grace might judge fit to make of them.

This last letter is inserted merely on account of the post-script, which gives great weight to the expressions of the foregoing.

To this new Administration the public was indebted for many beneficial measures; and the proof they gave of a due application to business will not be contested, when the effects of their labours are fully considered. Great temper was shewn towards the colonies by the repeal of the Stamp Act, a measure founded on good policy, and (as it was thought by many), on justice towards the Americans, who had committed, it must be owned, some violent outrages, on the arrival of the stamps. The ill advised regulations on the trade also were set aside, and all moderation was shewn towards the colonies, while the mother country was soothed by the declaration of the authority of Parliament over them in all cases whatsoever. Here I am sorry to add, as my belief, that the repeal of the Stamp Act could not have been carried, unless accompanied by the Declaratory Bill; so great was still the desire, both within and without doors, of drawing a revenue from America. It was not generally considered that, in fact, every coat or shoe the Americans put on, or saddle they rode on, &c., &c., were virtually paying, and largely, towards the taxes of Great Britain. Besides this most essential point, the long contested affair of the Canada Bills was settled to the satisfaction of the holders; and the Manilla ransom, long neglected by our predecessors, met with an issue which the claimants had nearly given up every hope of being able to attain. The demolition of certain fortifications at Dunkirk was attended with more credit to the nation than it ever had been, and not without proper liberality, and attention to the wholesomeness of the place. In the island of Dominica a free port was established, much to the joy of the American merchants; and in Europe a very advantageous commercial treaty was concluded with Russia [1].

---

[1] This seems to be a somewhat rose-coloured view of the performance of the Rockingham Ministry. The claims against France under the Canada Bills were settled satisfactorily, but the negotiations concerning the Manilla ransom were only revived, and the demolition at Dunkirk seems to have been partial.

By the death of the D. of Cumberland, which happened on the 31st of Octr. from a stroke of apoplexy, in the evening as we were assembling at H.R.H.'s house for a Council, we lost a support in the Closet which we all felt; for on the Duke's most honorable character we placed our hopes and our confidence[1].

The event, though melancholy, had been foreseen as approaching : and whatever real strength the Ministry had lost by it, they still proceeded as before.

About this time, an intimate friend of M^r. Pitt's and of mine[2] had occasion to write to him : I shall give, *in his own words*, the political part of M^r. Pitt's letter, in answer, as it appears to elucidate what was his intention regarding the public, and also with what description of men only he was disposed to act.

I have now troubled you enough, my dear Sir, upon my small private concerns : upon public and great things, (if great belongs to the affairs of so distracted a country), what remains for one so strangely circumstanced as I am, to say to a friend ? You well know how I was frustrated in my views for the public good : and a repetition of so unaccountable a story could have neither utility, nor amusement. All I can say is this; *that I move only in the sphere of measures.* Quarrels at Court, or family reconciliations, shall never vary my fixed judgment of things. Those who, with me, have stood by the cause of liberty and the national honor upon true revolution principles will never find me against them, till they fall off, and do not act up to those principles.

This letter will probably find you amidst additional perplexities of Court and city[3], from the late melancholy but long foreseen event. Many, no doubt, are the speculations upon the consequences of it ; but I am too far

---

[1] The Duke's position in relation to this Ministry was curious. He was present at all Cabinet meetings 'on a general request made to H.R.H., and approved by the king' (*supra*, p. 55). Lord Rockingham speaks of his Ministry as 'formed under your Royal Highness' protection' (*Memoirs*, i. 242). He consulted the Duke even in small matters (*ibid*. i. 241-3). The reputation which Rockingham and his colleagues have enjoyed for independence and capacity is in great measure a literary afterthought.

[2] The Hon. Thomas Walpole, second son of the first Lord Walpole of Wotterton ('Old Horace'). The letter which follows is printed in the *Chatham Correspondence*, ii. 242.

[3] Mr. Walpole was a merchant and banker in London.

off from the scene, and you are too near it, and too clear sighted for me to hazard any opinion of mine. I propose going to Bath in about a week, for which place I was on my way last Saturday, when I was stopt by the melancholy news[1], which broke the hereditary prince's journey thither. Wherever I am, I beg you will be assured that you have there a very sincere friend, and servant, who does justice to the steady spirit with which you stand up for a shaken country, feels all the value of the friendship with which you honor him, and who has a particular satisfaction in assuring you, &c., &c.

WILLIAM PITT.

BURTON PYNSENT, *Novr.* 5th, 1765.

The accounts from America were very alarming; our own disposition to restore peace and confidence was extremely strong, and measures had been proposed in the Cabinet for that purpose; but being anxious to know Mr. Pitt's sentiments, we commissioned Mr. T. Townshend[2] to go to him at Bath, and authorized him to say, not only that we requested to be favored with Mr. Pitt's advice on the measure then under consideration, but that we desired much to receive him at our head, now, or at any time he should find it suitable with his views for the public. Mr. Pitt's reception, though kind towards Mr. Townshend as well as those who had deputed him, was more cold than my colleagues expected. To myself, who perhaps knew better the manner of Mr. Pitt than they did, there was nothing to give me any doubt of his goodwill[3]. In his retired station, what could have been said plainer than this declaration, that he should look to *measures* and *not to men*, that those who acted on true revolution principles, would meet with his support; but so long only as they should not depart from them; that he had disproved of all the late Acts which had passed, relative to the colonies,

---

[1] The death of the Duke of Cumberland.

[2] Thomas Townshend, born 1733, afterwards first Viscount Sydney, and Secretary of State in the Shelburne Ministry, 1782, and again under Pitt, 1783-89. At this time he was M.P. for Whitchurch, and a Lord of the Treasury.

[3] The Duke over-estimated Mr. Pitt's goodwill. Pitt writes to Mr. Cooke, who had asked him whether he should accept an invitation to second the Address, expressing his resolve 'never to be in confidence or concert again with his Grace (Newcastle), nor accede to his Grace's Ministry' (*Chatham Corresp.* ii. 343.)

and that he should deliver his opinion fully to the House?
Nor could he be expected, after the ill use made of some
little encouragement [1] he had formerly given, to speak more
openly.   The reply of M[r]. Pitt was to me perfectly intelli-
gible and satisfactory.   And if he received only as a compliment our desire of seeing him at our head, it was not to
be wondered at; for from the king alone such an offer could
have been attended to by him.

The Session opened early in December [2]; but the king
having notified in the speech that all papers relative to the
disturbances in America should be laid before the Houses,
Parliament was adjourned till after the holydays; which also
gave time to fill up the many vacancies occasioned by those
who had accepted of offices [3].

The Parliament met, according to adjournment, on the 14th
of January 1766.   Previously to this [4], I delivered the subjoined paper to Lord Rockingham, as my humble advice,
recommending earnestly that a letter conforming to it should
be written by one of the king's ministers to M[r]. Pitt.   The
paper was in these words; 'That His Majesty would not press
M[r]. Pitt to come sooner up to London than was his intention, particularly as there must be some days allowed to
consider the American papers, after they are presented to the
Houses, before a decision upon them; but that the king
would be glad to hear his sentiments on the occasion, when
he arrived.'

On the day following, I presumed to recommend this step
to His Majesty, who had no objection to it, until he had seen
Lord Rockingham [5].   Anxious to know M[r]. Pitt's opinion of

---

[1] Probably the rumour that the Rockingham Ministry had been formed with
his approval.

[2] Dec. 17, 1765.

[3] The Speaker had not at this time
the power which he now possesses to
issue new writs during the recess. Consequently those members of the Commons
who had accepted office in July were
obliged to wait until December to offer
themselves for re-election.

[4] This must have been prior to the
9th of January, when the king wrote to
Rockingham declining to authorize
Grafton to say anything to Pitt
(*Rockingham Memoirs*, i. 266).

[5] This must be the matter which the
king in his letter of the 9th to Rockingham says he had considered most attentively, and resolved in the negative.

the most expedient plan for Government to adopt in the critical state of the colonies, I much desired to see him, and on the evening of the 16th I received the following answer to the letter I had written to him.

MY LORD,

I trust your Grace will easily believe that they are not words of compliment, when I assure you that nothing could flatter me more than the honour of your Grace's most obliging letters, and the kind sentiments of opinion and friendship which you are so good to continue to a real humble servant.

I am engaged this evening till towards nine, *from which hour*, I shall be proud and happy to be at your Grace's orders, being ever with the truest respect and attachment, your Grace's most

obed^t. and affectionate humble servant

WILLIAM PITT.

BOND S^r., Thursday night.

The interview with M^r. Pitt came fully up to the construction I had passed on his discourse with M^r. Thos. Townshend at Bath. He made no scruple of letting me feel, that he had no longer thoughts of Lord Temple at the Treasury. He was as open in declaring that the present set of ministers were the only men with whom he could desire to act. On the affairs of America, he should advise the most lenient measures, the very reverse of those which had been taken and pursued by the late Administration.

The following note, taken down in M^r. Stonhewer's handwriting, is likewise added, as it appertains to and gives the particulars of the same transaction.

Thursday Jan^ry. 16th. 1766. Lord Rockingham acquainted the Duke of Grafton that he had proposed and recommended, (according to agreement), to His Majesty that the Duke of Grafton should be authorized to go to M^r. Pitt, and to know from him on what plan he would enter into the king's service. Lord Rockingham added that the king's answer was, that he foresaw so many difficulties that he could not come into that proposal, and that he looked upon that point as absolutely decided. The Duke of Grafton, from the declarations he had made before, thought the whole affair at an end, and on his return that day from the House of Lords wrote to and appointed with M^r. Pitt a meeting at nine o'clock the same evening. At seven o'clock, the Duke of Grafton received a summons from the king to attend him at the Queen's House immediately.

On coming into the room, he found the king extremely agitated, who opened the discourse by declaring to him that, in return for the plain and open manner with which the Duke of Grafton had conducted himself during this negociation, he was determined to be as frank with him, and to assure him that however misinterpreted his own conduct might be, he acted most honorably by those whom he had called to his service; that whilst they saw a possibility of going on, he had [supported], and would support them to the utmost of his power; but as he saw it likely to be broken, he was determined to acquaint him with his design. The Duke of Grafton interrupted him by saying that he was from thence going to M^r. Pitt, in order that he might be better founded in the decisive answer His Majesty expected from him; that he was induced to it from two motives, first, the hopes that M^r. Pitt might authorize him to prove to His Majesty that he had been right in his construction of M^r. Pitt's declarations, viz. that M^r. Pitt was far from meaning a change of Administration; the next, that he thought it not impossible but that M^r. Pitt, if he had conversed with L^d. Temple, might have found that lord so connected as to be unable to take a part with him; the knowledge of which might determine M^r. Pitt to decline also, tho' he might express the desire of seeing the present establishment supported, being formed in a great measure of men whom he would wish to see in Administration. His Majesty then declared his firm resolution that no declaration should be carried to M^r. Pitt from him; and positively insisted with the Duke of Grafton that he should not deliver anything whatever from him: That he would wait to the next day to know from the Duke of Grafton whether he could not remain in his service. At nine o'clock M^r. Charles Townshend was with His Majesty, who could not persuade that gentleman to take a leading part in the forming a new Administration. On the contrary, M^r. Townshend endeavoured to prove to the king that M^r. Pitt alone was the minister who could put His Majesty's affairs into an easy and solid state. The Duke of Grafton was two hours that night with M^r. Pitt, who kept a great deal to the same language he had before held with M^r. Thos. Townshend, adding, however, that whenever he came into power, it should only be with those who had acted on the like principles and exerted themselves for the preservation of the constitution; that the difference in politics between L^d. Temple and himself had never till now made it impossible for them to act upon one plan; but that he would answer, that a difference upon this American measure would in its consequence be felt for fifty years at least; that, if he was called to form a proper system, it must be with the two present Secretaries, and first Lord of the Treasury[1], they *co-operating, willing,*

---

[1] It would appear from what passed later that Pitt did not contemplate the continuance of Rockingham in that particular office.

and *thoroughly confidential*; any honors or favors to be shewn to the Duke of Newcastle, but not to be of the Cabinet, as his perplexing and irksome jealousies would cast a damp upon the vigor of every measure. He condemned much the filling up the vacant offices, and particularly restoring L^d. G. Sackville to the Privy Council[1], at which he never would sit with his lordship. That he looked upon that measure as reproachful to the late king's memory, to his ministers, to Prince Ferdinand, and to the verdict of the court martial that had condemned him. He owned that he saw with pleasure the present Administration take the places of the last; that he came up upon the American affair, a point on which he feared they might be borne down.

M^r. Pitt was so good as to leave to my discretion the use that might be made of a long conversation.

Encouraged by the tendency of this discourse, I renewed, the next day, my humble advice to the king, to desire M^r. Pitt's assistance, at a time when the country stood in need of the abilities of the most experienced statesman. I ventured even to give my decided opinion that M^r. Pitt would not retire again from the Closet, '*re infectâ*,' on account of L^d. Temple, a point on which I had difficulty in persuading His Majesty, who had the condescension, nevertheless, to allow me to write to M^r. Pitt, to know when L^d. Rockingham and myself could wait on him with a message from the king, to which he returned immediately the answer which follows.

Bond S^t., Saturday, Jany. 18th.

My Lord,

I am honoured with a letter from your Grace acquainting me that your Grace and L^d. Rockingham are charged to deliver to me from His Majesty; and that you propose doing me the great honor to call at my lodgings. I shall remain at your orders, and be proud to receive your Grace and L^d. Rockingham there. I am with truest respect your Grace's most obed^t.

humble serv^t.
WILLIAM PITT.

---

[1] Lord George Sackville had been struck off the list of the Privy Council in April, 1760, after having been found by a court-martial to be unfit to serve the king in any capacity, in consequence of his cowardice at the battle of Minden. Rockingham obtained the restoration of this man to the Privy Council, and his appointment as Vice-Treasurer of Ireland. There is a curious memoir concerning Sackville in Fitzmaurice's *Life of Shelburne*, i. 356.

Having fully received the king's commands delivered to us, both being present, we left the queen's house in Lord Rockingham's carriage; but, on discoursing on our orders, I found that we had not the same conception of the essential parts; and, as we differed widely in opinion [1], I did desire that we might turn back, which we did from Constitution hill, when we entreated His Majesty to set us right. The king did not hesitate one moment; but told Lord Rockingham that he had mistaken his meaning. On going out of the king's room, I thought it right to put the two questions down in writing, in order to prevent any future altercation. After the explanation we had just received from His Majesty, L^d. Rockingham readily acquiesced in the words, after a trifling correction.

1st question—Whether, at this time, M^r. Pitt is disposed to come into the king's service?

2nd question—Whether, if L^d. Temple should decline to take a part, this will be a reason for M^r. Pitt's declining also?

M^r. Pitt receiving us with his usual politeness, we opened the purport of our commission. On the first article, he said that he was penetrated by His Majesty's kind opinion; that his life was devoted to his commands, wherever he thought it might be of benefit to the country; and that the men who now served His Majesty would be those with whom he should wish to act; but there must be a *transposition* of offices; which, as he repeated it several times, appeared to me to be ill received by L^d. Rockingham; but, as his lordship made no reply and I made no observation, this must be considered only as my opinion.

On the 2^d question, M^r. Pitt remarked that he had only to lament that he could not have the assistance of L^d. Temple; but he found that their opinions on the measures to be pursued were so widely differing as not to allow him to think of it at this juncture. M^r. Pitt dwelt long on the disgrace that the recall of L^d. G. Sackville to the Council had brought on the

---

[1] The difference was that Grafton wanted Pitt as a leader, while Rockingham wanted him as an ally.

nation, declaring over and over that his lordship and he could not sit at the Council board together. On our return we made immediately a faithful report to His Majesty; and tho' I never was able to make out how the business dropt[1] after having had so favorable an appearance, I shall never change my opinion in thinking that, under M[r]. Pitt's accession, the nation would have been brought to a conviction, at least, of the expediency of giving up all right of *taxation* over the colonies. He would have made the attempt at least; and should he have succeeded, what scenes of woe might there not have been avoided?

Things were in this state, when the Bill for the Declaration of the Right of Taxation, with that for the Repeal of the Stamp Act came under the consideration of both Houses. The Declaratory Bill[2] was strenuously opposed in the House of Commons by M[r]. Pitt, as also in the Upper House by L[d]. Camden: but they were supported by few voices in either. The Repeal was carried, however, handsomely, and the measure was much assisted by the active support which L[d]. Camden, L[d]. Shelburne and M[r]. Pitt brought to us on the occasion. Before I quit this subject, I must not conceal from you that the Repeal of the Stamp Act went heavily down with those, who passed under the denomination of *king's friends*; and

---

[1] 'How the business dropt.' The *Rockingham Memoirs* (i. 271) leave no doubt as to the cause. Pitt demanded 'a transposition of offices,' which would remove Rockingham from the Treasury. This was represented as 'impracticable' by Rockingham to the king.

In the *Rockingham Memoirs* (i. 271) a paper addressed by the king to Rockingham, undated, is treated as an answer to a request made by Rockingham on Jan. 15 and set out on the preceding page of the Memoirs, for leave to treat with Pitt. But it is, clearly, a direction to Rockingham as to the mode in which Pitt should be informed that 'the business had dropt,' Grafton having refused to be further concerned in the matter. How that direction was carried into effect is stated in Fitzmaurice, *Life of Shelburne*, i. 375.

[2] The Declaratory Bill might reasonably have been opposed on the ground that it was idle to assert a right which was not intended to be enforced: Pitt and Camden opposed it on the ground that as the colonies were not represented they could not be taxed. The rhodomontade of Camden on this subject (*Parl. Hist.* xvi. 179) exhibits a treatment of constitutional law and legal history astonishing in a man who enjoyed some reputation as a judge.

tho' most of them voted for the Repeal, yet it was done with so bad a grace, that they could not help seizing an opportunity by which they might affront an Administration growing every day up to popularity, and, at the same time, make their own consequence appear.   On an address to His Majesty praying that the governors might be directed to '*recommend*' to the assemblies to make good the losses which had by many been sustained, L^d. Bute himself rose, and moved for the leaving out of the word '*recommend*' and to substitute '*require.*'   The House divided, and the question was carried against us [1].

On the next day, much irritated with this usage, we went to Court with a strong disposition to resign our offices, if ample satisfaction was not given, on our complaint.   From the assurances we had from the highest authority, I believe that the plan had not been communicated to the king.   We attempted, nevertheless, the removal of one or two of those who had appeared to be the most hostile; and the failure of obtaining their dismission did not augur much good to our future consideration and favour at Court [2].   The Stamp Act repealed, and the Declaratory Act passed, together with some other laws beneficial to trade, cleared very satisfactorily the business in the two Houses.   Still men's minds were not at rest, while no prospect was open to bring forward M^r. Pitt, nor any step taken to gratify on that head the expectation of the public.   Many of my friends spoke to me under great concern, lamenting that this desirable object bore too much the appearance of being laid aside.   My uneasiness on this matter was equal to theirs; and was encreased by feeling that my character was at stake, and that I was called upon to prevent the present favorable moment from slipping in-effectually by.   It became incumbent on me to come to a full explanation on the subject with L^d. Rockingham.

On the 21st of April 1766, I found L^d. Rockingham in the evening, and was soon shewn into the dinner room, whence

---

[1] This must have taken place in Committee. The Address passed in the House without a division.

[2] See *Rockingham Memoirs*, i. 299, and Walpole, *George III*, ii. 288.

all the guests were retired, except Lord Albemarle, who staid the whole time, and who did not utter, as I recollect, a single word during our long conversation.

Three letters which passed between General Conway and myself, on this and the following days, give so natural an account of this interview, and the causes which led to it, that I prefer transcribing them to any description I could now give of the circumstances that attended it. With General Conway I had long been connected in cordial friendship and great intimacy[1]. But a violent attack of illness, from which he was just recovered at Park Place, deprived me of his assistance and advice, till the time of the date of these letters; for he was for a few weeks incapable of attending to business, and having often discoursed over with him my painful situation, I had avoided mentioning it to him at this moment, when it would have given him still further uneasiness.

PARK PLACE, 22d *April*, 1766.

MY DEAR LORD DUKE,

Having had a hint from a friend that your Grace is on the point of taking some final resolution on the present occasion of our political situation, I own it has alarm'd me much; tho' having heard nothing like it from yourself, but on the contrary a wish that we might meet and talk on the subject, I flatter myself it is not so; and, if your Grace has done nothing on it, do most earnestly entreat you, that you will be so good as to suspend any determination for a few days, till we may have an opportunity of talking it over. I feel myself so much interested and concern'd in what your Grace resolves, and think it of such consequence, not to ourselves only but to the king and the publick, that it does in every light deserve our thorough deliberation. I would have come to town even without summons; but to day I have no fires &c. order'd in my house; and to-morrow I must set out early in the morning, which I ought not, even to see you for a single half hour; and after that could not get back, but must enter into all the fatigue and business which I am not yet fit for; and most of all it would be impossible for your Grace after I had seen you, in that short interval before your setting out for Newmarket, to do or settle any thing. But yet my chief dependance is, that you will have the goodness not to take a final resolution, so deeply affecting us all, till we have had an opportunity of meeting, and especially as you have

---

[1] Grafton brought Conway into Parliament for Thetford.

not summoned for it. I have often been in hopes you might have found a few idle hours to have run down here; tho' I durst not ask it, not knowing how far it might appear importunate and interfering with your business or engagements. I will not trouble you further now, but shall really be much reliev'd and happy to hear we may have some little consultation before our system, be it what it may, is either form'd or dissolved.

I am with the highest esteem
Your Grace's most faithful humble serv^t.

H. S. CONWAY.

GROSVENOR SQUARE, April 22nd, 1766.

DEAR SIR,

A conversation which I had last night with Lord Rockingham makes me trouble you with a longer letter than I should otherwise do, if it was to acquaint you only that I shall go part of the way to-morrow night towards Newmarket, intending to return on Saturday. Any time on Sunday I am ready to talk over to you what my steps will probably be in the closet, and in which the conversation I am going to relate makes me see my way much clearer than I have hitherto done. Whatever my present designs may be, I would not call them resolutions, (tho' I must profess they approach very near to that in my mind), nor would I open them in the closet, till I have had an opportunity of communicating them to you.

I found L^d. Rockingham and L^d. Albemarle together, without any third person. They had din'd, and as the House of Lords had sat till seven, I believe L^d. Rockingham expected no one on business; and after some digressions came more to the point and with more openness as to one than I had ever known him do.

There was now no hesitation in him to declare that *he would never advise His Majesty to call M^r. Pitt into his closet, that this was a fixed resolution to which he would adhere* [1]. He added that he saw no reason why the present Administration, (if they receiv'd assurances from the king that people in office were to hold their posts at the good will of the ministers), should not carry on very well and with honor to themselves the king's business. The first of these I must consider as an absolute opposition to M^r. P. coming into the Ministry at all. We know that it is with the king alone that he can settle it, and I can feel M^r. Pitt's reasons to be strong on that head. I also feel very well that there is no quarter from which that advice can come to the king, if L^d. R. does not make a part. His lordship has often declared to me, that he wished to see

---

[1] Overtures had been made to Pitt in February through Nuthall, the solicitor to the Treasury, and through Shelburne, but always with the view of maintaining the existing Ministry. *Chatham Corresp.* ii. 399, iii. 9. Pitt's answer was on each occasion that he would act only on the commands of the king.

M^r. Pitt forming an Administration, but the hardship he then complained of was, that he was press'd to say beforehand that he would at all events form a part, whereas he desired that it might depend on the consistency he found it with his honor so to do, and that the leaving in or turning out such as he had press'd into office was to be his guide in that. As to the other measure, I differ extremely. The weakness of the Cabinet as now composed, the great bodies of men not included, many of ability, with a large share of those of property (even supposing M^r. Pitt and his friends neuter) present immediately such a determin'd opposition, that no point essentially right for this country can be carried through with certainty by Administration; and I know not whether it is more pitiful, or more the part of a slave, to be the whole sessions, and indeed the year out, fighting against such difficulties as will necessarily arise; knowing at the same time, that the very support, which has not come cordially from the closet, and on which hereafter you are to depend, may more likely deceive you; as it is indeed only to be obtain'd from the dread there is of seeing matters once more in confusion.

These are my objections against remaining on as things stand. If any of the great parties of men give their assistance by forming a part, my assistance would be superfluous, since there would be successors in plenty, and as I should not approve such a junction cordially enough to form a part, I could not be a voluntary actor in it. This would not, however, prevent my wishing heartily to see such a measure adopted, if unfortunately we are destin'd not to see the only man who stands sufficiently above the rest to be able allowed at this moment to give strength and stability to Administration. I own to you I have been deluded by the expectation that no such determination had been taken by L^d. R——. I was deceiv'd, my eyes are now open, and I shall probably take that step on Monday, (at least to acquaint the king with my resolution upon it)—that step I say, which nothing but a different idea of L^d. R——'s conversations with me had prevented my taking as soon as the Stamp Act was repealed, and which I have every hour repented that I had not done.

M^r. Stonhewer will call on you on Thursday even^g. I shall talk very fully on the subject to him, and any questions relating to myself he will be able to inform you upon. I am &c. &c.

GRAFTON.

PARK PLACE, 23^d April, 1766.

MY DEAR LORD,

Your Grace's letter of yesterday I must own gives me a good deal of alarm and uneasiness; as, if any Administration is to be continued on the present system or attempted, I foresee the greatest weakness, or rather impracticability, without your name and assistance; if it is weak now in

your opinion, what will it be when you leave it? For my own part,
I know not what to resolve; my desire on a thousand accounts is to
be out of this office, how much more now! yet I own I do not know how
to say we will break up and leave things, [in] or rather throw them
into, their ancient confusion, or a worse; it is such a dilemma as I can
satisfy myself in neither way. I shall certainly be in town to see your
Grace at your return, and talk all these matters over. I wish it were
possible you could give a little more time to so serious a consideration,
affecting so many of your friends, than that you have allotted, perhaps
you may yet do that.

I am with the greatest truth

Your Grace's faithful servant

H. S. CONWAY.

After the explanation with Lord Rockingham and his
declarations that he thought the present Ministry sufficiently
able and strong to conduct His Majesty's business without the
aid of M^r. Pitt; and that he had no intention of calling on
that gentleman any further for his assistance, I had little left
to inform M^r. Conway upon, when we met, as agreed, except
a repetition of the circumstances on which I had already
written [1]. There had been nothing more said to me on the
subject by Lord Rockingham; nor was there the smallest
hope that he would change his opinion. The *transposition*
of offices, talked of in our interview with M^r. Pitt, had not
been relished: but perhaps the declaration he had made of
never sitting at the Privy Council with Lord George Sackville
was still more galling. Here indeed Lord Rockingham had
been drawn into a perplexing dilemma. To have reinstated
him in the Council was open to great reproach: to have seen
him afterwards degraded a second time from it, would have
been dishonorable. General Conway could not but acknowledge my embarrassment; the footing I stood on with M^r. Pitt
and my connexion with him left me but little room for much
consideration. The Ministry, in the judgement of M^r. Conway

---

[1] The *Rockingham Memoirs*, i. 330,
and Walpole, *George III*, vol. ii. 321,
mention an application to Pitt at this
time, from Grafton, or from Grafton and
Conway together. Whether an interview
did or did not take place it certainly was
not authorized by Rockingham, who
seems now to have come to think that
he could stand alone.

as well as of myself, was weak as it stood; but I did not
admit that my retreat could affect it so sensibly, as he was
persuaded that it would; and I had every reason to think
that the marquis and his connexions were very confident that
it would be of little consequence.

On my audience of His Majesty on the Monday following,
and in presence of M^r. Conway, I stated to His Majesty the
reasons which prevented me from continuing longer in my
office, and my full intention and desire of giving his Administration every support I was able as long as they continued
to follow up those principles on which we had embarked.
Nothing could be more gracious than the king's obliging
declarations to me, and I left the seals in His Majesty's
hands, to the great concern, I believe, of the king and both
of us.

I had soon after the satisfaction of standing forward to
vindicate Lord Rockingham's Treasury against the attacks
of Opposition, who much blamed the taxes laid on in lieu of
the Cyder Tax, which had given such general alarm. Before
I concluded what I had to say on this occasion, I desired
the indulgence of the House to allow me a few words on
the condition of the country, and thence of the necessity
that there was, more than ever, for a junction of the ablest
and most experienced statesmen whom the country could
produce; that there were no pains nor trouble that would
appear too great, provided so salutary an object could be
obtained; and I recollect observing, that if every one would
join with me in declaring they would take up the mattock
and the spade[1] in so good a cause, it would be soon accomplished. This latter part was listened to and appeared to be
so well received, as to mark plainly how much it was in
unison with the general sentiments of the House.

---

[1] See Chesterfield, *Letters*, v. 510.
Pitt was much gratified. He writes to
Nuthall, June 1, 'I am indeed most
proud of the honour the Duke of
Grafton has done me. The testimony
is genuine, not the result of cabal; and
dignity and spirit of character meeting
with high rank, add every flattering
circumstance to the favourable suffrage
with which his Grace has been pleased
to distinguish his humble servant'
(*Chatham Corresp.* ii. 423).

LETTERS, 1765–1766

LORD VILLIERS TO THE DUKE OF GRAFTON

LONDON, Wednesday Night, *Jan.* 16th [1765].

MY DEAR LORD,

Mr. Rigby [1] has been so good to trouble himself with these few words to your Grace which I could not help writing to you. Our political concerns stand thus—on Monday comes on in our House, and I am told in your house also, the affair of the French prisoners : in this the declaration of the French has already been read to us, in which they promise to pay to us £670,000 during the course of about 4 years ; in lieu of our demand which is in reality £1,100,000, but which has been lowered to £900,000. I fancy little will be done in our House upon this question, and perhaps less in yours. On Tuesday comes the warrants, as you know ; on which day I wish we may make so good a figure as we ought ; Mr. Pitt is at present confined to his bed with the gout, and I question much whether he will attend us ; and C. Townshend, I hear, intends to vote, but not to speak on our side. So that I fear we must trust greatly to the goodness of the cause itself, which however to our comfort is good indeed. Now as to our further proceedings L^d. J. C——h has told me that they intend to move something in our House about the middle of next week concerning Conway [2], and he should be extreamly glad if your Grace would come to town, that the same might be moved in your House also, where he could venture to say you might have a great deal of support. He believes the D. of Richmond will either move or second anything upon that subject. I could not help mentioning this to your Grace as you desired to be informed of the plans in agitation. Nothing seems to have happened this week but Mr. Pitt's legacy [3] and what is confidently talked of, the demand of Mello for 6,000 men and ships to defend Portugal. I am not certain of the truth of this, but every

---

[1] Richard Rigby (1722–1788), a busy politician and jovial companion, attached to the Bedford party, whose political movements he to some extent directed, always with a view to his own interests.

[2] This related to the dismissal of Conway from office by Grenville, for his vote in the House. The contemplated motion came to nothing, see Walpole, *Memoirs*, ii. 45.

[3] Sir William Pynsent had just left his whole fortune, amounting in real and personal property to about £40,000, to Mr. Pitt.

body seems to believe it, and if it should prove true will turn us a little out of those contented notions of peace which we *have been told lately* is so well established in all parts.

I am, with the sincerest wishes for your health and happiness,

My dear lord,

Your most sincere friend,

VILLIERS [1].

LORD ROCKINGHAM TO THE DUKE OF GRAFTON

GROSVENOR SQUARE,
Thursday, Noon, 5 °Clock,
Apr. y° 25th, 1765.

MY DEAR LORD,

The Regency Bill is determined to be put off till Monday. I have just heard it in a manner that I can rely upon and have therefore sent a servant to stop your Grace, that you may not have an unnecessary trouble.

L[d]. Albemarle imagines that your Grace will receive an express from his R.H. to desire to put off Antinous and Herod's match—till the Saturday.

I hope in that case your Grace will be in London to give your assistance and weight on the present occasion.

I am ever, my dear lord, your Grace's

Most obed[t]. humble serv[t].

ROCKINGHAM.

LORD VILLIERS TO THE DUKE OF GRAFTON

GROSVENOR SQUARE, Friday [*May* 10th].

MY DEAR LORD,

I had fully determined to have written to your Grace each day after the debate in our House upon the Regency Bill, to give you some account of our proceedings there, not knowing whether any body else had undertaken to send you any information. But I was each time unexpectedly called away, and the post going to Wakefield only three times in the week, I consequently lost my opportunity. Perhaps it may not be too late to do it even now, nor improper, as the present state of that Bill is the cause of my troubling you with this express.

On Tuesday, upon the second reading of the Regency Bill (not a word having been said upon the first reading of it the day before), Lord John Cavendish made the same motion to address the Crown to name the

---

[1] George Bussy, fourth Earl of Jersey (1735–1805); he succeeded to the title   in 1769, and held from time to time various appointments about Court.

Regent, that I understood Lord Lyttleton did in your house. This was debated for some time, but I think with little spirit, and I suppose Lord John thought so too, for he let his motion be rejected without dividing the House. For my own part I am sorry he did, for in my opinion we should have been as strong upon that question as upon any other in the course of the whole Bill, notwithstanding the languid manner in which most had spoken. This being disposed of, the next question was upon the Comitment of the Bill. This was a more lively debate and produced some good speeches; among the best was Barré's. But as Conway and some others were for the Comitment, this question went also without a division. Mr. Pitt was not able to attend at all; I believe myself that he really was not, but you know the generality will always think his absence not owing to any real illness.

Upon our entrance into the Comittee of this Bill yesterday, Rose Fuller moved that the queen might be named regent; this you will easily guess was opposed, but the motion was well supported, and the debate a good one, such as I thought would have produced a better division, for our numbers were only 67 to 258.

Immediately after this, Mr. Moreton, seconded by Kynaston, and thirded (if I may use the word) by Martin, moved for the Princess of Wales to be inserted. You will be surprised perhaps when I tell you there was but little debate upon this, and it passed without a division. But the curiosity of it was that none of the B——d's[1] dare support what had been the opinion of their party in your House, and G. Gren. expressing by his looks and manner, which are not to be mistaken, how much he disliked the motion, spoke only ten words; that he dare say it would be agreable to His Mty. With this alteration, you see, it must come back to your House, and it is upon this account that I send this express, many of our friends wish to make a stand upon the occasion in the House of Lords, and to force matters to light, and make the divisions, was so apparently sown amongst the ministers, of some good to the country, by obliging the secret movers to step forwards. Your assistance therefore is much wanted, and you may possibly receive letters from other hands to the same purport as this; but I have taken this method (as by the post you could not have heard before Sunday) with the knowledge only of Lord Spencer, who joins with me in wishing much to see you here, and to do yourself that credit, which all sides agree in giving as your due from your last appearance in the House.

The Bill is to be read the third time in our House to-day, and I suppose you will have it on Monday.

Your Grace, I am sure, will excuse this application, as I can have but one motive in it.

---

[1] The Duke of Bedford's party.

I was exceedingly vexed not to have come to Newmarket, but racing matters, &c., I must defer to some other opportunity.

I am

Ever, my dear lord,

your most sincere friend

VILLIERS.

H.R.H. the Duke of Cumberland to the Duke of Grafton

CUMBERLAND HOUSE, *May y* 14th, 1765.

My Lord Duke of Grafton under the seal of secrecy I think my self obliged to acquaint you that an almost totall change is likely to take place here, the king being totally dissatisfied with the present Administration and inclined to remove them and fill up their places with those that you and I have formerly wish'd in Government at such a criticall time. I should be very happy to talk publick as well as personall affairs over if it were but an hour.

Ever your most affectionate friend

WILLIAM [1]

Lord Villiers to the Duke of Grafton

LONDON, Saturday Morn*.

MY DEAR LORD,

A report prevailed yesterday in so strong a manner that it gained belief every where of an immediate general change in the Administration ; I had before heard that the Parl[t]. was not to be prorogued, but only adjourned from time to time, w[ch] is a confirmation of the above report. I observed much remarkable whispering, and as remarkable a length of faces ; indeed it became at last the whole topic of conversation and as a determined thing even among persons of the present connections. I have yet heard no particulars.

The Weavers assembled again yesterday, much more riotously than the day before ; they attempted to pull down Bedford House ; and at last the Horse Guards were ordered to give them a general charge. This cleared and secured Bloomsbury Square and the avenues to it, but I do not find that any were secured, which is the material point. After this the mob adjourned to Carr, the mercer's, house, which perhaps by this time may be quite down : the last I heard of them was that they had

---

[1] There is a full account of these negotiations from the Duke of Cumberland himself in the *Rockingham Memoirs*, i. 185. The duke, whose political principles were not those of the king, for he was a strong Whig, seems to have acted a straightforward and generous part.

begun upon it and the Lord Mayor had applied for a battallion of Guards. What makes this mob more to be apprehended is that they are under the direction of one man who harangues them and whom they obey implicitly.

If any more news should fall in my way, I shall take the liberty of troubling your Grace with it. I am,

My dear lord,

Your most sincere friend,

VILLIERS.

Saturday Night.

A general change is now in every body's mouth, and it is looked upon to want only the forms.

LORD CHARLES FITZROY TO THE DUKE OF GRAFTON

DEAR BRO^R.   LONDON, Saturday Night, 19th *May*.

I met M^r. Ja. Grenville in the evening; and upon conversation with him, heard the following declarations, which he desired me to transmitt to you.

1st. That nothing like *carte blanche* has been offered to M^r. Pitt, nor was there any thing mentioned by H.R.H. in the visit to Hayes like an offer more than M^r. P. Sec^y. of State and L^d. Temple at the head of the Treasury, with some other things if asked for friends. 2dly. That nothing was convey'd that might have either for object or end, any thing like M^r. Pitt's settling an Administration upon his own plans; nor was there the least ground for M^r. Pitt to rest a belief, that such an Administration was designed. That even when the last proposal was sent to Hayes (which was far more at large), nothing like *carte blanche* was then offer'd; and the whole was broke off before H.R.H. knew M^r. Pitt's answer to the last proposal, *to which he acceded*.

That M^r. Pitt would be happy to see the D. of Grafton, as M^r. Gren. is convinced he could explain everything to him: if that cannot be, that I might go to Hayes and hear the whole from M^r. Pitt in order to transmitt to my Bro^r. That he is sure the plain truth would then appear to his Grace, and he would be able to detect him if he said false.

As for the reconciliation with G. Grenville, that was merely private family satisfaction, and did not regard the publick.

He profess'd M^r. Pitt's high regard for you, as far as you were personally concern'd. And upon my asking whether he was disatisfied with H.R.H. he said that personally throughout the whole he had acted handsomely, and repeated personally. I think he rather hinted an impossibility of ever being with the D. of Newcastle and his immediate friends (to whom I suppose he alluded when he repeated the word *personally*).

I think I have faithfully transmitted the substance of his conversation, and as he wish'd you should know it, in order to have things (as he said) clear'd up to you, I thought it my duty to acquaint you with it, that you may either see Pitt, write to him, send me to him, or draw what other use from it you chuse. As the thing strikes me, I think your interposition might lay a storm jealousy has raised.

. . . . . .

Ever faithfully
Your loving bro[r].
C. F. R.

PS.—Pray observe that is wrote not as an opinion of my own (for these diff[t]. accounts confound me) but as a repeated conv[n]. to which I do not add more credit than to report.

LORD CHARLES FITZROY TO THE DUKE OF GRAFTON

DEAR BROTH[R].

The inclosed I wrote in order to send it by Eylmore, but as there is no chance of knowing when he goes, as he is now out of town, I thought fit to send it by Jacob. I told L[d]. Rockingham the contents.

I am sorry to tell you that many people talk a language that is likely to make a breach between Pitt and others—which was contrary to your desire to Meynell and myself.

Meynell among many other people wish you to see M[r]. Pitt, and as he has given such an opening by M[r]. Grenville's conversation with me, they think your doing it might stop mischief that seems at present to be increasing, and may divide our friends. He tells me that he knows the K—— is at present most violent and at the same time miserable and ready to take any offer against the present set—and if you could but see Pitt it might prevent his going off from you and stop language that must breed ill blood. However I leave this, like the former, to your consideration, without making any remarks upon it.

L[d]. R—— thinks that since M[r]. Grenville held that conversation with me (and desired I would transmitt it to you) that I should be blamable in not doing, and you see I have no safe method of doing it but by a servant going to you.

L[d]. R. says the D. of Portland[1] and himself intend going to the birth day if you *will*, but desire to be guided by you.

Sincerely and faithfully
Your loving brother
C. FITZ ROY.

Monday, 4 o'clock.

---

[1] William, third Duke of Portland, was twice First Lord of the Treasury, in 1783 and in 1807, first as a Whig, then as a Tory. He held other high offices, but is not otherwise memorable.

LORD ALBEMARLE TO THE DUKE OF GRAFTON

MY DEAR LORD,

We have had strange doings here, nothing absolutely fixd about the ministers. I should rather think the present will remain, because M^r. Pitt could not be prevailed on to take a part. The Duke of Cumberland was five hours with him at Hayes. To-morrow I understand the king is to answer some questions put to him by the ministers, and as the duke is personally concerned in one of them, he begs your Grace will be so good as to come to town to give him your support. The king has been most insolently treated by his ministers, and shamefully abandoned by those who ought to have profited of this occasion of serving their king and country. I am, my dear lord, with the most perfect regard and esteem,

Your Graces
Most obedient, and faithfull
humble servant
ALBEMARLE.

CUMBERLAND HOUSE,
May 22^d, eleven o'clock.

LORD VILLIERS TO THE DUKE OF GRAFTON

LONDON, May 22^d, 1765.

MY DEAR LORD,

Your Grace will be sorry, but not surprised I am sure, to learn from me that the negotiation mentioned in my letter of Saturday, has met with the same fate which that of last summer twelvemonth did. The same person who was supposed to be the author of the failure then, may be the cause of the present miscarriage. In short, my dear Lord, on Sunday last H.R.H. the D. went to H——y's with, what was called in the world, *carte blanche*; how far it was fundamentally so I am at a loss to say. However, such as the terms were they were refused; assistance and support, it is said, was promised, if right measures were pursued; but neither of the brothers would come into office at present. In this state of confusion it has remained for two days, and a curious one it was : a greater variety of faces in point of length I never saw. In the mean time some of our friends have been endeavoring to form an Adminis. by themselves, but in vain, and yesterday H.R.H. told his M. that he could not succeed without Mr. P., and therefore recommended it to him to take the same into place again ; they had not, it is true, been turned out, but nothing seems to have been wanting except the forms. And now they are supposed to be reinstated, tho' upon what terms (for I heard they intended to make some) I cannot tell. And a circumstance

G

has happened, which makes some material alteration. G. Grenville and
L^d. Temple were reconciled yesterday, and it is said he is to resign
immediately—Chas. Town—d I have been told, and with some authority, has been offered the place of Chan. of the Ex. and has refused.
In this situation do things remain, as far as comes within the knowledge
of the public. The same person seems to be the object of most parties
at present, but it is difficult to know how he will be come at.

I wish most sincerely your Grace had been in town during the late
transactions, your advice would have had the greatest weight, and I dare
say would have put things in the channel we both wish them.

They say we are to be prorogued to-morrow or at least adjourned for
some time.

Whatever occurs, as you seem to desire intelligence, you may depend
upon hearing constantly, till the arrangement of matters has reduced the
conversation of the town to its usual stand.

The Weavers, who have for this last week alarmed the whole town as
much as if the French had been without our walls, and put the D. of
Bedford and his house in real danger, did not make the attack yesterday
onthe House of Lords which they were expected to do; but as nothing
has passed either to terrify or appease them, I fear they wait only for
the absence of the Guards to commit some fresh riot or insult.

Adieu, my dear lord, but I cannot conclude without lamenting that
from some mismanagement, such an opportunity has been missed of
gaining the most material point.

> I am
> Ever yours
> VILLIERS.

W. MEYNELL, ESQ., TO THE DUKE OF GRAFTON

MY DEAR LORD,

I should have wrote you word before of what was reported to be
going on in politicks, had I not imagin'd you would hear of it from those
who could give you much better information. Sunday the D. went to
Hayes by the K.'s desire, to tell M^r. P. that the people who were about
H. M—y were as disagreable to him as they were incapable of doing
anything for the good of the country; that it was impossible for him to
continue his affairs any longer in their hands, and that he therefore beg'd
M^r. P. would stand forth as minister and take upon himself the nomination to all the great offices. This was made publick by the desire of the
K. and the D. before the latter returned from Hayes, and all Sunday it
was taken for granted that the D. of Bedford and his friends would all be
out immediately, and that an administration would be form'd out of the
minority. Monday it was known that M^r. P. had declin'd accepting of the

K.'s offer; but it was said he had promis'd his support to any Administration that should be composed of men of the old Whig familys who had been in opposition to the late measures; and till this morning nobody seem'd to entertain the least doubt, but that the D. of Bedford &c. were to go out.   But to-day we are told, that all the old Administration continues, that L^d. Temple and M^r. Pitt have promist to support them, and that the D. says he will never more be concern'd in opposition; all which I believe to be true, tho' some of our friends that I saw just before dinner seem not to give absolute credit to it.   It is certain Geo. Grenville was at L^d. Temple's yesterday for some hours; that they are reconcil'd, and that L^d. Temple immediately after his brother had been with him, went down to Hayes, from whence he return'd this morning; and afterwards made a long visit to G. Grenville.   The D. of B. and his friends are so much irritated against L^d. B-te, that I conclude one condition of their continuance in His M.'s service is L^d. B.'s being banish'd his presence and all his friends turn'd out.   Many of our friends wear as melancholly aspect to-day as L^d. Waldegrave, Rigby, &c. have for the last three or four days; and countenances more dismal than theirs were till to-day you cannot well conceive.   Ascott begins the 10th of June, and I propose going down that morning.   I agree entirely with your Grace, that it is better to send Antinous to York, than to match him on any terms; and if he is well I shall be dissappointed if I do not win very considerably on him there.   Pilkington writes me word that all the horses are well except my colt; and that he sees rather better.   If any thing material happens, you may depend on hearing from me.   I am with all possible respect, my lord,

Yr. Grace's
most faithful
and most humble serv^t.
W. MEYNELL.

HILL STREET, May 22, 1765.

LORD ALBEMARLE TO THE DUKE OF GRAFTON

MY DEAR LORD,

I am commanded by the Duke to inform your Grace that H.R.H. is just come from Richmond, that M^r. Pitt was between three and four hours with His Majesty this morning, and was received in the most gracious manner, every thing he asked and wished in regard to home politicks was agreed, and given into, *particularly the favorite point of Chancellor for Lord Chief Justice Pratt* upon a vacancy.   M^r. Pitt insisted upon a triple alliance with the courts of Prussia and Russia, which His Majesty did not immediately agree to, alarmed at the consequences of so sudden a resolution, especially as M^r. Pitt had not engaged himself in His Majesty's service, and seeing the impropriety, if not impossibility of engaging or entering into such a measure, but thro' him. H.R.H. desires to see your Grace to-morrow morning, as he is directed by His Majesty to order M^r. Pitt to attend him again on Saturday morning. I have the honor to be, with the greatest truth and regard,

My d^r. lord,
Your Graces
most obedient
humble serv^t.

ALBEMARLE.

CUMBERLAND HOUSE,
Wednesday night, ½ past ten o'clock. [19th June, 1765.]

DUKE OF GRAFTON TO LORD ALBEMARLE

WAKEFIELD LODGE, *June* ye 20th, 1765.

MY DEAR LORD,

My inclination as well as my duty would always prompt me to run from the farthest corner of the world to pay my court to H.R.H and to receive his commands. In this situation I not only hope he will excuse my not coming up, but even will approve of my conduct in it when he hears the difficulty I feel myself under, which I am sure from your goodness to me you will convey to him. I mentioned, when I was last in town, the unsatisfactory part I had to act in carrying messages backwards and forwards to those persons who from their friendship treated me with an unreserved confidence I had no reason to expect. I must say now that a delicacy of honor on that acc^t. stops me in this instance from obeying H.R.H.'s commands, as I should (in fact) by entering into any scheme, or even delivering my poor opinion at this conjuncture, forfeit the truth of those assurances I had given, in hopes to give more weight to the conversation I had with him, and to the entreaties I added from myself, by declaring my resolution of leaving London the next day, and to wait the issue of the negociation in the country, particularly after I had given him leave to make use of my name (if necessary) as ready to enter His Majesty's service in the employment he should put me in, it renders it impossible, I think, as a man of honor, to be framing any other system, or even the appearance in me of consulting upon it, untill the time, if unfortunately that should happen, that this is at an end. To go to M^r. Pitt with any entreaties of mine *now*, would not only be of no weight, but would even take away the small fruits which had arose from the last conversation ; and he would have reason to treat me with as much coldness as he had with frankness before. Now, my dear lord, not to detain you any longer, I will only add, that every sentiment of mine I have delivered to H.R.H. in the most open manner. They are such which I am ready to put into execution, if the affair should go off; tho', I must own, our situation is not promising, if that must be our fate. I mean at present to be in town, ready to receive H.R.H.'s commands on Sunday morning by ten o'clock. If any thing which I do not foresee, or your lordship did not intimate should be the business on which H.R.H. would employ me, I could be in town by noon to-morrow. At all events I will send a servant to Dunstable to wait there till eight o'clock to-night, in hopes that your lordship will be so obliging to send me one line, and i will make me happy beyond expression to hear that H.R.H. is not offended at my conduct.

LORD ALBEMARLE TO THE DUKE OF GRAFTON

MY DEAR LORD,

The Duke is extreamly concerned that his summons should have given your Grace a moments uneasiness. H.R.H. sees and feels your delicacy, and thinks that if I had been a little more explicit in my letter last night your Grace would have seen the motives that induced H.R.H. to desire your assistance in town. It was not to assist in the forming of an Administration upon a supposition that M^r. Pitt could not agree with His Majesty on the next interview, it was to desire your Grace to use your weight at Hayes, and soften him a little upon his foreign politicks, by shewing him the impropriety, as I said before, of the king's going headlong into such a treaty by the advice of a person who was not in the king's service, nor in any shape engaged to serve His Majesty. The king wishes to employ M^r. Pitt, will submit to him as far as possible; he does not object to the system, but the precipitate mode of doing it, against the opinion of the ministers thro' whose hands the negotiation with the foreign courts must pass. H.R.H. is thoro'ly satisfied with the part your Grace has taken throughout this whole negotiation, and very sensible of your attachment and inclinations to him, and would by no means press you upon any point, where he thought your honor at stake, or when your Graces great and becoming delicacy upon that head suggested to you that it was in the least degree of danger. H.R.H^s. flatters himself that M^r. Pitt will be more reasonable upon that point of the tripple alliance next Saturday, and that he will undertake the administration for the ease and dignity of His Majesty, as well as the good and salvation of the country. This foreign point was the chief reason for H.R.H.'s wishing you in town, and that your Grace might have talked over with M^r. Pitt the diff^t. arrangements necessary to provide for the poor sufferers which H.R.H^s. is afraid M^r. Pitt could not consider so much as he wishes. H.R.H^s. commands me to repeat his thanks to your

Grace for the part you have taken in this affair, and for the noble manner in which you have engaged yourself. H.R.H⁸. still hopes and believes that matters will be settled to all our satisfactions on Saturday, and will not trouble your Grace before Sunday, unless some very unforeseen event should make him think it necessary to take that liberty. Excuse, my dʳ. lord, the hurry of this letter, and give me leave to assure your Grace of the very great regard and esteem with which I am, my dʳ. lord,

Yʳ. very faithfull
humble servant,
ALBEMARLE.

CUMBERLAND HOUSE, Thursday, 4 o'clock.

LORD ALBEMARLE TO THE DUKE OF GRAFTON [1]

MY DEAR LORD,

The Duke will be at Cumberland House this evening, and begs to see your Grace at seven o'clock. H.R.H. thinks His Majesty very well inclined, and disposed to do every thing that is right. I have the honor to be, with the greatest regard and esteem,

My dʳ. lord,
your Graces
most obedient
humble servant,
ALBEMARLE.

WINDSOR Gᵗ. LODGE, Thursday Morning. [27ᵗʰ June, 1765].

CONWAY TO THE DUKE OF GRAFTON

PARK PLACE, 16 *Apr.* [1766].

MY DEAR LORD,

Having just recouer'd a little the use of my hand, one of the first uses I make of it is to thank you for the favour of your last letter.

I hear with much pain and concern what has lately past in the H. of Commons; the account I have seems to me quite incredible in respect to the unprovoked violence with which Mʳ. Pitt is said to have arraign'd the Administration on the slightest occasion, evidently sought for, and with as much passion, as if the highest provokation had been offerr'd him. This is the first H. of Commons news I have heard since I was here, and indeed the first political, as to any point of our internal politicks. So that I am too much in the dark to aim at conjectures, except the general one that something done or omitted must have given him offence, which he sought the first opportunity to express, but that he wou'd have done it at

---

[1] This letter seems to refer to the resolution of the king to form a Whig Ministry on the failure of the negotiations with Pitt.

once, on so slight an occasion, and with so little reserve or candor as
I hear it represented I cou'd not believe. I had heard a gen. report that
he was angry at not being consulted, and on not having been *treated
with*; but being only report, and thinking both very improbable, knowing
your Grace on the spot and better inform'd, I omitted saying anything
on the subject, which I was two or three times on the point of doing,
from the anxiety which even the flying reports I mention'd had given me.
I thought indeed that, as soon as the holidays were over, some communication wou'd have been had with him; and especially as by what
I understood from L^d. Rockingham there seemed to be then a very good
disposition for it in the closet. All the rest remains still a mystery to me,
and I long to hear from your Grace the real state of the case and your
sentiments on what has past.

    And am in the mean time, with the greatest truth and respect,

Your Grace's most faithful

and obed^t. servant

H. S. CONWAY.

CONWAY TO THE DUKE OF GRAFTON

PARK PLACE, 20 *Ap.* 1766.

MY DEAR LORD,

    I had fix'd my journey to town for Thursday, which I am told is as
soon as I ought to think of it : I gather strength daily, but do not yet
feel equal to Court and Cabinet and Parliament business. I am griev'd
to be absent at this time, the difficulty and delicacy of which I perceive ;
and I wish much for an opportunity of talking to your Grace and L^d. R.
I must own M^r. Pitt's behaviour appears to have more passion and levity
in it than I cou'd have believ'd, and yet I shou'd be much for sounding
him, that we may appear consistent. Yet I hear he has already had
several conferences with L^d. Temple and G. Grenville ; all which surpasses
me. I shall be glad to know if your resolution holds for Newmarket on
Wednesday; if not shall hope to see your Grace on Thursday. If your
Grace thinks it of absolute necessity, I will obey your commands sooner,
to see you, but cannot otherwise be of much use.

    I will not defer your messenger any longer,

and am, with the greatest truth, your Grace's

most oblig'd and faithful servant,

H. S. CONWAY.

CHAPTER III

THE MINISTRY OF THE EARL OF CHATHAM

Feby. 19th, 1805.

MY DEAR EUSTON,

Since my arrival in London, I have had too many avocations, arising from business of various natures, to allow me leisure sufficient to proceed with the Memoir; but the reception you and some few friends have given to the work, as far as I have gone, encourages me to apply to it with encreased alacrity.

You have just seen that I was relieved from an elevated station, which I could no longer hold with honor or comfort to myself. You have before you also the cause of all my uneasiness; and posterity, if it ever reads this account, will judge whether, in this point, L^d. Rockingham or I was to blame. My desire, however, of giving every little support I was able to my former associates in office was as earnest as they could have wished it to be; and as long as in the material measures the Administration kept fairly to the principles which had originally united us, I should not have stumbled at all lesser things. It was evident, when the Parliament was up, even to the most common observer, that the Ministry, though composed of men of character and who possessed individually the general esteem of the public, could not hold long without some material accession of strength.

The Duke of Richmond filled my place[1]; but the general backwardness to embark with the Ministry was great.

Soon after the Parliament was prorogued I retired into the country, where the accounts daily received portended that there must be some essential alteration; and a letter from M[r]. Pitt desiring my attendance in London brought me directly up from Euston, near the middle of July 1766. In it I was informed only, that a new Administration would take place immediately on the most extensive and comprehensive plan, if His Majesty was not thwarted in his views, and in the formation of which there should neither be any exclusion of any man of ability and integrity, nor any listing under any banner whatsoever.

Travelling to London alone, I revolved well in my mind my own situation; and the result was, that I should be ready to undertake, and to my utmost properly to discharge, any office in which M[r]. Pitt should wish to place me; but that the situation of the first Lord of the Treasury, or that of Lieutenant of Ireland, were accompanied with circumstances so very disagreeable to me, that no consideration should induce me to embark in either.

I found L[d]. Villiers (now Earl of Jersey) in town. We went together to dine and sleep at Wimbledon that night; both of us, at that time, living much with our amiable and excellent friends Lord and L[y] Spencer[2]; whose good qualities both of head and heart were rarely equalled. Agreeing as we all did in our political wishes, and being without other company, we conversed in the most confidential manner during the course of that whole evening on all that was passing, and what might be expected. They all joined in combating my decision as to the Treasury, tho' ineffectually

---

[1] Charles Lennox, the third Duke of Richmond (1735–1806). The seals were first offered to Lord Hardwicke, and on his refusal his brother Charles Yorke, the Attorney-General, was suggested. Richmond had offended the king by protesting against an appointment which he considered unjust to his brother Lord George Lennox (*Rockingham Memoirs*, i. 339).

[2] John, first Earl Spencer (1734–1783), a staunch Whig. Lady Spencer was a daughter of Stephen Poyntz of Midgham in Berkshire.

to the last, when I was stepping into my phaeton to proceed to North-End [1], where M[r]. Pitt then was; and it was my intention to return with my report in the afternoon.

I found M[r]. Pitt very anxious to explain to me what had passed at Court, in as concise a manner as the business admitted. He was perfectly satisfied that the ground was firm under him; that the king heartily adopted, and would support M[r]. Pitt's determination of standing in the gap to defend the Closet [2] against every contending party. He added, that His Majesty had given him full powers thus to form a Ministry which might be generally approved by the nation. M[r]. Pitt came soon of course to mention the office His Majesty had approved for me: and this office was no other than the Treasury. Though I was prepared with my answer, for a long time neither of us could be driven from our ground; and I felt, for a moment, happy with the hope of retiring with my negative admitted and acquiesced in. At last M[r]. Pitt, shewing strong marks of disappointment, rose from his chair, and declared that he must fairly tell me, that his whole attempt to relieve the country and His Majesty was at an end; and that he must acquaint the king, that he was once more frustrated in his endeavors to serve him; and that he should recommend to His Majesty to employ others; for that he could do nothing, if he had not my assistance at the Treasury; his own health allowing him to enter into no office except that of Privy Seal. Here all that I wished to see established, together with all that I dreaded for myself, crowded at once on my mind, already too much agitated for due consideration. If M[r]. Pitt's threatenings were realized, it was easy to

---

[1] Pitt arrived in Town on July 11 after a hurried journey from Somerset. He slept in Harley Street at the house of Captain Hood, and waited on the king at Richmond on the 12th. The hurry of his journey upset him, and he went to Mr. Dingley's house at Hampstead on the 13th or 14th.

[2] Pitt's ideas as to combining with the great Whig families seem to have undergone a gradual change. In 1763, when consulted by the king as to the formation of a Ministry, the restoration of the great Whig families to office was an essential part of his programme (*Lif of Hardwicke*, iii. 378). In 1765 'he talked much of revolution families, from their weight, but unconnected' (*supra*, p. 51). In 1766 he seems to adopt an attitude definitely hostile to them.

foresee the confusion into which the country would be plunged, and possibly that I should be marked as the principal cause of the disaster. I still remained as firmly persuaded as ever, how little suited the post was to my inexperience and my feelings. I yielded however, at length, tho' with reluctance, to M^r. Pitt's solicitation. His views were great and noble, worthy of a patriot; but they were too visionary to expect that ambitious and interested men would co-operate in promoting them. He had persuaded himself, that his weight as a statesman, together with his present popularity, and the cause well supported by His Majesty, would be able to reconcile every man to those posts which he had designed for them [1].

M^r. Pitt's plan was Utopian, and I will venture to add, that he lived too much out of the world to have a right knowledge of mankind. His turn of mind was to be suspicious and jealous, tho' perfectly forgiving. On the present occasion, to men, who came to him from almost every quarter, he held a language which could not but be approved by them in principle; though certainly not palatable to the interested expectation of their friends. M^r. Pitt attributed more efficacy to these flattering visits than they merited. No doubt could be entertained on the position, that it was a desirable object for the country that the men of the best talents and fortunes and highest rank, taken from every party, should unite in one common cause. But in the heighth of his spirits, M^r. Pitt flattered himself with succeeding in an undertaking so very difficult; indeed, from his statement of the disposition he had found in some of the principal characters with whom he had

---

[1] An illustration of this may be seen in his dealings with Temple, Townshend, and Dowdeswell. He knew the self-importance of Temple, and must also have known that on the great question of American policy they differed profoundly, yet he desired Temple to take office and would allow him no voice in the formation of the Ministry. His peremptory method was perhaps the best way of dealing with the vacillating Townshend (Walpole, *Memoirs*, ii. 346). Dowdeswell had been Chancellor of the Exchequer under Rockingham. Pitt offered him a place at the Board of Trade, or a joint paymaster's place, and called on him to decide in a few hours. He declined both (*Chatham Corresp.* iii. 22).

conversed, I was led myself to give in to the like persuasion ; until the intrigues of party breaking out in various ways, discovered to us our short-lived delusion.

I do not recollect whether it was the next or the following day that I returned to North-End, when the conversation chiefly turned on the particulars of the intended arrangement. M^r. Chas. Townshend had paid great attention to me, especially since I resigned the Seals. He possibly might consider me as a rising man, and worthy of more than ordinary attention. His talents had captivated me, I grant ; but it was not till afterwards that I discovered his knowledge to be more confined than I had rated it. His powers, as a speaker, were brilliant. In the forementioned interview I much pressed M^r. Pitt that M^r. Townshend might be the Chancellor of the Exchequer[1]. M^r. Pitt, who knew the gentleman much better than I did myself, said everything to dissuade me from taking, as a second, one from whom I should possibly meet with many unexpected disappointments. I had seen M^r. Townshend and was weak enough to persist in my desire, as I had found him eager to give up the Paymaster's place for this office. M^r. Townshend might possibly view this situation as the readiest road to the upper seat : and his professions had gained me over to expect every assistance from him. The credit I gave M^r. Townshend made me very unwisely persist in my first wishes ; and M^r. Pitt at last gave way, though much against his inclination, as well as his opinion. M^r. Townshend, however, was not to be called to the Cabinet ; a point on which he was so sore, that he was not at rest till he had, through me, teazed M^r. Pitt to admit him there, just as that gentleman was setting out on his most unfortunate journey to Bath. The first Cabinet was composed as follows,

---

[1] The vacillations of Townshend about this office may be gathered from the *Chatham Correspondence* (ii. 452, 456, 459, 462, 464). The paymaster's place was the more valuable by some £4,000 a year : but when Pitt seemed ready to acquiesce in his refusal of the Exchequer his vanity got the better of his interest, and he became urgent to be Chancellor of the Exchequer.

Lord Camden	Chancellor.
Lord Northington	President.
M^r. Pitt, created Earl of Chatham	Privy Seal.
D. of Grafton	First L^d. of the Treasury.
Lord Shelburne	Southern Sec. of State.
L^t. Genl. Conway	Northern Sec. of State.
Lord Granby[1]	Commander in Chief.
S^r. Chas. Saunders	First L^d. of the Admiralty.

It was not the intention to remove Lord Egmont from the Admiralty[2]; but he chose to resign; and I believe from a general dislike of M^r. Pitt's politics.

Lord Camden was on the circuit—I had but little acquaintance with him at that time; but the state of his mind during this impending arrangement, as well as his view of the business, may be well collected from the following letters, which were written to a particular friend of both, who presented them to me, desiring that I would make such use of them as I thought proper. They may be acceptable in this place.

July 19th, 1766, LEICESTER.

I am arrived late at this place, and find letters from you and Nutthall, pressing me to leave the circuit. I am willing enough to quit this disagreeable employment; but I think I ought not, upon a private intimation, depart from my post. If you will by letter, or by express, if you please, only tell me, that M^r: Pitt would wish to see me, I will post to town at a moment's warning. L^d. Temple is gone. If M^r. Pitt is not distressed by this refusal, or if he is provoked enough not to feel his distress, I am rather pleased, than mortified. Let him fling off the Grenvilles, and save the nation without them[3].

Yours, &c.

CAMDEN.

I shall be at Warwick on Wednesday next.

---

[1] Eldest son of the third Duke of Rutland: the most popular military figure of our Continental war in 1758–1760. He died in his father's lifetime, Oct. 1770.

[2] John, second Earl of Egmont (1711–1770), sat in the House of Lords as Lord Lovel and Holland. He had been of the Household of Frederick, Prince of Wales, and was a friend of Bute. Walpole (*Memoirs*, ii. 193) is wrong in saying that he became First Lord of the Admiralty in the Rockingham Ministry. He succeeded Sandwich in 1763. He now resigned, not from loyalty to Rockingham but from dislike of Pitt (Walpole, *Memoirs*, ii. 360).

[3] This is the first intimation in the autobiography of the quarrel between Temple and Pitt.

July 20th, 1766, LEICESTER.

DEAR SIR,

I have slept since I wrote to you, and having taken the advice of my pillow upon the subject of my coming to town, I remain of the same opinion, that I ought not at this time to quit my station, uncalled and uninvited. If M^r. P. really wants me, I would relieve his delicacy by coming at his request, conveyed to me either by you or Nutthall; but I suspect the true reason why he has not desired me to come is because, as things are just now, he does not think it fitting. Sure M^r. P. will not be discouraged a second time by Lord T.'s refusal. He ought not for his own sake; for it does behove him now to satisfy the world that his greatness does not hang on so slight a twig, as T. This nation is in a blessed condition, if M^r. P. is to take his directions from Stowe. A few days will decide this great affair, and a few days will bring me back of course. In the mean time, if my sooner return should be thought of any consequence, I am within the reach of an express. I understand L^y. Camden has paid her comp^{ts}. to M^{rs}. ——, which I look upon as a ratification of the treaty between the two families. I was catched at Chatsworth by the D. of Devon [1] and his 2 uncles, and very civilly compelled to lye there, where I had the pleasure of seeing L^d. and L^y. ——, but not one word of politics, or the great change.

I am, &c.

CAMDEN.

Take care, that I do not break in again upon your foreign correspondence: but let me have an inland letter.

WARWICK, *July* 24th, 1766.

I am much concerned to find M^r. Pitt's illness hangs upon him so long, and the wishes of the public by that means retarded. He must set his hand to the plough; for the nation can not be dallied with any longer. L^d. T.'s wild conduct, tho M^r. P. is grievously wounded by it, may, for aught I know, turn out to be a favorable circumstance, to reconcile him more to the present Ministry, out of which corps he must form, as he always intended, this our Administration. Indeed this inclination is one of the principal grounds of difference between the two brothers; L^d. T. having closely connected himself with that set of men whom he opposed so inveterately. I have heard very authentically from the Stowe quarter that one of the chief points upon which they broke was upon the promotion of L^d. Gower [2] recommended by L^d. T. to be Secretary of State, under the color of enlarging the bottom and

---

[1] William, fifth Duke of Devonshire (1748-1811).

[2] See letters from Temple to George Grenville and to Lord Gower (*Gren-ville Papers*, iii. 267-272). It is worth noting the belief of Camden that Pitt would desire to form a Ministry of the Rockingham Whigs.

reconciling all parties. That since he asked nothing for his brother George he had a right to insist upon this promotion. The other, on the contrary, put a flat negative upon all that connexion. L^d. T. was very willing to go hand in hand with M^r. P. *pari passu*, as he called it, but would acknowledge no superiority or controul. This was continually and repeatedly inculcated, not to say injudiciously, if he really intended to unite, because such declarations before hand must create an incurable jealousy, and sow disunion in the very moment of reconciliation. He taxes M^r. P. with private ingratitude, and is offended that two or three days elapsed before he was sent for. This is public talk at his Lordship's table, and therefore requires no secrecy. There are now, or will be in a few days, at Stowe the two Dukes of B. and M. with their ladies, S^r. J. Amherst, and the royal guests[1]. Therefore L^d. T. is declared not the head of that party; for that is an honor he must never expect, but a proselyte received amongst them. Let not M^r. P. be alarm'd at this formidable gathering of great men. The king and the whole nation are on the other side. I hope to be in town next Wednesday. I received your last on Saturday night at Leicester, where the post comes every day, and answer'd on Sunday morning, so that it arrived very regularly in town on Monday morning and was not opened. I shall call at Nutthall's in my way.

In the mean time believe me,

With utmost sincerity y^r. most obed^t.

faithful servant

CAMDEN.

On the Sunday after his Lordship's arrival in London, I received the annexed letter from M^r. Pitt.

HARLEY STREET, past 2 °clock, Sunday [July 27th].

MY LORD,

All being entirely fixed with M^r. C. Townshend, who has accepted the office of Chancellor of the Exchequer, your Grace is desired to be at the queen's house to-morrow at twelve. His Majesty's intention is, that we should arrange things for kissing hands on Wednesday, which may very well be, if your Grace should be of that opinion. I think it imports the king's Government, that this kind of *inter-ministerium* should not be protracted. I shall be to-morrow at the queen's house; where I hope to have the honor of seeing the Duke of Grafton perfectly well, and perfectly satisfied with his Chancellor of the Exchequer.

I took my chance to-day at Lord Rockingham's door[2]; but found his

---

[1] Lord Temple entertained at Stowe the Princess Amelia, and the Dukes of Bedford and Marlborough.

[2] For an account, more or less exaggerated, of this episode, see *Rockingham Memoirs*, ii. 4; *Grenville*

Lordship going out, so was not let in. I meant to make a visit of respect, as a private man to Lord Rockingham, and had I found his lordship, to have told him, as Pitt to Lord Rockingham, what I understood to be the king's fixed intentions. I am ever, with respectful and warm attachment,

My dear Lord Duke's

Most humbly devoted servant

WILLIAM PITT.

Turn over.

I saw M#. Yorke yesterday; his behaviour and language very handsome: his final intentions he will himself explain to the king in his audience to-morrow[1].

I make no apology for adding here a letter from M#. C. Townshend, written to me at that time.

MY DEAR LORD,

In performance of my promise, I report to your Grace the result of the audience which I had this day; in which I found that M#. Pitt had renewed the subject of our last conversation, and informed His Majesty that he earnestly wished that I might be the Chancellor of the Exchequer. I then stated the difference of the offices in real income and supposed rank: I frankly declared my resolution to act as the king should command; and professed my ambition to prefer the honor (for such I think it is) of contributing, with M#. Pitt and your Grace, to the stability of government, to any emolument or any ease. The king, in the kindest manner, left me to consider and decide, only adding that my manner of acting was too liberal to permit him to press me, as he would do other men. I have since received the most friendly and honorable letter from M#. Pitt, and on Sunday I shall again see the king. In the mean time, your Grace may be assured that I shall accept; still desiring to be understood that I relinquish my own natural inclination and evident interest, upon the hope of being known by you, M#. Pitt, and the Crown to sacrifice, with chearfulness and from principle, all that men usually pursue to the veneration I bear M#. Pitt, my plan of union with your Grace, and my gratitude to my sovereign. Here let this anxious matter rest. If you feel it as I do, words are useless. God prosper our

---

Papers, iii. 283; Walpole, *Memoirs*, ii. 355. Pitt was prevailed upon by Conway at the instance of the Cavendishes to call on Rockingham, who refused to see him.

Either Rockingham's followers misunderstood him, or they must have deliberately induced Pitt to subject himself to a rebuff: for it is clear that Rockingham regarded Pitt as the cause of his dismissal, and was very angry, while Pitt had been told that Rockingham would be gratified by the attention of a call.

[1] Mr. Yorke resigned his place as Attorney-General.

joint labors, and may our mutual trust, affection and friendship grow from every act of our lives.

> I am, my very dear lord,
> Your Grace's affect[e].
> and faithful humble ser[t].
> C. TOWNSHEND.

July 25th, 1766.

Being appointed to the queen's house[1], I found Lord Northington and Lord Camden already there. Mr. Pitt was in with the king. The two lords appeared to be in most earnest conversation, and much agitated. On perceiving it, I naturally was turning from them, after my bow; but they begged to impart to me the subject of their concern, asking me whether I had any previous knowledge of M[r]. Pitt's intention of obtaining an earldom, and thus placing himself in the House of Lords; whereas our conception of the strength of the Administration had been, till that moment, derived from the great advantage he would have given to it by remaining with the Commons. On this there was but one voice among us, nor indeed throughout the kingdom[2]. When M[r]. Pitt left the Closet, we had only to receive notice of the measure, as a matter fixed, and not for deliberation. The reception we gave to the communication was so evident, that it could not escape a penetrating eye; for we were all struck with the idea of the prejudice it would do to his new Administration. Other necessary matters being arranged, we entered on office on the day which had been named for kissing the king's hand.

M[r]. Pitt, now become Earl of Chatham, who was bent on the salutary measure of a great alliance in the North, consisting of Prussia, Russia, Great Britain, and including Holland, was confident that he should be able to effect such a treaty of alliance, as a proper counterpoise to the famous *Pacte de*

---

[1] July 28.

[2] Not only in the kingdom but abroad was the mistake noted: see a remarkable letter from Choiseul to Guerchy (Fitzmaurice, *Life of Shelburne*, i. 412). Choiseul fears lest Chatham should seek to regain his lost popularity by schemes of conquest. He is also sceptical as to the continuance of the quarrel between Chatham and Temple.

Famille; and M^r. Stanley was commissioned to negociate this important business. Some have thought that, if Russia instead of Prussia had been the power to which we had applied, it might have succeeded. I do not think that this circumstance would have made the least alteration. Lord Chatham had the mortification to find, that M^r. Pitt had more weight with Frederic, who wanted him, than the Earl of Chatham had, whom he did not want at that particular moment [1]. The opening to an alliance, which must have appeared desirable for the independance of Europe, having at the present moment failed, the Ministry thought it adviseable to wait a more favorable opportunity. If I was to hazard an opinion on the coldness shewn by the Court of Berlin in particular, I have since attributed it to the plan, which might already have been formed in the K. of Prussia's head, and which he knew would be objected to by the Court of St. James's, namely, the dismemberment of Poland.

Among the other events of the year there appeared none which more merited the attention and good management of the Administration than the great and extensive acquisitions obtained in the East Indies. I heartily joined in L^d. Chatham's opinion, that it was idle to be talking on terms and arrangements with the Company, while the great point had not been decided in Parliament, namely, who had the right to the territorial possessions in India? that it was preposterous that the right could lye in the Company; and that the Imperial Crown of Great Britain, (not the king) had the sole territorial right [2]. Beside this, the steps taken of laying an embargo on all vessels laden with corn, which prevented a scarcity here,

---

[1] Mr. Stanley was intended to supersede Sir George Macartney at the Russian Court, and on his way thither to discuss, at Berlin, the scheme for an alliance of the Northern powers. Sir Andrew Mitchell, our representative at Berlin, found that Frederick was disinclined for such an alliance, and Stanley's mission never took place. Frederick's reasons were substantial.

We had treated him badly in 1762 : our frequent changes of Ministry made our foreign policy disconnected and uncertain ; and there were many chances of a collision between England and the Southern powers which would not interest Prussia (*Chatham Corresp.* iii. 36, 46, 67, 80, 82, 139).

[2] This question of territorial right was settled by 53 Geo. III. c. 158.

became a subject for much parliamentary debate. The Opposition acknowledged the rectitude of the measure ; but we were not to be justified on the ground on which the Cabinet thought fit at first to take up the business, by supporting it as maintainable under the *Salus Populi Suprema Lex*; and we had the mortification, after two days' debate, to stoop to a Bill of Indemnity, which ought to have been proposed in the beginning[1].

It has been mentioned that Lord Egmont quitted the Admiralty on Lord Chatham's appointment. The first person thought of as his successor was Lord Gower; and Lord Chatham desired that I would be the negociator. As such I embarked, with more desire, I confess, than expectation, of success; and my letter from Wakefield was written to Trentham, and drawn out according to the directions of this letter of Lord Chatham's.

> BOND STREET,
> Wednesday, Augt. 20, 1766.
>
> MY LORD,
>
> It is with very real concern that I find your Grace's indisposition so considerable as to prevent your much wish'd return to S^{t}. James's. I am commanded by the king to express in His Majesty's name, how sorry he is to hear your Grace is ill; and I should not do justice to His Majesty, if I did not add that the king's expression and manner was full of the most gracious attention towards the Duke of Grafton.
>
> Inclosed your Grace will find the Duke of Bedford's letter to you[2]: I have related the contents of it to the king. His Majesty is of opinion, and I applaud the judgement, that your Grace should, without loss of time, sound Lord Gower *directly* with regard to the Admiralty, and bring

---

[1] The Act of Indemnity, 7 Geo. III. c. 7 covered the ministers who had advised the Order in Council which imposed the embargo, as well as those who acted under it. The Bill should, as the Duke says, have been proposed at once, but there was a great deal of affectation in the solemn constitutional discussions which ensued, and Lord Mansfield, though no friend to ministers, thought at first that the embargo was lawful (*Grenville Papers*, iii. 337).

[2] The negotiation began with a conversation between Lord Tavistock and Grafton, the substance of which is given in the *Bedford Correspondence* (iii. 342). The Duke told Lord Tavistock that 'Lord Chatham's idea was a great and conciliating plan': but the Bedford party were to get no more than the appointment of Lord Gower to the Admiralty. The Duke of Bedford was informed of this and declined, in the letter referred to in the text, 'to be a middleman between the Administration and Lord Gower' (*Bedford Corresp.* iii. 344).

on a clear decision of a matter which cannot remain in suspence. The king rests entirely on your Grace's prudence and address, not to commit His Majesty in opening this offer to Lord Gower. It is taken for granted that your Grace will dispatch, in some proper way, this proposal to Trentham, and save as much time, as may be, with propriety in an affair of this nature. I am far from well myself, and write in much haste. I will only add to your Grace's trouble at present, by saying that, if the Duke of Grafton will be so good to bring himself back in perfect health, he will more than compensate the shattered state of his Grace's

most truly devoted

humble servant,

CHATHAM.

To the letter I wrote to Lord Gower I received the following answer.

TRENTHAM, *Aug*st. 22nd, 1766.

MY DEAR LORD,

I received your Grace's letter[1] last night at ten o'clock, the contents of which I had been appriz'd of two days ago by a letter from the Duke of Bedford, communicating to me what had past in London between your Grace and Lord Tavistock. I am extremely honor'd and flatter'd by your Grace and the chief of His Majesty's servants in thinking me a proper successor to the Earl of Egmont at the Board of Admiralty, and I need not inform y^r Grace how happy it would make me to be a *pars parva* of an Administration of which your Grace is so considerable a member; but so uninformed as I am at this distance, and so very unexplanatory as your Grace's letter is, and I therein call'd upon for a clear decision, I find myself necessitated to decline the acceptance of the office. For, tho' I am acquainted with the commanders in chief of the Administration, and I do assure your Grace that I have not the least personal objection to any one, yet your Grace must know how unpleasant it is to be in a *responsible* office (and such is the Board of Admiralty), unconnected with the individuals who compose that Administration, and finding myself, as M^r. Beckford would say, *Isolé*; nay, your Grace has not given me the least hint, who are to be the mariners in the vessel, on board of which it is propos'd that I should embark. Your Grace says that a fundamental principle on which the present Administration have embark'd is to conciliate and unite; it gives me infinite pleasure to hear that intention is such, for it is the only principle which can give stability to Administration, or ease to the Crown; and

---

[1] This is the letter described by Temple as 'not very wise' (*Grenville Corresp.* iii. 321). It does not seem to have erred on the side of indiscreet disclosure.

that this was my opinion, I had the honor to tell your Grace more than once last winter. Give me leave to add (least improper motives should be suppos'd to have influenc'd me upon this occasion), that I do not decline entering into the office propos'd to me from any dislike to any one member whatever of the present Administration : I know their abilities, and I honor their characters ; nor from my name having been some time since mention'd for a considerable post which was not acquiesc'd in [1]; for as it was proposed without my knowledge, so would it have been accepted against my inclination ; nor do I do it in consequence of any one opinion but my own, and consequently very likely to be wrong. I cannot conclude without acquainting your Grace, how unhappy I feel not to embrace with eagerness a proposal of this kind which comes from or thro' your Grace, as no one is

with more sincerity y^r Grace's

most obliged and most obedient servant,

GOWER.

I hope this letter will find y^r Grace in better health.

His lordship dined with me at Wakefield Lodge a few days after, when we had the subject over and over, in every light in which it could be presented ; and we parted in the best humour possible with each other, and as old friends. In the meantime, the answer from Lord Gower was forwarded to Lord Chatham [2], from whom I soon received the letter which follows :

NORTH-END, Saturday, 4 o'clock.

MY LORD,

I have the honor to agree entirely with your Grace, in the view of the declining of Lord Gower : the issue is not what I expected. The fruit of the offer will be full of advantage ; and if His Majesty shall be pleased to form an Admiralty with S^r. Charles Saunders, and M^r. Keppel [3] (S^r. Charles first Lord Commissioner), I have no doubt that the publick in general, and the sea-service in particular, will receive such an arrangement with satisfaction and applause : the fleet will be well filled and served, and harmony insured at the Board. Confirmed in these sentiments by your Grace's full concurrence, I have presumed to write to the king this day, to submit most humbly this arrangement to His Majesty's wisdom. It is necessary for me to be to-morrow at S^t. James's, which will

---

[1] The post of Secretary of State. See Camden's letter, p. 94.

[2] *Chatham Corresp.* iii. 54.

[3] Saunders and Keppel were Whigs of the Rockingham party : they both resigned on the dismissal of Lord Edgecumbe in November of this year. Sir Charles Saunders died in 1775. Augustus Keppel, second son of the second Earl of Albemarle, was made Viscount Keppel, and became First Lord of the Admiralty in 1782. He died in 1786.

oblige me to defer the honor of receiving your Grace's commands, as you
pass. I trust to heaven we shall have your Grace confirmed safe and
well by Sunday. The next week we all hope to fill with important objects.
Meetings upon E. India affairs, (the greatest of all objects, according to
my sense of great), as well as the whole outline of the ensuing Session.
The Duke of Rutland[1] has in the most handsome and noble manner,
thro' Lord Granby, offered his office for the accomodation of the king's
affairs. Lord Hertford[2] has been spoke to by His Majesty upon the
subject, of which his lordship will more properly give your Grace an
account. The answer from Berlin is anxiously expected. That our
expectations of seeing the Duke of Grafton well, may be answered
to-morrow, is the ardent wish of your

Grace's most respectfully
and affectionately devoted humble servant,
CHATHAM.

This intercourse with the Duke of Bedford's party was
renewed in autumn, at Bath, where his Grace often saw Lord
Chatham, as well as Lords Northington and Camden[3]. By
what passed there, and by the good disposition shewn on
both sides to an honorable junction, I had no doubt of the
interviews Lord Chatham had, in the beginning of winter,
with the D. of Bedford ending with satisfaction. It proved
otherwise: and Lord Chatham found the duke rising in his
demands on every attempt to provide suitably for his friends:
which may be attributed in a great manner to the weight of
M[r]. Rigby, who did not see that office within his reach
which might answer his wants, as well as his ambition.
The approaching Session assisted this gentleman's endeavors;
tho' it was thought that the Duchess, L[d]. Tavistock, Lords
Gower and Ossory were earnest for the junction. So much
for these unsuccessful parleys and negotiations, on which
I shall perhaps be considered as having dwelt too long already.

---

[1] John, third Duke of Rutland (1696–
1779), was now Master of the Horse;
he placed his office at Chatham's disposal, who was thus able to offer it to
Lord Hertford, and so obtain the Lord-
Lieutenancy of Ireland for Lord Bristol.

[2] Francis Seymour Conway (1719–
1794), first Earl and Marquis of Hertford.

He had been appointed Lord-Lieutenant
of Ireland in 1765. He now became
Master of the Horse, and in December
of this year Lord Chamberlain.

[3] The Duke of Bedford left an account
of these interviews (*Bedford Corresp.*
iii. 348–354).

S^r. Charles Saunders, on Lord Gower's declining, became First Lord of the Admiralty: unfortunately, he held that important office for a short time indeed; and was succeeded by S^r. Edward Hawke in December following.

Lord Chatham, with his superior talents, did not possess that of conciliating mankind : he was admired, but was rarely liked. So far from succeeding in smoothing away all party divisions, as had been his first and great declaration, he contrived to irritate and offend most.; and his mistrust of the friends of the Duke of Newcastle was greater than could be conceived. While he continued to honour them for the political principles by which they professed to be actuated, he suspected that they were not well-wishers to him, in which he was probably not mistaken; but he at length put their patience to a trial, which could only be received by that party as a declaration of hostility. I was not the only person among his friends, who ventured to dissuade him from his design of removing Lord Edgecombe from his office[1], and giving his stick to M^r. Shelley, the nephew of the Duke of Newcastle, whom he had some time quitted in order to attach himself to M^r. Pitt.

You will not be displeased, that I should here introduce a letter from M^r. Chas. Townshend. It will be read with satisfaction, at the same time that it is creditable to him. I wish that I had many of the sort to produce.

MY DEAR LORD,

Having dined this day with M^r. Conway and had the opportunity of reading his letter to Lord Chatham, and Lord Chatham's answer, I cannot resist my own apprehensions, least the matter which you have left depending should end unfortunately. The generosity of Lord Besborough[2]

---

[1] George, third Lord Edgecumbe, created Earl of Mount Edgecumbe in 1789, had served with distinction in the Navy, and was at this time Treasurer of the Household. Chatham wanted the place for Sir John Shelley, who had the merit of having deserted Newcastle for Pitt. Edgecumbe was offered a Lordship of the Bedchamber, which he refused : he was thereupon dismissed. He commanded four boroughs, and was intimate with the Rockingham Whigs. Conway remonstrated strongly with Chatham (*Chatham Corresp.* iii. 120).

[2] Lord Besborough had offered to give up to Lord Edgecumbe the place

can never be enough celebrated by every real friend to public tranquility, the union of the Whigs, and the common cause of those great persons and families who have acted together, ever since the reality of a Whig party. M^r. Conway has communicated the idea of a new arrangement, with the utmost delicacy and good sense : but a motive of accomodation seems to have been construed into a plan of authority, and what was designed to express good humour and prevent connexion has been disliked as stipulation and presumption. I confess I cannot adopt the interpretation; I lament the ill success of so promising a ground of reconciliation; and I beg leave to repeat my earnest and most anxious wishes, such as I am, that disunion may be prevented among men, who cannot separate without weakness to the public. It is mean to think of private situations when so general an interest is at stake : but every honest man who has a heart worthy of respect will be comfortless in his station, whether that be in government, or out of it, if the ancient Whig families should, in the opening of a Ministry so popular, so able, and so sure of success, be divided, and each part be obliged to form an entire Administration or a settled Opposition. The settlement of the times, the peace of the king's mind, the hopes of the country will all be once more dissolved, and for what? It may double M^r. Shelley's income; it may do the work of former ministers, it may gratify our enemies; but it cannot answer the ambition of any man we love, nor the expectation of the people. For these reasons, I cannot help renewing my entreaties, that you will persevere in your powerful endeavors to obviate the stroke. It will be your own work, and it is worthy of you. I am with the sincerest affection,

My dear lord, your Grace's, &c.

CHS. TOWNSHEND.

DOWNING STREET, Friday evening.   [Novr. 25th.]

M^r. Secretary Conway was properly the servant of the Crown, to take the lead in the House of Commons. It was with him that Lord Chatham ought to have been really confidential in his different purposes. How could it be expected that, with coldness towards M^r. Conway, his Ministry could ever move with comfort to any part of it? M^r. Conway felt disappointed on this treatment from the beginning; his complaints to me were daily, and these were much fomented by Lord Rockingham, the Duke of Richmond [1], and

of joint Postmaster which he held, and to become a Lord of the Bedchamber. This was refused, and all the Rockingham Whigs who had retained office

under Chatham now resigned, except Conway.

[1] The efforts of Rockingham and the Cavendishes to induce Conway to resign

the Cavendishes, while his brother, M^r. Horace Walpole, and myself strove all in our power to reconcile him to his situation. Mr. C. Townshend perceived M^r. Conway's uneasiness; tho' he might not exactly attribute it to its true cause. He was no longer within the lash of M^r. Pitt's formidable eloquence; and took more on himself in the House than he would have ventured under any other circumstances.

On the night preceding Lord Chatham's first journey to Bath, M^r. Chas. Townshend was, for the first time, summoned to the Cabinet. The business was on a general view and statement of the actual situation and interests of the various powers in Europe: Lord Chatham had certainly taken the lead in this consideration in so masterly a manner, as to raise the admiration and desire of us all to co-operate with him in forwarding these views. M^r. Townshend was particularly astonished, and owned to me, as I was carrying him in my carriage home, that Lord Chatham had just shown to us what inferior animals we were: and that, as much as he had seen of him before, he did not conceive, till that night, his superiority to be so very transcendant. M^r. Townshend, however, soon forgot the great and extensive mind of the minister; and I had daily to hear, or to read his train of grievances, among which the disappointment he had met with in his application for a peerage for Lady Dalkeith was not the least.

Excepting our vast acquisitions in India, and the embargo laid at home on the ships laden with corn, there was not anything that occurred to arrest materially the public attention. The ministers, however, who remained in London were by no means idle, tho' very uncomfortably situated, in the absence of the President, Lord Chancellor, and Lord Chatham, who were all at Bath; and we had the mortification of receiving from them the draft of a speech, drawn up on a ground which some much disapproved[1]; but which was conformed

and the successful persuasions of Horace Walpole which induced Conway to retain office, are described by Walpole (*Memoirs*, ii. 377).

[1] The king's speech dwelt mainly on the prevailing scarcity of corn.

to, thro' deference to the authority of those from whom we had received it.   In the debates which took place at the opening of the Session it was curious, in the struggle for and against the necessity of passing the Indemnity Bill, to see Lord Mansfield bestriding the high horse of liberty[1], while Lord Chatham and Lord Camden were arguing for an extension of prerogative beyond its true limits.   And it was in these debates that this upright chancellor, in the warmth of speaking, inadvertently made use of the expression ' that, if it was a tyranny, it was only a tyranny of forty days.'

The desire of acquiring the support of the Duke of Bedford and his friends was not dropt by Lord Chatham, even after the first days of the opening of the Session: as will appear from the following note and letter to myself from his lordship[2]. Sᵣ. Chaˢ. Saunders and Admiral Keppel resigned

---

[1] Lord Mansfield's doubts as to whether the embargo was not lawful have been mentioned, *supra*, p. 99.

[2] The early troubles of the Chatham Ministry, indicated in these letters, may thus be summarized.   The offer of Lord Besborough to change offices with Lord Edgecumbe was notified to Chatham at the beginning of the week of Nov. 25.

On Tuesday, November 25, Beckford, in the House of Commons, moved to take into consideration the affairs of the East India Company.   This was opposed by Grenville, Rigby, and the Rockingham Whigs.

On Wednesday, November 26, Chatham wrote to Grafton doubting whether Rigby 'is after yesterday's vote admissible.' (See letter on p. 107.)

On Thursday, November 27, the Duke of Portland, Lords Scarborough, Besborough, and Monson resigned. Gower had an interview with Chatham, and received offers which he was to communicate to the Bedford party.

On Friday, November 28, the Admiralty Board, Saunders, Keppel, and Meredith, desired to resign, and only

deferred a formal resignation until the following Monday at Chatham's request (*Grenville Papers*, iii. 390).

On Saturday, November 29, Gower returned from Woburn and saw Chatham. The king is indifferent or averse to the the negotiation (*Chatham Corresp.* iii. 135).

On Monday, December 1, Bedford came to London and met his followers to consider Chatham's offer: i.e. Gower to be Master of the Horse ; Weymouth, joint Postmaster ; Rigby, Cofferer ; the Duke of Marlborough to have the Garter at an early date.   Bedford saw Chatham and asked for some further concessions (*Bedford Corresp.* iii. 359).

Tuesday, December 2.   The Duke's demands were refused, all negotiations broken off, and the Admiralty Board was filled, Sir Edward Hawke being first Lord.

Thus in a week Chatham had alienated the Rockingham and Bedford groups, and stood alone, with Grafton, Camden, Conway, Shelburne, and some placemen and king's friends.

at the same time with the Duke of Portland and Lord Rockingham's other friends, on the dismission of Lord Edge-combe from the Treasurership of the Household.

Lord Chatham, with most real concern, begs to inform the Duke of Grafton, that his Grace's intelligence with regard to Sʳ. Chaˢ. Saunders and Mʳ. Keppel was too well founded.

Lord Gower received the offer made to him with all the duty to the king, as well as all the genteelness and excellent good sense natural to his lordship, and proposes to go to Woburn to-morrow morning; after which his lordship will make his answer. This is all that could be expected; Lord Chatham does not hazard any conjectures on the final issue.

BOND STREET,
 Thursday night (*November* 27).

Wednesday (*Novᵇʳ*. 26).

MY DEAR LORD,

I beg to return your Grace many thanks for the obliging trouble you are so good to take, and to express at the same time my just sense of the friendly and kind intention of the correspondant, whose note your Grace takes the trouble to inclose. As to the present crisis, I view it in its whole extent, but knowing *where there is firmness*, I cannot consider the journey to Woburn as matter of alarm. I doubt much, whether Mʳ. Rigby is even, now after yesterday's vote, admissible: if he is, it is as much as can be said; and that only on condition of another conduct. Unions, with whomsoever it be, give me no terrors: I know my ground, and I leave them to indulge their own *Dreams*. If they can conquer, I am ready to fall; but I shall never consent to take any premature step from the consideration of what Rigby's *manœuvres* may produce. I repeat again, that I doubt whether the abovesaid gentleman can be admitted: the consideration of the Duke of Bedford and Lord Gower alone can bring that about. To sum up all in two words: *faction will not shake the Closet, nor gain the publick.* I wait the issue without the possibility of change in my sentiments. Give me leave, my dear lord, under these considerations, to decline taking any step, but that of advising the king to fill up the offices as they shall become vacant, by the *most eligible* who will accept them. I depend on the Duke of Bedford's rectitude and wisdom, and I have every good to expect from Lord Gower's knowledge of things, his discernment, and his excellent sound understanding. I fear your Grace may think me foolhardy and presuming. Indeed, my lord, the Closet is firm, and there is nothing to fear. I am ever with truest respect and attachment, my lord,

Your Grace's most devoted serᵗ.

CHATHAM.

Previously to Lord Chatham's coming up from Bath about the 4th of Nov[r]., his Lordship had received several letters from me; in many of which I had represented to him the circumstances which indicated that no light clouds were collecting to disturb the political horizon; and which to disperse would require, in my best judgement, all Lord Chatham's dexterity and management. I transcribe a letter from his lordship, in order to shew the sense he had of his own political situation.

BATH, Oct[r]. 19th, 1766.

MY DEAR LORD,

It is with much difficulty, and at the same time with particular pleasure, that I attempt a few lines to return your Grace many respectful and warm thanks for the honor of several most obliging letters. That of the 17th [1], just received, gives me great satisfaction, as it informs me of a very agreeable conclusion to a matter, which, I confess, gave me much uneasiness [2].

As to the phalanx your Grace mentions, I either am full of false spirits infused by Bath waters, or there is no such thing existing. The gentleman your Grace points out as a necessary recruit, I think a man of parts, and an ingenious speaker [3]. As to his notions and maxims of trade, they can never be mine. Nothing can be more unsound and more repugnant to every true principle of manufacture and commerce, than the rendering so noble a branch as the Cottons, dependant for the first material upon the produce of French and Danish Islands, instead of British [4]. My engagement to Lord Lisburne [5] for the next opening at the Board of Trade is already known to your Grace; nor is it a thing possible to wave for M[r]. Burke. M[r]. Hussey [6], I believe, is in Cornwall. That gentleman's ability and weight are great indeed; and my esteem and honor for his character the highest imaginable: I flatter myself with some share in his regard: but, as to his intentions, my Lord Chancellor may possibly be

[1] This letter is printed in the *Chatham Correspondence*, iii. 110.

[2] Lord Cardigan, who had been promised a dukedom, was prevailed upon to give up the office of Governor of Windsor Castle on becoming Duke of Montagu (*Chatham Corresp.* iii. 101, 107, 110). The king wrote to Grafton expressing his 'thorough approbation of the delicacy you have shown in the course of this affair.'

[3] The Duke pressed the claims of Burke, as 'the readiest man upon all points perhaps in the whole House.'

[4] I do not know when or where Burke expressed this opinion.

[5] Lord Lisburne was offered a place at the Admiralty Board when Keppel and Meredith resigned, but his seat was too insecure to allow him to accept it.

[6] Richard Hussey (1715–1770). Attorney-General to the Queen and Counsel to the Admiralty, a politician of Whig principles and high character.

more able to inform your Grace, when you meet, than I can presume to do.   M[r]. Nugent[1] I have not yet seen, having missed him when he was so good to call.

The inclosed draft, which is submitted to the consideration of your Grace, the Secretaries of State, and M[r]. Chancellor of the Exchequer, has the approbation of Lord Camden and Lord Northington.   If new matter should arise before the meeting, the speech will, to be sure, adapt itself to the event.   I have the most sensible joy in being able to acquaint your Grace, that Lord Spencer has, with infinite goodness, listened favorably to my earnest intreaties, and will move the Address.   Your Grace will be so good as to think of a seconder.   I think of going about Wednesday next for one day to Burton-Pynsent; and hope to pay my respects to your Grace in town, about the 4th of November.

My hand recovers very slowly, but my general health is mended by the waters; and I trust that a second reprise of ten days will help my hand.

> I am, with truest esteem and respect,
> > Your Grace's
> > > faithfully devoted,
> > > > most humble servant,
> > > > > CHATHAM.

I hope the Special Commission will not be delayed.

When Lord Chatham set out on his fatal journey to Bath, he was not sensible, nor would he be persuaded, of the many difficulties under which his Administration labored, though they were viewed with real concern by the nation at large, who perceived an union of parties, sufficiently powerful to embarrass every measure.   But he had also internal dangers to expect.   M[r]. Conway was not satisfied in his situation; and M[r]. Townshend was never settled in any; and these two gentlemen saw the management of the E. India business in a very different light from what Lord Chatham had wished.

They were for waving the decision on the right, and for bringing forward a negociation with the Company, without entering on this essential point, which Lord Chatham, together with the rest of the Cabinet, wanted to see decided in the first instance; and which M[r]. Ald[n]. Beckford[2] had undertaken to move in the House of Commons.

---

[1] Afterwards a peer of Ireland, Viscount Clare.

[2] Beckford (1709-1770) represented the City from 1753 until his death, and

Lord Chatham's illness, and indeed his constant bad state of health, often making it impracticable to talk with him on business or even to get access to him, brought a weakness on the Ministry which will be easily conceived; and placed us, who wished to forward his views, in the most uncomfortable and perplexing of all situations, scarce knowing what line to adopt; for Lord Chatham did never open to us, or to the Cabinet in general, what was his real and fixed plan. He would have found Lords Northington, Camden, and Shelburne, together with S^r. Edwd. Hawke and myself, full of zeal to support him.

I shall transcribe a letter of Lord Chatham's to myself, when he was preparing for his journey. There is no other date to the letter, than *Sunday night*; tho' a docket in my handwriting, I see, puts it to December 7th, 1766.

MY DEAR LORD,

I grieve most heartily at the report of the meeting last night. If the enquiry is to be contracted within the ideas of M^r. Chancellor of the Exchequer[1], and of M^r. Dyson[2], the whole becomes a *farce*, and the *Ministry a ridiculous phantom*. M^r. Beckford will move his questions, (waving for the present the bonds and transfers), and upon the issue of Tuesday must turn the decision of the present system, whether to stand or make way for another scene of political revolution. M^r. Dyson's behaviour cannot be acquiesced in. M^r. C. Townshend's fluctuations and incurable weaknesses cannot comport with his remaining in that critical office. Your Grace will not, I trust, wonder at the pain I feel for the king's service and personal ease, as well as for the *redemption* of a nation, within reach of being saved at once by a kind of gift from heaven; and all marred, and thrown away by fatal weaknesses, co-operating with the most glaring factions. What possible objection, fit to listen to, can be made to the bringing the revenues in India before the House? I hope M^r. Beckford will walk out of the House, and leave the name of an enquiry, to amuse the credulous, in other hands, in case this

was Lord Mayor in 1761 and 1769. Though a friend of Chatham he was a vain and noisy politician.

[1] Charles Townshend showed more than his usual instability on this Indian question, but in the debate which arose on Beckford's resolutions on Dec. 9 he took a more decided line, having,

as Walpole said, 'been chid by the Duke of Grafton for his variations' (*Memoirs*, ii. 408).

[2] Jeremiah Dyson (1722–1776) at one time clerk of the House of Commons and now M.P. for Yarmouth and a 'king's friend.' A busy underling.

question be not fully supported and carried. For my own part, I shall wash my hands of the whole business, after that event. Pardon the zeal, my lord, of a man in earnest for the king and for the community, and believe me, in all events, with the utmost respect and attachment, my dear lord,

Your Grace's most obedient and

devoted humble servant,

CHATHAM.

Sunday night.

All negociations with the Duke of Bedford having failed; and no accession of strength having fallen in to fill up the great chasm made by the resignation of the Duke of Newcastle's and Lord Rockingham's friends; and having the Grenvilles more bitterly hostile than any other faction, we, depending on our own best intentions for the public welfare, were preparing to meet the Parliament after the recess, with the firmness derived from a consciousness of the uprightness of all our endeavors. Judge then of the increased intricacy of our situation, when, in addition to all other concerns, we received the account of Lord Chatham's being seized again with the gout, and obliged to turn back from Marlborough to Bath; and the following letter from his lordship of the 10th of January will shew the flattering expectations he had given us of coming to our immediate relief.

(PRIVATE.)

BATH, *Jan'y*. 10th, 1767.

MY DEAR LORD,

It is with very real concern that I learn from the honor of your Grace's letter you had brought back from the country the indisposition which troubles you but too often; and I feel myself more particularly obliged to your Grace for having the goodness to write to me, under so painful a circumstance. Tho' I trust this will find your Grace in perfect health, I will not detain you with a long letter, as I propose setting out for London in a day or two, and shall principally mean at present to express my best thanks to your Grace for the communications you have done me the honor to give me, with regard to East India affairs[1]. I wish, my

---

[1] For the communications which passed between Chatham and Townshend on the dealings with the East India Company, see *Chatham Corresp.* iii. 149–158. On Jan. 8, 1767, Grafton sent to Chatham a paper delivered to him by the Chairman of the Company (*Chatham Corresp.* iii. 163).

dear lord, I could see cause to express any thanks to the good chairman and deputy chairman for their communication to your Grace. I will say but a few words upon their *captious* and *preposterous* paper. The points, on which the committee are of opinion it is requisite and necessary to treat, entirely pass by the great objects of parliamentary enquiry and national justice; and, to render the disingenuity of the proceeding more gross, all this is, (according to the words of the reference), *in pursuance of the resolution of the General Court.* On this self-evident state of the thing, I am forced to declare I have no hopes from the transaction; my only hope centers in the justice of Parliament, where the question of right can alone be decided; and which cannot (upon any colourable pretence) be in the company. The temper and turn of your Grace's answer, upon this occasion, may be more discreet than such an one as, I confess, I should have made in like circumstances; for I should have desired the gentlemen to dispense me from *receiving a resolution of the committee, not admissible* as the opening of a treaty, because *taking no notice of the revenues in question.* I hope soon to be at your Grace's orders in town, though I see not the least use I can be of in this matter; possibly rather in the way of others, from whom I have the misfortune to differ *toto coelo* upon these matters. With regard to M^r. Ch. Price, I beg leave to defer that consideration till we meet; only suggesting to your Grace at present, that whatever shall be resolved, the agreement had better be specifick, and must have the king's approbation. Allow me to beg the favour of your Grace to tell Mr. Townshend I apprehend my account will not have pass'd soon enough for his view: no time shall be lost.

I have the honor to be, with truest respect and attachment,
My dear lord, your Grace's
most obedient and most faithful humble servant,
CHATHAM.

A note to me, dictated by Lord Chatham, dated Bath, Jan^{ry}. 15th, 1767, brought us an account that his lordship on the Sunday preceeding had attempted the journey, but that he was compelled through excess of pain to return to his bed at Bath. This melancholy event discovered all the weakness, which was to be expected in consequence of Lord Chatham's absence, at a moment when his presence was so peculiarly wanted. Indeed I may say that the accident was fatal to the king's affairs. His Majesty appeared to be duly sensible of this misfortune, and that it was singularly detrimental to the affairs of the public as well as to his own personal comfort.

Lord Chatham was not more earnest, I may say, than His Majesty himself in thinking that in Parliament alone could be determined the great point of right to the territorial acquisitions in India.

The letter following was the next account we had from Lord Chatham, and which will be best related in his own words :

BATH, Friday evening, *Jan^{ry}*. 23^d.[1]

MY DEAR LORD,

Having been taken up for the first time yesterday, I can hardly use my pen. Give me leave to begin this short letter by begging your Grace again to lay me most dutifully at the king's feet, together with every sentiment which can fill the heart of a most devoted servant, deeply penetrated with the infinite condescension and gracious goodness of a most humane and indulgent sovereign ; expressing at the same time my extreme solicitude to hear that His Majesty's cold is entirely removed, to which, I trust in God, this more favorable weather will have greatly contributed.

As to East India affairs, my last letter to your Grace, as well as two I wrote to M^r. Townshend, shew how unpromising I think that matter is. Allow me, my dear lord, to say, that it is not my absence which affects this business, but an unfortunate original difference of opinions among the king's servants, which, totally contrary to my notions, by enervating at the outset the principle of the Parliamentary enquiry, shook the whole foundation of this great transaction, and has, in my opinion, thrown it into confusion inextricable ; *for* the consideration of the Company's right to the enormous revenues is the hinge upon which must turn the very essence of the question, namely, *whether the Company is to receive,* on this head, *indulgence and benefit from Parliament, or whether the Company is to make a grant to the public.* This right must, of necessity, be admitted or decided one way or other, before a just rule can be laid down whereby to judge if the proposal, when made, be adequate. The aim of the Company seems to be, to give the change, and, by making an inadmissible proposal, to reduce the king's servants to make demands upon the Company, with regard to the revenues in India, instead of

[1] The business part of this letter appears in the *Chatham Correspondence,* iii. 199, with a note—'from the original in Lady Chatham's handwriting, and with a date assigned by the editor' [Feb. 9, 1767].

I think that this date is wrong, and that it was assigned on the supposition that this letter was an answer to Grafton's of February 8, printed below, and also in the *Chatham Correspondence.* But the answer to Grafton's letter of Feb. 8 now appears for the first time in the letter dated Feb. 9 on p. 116.

receiving from them applications to supply a want of title, and to indulge them with a princely establishment civil and military, over and above many beneficial extensions in point of trade, which the commercial policy of their charter, and the wisdom of their institution suggest. If this be the project, as I believe, of this notable negociation, I know one of the king's servants who will beg to be excused running his head into such a snare; in this case Parliament alone can decide, and fix the public lot. As for any reviving hopes of particular factions, I confess, my dear lord, they are all indifferent in my opinion, and engage but little my thoughts. My whole mind is bent to acquire, by the prosecution of national justice, such a resource, once for all, as must give strength, ease, and lustre to the king's reign. If this transcendent object fails, it will not be by the force of factions from without, but from a certain infelicity, (I think incurable), which ferments and sours, (as your Grace has observed), the councils of His Majesty's servants. Nothing, I am persuaded, my dear lord, ever was or will be wanting on your Grace's part for the king's service, or the public good : but for all these generous and salutary endeavours things can hardly go on, till there is more agreement, or more acquiescence.

I am ever with truest respect and attachment,

My dear lord, your Grace's

most faithfully devoted humble serv^t.

CHATHAM.

Here I am of opinion that I cannot do better than to lay before you the letters which passed between Lord Chatham and myself previously to his arrival from Bath to London, as his lordship's will best indicate the state of his mind on the great India business.

GROSVENOR SQUARE, Feb^ry. 8th, 1767.

MY DEAR LORD[1],

I am not without hopes that this letter may meet your lordship on your journey to London, where, give me leave to say, your appearance was never so much wanted as at this time. There is no interpretation that the ill-wishers to the present system do not endeavor to give to your absence, and, I am sorry to say, they succeed so far, as to make every one feel the languor under which every branch of the Administration labours from it. My Lord Chancellor, the Lord President, and myself have within this day or two conversed a good deal on the consequences it may bring on, and as much as we are acquainted with your lordship's zeal in the cause you have so nobly undertaken, yet are we most thoroughly convinced that your presence is absolutely necessary to give dignity to the Administration, and to carry thro' this affair (the

[1] Printed in *Chatham Correspondence*, iii. 194.

most important of all) of the East India Company, in which they all
think that there is no stirring without your assistance and concurrence :
and on my part, I am ready and desirous to declare that whatever shall
appear to you to be the most eligible mode to terminate it, that same
shall I most thoroughly join in : not that I imagine any present difference
of opinion on the subject between us, but meaning only to observe that,
if there should be, I should frankly open to your lordship my reasons,
and then be ready to fall into the measures which your experience and
ability will always call upon me to prefer to all others.

Since the time of my writing last to your lordship, I have had no sort
of intercourse with or intelligence from any one person concerned in the
East India direction until the night before last, when I received a note
from the East India House that the chairman and deputy would wait
on me in the morning.   They came accordingly yesterday at ten o'clock,
and opened their discourse by telling me that they came *authoriz'd* by
their Treasury Comittee to lay before me *the ideas* on which they thought
the revenues, &c., in the East Indies might be terminated with mutual
advantage to the publick and the company, desiring me to communicate
them to the principal of His Majesty's servants.   Before they open'd
the contents of the paper, (a copy of which I inclose), I observed to
them that it was my duty certainly to receive their *ideas*, and to communicate them to the Cabinet, which I was glad to express to them before
I was inform'd of the contents of the paper, that they should not interpret
my doing it even to my personal avowal of the admissibility of this
proposal.   M^r. Dudley then said that, their being somewhat declaratory
of their opinion in regard to the right of those acquisitions, he was
order'd to say that it was expected that no use would be made of their
opinions against themselves, in case their ideas should be totally rejected :
as such was the opinion of them as individuals, and on which their
constituents had not authoriz'd them to decide.   My answer was, that
I should not fail mentioning this request of theirs, when I open'd their
scheme to His Majesty's servants, and that I would be frank enough to
deliver it as my opinion, that a confidential avowal of the way of thinking
of individuals ought not to be turned against them ; but that I would be
answerable for no one but myself, who, if they told me their opinion in
confidence, would look upon myself as obliged not to declare that I had
receiv'd it from them.   But to this I added that, if call'd upon in Parliament as a servant of the publick, I did not see how it could be avoided.
To which M^r. Rous observed that they were directed to say this, but that
he saw that, in the case I mentioned, it was unavoidable.   I will not
make my remarks on the contents of this paper, tho' I think there are
many objectionable parts : the length of the term, and the want of direct
application of the company's moiety I think are capital ones.

Your lordship will observe that the idea of blending the profits of the revenue, &c., and that arising from their trade, and dividing them with the publick are new, at least they are so to me. Lord Northington, to whom, and to whom alone I have had an opportunity of communicating the paper as yet, perfectly agreed with me that your lordship should have a copy of it sent to you; and that I should not lay it before the Cabinet till your lordship comes to town. Though not in direct words, I think I could gather from the directors *that they might go further.* I shall think it incumbent on me to lay it to-morrow before the king.

That I may soon have the honor of seeing your lordship, and well recovered, is the sincere wish of him, who is with the most perfect respect

Your lordship's &c.

GRAFTON.

BATH, *Feb*ʳʸ. 9ᵗʰ, 1767.

MY DEAR LORD,

I have very many thanks to return your Grace for the honor of your obliging letter, accompanying the proposal from the Committee of the East India Directors. If my wishes to be where I might be of a little use, were not what they are, your Grace's kind exhortations, and those of the Lords you mention, would be effectual spurs to me to quicken my motions. I can venture to assure your Grace, that the same *duty* and *devotion to the king* which animated me to attempt, and *sperare contra spem* still prompts me to struggle, under bodily infirmities, and equally incurable disadvantages which certain infelicities of the age throw upon publick business. As soon as I can recover strength enough, I will set out; but I cannot imagine the least utility, in my lying short by the way, or being confined to my bed the moment I reach London. In the mean time, reports about my absence seem quite immaterial: those of my not being satisfy'd with certain notions, and with a conduct consequential to them, from the beginning of the East India enquiry to this hour, I should be sorry to remove: on the contrary, I would have this clearly understood: but instead of this *dissatisfaction* being a cause of prolonging my absence, it would most certainly accelerate my return. My present state will hardly allow me to hope I can be in town before the 18ᵗʰ, nor can I see the importance of a week, more or less.

I now come to the papers of the 6ᵗʰ of Febʳʸ. from the Committee of Directors. I shall not enter into the merits of the proposal. Parliament is *the only place* where I will declare my final judgement upon the whole matter, if ever I have an opportunity to do it[1]. As a servant of the Crown, I have no right or authority to do more than simply to advise that the *demands* and the *offers* of the Company should be laid before

---

[1] This is a characteristic statement. Apparently Chatham, though Prime Minister, did not propose to acquaint his colleagues with his views on an important question of policy until he had in the first instance confided them to Parliament.

Parliament, referring the whole determination to the wisdom of that place.

But tho' I abstain at *present* from entering into the *merits* of the above paper, I must take notice of the *manner* of this transaction. The paper begins by asserting *that the Committee have already offered to the consideration of Administration several articles in which their commerce seems to require new regulation and present relief.* This refers (most ingenuously) to a paper put into your Grace's hands, upon your return to town, *to show respect* and only *for communication to your Grace*, requiring *no answer.* Well then, to take these gentlemen at their word, and according to their own sense of the thing, these articles requiring regulation and present relief cannot possibly be withheld from Parliament, and must, in due time, be laid there. Next, I come to the notable attempt to render the *proposal* relating to the revenues only an *idea*, and unauthorized by their *constituents*; the transaction too to be *a secret.* Was ever anything so puerile and ridiculous as this state artifice? Who can abet these gentlemen in so captious and offensive a proceeding? I cannot talk seriously upon such a farce of negociation. To sum all I have to offer upon this affair, I beg to *acquit myself* by *submitting it as my clear opinion*, that Parliament is *intitled to be inform'd what steps have been taken by the directors* in *consequence* of the *resolution* of the *general Court, and that the servants of the Crown* are *indispensibly bound in duty not to suppress any* [facts], *but to lay them in due time, even uncall'd for, before the House; besides their general duty, it is become still more incumbent, if possible, from the proceedings of the Committee of Enquiry being stopt, with regard to printing the papers, by a formal declaration of an expected proposal.* Thus much I think necessary to say with regard to the secrecy of this strange business. Now, my dear lord, give me leave to beg your Grace's forgiveness for this diffuse, prolix letter; the matter fills my mind and heart; the manner of proceeding of the committee is insidious; the proposal deserves no other observation, than that it is *enormous* and *unconscionable, even to effrontery.* Thus, my lord, your Grace sees, I can declare to the Duke of Grafton a direct opinion, out of Parliament. As to the poor cunning of these pedlars in negociation, I am much mistaken, if they are not already taken in their own snare; for they have done enough to lead, bye and bye, to the dénouement in Parliament, with more advantage to the friends of the publick, against the advocates for the alley.

I am ever, with the truest sense of your Grace's great goodness to me, my dear lord,

Your Grace's most humbly
devoted serv^t.
CHATHAM.

GROSVENOR SQUARE, *Feb^y*. 15th, 1767.

MY DEAR LORD,

Lord Granby, who is confined (by advice) on account of his leg at Knightsbridge, has asked me much to call upon him, and as Lord Shelburne informs me that a messenger sets out this afternoon from his house with a packet to your lordship, I must be obliged to put in as few words as possible what pass'd at the Cabinet last night on the consideration of the paper from the directors which I sent to your lordship some days ago. Every one agreed that it was so general and unintelligible, that no one would venture to pronounce even an opinion on what they protested they did not understand. To all it appeared *extremely* objectionable, to most *totally* inadmissible, to some insidious, nay almost impertinent, considering the time they had taken to make up so incoherent a proposition, and which was for the consideration of the king's servants. On the whole it was agreed that, explanation being necessary even for a dismission of the proposition, such questions should be put to the directors for their answer as the dark parts of it required. It was doubted whether the questions agreed upon, and herein inclosed, were such as could allow them to continue a negotiation; but as they were necessary to be asked in justification to the decision of the king's servants, the consequences were to turn out as they might; for it would have been indeed sufficient and a good handle for opposition to have heard the ministers declare that they had decided on proposals they understood not, without requiring an explanation.

I have written by the direction of the Cabinet to desire the chairman and deputy to call upon me to-morrow, when I am to deliver a copy of the inclosed *in writing*, it being determined that if they choose to complain of the treaty with them being broken off, they should at the same time be obliged to confess that they had throughout met with the most regardful reception from Administration. I will only add that the whole passed last night with a cordiality which *Cabinets* of late have not shewn, and owing greatly, as I think, to the presence of my Lord President, whose manly conduct and experience have been of the greatest service. I am of opinion that the explanation of their sense of the word *annexation* will puzzle the gentlemen so much who hoped to be screened under it, that your lordship will find, I think, this affair going on under a parliamentary enquiry, and the only one in which it can end properly for the advantage of the publick.

I am very anxious for your lordship's return, which I am confident you are not less concerned about yourself. Believe me to be, with the truest esteem and respect,

My dear lord, &c.

GRAFTON.

The gout having returned so severely upon Lord Chatham at Marlborough as to confine him to his bed, he desires, with his best respects to the Duke of Grafton, that his Grace will be so good to lay him at the king's feet, and acquaint His Majesty with his situation, which detains him, so unhappily for himself, from attending his duty at this very critical conjuncture. The moment he is able to move he will endeavor to reach London.

In the mean time, Lord Chatham humbly submits, as his opinion, that it is adviseable, and even necessary, to put off the proceedings in the enquiry 'till the *final intention* of the Company, and their *application* to Government, in consequence of the resolution of the General Court, can be brought to maturity enough to be laid before Parliament. If the Duke of Grafton and the rest of the king's servants should concur in this opinion, Lord Chatham begs the Duke of Grafton will see M^r. Beckford, as soon as conveniently may be, and apprize him of what shall be agreed upon.

MARLBOROUGH, Monday, 16th *Feb^{ry}*. 1767.

Lord Chatham continues much in the same state he was yesterday, and quite unable to enter into any detail of things; he therefore only begs leave humbly to submit his opinion, that the proposal from the East India Company, vague and extravagant as it is, should not finally be dismiss'd by the king's servants, but, on all accounts, left to the conclusive judgement of Parliament. Lord Chatham is also of opinion, that it seems most adviseable and indispensible, that the first proceeding in the continuation of the enquiry should be, to desire to be informed if any applications, and what, have been made from the directors of the East India Company to the servants of the Crown, relative to the state of the Company's affairs in consequence of the resolution of the General Court.

With regard to New York, Lord Chatham desires to submit his opinion, that the disobedience of the assembly of that province to the Mutiny Act is a matter so weighty and big, with consequences which may strike so deep and spread so wide, that it ought, on no account, to rest on the advice of meetings of the Cabinet and the course of office; but that the memorial, transmitted by the Governor of New York, relative to this event ought, in the proper manner, to be laid before Parliament, in order that His Majesty may be founded in, and strengthen'd by, the sense of his grand council, with regard to whatever steps shall be found necessary to be taken in this most unfortunate business.

Lord Chatham humbly offers to the consideration of the king's servants the above opinions, and also begs that they may be laid with all duty and submission at His Majesty's feet.

Lord Chatham begs the Duke of Grafton will accept of his best respects, and many thanks for the honor of his Grace's very obliging letter.

MARLBOROUGH, Tuesday, *Feb^{ry}*. 17th, 1767.

GROSVENOR SQUARE, *Feb^ry*. 22ⁿᵈ, 1767.

MY DEAR LORD,

The East India directors brought to me yesterday the inclosed paper as an answer to the questions on the meaning of their former paper, which, by directions of the king's servants, I had delivered to them. I know not how satisfactory they may appear to the other lords of the Cabinet, but I profess that I thought I could *guess* better at the meaning of their propositions before than *now* I can after their explanations. In short, my lord, it seems now that our thoughts must be turned to the most adviseable steps to be taken upon this great affair by the king's servants in Parliament, where the decision of the right must, I think, be in the first place determined. Resolutions to be moved on this business must be well weighed and worded, so as to carry the effect that Administration aims at. When you are free from pain, I am confident you are turning this thoroughly in your thoughts, as I am certain that your plan is much desired by all the ministers in general, many of whom, among which I am, would not willingly give into any other, until they know your sentiments. If your lordship acquaints me that you are likely to be detained still at Marlborough, I am ready to run down there, to talk this whole matter over with your lordship, and to receive and communicate your wishes upon it. If you would have me come, let me know the time of day that I shall arrive there, to be the least inconvenient for you to see me, who have the honor to be,

&c., &c.

GRAFTON.

PS. Your lordship has certainly been informed that the day stands fixed for Friday se'ennight.

Lord Chatham's best respects attend the Duke of Grafton, with many acknowledgements for the honor of his Grace's very obliging letter. Nothing can be more kind than the offer the Duke of Grafton has the great goodness to make, of which Lord Chatham desires to express the humblest and warmest sense. At the same time his Grace will give him leave to suggest that, until he is able to move towards London, it is by no means practicable for him to enter into discussions of business. He desires farther to add, that, with regard to East India regulations, his fix'd purpose has always been, and is, not to be a proposer of plans, but, as far as a seat in one House enables, an unbiass'd judge of them. Friday se'ennight, the day mention'd in the Duke of Grafton's letter as fix'd for the enquiry in the House of Commons, being the 6th of March, leaves room to hope the gout may before that time be enough abated to admit of my getting to London.

As to the proposal from the East India House, with their explanation, Lord Chatham begs leave to refer to his former clear opinion, transmitted to his Grace by Cleverley, with regard to the full information which Parliament indispensibly ought to have concerning this transaction.

MARLBOROUGH, Monday, 23rd *Feb'y*, 1767.

I do not recollect, nor do I find among my papers, that any other letters passed before Lord Chatham arrived himself in London, which must have been about the first week in March[1]. The sixth was the day fixed for entering into the East India business in the House of Commons[2]: Mr. Conway previously to this, finding that he differed in opinion on this head from Lord Chatham, myself, and other of the king's principal servants, presented his opinion to His Majesty in writing, and conceived in these terms:

I am of opinion the propositions made by the directors of the East India Company ought to have been admitted, as a ground of further treaty:

1. Because, by consenting that the possession of their territories in India should be annexed to the exclusive charter, for such a term as the Parliament shall think proper to grant them, they do in effect give up *their claim* of right.

2. Because they offer now, in the first instance, one half, not of the Dowannee only, but of all the territorial revenue in India, together with the half of the clear profits arising from their trade, after all expences civil and military are defrayed, and all necessary charges at home deducted, which article, tho' not now sufficiently explained, cannot fail, when properly ascertained, of producing a very considerable clear revenue for the use of the public, and might probably, on further treaty with the directors, be not only explained to the satisfaction of Government, but altered or improved so as to be free from every objection now made to it.

3. Because the directors, by proposing to fix the quantum or rate of the dividend on their stock hereafter, do in effect thereby take away in great measure the immediate interest of the Company even in *their half* of the nett surplus, and necessarily constrain and induce the employment

---

[1] It must have been on March 2 (Walpole, *Memoirs*, ii. 426).

[2] The Ministry were strangely divided on this question. Chatham and Grafton seem to have wished that the proposals of the Company should come before the House of Commons with no indication of the wishes of the ministers, and so should obtain an independent condemnation. Townshend was inclined to deal easily with the Company, and was not wholly free from the suspicion of speculating in East Indian Stock. Conway thought that the proposals should have been considered. It came out in debate that the Cabinet had already rejected them (Walpole, *Memoirs*, ii. 430).

of whatever shall remain, after the dividend is paid and their present debts satisfied, to some purposes advantageous to the public, either by extending or improving their commerce, or by disposing it in loans to the Government at a low interest, in such manner as may be hereafter settled.

4. Because, by pursuing this method of negociation, all the difficulties which attend a Parliamentary decision of this question may be avoided as well as the great inconveniencies that must follow from a breach with the Company, or even a delay in making some proper settlement of their affairs, both for the Company's and the public benefit [1].

Lord Chatham, on his arrival in London, was much concerned to find that M[r]. Conway differed so essentially from him in the manner of conducting the East India enquiry in Parliament. He did not, (for no man could), question the sincerity of the general's views; but felt how much the leading minister in the Commons, differing from the king's other servants, lessened the general efficacy of their measures. As to M[r]. Townshend's behaviour, Lord Chatham considered him as the man who had marred the business in the outset; inasmuch as he had held language to the directors and others quite improper, and unbecoming his situation. This was not all that excited Lord Chatham's anger. Mr. Townshend had lost the question on a land lax at 4 shillings in the pound, which was proposed by him [2]. The failure was very generally imputed to a want of exertion on his part.

Lord Chatham received the account of this defeat with an increased indignation against the whole conduct of the Chancellor of the Exchequer; and he had no difficulty to obtain the king's leave to speak to Lord North, and to encourage him to become the successor of Mr. Townshend. Lord North, however, after a long conversation with the minister, declined the offer; of which I informed the king, whose commands I received to wait on Lord Chatham the

[1] The proposals made by the Company to the Government are to be found in the *Chatham Correspondence*, iii. 150, 196.

[2] On February 27 the country gentlemen, headed by Dowdeswell, carried a reduction of the land-tax from four shillings in the pound to three. Dowdeswell had been Chancellor of the Exchequer in the previous year, and must have known that the Government could not afford such a reduction. Burke did not vote.

next day, to hear whom he would recommend to be the Chancellor of the Exchequer, and I was directed to prevent Lord North from coming to His Majesty, in order that his refusal should not be suspected[1]. The same idea had struck Lord North himself, as appears by the following letter :—

MY LORD,

As I returned from your Grace's this evening a reflection suggested itself to me, which I think I ought to communicate to you. What has passed this evening between your Grace and me need not be known to any, but His Majesty and ourselves. But if I wait on the king at the queen's house to-morrow, the negociation will become public. It will soon be known that I have declined the offer, and such a report will, I am afraid, be an additional weakness to Government. I have the highest sense of gratitude both for the honor of being thought by His Majesty worthy of so great an employment, and for the very gracious manner in which the offer is intended to be made. But, as my resolution is fixed upon a thorough conviction that my acceptance of the seals will not be of any real service to the king, I should think it adviseable that they should not be publickly offered to me, or indeed to anybody else, before it is certain that they will be accepted.

I submit this consideration to your Grace out of a sincere goodwill to Government, and a grateful sense of my duty to the king. If it should appear of any weight to His Majesty or your Grace, I hope to have a line from you before half an hour after eleven o'clock to-morrow morning. If I hear nothing from you before that time, I will then set out for the queen's house, in obedience to His Majesty's commands delivered to me this evening. I am with the greatest respect, my lord,

Your Grace's most faithful,
humble servant,
NORTH[2].

PAY OFFICE, Wednesday night.

---

[1] Yet Townshend seems to have heard of the offer.

Shelburne tells Chatham on March 13 that Townshend had assured the Cabinet on the preceding evening that he had promised the House of Commons to raise a revenue from America. Shelburne further says that Townshend's conduct seemed incomprehensible 'till I afterwards understood that he declared he knew of Lord North's refusal, *and from himself*' (*Chatham Corresp.* iii. 232). It is to be hoped for the credit of Lord North that Townshend's statement was as imaginative as many of his public utterances seem to have been.

[2] Frederick Lord North, eldest son of the first Earl of Guildford, Chancellor of the Exchequer, Sept. 1767; First Lord of the Treasury, Jan. 1770–March, 1782; Secretary of State, April–December, 1783. His best friends can say little more for him than that he

I have not, at this distance of time, the recollection that any other was proposed for the post, wherefore I conceive that there was none ; and that Mr. Townshend, owing to the violent illness of Lord Chatham taking place soon after, remained in his office, quite uninformed of Lord Chatham's intentions in regard to himself. On some day previous to the transaction, the note which I transcribe here was received by me, sufficiently marking the minister's anger against M^r. Townshend.

BOND STREET, Wednesday[1].

Lord Chatham has the honor to agree entirely with the Duke of Grafton and other servants of the Crown that a meeting of Cabinet should be had, upon the East India business—the capital *object of the publick*, upon which Lord Chatham will *stand* or *fall.* Report, not rumour, is unjust indeed, if M^r. Townshend did not give up the enquiry yesterday, and clearly convey his opinion *not to call for more* lights, or at least, *not to lay open the whole.* If this be so, the writer hereof, or the Chancellor of the Exchequer aforesaid, cannot remain in office together, or M^r. C. Townshend must amend his proceeding. Duty to the king and zeal for the salvation of the *whole* will not allow of any departure from this resolution.

If to-morrow night should be agreeable to the Duke of Grafton, Lord Chatham desires the favor of his Grace to appoint the meeting at his Grace's house at *seven* in the evening ; being the house from which firmness, candour, and salvation is to be hoped, if anywhere, in these factious times.

A suppressed gout falling on his nerves, to a degree sufficient to master his resolution, soon rendered Lord Chatham unwilling, and indeed unfit to receive any of us on business. Had his health allowed it, I have no doubt that he would still have weathered those difficulties which presented themselves from all quarters to resist his views for the public. From this time he became invisible, even to the Lord Chancellor and myself; and he desired to be allowed to attend solely to his health, until he found himself to be equal to any business. Here, in fact, was the end of his Adminis-

was a man of good business capacity, and cultivated understanding, very amiable, indolent, and unfortunate in everything except the length of his tenure of place.

[1] Probably March 11.

tration; tho', relying on the hopes of his recovery, we were struggling to the end of the Sessions, in order to prevent, if possible, the government of the country from falling into other hands.

I have often thought that, if certain steps had not been taken and others not omitted, the confusion into which Lord Chatham's illness plunged the Ministry might have been totally avoided. Who will venture to assert that the state of the country might not have been very different at this crisis, in case Lord Chatham had not quitted the House of Commons, where he was looked up to as the *great commoner*, and where he would effectually have controuled all the unsettled behaviour of the Chancellor of the Exchequer? if he had shewn confidence towards M^r. Conway, who was worthy to be trusted by him? and if he had conciliated the friends of the Duke of Newcastle and Lord Rockingham, which might have been attained without receiving the former into the Cabinet? But it is in vain to look back, and unavailing to lament: still I must observe that I never had but one opinion on the unhappy impolicy which guided these different measures, and this opinion can never be erased from my mind.

I must now turn again to the drudgery of Parliament, for such it truly was to the very end of the Session.

After much cavilling with the India Company, a temporary agreement was adopted, rather than to pursue the right forward road, on which Lord Chatham had laid the greatest stress, and which I earnestly wished to follow. But while this was depending, the attempts of the general courts to run up the dividends to an enormous height compelled me to submit to the king's servants the necessity of rescinding the resolution of the general court, and restraining the dividend to 10 per cent., during the continuance of the agreement which had been entered into under the sanction of Parliament. This, as a regulation of finance, fell naturally under my department, and the full support I received from the court, and from all my colleagues, except M^r. Secretary

Conway and the Chancellor of the Exchequer, enabled us
to get the Bill through both Houses[1].

The measure undoubtedly was a strong one, but so necessary that I was and am persuaded that encreased dividends
would in a short time have produced an East India bubble,
which would have gone much farther in its mishievous consequences than even the well known and infamous transactions
of the South Sea Company in 1720; and I had the satisfaction
to find that the steps taken to prevent similar distresses met
with public approbation.

The Act also which prohibited the Governor, Council, and
Assembly of New York from passing any Act, until they had
in every respect complied with the requisition of Parliament
on the quartering, &c., of the troops, was considered to be
a temperate, but dignified proceeding, and purposely avoiding
all harsh and positive penalties. Had such a conduct been
uniformly observed, every day would have encreased, and not
have alienated, the affections of the two countries from each
other. Such were the genuine sentiments of the king's
servants, when, in an ill-fated hour, M[r]. Townshend chose to
boast in Parliament that he knew the mode by which
a revenue might be drawn from America, *without offence*[2].
M[r]. Grenville fixed him down directly to pledge himself
on the declaration, which was received with such welcome
by the bulk of the House as dismayed M[r]. Conway, who
stood astonished at the unauthorized proceeding of his vain
and imprudent colleague. On being questioned by the
Cabinet on the evening following, how he had ventured to

---

[1] It did not pass the Lords without
a strong protest signed among others
by Temple, Gower, Portland, and
Rockingham (*Parl. Hist.* xvi. 351).

[2] Charles Townshend made this statement in the debate on the army extra-
ordinaries, Jan. 26, 1767. This is not
clearly brought out in the accounts of
the debate in Walpole, *Memoirs*, iv.
414, and the *Grenville Papers*, iv. 211.

But Townshend had pleased Walpole
by making fun of Grenville, and had
pleased Grenville by a general concurrence in his policy of taxing America.
It is clear that he then pledged him
to find a revenue from the colonies
(*Chatham Corresp.* iii. 178, 185). The
details of his plan were laid before the
House on May 13 (*post*, p. 176).

depart, on so essential a point, from the profession of the whole Ministry, M^r. C. Townshend turned to M^r. Conway, appealing to him whether the House was not bent on obtaining a revenue of some sort from the colonies. M^r. Conway acknowledged that such a disposition had been indicated by the House in a very decided manner, though I never understood that any symptom of such disposition appeared, before Mr. Townshend had himself given to Mr. Grenville the ground on which with eagerness he set his foot. No one of the Ministry had authority sufficient to advise the dismission of M^r. Chas. Townshend, and nothing less could have stopped the measure, Lord Chatham's absence being in this instance, as well as others, much to be lamented.

To render the business as little offensive as possible, articles were thought of which came within the description of *Port* duties [1]. A Board of Customs was proposed to be erected in some central spot of the colonies, and I was not aware of the mistrust and jealousy which this appointment would bring on, nor of the mischief of which it was the source: otherwise it should never have had my assent, and I must here confess my want of foresight in this instance. The novelty of the situation in which I was placed may perhaps afford some excuse for me, and for those who then acted with me. The right of the mother country to impose taxes on the colonies was then so generally admitted, that scarcely any one thought of questioning it, tho', a few years afterwards, it was given up as indefensible by everybody.

As the Session proceeded, the want of cordiality among the king's servants in the House of Commons was remarkable on every debate. The Chancellor of the Exchequer often in a minority with the Secretary of State, and sometimes likewise on different sides. M^r. Conway and myself continued in our usual intimacy and friendship, though we differed in

---

[1] The American colonists had, in 1766, drawn a distinction between duties on imports and direct taxes such as Grenville had imposed. The distinction was one well known in our own Constitutional History. But Townshend had treated the matter in a tone calculated to irritate and alarm.

the conduct of the East India business, as well as in our confidence in Lord Chatham. The general leaned to the Marquis of Rockingham and his friends, and had never been easy in his own situation since the fatal breach with them.

M[r]. Townshend had other views : he found that Lord Chatham was little likely to appear for some time on the political stage ; and therefore all his ambitious views prompted him to strive in every mode he could devise to attain their object. His lively imagination was for ever on the stretch, and turned him to pay the greatest court, wherever the political appearances of the day seemed most to invite him. He lived but a short time to enjoy the satisfaction he had in having obtained the Peerage of Greenwich for Lady Dalkeith [1].

LETTERS, 1766

LORD NORTHINGTON TO THE DUKE OF GRAFTON

GRAINGE, 31 *Aug.* 1766.

MY LORD,

I had the honor of your Grace's letter of Friday evening's post and therefore could not answer it till this day. I am much obliged to you for the authentic information of what hath passed relative to Government since I left London, as I was too ill when I left that place for taking any consideration of establishing a correspondence in my absence.

I own I was surprized with the confirmation of Lord Egmont's resignation and the manner of it ; importing a total disapprobation of Ministry and an offer to support their measures, which the offer of taking the Bedchamber, to any man of sense must imply, as it is impossible for any Ministry in this country to carry on the business of administration without the confidence of their fellow servants.

I was not surprized that Lord Gower did not take the office of 1. 'Comm.' ; as it was an office so important to the State and the business

---

[1] Lady Caroline Campbell, daughter of John, Duke of Argyle. Her first husband was Charles, Earl of Dalkeith. Her peerage expired with her, for she outlived her two sons by Charles Townshend, and died in 1794.

of which, I suppose, he was altogether to learn : however I was pleased to see that he took in a proper sense the offer, and as he is a person of a very good understanding, and respectable, I shall be glad to see him in a proper office.

Y^r. Grace knows it hath been my constant opinion, that in the present circumstances of this country, the true interest of it and the honour of the Crown can only be maintained, by the most impartial supply of offices : and I am fully persuaded that the king's Ministry persisting in that resolution, will get the better of faction, the bane of everything great, manly or vertuous in Government.

I understand from Lord Chatham his intentions with respect to the Earls of Hertford and Bristol[1] ; I allways approved the plan of constant residence and I only doubted the last Earl's health to manage the rudder of so turbulent and bacchanalian a State.

Your Grace is very wise in the attention you have paid to the present condition of the E. I. C^o. and I don't doubt its being attended with salutary effects.

I come now to that part of your Grace's letter which more immediately relates to my office : the revival of the prohibition of the exportation of corn, by order of Council pursuant to the late Act, which I have not here. And I am of opinion *that* is absolutely fit and necessary as I stand at present informed.

As to the question concerning the revenue of Canada I am a stranger to the state of it.

But I am very desirous of coming to London to give my personal concurrence in those measures : tho' I can with difficulty set out till Friday next, as I have blisters on me for an attack of the gout in my head, notwithstanding I am better than when I left London ; I will therefore be in town to attend a Council Saturday next or Monday sennight as your Grace shall advise me which day will be most agreeable to the king's serv^{ts}. that are in London.

I have not spent my time here without regard to my new employment, having perused the business, the papers relative to w^h. I brought down and which have been long in arrear.

I am sorry Lord Chatham is laid up, & shall only add that I think no journey inconvenient w^h. tends to the king's service, or to express the great personal regard with w^h. I am

My d^r. L^d.

Y^r. Grace's

Most obedient & hum^b. serv^t.

NORTHINGTON.

---

[1] Lord Bristol was to take Lord Hertford's place as Lord-Lieutenant, Hertford becoming Master of the Horse.

K

THE KING TO THE DUKE OF GRAFTON.

DUKE OF GRAFTON, Tho I can on all occasions rely on your punctuality, as well particular attention to me, yet as you did not hold last winter your present employment, I am uncertain whether you are appriz'd that it has ever been the usual practice of your predecessors to send me the morning after the meeting of the Lords [1] a list of those that attended : I shall therefore expect it to-morrow morning, and that evening a note from you with the contents of that day's debate.

GEORGE R.

QUEEN'S HOUSE,
Novr. 10th, 1766.
$\frac{m}{58}$ P. 3 p.m.

QUEEN'S HOUSE, Novr. 1766.
$\frac{m}{5}$ past eleven a.m.

DUKE OF GRAFTON, I see several names in the list you have sent me that I did not expect, & remark that altho the Bedford party speak civily none of them appeared on this occasion ; L^d. Egmont's name not being in the list rather surprizes me, and makes me fear he is more adverse than I had flatter'd myself unless he may have staid away from his disapprobation of the embargo, and thinking it therefore more civil not to attend and object to it.

Lieut. Gen..Conway has acquainted me that my Ministers wish the Privy Council may attend me this Evening if the House of Commons is up in any reasonable time, that the embargo may be instantly prolong'd on wheat, & be extended to barley and malt. I have therefore desired the addresses may be brought to me on that subject as early as possible this evening, and that the Council may meet here any time before eleven.

LORD CAMDEN TO THE DUKE OF GRAFTON.

Oct. 4th. 1766, BATH.
MY LORD,

It is some time since I had the honour of your Grace's letter, wch. w^d. have been answered sooner if L^d. President or myself c^d. have

---

[1] A meeting held at the Cockpit, Whitehall, immediately before the opening of Parliament, to hear the speech which would be delivered on the next day from the Throne.

procured by any information here a choice of Scotch or Irish titles to have submitted to His Majesty, for it is not very easy without having recourse to the College of Arms or some books of heraldry either to recollect what titles have been born by the Blood Royal or to suggest any new ones that are not already possessed by the nobility of Ireland or Scotland[1].

With respect to the latter I am informed that Strathern w[h]. is a kind of County Palatine has been heretofore a Royal title, and has laid dormant for some generations, and that this is the only one of the sort that L[d]. Buchan, to whom I have applied, can recollect. That if a new title should be thought proper—either Inverness or St. Andrews are open. The first if I mistake not has been taken up by the Pretender, in w[h]. respect possibly not so fit to be adopted by His Majesty upon this occasion, as it is a new title. The other, that of St. Andrews, is described to me as a place of dignity and antiquity : the seat of y[e] Primate formerly, and y[e] oldest University in Scotland. As to Ireland for want of better information we are able to mention no title of sufficient *eclat* but that of Dublin or Ormond. If the first is unpossessed, as we believe it is, it recommends itself enough by being the metropolis of that kingdom. The latter is dignified enough, and not unworthy to be assumed by His Royal Highness : unless it sh[d]. be thought that this choice might give umbrage to the heir of y[e] Butlers.

My Lord I am afraid L[d]. President and myself are rather out of our element upon this occasion and may ignorantly propose some names that upon further inquiry may be liable to objections unknown to us : in which case the Earl Marshal or the College of Arms might be able to furnish better materials and more certain information. We have ventured however to submit these titles and if the precedent of his Royal Highness' 2 brothers is to be followed Prince Henry must be created a Duke by his English and Scotch titles, and an Earl by his Irish title.

My Lord Northington has been pleased to compliment me as y[e] greater person with the honour of answering your Grace's letter to both of us, w[h]. I am forced to accept as Chancellor but utterly disclaim as Lord Camden.

His Lordship is mending every day and begs his respects to your Grace.

Lord Chatham too is growing well apace, goes abroad every day, and has begun to drink the waters at home.

I am my Lord with the highest respect your
Grace's most obed[t]. faithful serv[t].
CAMDEN.

---

[1] This letter concerns the choice of a title for Prince Henry, the third brother of the king, who attained his majority in this year. He was created Duke of Cumberland and Strathern, and Earl of Dublin.

CHAPTER IV

1767

THE EFFACEMENT OF CHATHAM

EVERY day's additional acquaintance brought me on a more confidential footing both with Lord Camden and with Lord Northington. We all perceived, and much lamented the distressful dilemma into which we were brought, and we had many consultations on the part which it became us, as good subjects and as men of honor, to act. We could get no access to Lord Chatham, and we were perfectly agreed, that the present system, circumstanced as it stood, neither could nor ought to proceed. It was therefore our duty to state to the king that, in spite of our best endeavours and these well supported by His Majesty, his Administration was in fact dissolved. We ventured to recommend to His Majesty, since all our attempts to see, or hear from Lord Chatham had proved ineffectual, that he would be pleased to call upon his lordship for his advice on the present urgent occasion. The king was so gracious as to listen to our joint representation ; and though it was determined, that the Administration should be considered as at an end ; yet it did not appear in the many debates we had in Parliament, that this secret ever got beyond the few persons who were intrusted with it. I was directed to write a pressing letter to Lord Chatham, earnestly desiring to lay before him, the plain state of His Majesty's Administration ; and of the impossibility of carrying it on, unless his lordship could suggest his advice to the king in a situation so difficult, and on which I earnestly entreated to be allowed to wait on him, in order to receive his commands, together with the advice he could offer to the king. To this letter [1] I received the answer which follows, and written in Lady Chatham's hand.

NORTH END, *May* 27th : 1767.

Lord Chatham still unable to write, begs leave to assure the Duke of Grafton of his best respects, and at the same time to lament that the continuation of his illness reduces him to the painful necessity of most earnestly entreating his Grace to pardon him, if he begs to be allowed to decline the honor of the visit the Duke of Grafton has so kindly proposed. Nothing can be so great an affliction to him, as to find himself quite unable for a conversation, which he should otherwise be most sincerely proud and happy to embrace.

Lord Chatham takes the liberty to send the Duke of Grafton his proxy signed, which he begs his Grace will do him the honor to have filled up with his own name, and entered.

His Lordship's proxy sent to me in this manner, had something in it satisfactory : but nothing that could take off from the disappointment Lord President and I felt on Lord Chatham's declining to receive me at North End. We had a long consultation, and concluded, that a letter from the king himself, desiring that he would see and converse with me, on the measures immediately necessary to be taken, would be the most likely circumstance to rouse Lord Chatham to admit a political conversation. His Majesty condescended to receive our humble advice; and on the 29th of May wrote to Lord Chatham to this purpose. I thought it right to send a letter at the same time, in Lord Northington's and my own name, and I should have added Lord Camden's also, if he had been in London. It is right to insert here the copy of my letter, and of the answer, which was in Lady Chatham's handwriting.

---

[1] The letter appears in the *Chatham Correspondence*, iii. 255. Grafton says, 'If I could be allowed but a few minutes to wait on you it would give me great relief: for the moment is too critical for your lordship's advice and direction not to be necessary.'

GROSVENOR SQUARE, *May* 29th : 1767.

MY DEAR LORD[1],

I sufficiently expressed to your lordship by my letter of Wednesday last, how very necessary I thought it for the well-being of the king's affairs, indeed, almost for their existence, that I should be permitted to deliver some advice from you, on a situation of affairs that appeared to me, to be pressingly critical. Disappointed of such an interview, and thus deprived of an assistance which I never expected to have been without to direct me in the difficulties that might arise, I thought the state of affairs too serious, not to wish as a man of honor to apprize His Majesty of my thoughts upon them, that the king might consult others of his servants, and decide what was most judicious to be done. I found, on imparting my ideas, the night before last to my Lord President, that his lordship saw the king's affairs at least as embarrassed as I did ; and that the king might find *factions united* intruding themselves upon the closet, before he might be expecting so offensive an event. We judged it thoroughly proper to lay fully our opinions before His Majesty who would have cause most truly to blame a silence on this head from those in his service, who were in a situation to form some judgment on the present state of things. We yesterday separately laid before the king the real state of his Administration ; in one House acting from the beginning of the Session in direct contradiction to all Cabinet decisions : in the other, by the prevalence of faction brought to such a crisis, as to carry questions in a very full House, by majorities of three only, and even those made up by the votes of two of the king's brothers, and some lords brought down from their very beds. The king was of opinion that your lordship's presence and advice could still reinstate, and give Administration some consistence again. Unfortunately your illness deprives us of the first, and unless your lordship's experience and abilities can suggest any measure for bettering the state of things, and in support of your Administration, all our powers and faculties having been tried, we see no possibility of serving His Majesty with effect, honor, or justice, to him or to the public. It is in conjunction with my Lord President, that I have the honor of writing this to your lordship, whom I met by the king's orders for that purpose ; and I believe I do not go beyond my authority, when I say His Majesty has no expectation of being relieved from this embarrassing dilemma, but by your counsel and advice. What I felt in this situation, I leave your lordship to judge ; but disagreeable as the task is, to carry the opinions of others on so delicate a subject, I am ready to undertake it, if you prefer that mode to a letter. Pray send me your commands, indeed, my lord, your thoughts and advice in such a situation are due

---

[1] This letter appears in the *Chatham Correspondence*, iii. 257.

to the king, and to those who have supported to their utmost in your absence every view of yours. I have the honor to be with the most perfect esteem and respect

My dear lord,

Your &c.,

GRAFTON.

P.S.—We should have desired Lord Chancellor to have been with us last night, but unfortunately he was gone into the country, to profit of the adjournment.

NORTH END, May 29th: 1767.

Lord Chatham continuing under the same inability to write which he was under the unhappy necessity of conveying to the D. of Grafton so lately; begs again his Grace's indulgence for taking this method of repeating the same description of his health, which for the present renders business impossible to him. He implores the D. of Grafton to be persuaded that nothing less than impossibility prevents him from seeing his Grace (which he so ardently desires) and entering into the fullest conversation with him. At present, all he is able to offer in true zeal for His Majesty is, that the D. of Grafton and Lord President may not finally judge it necessary to leave the situation they are in. The first moment health and strength enough, at present denied him, return, Lord Chatham will most humbly request permission to renew at His Majesty's feet, all the deepest sentiments of duty, and most devoted attachment.

These answers from Lord Chatham perplexed the business more and more ; and it appeared that all that could be done by us could go no farther than to keep matters from falling into confusion while His Majesty should be forming such a Ministry as might give contentment to his people. But the difference of opinion, so decidedly maintained by one of the ex-parties against the other ; and especially on the American Stamp Act, seemed to render all junction between them almost impracticable ; at least, it never could be expected to be cordial. Lords Northington, Camden, and Shelburne, with myself, and I believe, Lord Granby, would have declined any office, that might be offered to us ; showing thereby our steady attachment to Lord Chatham, with whom we desired to be considered as acting.

His Majesty, aware of the consequence and necessity of

our being informed of Lord Chatham's present intentions, and
of the advice, which he might have to give, wrote to him so
pressing a letter [1], that I received the note following, written
in Lady Chatham's hand.

> 'Lord Chatham presents his respects to the Duke of Grafton, and
> begs to have the honor of seeing his Grace to-morrow morning at North
> End, at eleven.   Unfit as he is, for the favor of such an interview, he
> can only hope his Grace will attribute this liberty, to the most real
> respect for his Grace's person, and to the truest zeal for His Majesty.
>
> 'NORTH END, Saturday even⁵.'

I readily obeyed this summons, which I received in consequence of the letter with which he had been honored by
the king.   I carried to North End the most zealous disposition to exert myself on any practicable plan, which his
lordship might be able to suggest, as capable of giving expectation of carrying on with credit the king's Government,
until Lord Chatham could feel himself well enough to resume
the reins.   My own determined objects were, either to assist
his lordship, *in his absence*, in such a manner, as to enable
him to return to the head of affairs; which was my first and
ardent wish; or on the other hand, to retire myself to a
private station, until some more favorable opportunity of
being serviceable to the country should call me forward.

Though I expected [2] to find Lord Chatham very ill indeed,

---

[1] The king's letter is printed in the
Chatham Correspondence, iii. 260.   It
describes the troubles of the Ministry
as formidable.   Majorities of 6 and of 3
in the House of Lords, though the
king's brothers were ordered to vote,
and the House was full.   This was on
the mode of dealing with an Act of the
Assembly of Massachusetts (*Parl. Hist.*
xv. 360).   In the Commons the majorities were large, but on the East India
question, Conway, the Secretary of State,
and nominal leader of the House, and
Townshend, the Chancellor of the Exchequer, voted in the minority.   As to
Grafton the king says, 'I fear I cannot

keep him above a day unless you would
see him and give him encouragement.'
The President and Chancellor are
described as of the same mind with
Grafton; Shelburne as a secret, and
Townshend as an avowed enemy.   Conway as anxious to retire, 'though without any view of entering into faction.'

[2] Chatham's illness seems to have
been regarded as mysterious by his contemporaries.   Walpole thought he was
mad (*Memoirs*, iii. 41).   Later, when
his general health improved, it was
believed that he was acting a part
(*Grenville Papers*, iv. 311).   It seems
probable that the anxiety and excite-

his situation was different from what I had imagined; his nerves and spirits were affected to a dreadful degree: and the sight of his great mind bowed down, and thus weakened by disorder, would have filled me with grief and concern, even if I had not long borne a sincere attachment to his person and character. The confidence he reposed in me, demanded every return on my part: and it appeared like cruelty in me to have been urged by any necessity to put a man I valued, to so great suffering as it was evident that my commission excited. The interview was truly painful: I had to run over the many difficulties of the Session: for his lordship, I believe, had not once attended the House, since his last return from Bath. I had to relate the struggles we had experienced in carrying some points, especially in the House of Lords; the Opposition also, which we had encountered in the East India business from M^r. Conway, as well as M^r. Townshend[1]; together with the unaccountable conduct of this latter gentleman, who had suffered himself to be led to pledge himself at last, contrary to the known decision of every member of the Cabinet, to draw a certain revenue from the colonies without offence to the Americans themselves: and I was sorry to inform Lord Chatham, that M^r. Townshend's flippant boasting was received with strong marks of a blind and greedy approbation from the body of the House[2]. I endeavoured to lay everything before his lordship, as plainly as I was able; and assured him, that Lords Northington and Camden had both empowered me to declare how earnestly they desired to receive his

---

ment of the years 1757–1762 had told upon his health, and had left him more liable than ever to his constant malady, the gout. The effort of forming a Ministry completely broke down his nervous system. He had, in fact, undertaken a task difficult in itself and unsuited to his peculiar genius, at a time when his constitution needed entire rest. The breakdown is not surprising.

[1] It should be borne in mind when Grafton's conduct in relation to Con-

way is criticized, that Conway, though nominally leader of the House of Commons, had failed to support his colleagues on more than one occasion. In fact, the Chancellor of the Exchequer and the Secretary of State acted from time to time in complete independence of one another, of their colleagues, and of their party.

[2] For an account of this debate, see Walpole, *Memoirs*, iii. 28.

advice, as to assisting and strengthening the system he had established by some adequate accession, without which they were confident, it could not, nor ought to proceed.

It was with difficulty that I brought Lord Chatham to be sensible of the weakness of his Administration; or of the power of the united factions[1] against us; though we received every mark we could desire of His Majesty's support. At last, after much discourse, and some arguing, he proceeded to entreat me to remain in my present station; taking that method to strengthen the Ministry which should appear to me to be the most eligible; and he assured me, that, if Lords Northington and Camden, as well as myself, did not retain our high offices, there would be an end to all his hopes of being ever serviceable again as a public man. His lordship doubted not, that we should find also every support from Lord Shelburne. I answered Lord Chatham, that without some material accession of Parliamentary strength could be properly obtained, we were all decided that the Administration would have too much to contend with; and that M[r]. Townshend's oratorical abilities would add to the power of our opponents, though it had been so little useful to the measures of the Cabinet. I observed, that a junction with the Bedfords or the Rockinghams appeared to me to be the only steps that could now be effectual : to which his lordship assented, though he inclined to prefer entering into negociation with the former[2]. Hopeless as I was, from all appearances, that I might see Lord Chatham restored to health in any but

---

[1] The lists of speakers in the debates in the House of Lords in June, 1767 (*Parl. Hist.* xvi. 347), show how the Grenville, Rockingham, and Bedford parties combined to attack the Ministry. In one list appear Temple, Lyttelton, and Mansfield, Newcastle and Richmond, Bedford and Weymouth.

[2] The preference expressed by Chatham for the Bedford party, as against the Rockingham party, is at first sight strange to us who, in the light of sub-sequent events, see how important was the American policy in which Chatham and Rockingham were agreed. On two cardinal points there was a deep differ-ence between Chatham and Bedford: the latter was for a pacific policy towards France and Spain, and for dealing sharply with the colonies. But Chat-ham seems above all things to have mistrusted Newcastle, and to have re-garded the Rockingham Whigs as a clique.

a most distant day, I was cautious of committing myself to him, under any assurance, that I would do my best to fulfill his wishes. In entreating me to proceed in office, if I could bring my mind to undertake the charge, Lord Chatham assured me, over and over, that I might depend on his giving all his support to the measures I should bring forward in his retirement; and on a return of health, that he would smooth over any which he might have disapproved, knowing that they had arisen from the purest motives. Our interview must have lasted two full hours; and we parted with the most cordial professions of good-will and attachment to each other.

Returned to London, I lost no time in communicating the particulars of this transaction, in the most ample and open manner, to the king, Lord Chancellor, and the Lord President. There appeared to us, so little chance of a disposition of either of the great parties to associate with the Ministry, considered by them in a manner dissolved, from the circumstance of the very sad illness of Lord Chatham, that we joined in advising the king to see one of the leaders of these parties, and to hear how that Administration would be composed, which either of them had to recommend. His Majesty preferred the communication with Lord Rockingham[1], which he knew likewise would greatly conciliate General Conway. A measure of this nature we had some reason to think would disunite the parties among themselves: and the desire of the Lords Camden and Northington was as earnest as my own that we should do everything to assist the king, during this negocia- tion; and to prevent all unbecoming conditions being exacted from His Majesty: for we were still his servants, and in the highest offices. Lord Camden's sense of the state of his friend's illness, and of the line he wished me to follow will be

---

[1] The king seems to have feared that a junction with the Bedford party might bring back George Grenville. Walpole (*Memoirs*, iii. 51) says that Grafton 'told Mr. Conway and me that he had never seen the king so much agitated: that His Majesty was not disinclined to take Lord Rockingham, but protested that he had almost rather resign his crown than consent to receive George Grenville again.'

best explained by the subjoined short letter, which I received,
as I was stepping into my phaeton to go to North End.

MY LORD,

I am leaving London, but shall be within call, to wait your Grace's
commands at a moment's warning.   It is very uncertain what may
happen during my absence; but I should hope, that your Grace will
keep your future decision in your own power, during the remainder
of the Session.   Every thing depends on your Grace's determination.
Lord C——m may recover; but if he recovers only one moment after
you are decided, he recovers too late.

I am with the most perfect esteem and respect,

Your Grace's most obedient faithful ser\.

CAMDEN.

June 4th, 1767.

Under these untoward circumstances, we carried forward the
remaining business in Parliament, till an end was put to this
long Session by prorogation on the 2^d. July, 1767.   As soon
as the Parliament was prorogued, the different parties became
more alert to reconcile their jarring opinions, and interests,
and they expected daily to be applied to, in order to form
a comprehensive Administration.   At the same time His
Majesty continued to receive the same advice from us, as
before; which was more approved, as we gave the king
assurances that we would remain in our offices until the
negociation with the Opposition should take a favourable, or
an unsuccessful turn.   We desired, however, that His Majesty
would be pleased to consider the part we were taking, as
intended to facilitate an honorable and just settling, and to
carry this on, with more decorum to himself.   The Lord
President, from infirmities of age, wished to give notice at any
rate of his intended retreat.   There was no one from whom
I received so just accounts of the schemes of the various
factions (for, I must so style them on the present occasion)
than from Mr. Horace Walpole, who since became Earl of
Orford.   His friendship, and attachment to Mr. Conway had
been constant, and he was well known; and his zealous desire,
that we two should be more closely united, urged him to sift
out the designs of those who were counter-acting his active

endeavors: and no person had so good means of getting to the knowledge of what was passing, as himself. The letter from him, which I transcribe, will give you a just representation of M^r. Conway's difficulties, and flings some light on his final determination.

ARLINGTON STREET, *May* 23^d, 1767.

I must intreat your Grace, to look upon the trouble I give you, with your usual indulgence; and as my zeal to serve you, has been hitherto attended with success, I will beg you to hear me with patience, when things are come to such a crisis, that my endeavours to prevent Mr. Conway's resignation are almost exhausted. Your Grace knows his honor and delicacy, and I may be bold to tell you, who are actuated by the same motives, that it is the character I hope he will always maintain. I had much rather see him give up every thing and preserve his honor, than stay with discredit. But in the present case, I think him too much swayed by men who consult nothing but their own prejudices, passions and interests, to which they would sacrifice him and the country.

I need not tell your Grace, that on the dismission of Lord Edgcumbe, M^r. Conway declared he would not remain long in the Ministry. With infinite pains I have prevailed to keep him in place to the end of the Session. He now persists in quitting, but the extravagance and unreasonableness of his old friends, I think, ought to discharge him from all ties to them. They have abused him in print, reflected on him in Parliament; and I maintain have broken all their engagements to him. I will name nobody, but was witness in the Summer, to repeated promises from them *that they would (tho' taking liberties with L^d. Chatham) distinguish M^r. Conway, commend him, and openly in their speeches avow their abhorrence of M^r. Grenville.* The world have seen how they have adhered to these declarations. What is worse; when M^r. Conway came over to them in the American business and professed publicly his disposition towards them, was it not notorious that they received him with the utmost coldness and indifference? They not only avoided a single expression of good will to him, but sat still, and heard him abused by Grenville and Rigby. He was thoroughly hurt at this behavior, and I would beg your Grace to paint it strongly to him.

In many late conversations with him, they have shewn the utmost extravagance: they not only aim at every thing, but espouse M^r. Grenville, and tho' they say they do not like him for first minister, would absolutely make him a part of their system. M^r. Conway objected strongly and I went so far as to reproach them with this contradiction to all their declarations, and with adopting so arbitrary and unpopular a man.

Having stated these facts, I will now take the liberty of informing your Grace of my motives of writing you this letter. I told M^r. Conway, *that if his friends would not come in, I could not conceive why he was to go out;* and that I thought the question turned singly on this. When he made his declaration to them, he, at the same time protested against entering into opposition. If they therefore will not come in but by force, does not their refusal put an end to his connection with them? Nothing therefore seems left but to drive them to this refusal. Accordingly, I have begged M^r. Conway, to open his mind to your Grace, and I thought it right to apprize your Grace, of what he will say to you, that you may not be surprized, and may be prepared with your answer. Your kindness to him, my lord, has been invariable, and I am sure will continue so on this occasion, which I flatter myself may preserve the union of two men who have the strictest honor, and most public spirit of any men in England. The more indulgence your Grace shows to his scruples and delicacy, the more he will feel the wildness and unreasonableness of his other connexions. Pray my lord, forgive the extreme liberty I take of suggesting behavior to your Grace; but knowing M^r. Conway as I do better than any body does, I am called upon to paint to your Grace the best method of treating with him. If you should be so good as to tell him that you are willing to assist his delicacy, and to contribute to bring in his friends on reasonable terms, and that you hope he will not gratify them in any unreasonable hopes; it will open the door to a negociation, in which I can venture to say they will be so immoderate in their demands, that it will not only shock him, but be a strong vindication to His Majesty's rejection of them, and what is most at my heart, may, I hope, conduce to retain M^r. Conway in the king's service, when his other friends have shown that they mean nothing, but to engross all power in league with the worst men, or to throw the country into the last confusion.

If I can but prevail to keep M^r. Conway united with your Grace and acting with you, it is the height of my ambition; and if your Grace is so good as at least to accept my labours favorably, I shall be overpaid, for I have most undoubtedly no views for myself but those of being approved by honest men; and as there is nobody I can esteem more than your Grace, I am not ashamed, my lord, tho' you are a Minister, of professing myself,

Your Grace's
Most obed^t. and devoted humble servant,
HOR. WALPOLE.

With the king's permission and approbation I had a meeting first with Lord Gower, which produced a conference, as open as either of us could wish; so much so, that many parts of our discourse were to be considered as unauthorized, as the communications of two old acquaintance who had a true regard for each other. The situation in which the friends of the Duke of Bedford viewed the Administration gave them such confidence, as rendered them quite unreasonable[1]; and it was soon found that all the other parties were equally so, and they appeared to have forgotten how difficult would be the reconciling each other to the measures that were to be proposed in regard to cultivating once more a good understanding with the American colonies. Except his Grace, the Bedford party were less difficult on measures, than on influence. This was not the case with Lord Rockingham and many of his friends; who always wished to act on principle. It is to be lamented, that he was too often swayed by those, whose judgment was not equal to his own. Lord Temple's, and M[r]. G. Grenville's opinions were not so supple as to be formed into a different mould; and I believe, that those, who knew best the characters, would agree that an union of sentiment with Lord Rockingham on American politics could never have been settled between these wide differing statesmen. After this I received His Majesty's commands to see Lord Rockingham, taking Gen[l]. Conway with me, as we had both long lived with the marquis in the greatest intimacy. Our conversation lasted long; and it chiefly turned on the propriety of Lord Rockingham being sent for previously to his laying a plan before His Majesty[2], as a foundation for an able and solid Administration; or when he should be prepared to lay his plan before the king. The latter mode was required by His Majesty, and the marquis with great propriety gave way. The following were the letters which I was

---

[1] This meeting, which took place during the Whitsuntide recess, at Wakefield Lodge (Walpole, *Memoirs*, iii. 56), and a later meeting at White's Club (*Grenville Papers*, iv. 36), served to show the close union which at this time subsisted between the Bedford and Grenville parties. The negotiation broke off in each case on the inclusion of the Grenvilles.

[2] Rockingham took the modern view of the position of a Prime Minister. He desired to receive the king's commission to form a Ministry. George III wished to have suggestions made to him, which he might accept, reject, or modify.

directed to write to Lord Rockingham, and his lordship's answer.

GROSVENOR SQUARE, *July* 15th, 1767.

MY DEAR LORD [1],

After having delivered to His Majesty the answer which your lordship communicated to Gen[l]. Conway and myself this morning, I was commanded to acquaint your lord[p]. that the king wishes your lord[p]. would specify the plan on which you and your friends would come into office, in order to extend and strengthen his Administration; that His Majesty may be enabled to judge, how far the same may be advantageous to His Majesty's and the publick's service. I have the honor to be &c. &c.

GRAFTON.

MY DEAR LORD,

I have the honor of your Grace's letter by which your Grace acquaints me *that His Majesty wishes me to specify the plan, on which I, and my friends would propose to come in, in order to extend and strengthen his Administration.*

I hope your Grace will do me the honor to explain to His Majesty, that the principle on which I would proceed should be to consider the present Administration as at an end, notwithstanding the great regard and esteem which I have for some of those who compose it [2].

If His Majesty thinks it for his service to form a new Administration on a comprehensive plan, the general idea of which has already been opened to your Grace, I should then humbly hope to have His Majesty's permission to attend him, in order to receive his commands, it being impossible to enter into particulars till I have His Majesty's leave to proceed upon this plan.

I have the honor to be, with great respect and regard
Your Grace's most obed[t]. and most humble serv[t].

ROCKINGHAM.

GROSVENOR SQUARE,
Thursday, P.M. 2 °Clock, *July* 16th, 1767.

GROSVENOR SQUARE, *July* 17th, 1767.

MY DEAR LORD,

I have laid your lordship's letter before His Majesty, and have the satisfaction of acquainting your lordship, that the king's gracious senti-

---

[1] The original draft of this letter appears in Walpole, *Memoirs*, iii. 69. Horace Walpole amended it where it seemed open to misconstruction, and drafted Grafton's second letter to Rockingham. His memoir serves to show how intensely personal were the politics of this time.

[2] Walpole says that 'nothing could surpass the insolence' of Rockingham's answer. The insolence consisted in his assumption that the Grafton Ministry was at an end, and that he was prepared to undertake the formation of a new one (*Memoirs*, iii. 71).

ments concur with your lordship's in regard to the forming of a comprehensive plan of administration, and that His Majesty desirous of uniting
the hearts of all his subjects, is most ready, and willing to appoint such
a one as shall exclude no denomination of men attached to his person
and government.

When your lordship is prepared to offer a plan of administration formed
on those views His Majesty is willing that your lordship should yourself
lay the same before him for His Majesty's consideration.

I have the honor to be, with the most perfect esteem and regard
my lord

Your lordship's &c. &c.

GRAFTON.

M. of Rockingham.

After a few days I received the following [1],

[1] MY DEAR LORD,

As I propose desiring an audience of His Majesty I much wish to
see your Grace previously. I shall therefore desire that your Grace will
either appoint a time, that I could wait upon you, from 11 to 1, or that
you would call for a moment here, whichever best suits your convenience.

I am, my dear lord, with great truth and regard
Your Grace's most obed[t]. and most humble serv[t].

ROCKINGHAM.

GROSVENOR SQUARE,
Tuesday Night, *July* 21st, 1767.

Lord Northington, who had been so much my coadjutor
through this whole business, was gone down to the Grange:
and anxious as I knew him to be for some account of our
proceedings at this critical moment, I wrote to him the letter
which follows; and which I had luckily at the time desired
M[r]. Stonhewer to copy. I lay the letter before you with
greater satisfaction; because I can depend more on the accuracy of its contents, than from anything I could be able to

[1] For an account of the negotiations
which took place between the various
sections of the Whig party, see *Bedford
Corresp*. iii. 382–385; *Rockingham
Memoirs*, ii. 5; and Walpole, *Memoirs*,
iii. 80. It is plain that when a combination in which Rockingham and
Grenville were to take part came to be
seriously discussed, colonial policy was
certain to be a stumbling-block. Not
only measures but men caused difficulty.
Bedford would not accept so incompetent a leader in the Commons as
Conway, and Rockingham, who saw
that Grenville was the necessary alternative to Conway, broke off on this
ground.

draw, at this distance of time, from recollection, on transactions so very intricate.

GROSVENOR SQUARE, *July* 18th, 1767.

MY DEAR LORD,

By the last letter which I had the honor of writing to your lordship, you will have reason to expect, that the D. of Bedford's friends did not quite answer to the reasonable dispositions, which they have so often flung out to us; and which your lordship and myself have as constantly found to be otherwise, whenever we came more to the point. Thus it proved on the last attempt where Lord Gower whom I talked with, professed that he was unauthoriz'd, but that he believed that the Duke of Bedford and Lord Temple would willingly confer with myself on the grounds of forming a solid and extensive Administration; that he did not imagine they had any objection to my remaining at the Treasury, but, that if Lord Temple came into any other great office, then the Administration must greatly hold out the complexion of being his; for, continued he, how can he think of having less weight in this, than in one last year which he would not enter into unless *pari passu* with Lord Chatham?

Your lordship will certainly conceive that such a formation could not keep me where I am; nor did it satisfy His Majesty; particularly as Lord Gower told me that the openings must be large indeed. Thus failed this attempt, which some moderation from that quarter might have brought to bear, and to have formed the best Ministry (in my opinion) which this country is now in a condition to receive. By the intimation of Gen¹. Conway to the king, and by his firm belief of the favorable disposition to the Marquis of Rockingham, His Majesty was induced to order the Gen¹. and myself to meet his lordship, in order to know from him *the plan on which his friends and himself could honorably to themselves come in to assist the king's Government together with the Chancellor and the remains of the present Administration.* Your lordship may imagine that the conversation was long and very diffuse; many questions asked upon particulars which were answered by saying that the time was yet too early to go into them till his lordship offered his plan. On his enquiring whether the plan was to be confin'd to his own people or whether it was to comprehend the Bedfords and even the Grenvilles; my answer was that the king had particulariz'd no one, but that if his lordship went to the including both parties as well as his own, I could not make out, how it could possibly be consistent with His Majesty's most gracious opening to his lordship where the remainder of the present Administration together with the Chancellor was to be the foundation of it. After much conversation the words I was directed to report to His Majesty from Lord Rockingham were these ' *That his lordship and his friends on considering the opening His Majesty had honored them by making, were of opinion* *that they would not do right to come into Administration without it could be made to comprehend Lord Rockingham and his friends, the Duke of Bedford and his friends, such of M^r.* Grenville's *also as chose to come into office; for as to the particular determination thereupon of Lord Temple or his brother personally his lordship did not take it upon him to answer.'* To which message of his lordship I returned the answer, the next day, mark'd N°. 1. This brought his lordship's answer to it the day following N°. 2, and on my sending with the king's approbation the letter mark'd N°. 3 [1], his lordship call'd upon me at night to say that he certainly now must go to work in order to produce his plan; disagreeable as the task appear'd to him: that his wish was, still to have been admitted previously to the king, which he dropped on my assuring him, that I had, from orders, endeavored to make it clear that His Majesty neither designed, nor ought to grant that request.

Your lordship will take notice that the former part is wrote on the 18th as I was interrupted before; and that I am now finishing my letter on the 19th. I mention this, that you may not think the messenger has been faulty in delivering the letter.

I understand that they are now employed in making out their plan to be offer'd to His Majesty's consideration, a work, which before it can be brought to birth, seems open to so many accidents, that I am, I own, not without thinking it possible, that it may disunite parties freshly and loosely cemented, and that some one among them may find it for their interest, as well as credit, to fall in honorably with the present Administration. If resentment comes in aid on account of too little consideration shewn to some, or too much power grasp'd at by another, this event may still be the more likely. The Duke of Bedford, I understand, is sent for from Woburn, to assist at this work, which I fear they will offer on such enormous terms that no one can wish His Majesty to accept; for it is too preposterous to suppose that a solid Government is to be attain'd if it should be so composed as to drive, in the divided state of this country, the king's inclination towards those who would be opposing his Administration. M^r. Grenville and Lord T. have been those who in this affair have acted as the wiser politicians.

On the opening of this matter to them by Rigby dispatched from Woburn, where the D. of Bedford and Lord Rockingham were, their answer was, that they should be glad to see an Administration where the D. of Bedford's friends should have a great share; that they should be *well-wishers* to it, and desirous that *their friends* should have places under it. They appear to me to be waiting only the moment to pave their way towards reconciling the closet by a moderation now, when others take up *their* violence, and seem to have laid in for joining

---

[1] These are the letters set out above, dated July 15, 16, 17.

effectually with the king's friends, and Lord Chatham's, who both must be proscribed, if I can guess at Lord Rockingham's views; and thus the Grenvilles see the *comers in* weaken'd by their own scheme, and raising to themselves opponents capable of making head against them; even if they had His Majesty's support farther than they have any right to expect, their principle being *not to trust that they shall have it, but to make it impossible for the king not to give it to them.*

Your lordship will call this, most likely, too much refining on the conduct of these different gentlemen. My only excuse is, that on the occasion, I write as I think to your lordship.

I now come, my dear lord, to the point I am most concern'd in, and where you have so obligingly assisted me with your advice. M^r. Conway sees the extension of Lord Rockingham's connexions in the same light as myself, and I believe there is nothing he would not do to prevent such a Ministry from taking place under the certainty of bringing the country into fresh difficulties. He presses me much not to retire. My only answer has been that which your lordship knows : however by the king's most gracious proposals to these different sets of men, so *strangely* receiv'd by them all, I think the case greatly alter'd, and that there is a great deal to justify those, who shall endeavor to carry on Administration on a narrower ground than they could wish. I have told the king on his repeated requisition to me to remain at the Treasury, that one previous point must be attained to make it possible and that, even then, it would labor to a great degree, perhaps too much to move forward. That previous point in such case must be M^r. Conway's retaining the lead in the House of Commons. In consequence of this His Majesty has much employed his brother to press him so to do : and though he is determined to resign, which he will do on Wednesday, it is not impossible but they may still prevail on him; so much he apprehends the consequences of the other event. Your lordship sees that my fate remains still undecided, or rather dependent on what M^r. Conway can bring himself to. In truth, my lord, Messrs. Grenville and Conway are the only two men able to lead the House of Commons; and you will see that the latter thus taking on in his own cause is not liable to that leaning to another party which last year brought on half the mischief of it.

If this does take place; one favour I must entreat of your lordship, who considering the consequence it is of to the publick must not refuse, which is, tho' out of office, to assist the Cabinet and particularly myself, with the advice which your ability and great experience in public affairs will make so essential to the king's service. I have trespass'd so long that I have tired your lordship as well as myself; I shall only beg now to assure you of the sentiment of the truest esteem and respect with which I have the honor to be &c. &c.

GRAFTON.

It will be proper also to introduce here Lord Northington's answer. We lived in full and mutual confidence in each other: he had about him the genuine principle of a Whig: and in all transactions I found him to be a man full of honor, a disinterested gentleman, and though much devoted to the king, with great zeal for the constitution. As a lawyer, his knowledge and ability were great; but his manner and speech were ungracious. I shall ever do honor to his memory, wherever I hear his name brought forward.—But,—for his letter.

MY DEAR LORD,

I think myself much obliged to your Grace for communicating to me, in so clear and historical a manner the progress of political matters, since I left London. It gives me not only a view of their present state, but affords a kind of prospect of the event and end of them : and considering the strange state of men and times not a displeasing one. I was not surprized at the forbidding language of Lord Gower on this delicate subject, it being uniform to what he held to me, and which I told your Grace I considered as an end of treaty ; as it in effect required a surrender of not only servants, but of the master. This would have been ignominious indeed; but what is if possible worse, useless. For it is impossible, that the several parties, so numerous and extensive, can ever agree; and besides, I always thought, and do think, that the king's friends would, together with the remainder of the present ministers, have carried out more power and abilities to distress, than all of them could have brought in to strengthen Government. However, I think His Majesty has acted with great wisdom in pursuing every means to obtain an Administration that might, as much as possible, conciliate and destroy faction, the bane of Government, so disastrous to this country. I must however, conclude that the opening to the Marquis of Rockingham wise in its commencement, will be attended with the same impracticability as that to Lord Gower ; and with the insupportable consequences I have mentioned above ; for I cannot be at a loss to conjecture what advice will prevail in framing the answer. But His Majesty must by this conduct, so royal and gracious, fix the eyes of the public on the true object, and awaken the zeal of his faithful subjects, which next to his own, will be the best support he can afford to the Ministry he shall, in his royal wisdom, think fit to establish. In this embarrassed situation of the king and country, in this opposition so boldly and unbecomingly founded, I cannot sufficiently admire your Grace's reluctance in quitting the service of our amiable sovereign. I am satisfied, it will redound to your honor and glory with the public, afford your Grace the highest pleasure, self-approbation, and I verily believe, attain the desireable end of preserving a constitutional Government. I shall be happy to find, you have the support of Mr. Conway's abilities in so laudable an undertaking.

As to myself, my lord, I thought it my duty frankly to open my state of health, and its insufficiency to an office so extensive and of so much attendance : it was but just both to the king and to his ministers, as I was, and am, morally certain, I shall never re-establish my strength to sustain that burthen : but, I desire to be laid at the king's feet, as one that, out of office, will be as zealous as in, and as one that will ever to the best of his abilities, support His Majesty's Government ; and, without a compliment, never with so much pleasure, as when your Grace is at the head of it.

I have the honor to remain, with most perfect respect, my dear lord,
Your Grace's most obedient
& most humble serv[t].
NORTHINGTON.

20th *July*, 1767.
GRAINGE.

On the 22nd Lord Rockingham had the audience of His Majesty : I was at Court, and his lordship conversed with me with his usual civility both before and after he saw the king ; and said that he doubted whether His Majesty would enter into his views for forming an Administration. His Majesty soon sent for me into the closet, and I heard from himself what had passed, as well as the king's opinion that it went to the total overthrow of the system Lord Chatham had established.

A few notes of my own, forming a kind of short diary, and overlooked, I shall add here, as they may help to elucidate and confirm the former recital. I have often lamented, that I had so much *neglected* this method, which would have furnished information which must surpass what even the most retentive memory can produce. What differences there are, will be found to be on no material points, though the diary descends into some more particulars.

1767.—July 2nd. I delivered to His Majesty the fair draft of a paper [1] which Lord President and myself sketched out

[1] There is no copy of this draft among the Grafton MSS., nor is there any record of communications of this date in the *Chatham Correspondence*; but in vol. iii. pp. 266-8, there is a letter from the king enclosing a paper

the preceding evening, in order to shew the situation in which we stood in the king's service; unable to assist His Majesty in patching up the Administration temporarily, till Lord Chatham's health allowed him to return ; a measure we could neither justify to the king, to the country, nor to ourselves.

His Majesty determined on this to word a letter to Lord Chatham in such a manner, as either to incite him to exert himself to forward the measure he recommended by filling up the offices, in effect vacated [1] ; or to draw from him an avowal of the necessity the king lay under of calling in other assistance.

July 4th. His Majesty honored me with a communication of the answer from Lord Chatham, penned by her ladyship ; wherein his health is represented as still worse, with many expressions of his unfortunate state, which renders him *at present* absolutely useless to advise the king.

His Majesty feeling the necessity of some step being taken, and that advantage was every moment given up by delay, ordered me to sound Lord Gower on the hopes there might be of the Duke of Bedford and his friends coming in to join the remains of the present Administration, in a manner honorable to themselves.   The idea of Lord Temple or M[r]. Grenville in a great office was no ways a hindrance in the king's mind ; if, by it, I could remain in my post ; and by that make it bear the appearance of an accession to, and not a defeat of, the present Administration.

drawn up by Grafton and Northington, and with an answer from Lady Chatham.

The purport of these documents is precisely the purport of those referred to in the text, but they are dated June 2. It seems probable that the Chatham papers are misdated by a month, for Grafton had seen Chatham on May 31, and there is another letter of the king to Chatham of June 2, merely inquiring after his health.

[1] The king's letter to Chatham, dated in the *Chatham Correspondence* June 2, names the following vacancies as about to occur :—

'The resignations pointed at are the Lord President and lieutenant-general Conway; besides the Duke of Grafton finding it impossible himself to undertake the forming a temporary Administration; so that the present one will infallibly fall into pieces in less than ten days unless you point out proper persons to fill the vacancies that may arise. Indeed M[r]. Townshend may be added to the list of those retiring unless additional strength and ability be acquired.'

Lord Gower this evening enlarged so much from the style of our conversation at Wakefield, that, though unauthorized as we both declared ourselves to be *to treat*, it was clear to make out, that the openings to be made would be great; and that the Ministry must bear to a considerable degree the marks of Lord Temple's weight, if the Duke of Bedford and Lord Temple should talk with me on the formation of an extensive and solid Administration.

I had liberty to mention this part to His Majesty; and, without giving any opinion of my own, that might lighten the difficulties I foresaw, we parted with this declaration from me, that my part in the Treasury, upon such a footing, would require at least the reflexion of one night before I could answer it even to myself.

July 5th, 1767. His Majesty received from me at Richmond an account of my conversation with Lord Gower; and considered it so much as the grounds of an Administration to be formed by, and under, Lord Temple, that he immediately expressed the greatest objections to it, and did me the honor to ask, how I should conduct myself if he could think well enough of the scheme to lean to carry it into execution. My answer was, that it was so loaded with objections which I, as an individual, more particularly felt, that I should look upon myself as acting very inconsistently with the professions I made to His Majesty, and to Lord Chatham, on my coming to the Treasury, to act the same part under men so very opposite ; that my honor forbade me also to do it, where persons who had deserved my little support, were by this plan given up.

The king's desire was, to see Gen¹. Conway to-day, that he might hear from him the possibility there might be of finding Lord Rockingham's friends practicable.

At night, in communicating to Lord Gower, that I did not find a desire of making so total a change as his conversation led to conclude, I chiefly rested it on the impossibility of my own standing in such a situation in a Ministry, which, in fact, would be a Grenville one [1].

---

[1] Here the separate memoranda come to an end.

While it was problematical in what shape the new plan of Ministry was to appear, which was to be offered by Lord Rockingham for the king's approbation, or whether the changes called for might not be so extensive as to endanger the failure of the whole, it was most natural, and indeed most incumbent on me to consider, what, in the last of these cases, was our duty, and especially mine, to yield to in this serious state of things; and what could be done to extricate the king and the country, with some satisfaction, out of the mischiefs of threatening internal dissensions. As much as I desired to be released from my office, I foresaw, that circumstances might arise, so as to compel me to comply with that which might appear most beneficial to the public. However, I should not, even then, be able to answer to myself the continuance at the Treasury; unless General Conway, who earnestly wished me to remain, should undertake to be the Leader in the House of Commons. The friends of us both pressed earnestly that we should mutually decide, according to their zealous wishes.

After many expedients proposed, and declined as soon as well considered, M^r. Conway and myself yielded to the entreaties of our friends, unwilling as we were to see the king and country deserted: when such assistance as we could bring, was thought by very many independent men, capable of giving essential relief. M^r. Chas. Townshend after a great favor granted to his lady[1], and his brother coming over, in order to be sent Lieutenant to Ireland[2], promised his assistance also with every profession of attachment. His death followed so soon that it would be too uncandid to call his sincerity in question. I cannot say that Lord Shelburne (M^r. Conway's colleague) took much part in what was going forward. His lordship probably saw that the Ministry still bore so much the seal of Lord Chatham's, that he could not

---

[1] *Supra*, p. 128.

[2] George Viscount Townshend (1724–1807); he succeeded Lord Bristol as Lord-Lieutenant of Ireland in August, 1767. He was created Marquis of Townshend in October, 1787. His career as Lord-Lieutenant began well, but ended in disaster. Lecky, iv. 401.

well be justified in quitting under these circumstances his post, though he was never cordial with us[1]. Matters were sufficiently arranged, before the end of the month, to enable me to write the following note to Lady Chatham with the view of her ladyship's acquainting Lord Chatham with our decision, whenever she thought the moment to be proper.

GROSVENOR SQUARE, *July* 31st : 1767.

The Duke of Grafton's best respects wait on Lady Chatham, and begs to inform her ladyship, that General Conway has given him authority to say, that (though the particular situation is not fixed on) he is determined to stand forward in the House of Commons to carry on the king's business, having been assured that no consideration whatever could induce the Duke of Grafton to remain in his present post, in order to wait the return of Lord Chatham to the head of affairs, if the general was not the person on whom he could place his confidence in that House. The distressful state, to which the Crown must have been reduced, has actuated them both to take this part ; and to struggle with the difficulties that surround them.

The hopes that this account may give some satisfaction to Lord Chatham, is the occasion of the trouble the Duke of Grafton gives to her ladyship.

He must add, that no motive weighed so much with himself, as the reflexion of the just accusation he should draw on himself, if, on Lord Chatham's recovery, he should find that it proved some months too late to do the good which his superiority can alone effect.

Without disturbing Lord Chatham, the Duke of Grafton entreats him only to think that, where he cannot immediately approve, he would consider him as acting for the best, and often in these intricate times, compelled to make the lesser evil the more eligible measure[2].

The messenger brought me back her ladyship's answer.

Lady Chatham presents her best compliments to the Duke of Grafton

---

[1] Lord Shelburne had ceased at this time to attend meetings of the Cabinet, and was endeavouring to carry out a firm and conciliatory policy towards the colonies. Fitzmaurice, *Life of Shelburne*, ii. 38; and see Shelburne to Lady Chatham, *Chatham Corresp.* iii. 294, where he describes his isolation from his colleagues during the summer of 1767.

[2] This letter and the answer to it appear in the *Chatham Corresp.* iii. 281, 282. Grafton uses the argument with which Camden had pressed his retention of office : that so long as he was at the Treasury the way was kept open for Chatham's return.

with many grateful acknowledgments to his Grace for his great goodness
to Lord Chatham in the most obliging attention shewn to his present
unfortunate state of health.   She begs also to express how sensibly she
feels the honor done her by his Grace, in the note intrusted to her.   She
persuades herself from the experience of the D. of Grafton's friendship
to Lord Chatham, that she shall be forgiven by him, if she intreats to be
permitted to withhold the contents till some little degree of amendment
in Lord Chatham's health may render it less anxious to communicate
anything of business to him, especially upon a point which cannot fail of
turning his thoughts upon the whole of things, which till he has recover'd
more strength must be prejudicial to him.   This, Lady Chatham is clear
the Duke of Grafton knows, without her taking the liberty to assure him
of it, that Lord Chatham's opinion has been constantly, that his Grace's
stay in his present post is essential to the well-being of the king's affairs,
and the good of the whole.   She therefore judges whatever confirms that
most desired circumstance will be heard with infinite pleasure by Lord
Chatham.

   She hopes his Grace will believe she is under the greatest confusion
in hazarding so much from herself, and that she is conscious nothing
less could excuse it than her apprehension for Lord Chatham, whose
illness has rather encreas'd for some time past, and who is to-day under
physical operation.   This she flatters herself will plead her pardon with
the D. of Grafton.

N. END, July 31st: 1767.

A much greater degree of responsibility you see directly
devolved on my shoulders ; and you will consider this hour,
as having opened a fresh æra in my life.   I hope I am not
too presuming in thinking, if the same disposition for moderate
councils had been pursued by my successor, that this country
would readily have settled all its disputes with our colonies ;
have released America from the fetters of their old charters,
and in conjúnction with them bid defiance to all our enemies ;
or what would have been far preferable, employed our
strength and weight to maintain the blessings of peace to
many countries.   What a retrospect for us, who now see
Great Britain detested and insulted throughout Europe ;
threatened by a formidable enemy, and sinking under heavy
and vexatious taxes, the consequences of our repeated follies,
if not of our iniquities !

   It is a great comfort to a public man to be able to say that his best endeavours were exerted to prevent the mischief and the sad policy which future ages will join to condemn.

I am now to enter upon the most arduous part of my undertaking; and I am sensible of the many difficulties which may be expected to arise. However being determined to do no injustice to any person, nor more than justice to myself, I shall not be afraid to bring forward every material truth. You will bear in mind, that you are not to look into this memoir, for a general history of the times, but of those transactions solely, in which I was more immediately concerned; and of which I can give the best authenticated accounts. To the debates in Parliament, and to the professed histories of the king's reign, I shall beg leave to refer you for all information, which does not come within my recollection, or cannot be supplied from my papers.

The various parties, declaring themselves in opposition to the Administration, circumstanced as it stood, were formidable indeed, whether they were to be considered from the landed property they possessed, from the numbers they were composed of, or from the weight of their abilities.

On our side, we had the satisfaction of seeing a great and very independent majority in the House of Commons, which gave us credit with the publick.

The declaration also of our readiness at any time to extend, without exclusion of any, the Administration to as comprehensive a plan as could be effected, gave a good impression of the moderation of our characters : and the hopes, though distant, of the recovery of Lord Chatham, brought some accession to our cause: and the list annexed will shew, that my colleagues, who still composed the Ministry, though they were deprived of Lord Chatham's aid, were most respectable for their talents and abilities. For Lord Camden was Chancellor, Lord Northington President, Lord Chatham, (but unfortunately absent) Privy Seal, Lord Shelburne, and M^r. Conway, Secretaries of State, M^r. Charles Townshend Chancellor of the Exchequer, Sir Edwd. Hawke at the head of the

Admiralty, and Lord Granby Commander in Chief. But, to proceed: the affairs of Ireland called for our early attention; the Lord Lieutenancy was vacant, and a new Chancellor was to be appointed. Lord Townshend was entrusted to discharge the duties of the former important office, under the same stipulations for permanent residence as Lord Chatham had intended [1]: for it was my earnest wish to adhere to his lordship's plans, as far as I was acquainted with them. Lord Chatham saw that it was highly expedient to bring a distinguished officer to the command of the army in that kingdom, where parliamentary favor led too often to pernicious partialities. With a view of placing Sir Jeffry Amherst [2] in that situation his lordship had desired to see him: but was much disappointed and discontented when he found that the attempt to persuade him was in vain. No officer in the service could have been thought of so proper as Sir Jeffrey to discharge this; and whose talents were particularly calculated to enforce strict discipline and due subordination.

Lord Chatham likewise inclined to concede to the Irish Ministry the three or four points at which they principally aspired. To shorten the duration of their parliaments was an essential object; and justly to be demanded by a free nation; and on that ground would have received his sanction.—You well know that the life of the king was the period of its former duration.

Lord Townshend was no sooner named to be the Lord Lieutenant, than he was surrounded by Irish advisers [3]; and

---

[1] Fitzmaurice, *Life of Shelburne*, ii. 93, says that Townshend had not been made aware of this requirement. The residence of the Lord-Lieutenant was designed, among other things, to take the control of Irish business out of the hands of the Lords Justices who had hitherto conducted the government. Chatham proposed also to limit the duration of the Irish Parliaments, which had hitherto lasted the king's life unless sooner dissolved by an exercise of prerogative; and to assimilate the tenure of the judges in Ireland to that of the English judges.

[2] Jeffrey, first Lord Amherst (1716–1797), had commanded with brilliant success in America during the years 1758–1762. He was at this time the non-resident Governor of the colony of Virginia.

[3] For a description of Irish politics and Irish statesmen at this period, see Fitzmaurice, *Life of Shelburne*, vol. ii. pp. 93–117.

some of them, as was thought, not the most disinterested. Through the medium of these men he viewed the various proposals offered, or rather pressed on him. The first point his lordship was anxious to carry, was the appointment of a Chancellor from the Irish Bar. I believe, that I was not at first aware of the objections, or leaned perhaps too strongly to gratify Lord Townshend in his wishes; as I might also in my letter to Lord Camden, though my determination was, not to proceed in it without the concurrence of the Lord Chancellor, to whom, at Bath, I transmitted Lord Townshend's long letters and papers, and from whom I received in return the well considered letters, which follow.

BATH, *Sepr.* 27th, 1767.

MY DEAR LORD DUKE,

   I have since the receipt of your Grace's letter turned my thoughts upon the subject of it, with the most serious attention ; and am displeased with myself for not agreeing altogether with your Grace in conferring the Irish Seal upon an Irishman. I will readily confess, that I am not a competent judge of this question, for want of knowing the true state of that country ; the manner in which it has been governed of late years, the power and influence of the several connexions, and above all, the importance of the Irish Barr in the House of Commons there : and therefore it is very likely that your Grace may be much better enabled than myself, to form a true judgment upon the utility and policy of complimenting the Irish, with the high office. Your Grace, however, has a right to my poor opinion, such as it is; and indeed, my lord, I am very loth to give up to the unreasonable demands of two or three barristers (however eminent) the last, as well as most important law office in that kingdom, which England hitherto has thought fit to reserve to herself. All the chiefs upon each bench were formerly named from hence : the Irish have acquired the King's Bench; and the last Lord Lieutenant for the first time made them a present of the chief baron ; and there has not for many years been an instance of a puisne judge sent from this country : I believe Baron Mounteney was the last[1]. .

   Thus, by degrees, has this country surrendered up all the great offices of the law, except only the Common Pleas, and the Great Seal; and I much doubt, whether this country acquired any advantage by all these concessions.

   In the last Session, Mr. Flood[2] moved a general censure upon the

---

[1] He was appointed in 1741.   [2] Henry Flood (1732-1791) entered

characters and capacity of the judges sent from England, with a view, no doubt, of inflaming the people against all these nominations, in hopes of extending their encroachments to a total exclusion of the English from the Irish bench : and now, such is the danger of precedent, they threaten general opposition, for so I understand from Lord Clare [1], if this favour is refused and your Grace seems to think it will be an *affront* upon the Great Council there.

Jocelyn and Bowes, though both Englishmen, are honored with the appellation of Irish for the present purpose, and are cited as precedents in their favour [2].

I am very apprehensive, that if your Grace should indulge now the Irish in this *demand* (for I can call it by no other name) the precedent will bind England for ever : for national favours once conferred, can never be resumed. Ireland has reason enough to be discontented with the mother country : the popular party are sure to distress the Castle to some degree every Session, and the method has been hitherto to win over the leaders in the House of Commons by places, pensions, and honors, which has enabled the Lord Lieu[t]. for the time being, to close his particular Session with ease to himself : at the same time that it has ruined the king's affairs, and enraged the people. The next successor is involved in the same difficulties, and his convenience has been complimented with the like measures, till, at last, by this profusion of rewards, the Government has nothing to give ; and is left beggared, and consequently unsupported. In such a state of things, would your Grace wish to pursue this plan, and grant now, before the opening of Session, the highest post in the law to one member only of the H. of Commons (for only one can have it) whose removal afterwards to make room for an Englishman (let his behavior be ever so obnoxious) would be a most odious and unpopular measure in that country? An Englishman in the office is expected to remain an Englishman, and is permitted : an Irishman anglicized would never be endured.—Indeed, my lord, the very yielding, in my humble opinion, would be a weakening of Government, and be more pernicious, than the most troublesome Session.

I am truly sensible of Lord Townshend's embarrassments, and foresee, that if he should not obtain this boon, he must expect to meet with some very disagreeable struggles. But I daresay his zeal, courage, and ability are equal to the whole ; and, I am sure, he will chearfully undertake

the Irish Parliament in 1759 where he was for some time leader of the popular party. Acceptance of office lost him this position which was occupied by Grattan and never regained by Flood. He entered the English Parliament in 1793, but made no great figure there.

[1] Robert Nugent (1702-1788), Viscount Clare (1766), and afterwards Earl Nugent, in the peerage of Ireland.

[2] Jocelyn was Chancellor 1739-1756, and Bowes 1756-1767.

what he has accepted, though your Grace should adhere to our first opinion, of keeping the Seal for the present in commission.

Your Grace takes it for granted, that no proper person can be had from hence at present : S^r. T. S.[1] (who was not perhaps the properest) has refused, and no other person has yet been applied to. Suppose the Attorney and Solicitor[2] should decline it, perhaps M^r. Justice Bathurst[3] might accept. I am sure Messrs. Justices Aston[4] or Hewitt[5] would be pleased with it; who, if not of the most shining parts, are yet good lawyers, and sensible men, and I a sure of very sufficient abilities to command respect from the Irish Bar : and I should not for my own part have had difficulty in the nomination of either of them *at this* time : but I submitted to the opinion of others for the Commission, thinking that this expedient might be a means of carrying Lord T. through the Session with more facility.

Your Grace will be pleased to consider, that the Chancellor, Chief Baron, and Chief Justices, are called to the Council in Ireland, in the quality of statesmen, and that the Council in that country is an assembly of equal importance with either of the branches of the Legislature. If the Lord Lieu^t. is surrounded with Irish only, filling these offices, at that board he is subject to be over-ruled in every quarter by the great chiefs of the law, in which case, I doubt he must submit.

[1] Sir Thomas Sewell, Master of the Rolls, a lawyer and judge of considerable reputation.

[2] William de Grey, the first Lord Walsingham, who succeeded Wilmot as Chief Justice of the Common Pleas, was Attorney-General 1766-1771. He was a good lawyer and possessed an extraordinary memory. Fosse, *Lives of the Judges*, viii. 264.

Edward Willes, son of Sir John Willes, Chief Justice of the Common Pleas, was at this time Solicitor-General. Mr. Fosse says that Willes would have liked to accept the Chancellorship of Ireland, but that Camden had promised the place to Hewitt, whom Willes succeeded as a Judge of the King's Bench.

[3] Henry Bathurst, 1714-1794, afterwards Lord Apsley and second Earl Bathurst, was at this time a Judge of the King's Bench. He was a Commissioner of the Great Seal in 1770, and became Lord Chancellor in 1771

as Lord Apsley. He succeeded to the earldom of Bathurst in 1775, and resigned the office of Chancellor in 1778. He was afterwards President of the Council 1779-1782.

[4] Richard Aston had been Chief Justice of the Common Pleas in Ireland 1739-1765, when he was removed to the King's Bench in England. He was Commissioner of the Great Seal with Bathurst and Smythe, J.J., in 1770. He is described as a good lawyer, with a rude and overbearing manner. Fosse, *Lives of the Judges*, viii. 237.

[5] James Hewitt, afterwards Lord Lifford, was at this time a Judge of the King's Bench. He had been a tedious speaker in the House of Commons, but his Whig principles commended themselves to Camden, whose promise to him of the Irish Great Seal, if, as alleged by Fosse, it had been already made, throws some light on the correspondence.

But, if your Grace should at last be determined to name an Irishman, you will please to consider, whether S^r. A. Malone[1] is not clearly the properest person. He has not indeed applied for it : but, I understand he would be happy with the offer: and such is the deference to his superior character, that every one of those gentlemen, who have applied, have put themselves only in the second place after him. So that, if your Grace is resolved upon an Irishman—' Detur dignissimo ! ' Let it carry with it a mark of publick spirit, at the same time that it is a management of parties. I know your Grace will forgive my frankness : this is my present opinion, though I shall most willingly submit to a contrary determination, and when your Grace has done it, shall say in public that it is well done: indeed, I shall go near to think so, because, I am sure the decision will be taken by those who understand Ireland better than I do.

I presume your Grace has asked Lord Northington's opinion upon this subject; that will have great weight with me, as well as your Grace. He used to think as I do, as did Lord Chatham, but different circumstances may well bring about a change of opinion.

I know your Grace will be anxious to hear some news of Lord Chatham : if I had been able to have given you any authentic intelligence of his amendment to any considerable degree, I should have wrote before. The whole country in his neighborhood report him much better, but his knocker is tied up, and he is inaccessible. I read a letter from Lady Chatham yesterday, who is so fearful of owning my lord to be better, that she retracts it, even while she is admitting it in the same sentence, and conveys hopes of his recovery while she forbids them. I verily believe he is considerably mended.

I propose to be in town on Wednesday morning the 7th of next month, to prorogue the Parliament at 11 o'clock in the morning: if your Grace will be so good as to order the proper preparations—to go to Court—to swear in Lord North[2] and set out immediately for my return; I hope this will be permitted.

I have the honor to be, with the most perfect respect and esteem, your Grace's

Most obedient faithful serv^t.

CAMDEN.

---

[1] Antony Malone, 1700–1776, had been Prime Serjeant 1740–1750, and Chancellor of the Exchequer 1757–1761. He was dismissed from this latter office because he had supported the contention that Irish money bills should originate in the Irish House of Commons and not in the Irish Privy Council (Lecky, *Hist. of England*, iv. 359).

[2] On September 10 Lord North had accepted the Chancellorship of the Exchequer in succession to Charles Townshend, who died on the 4th.

M

Secret—BATH.

MY DEAR LORD DUKE,

Since I had the honor of writing last to your Grace, I have had a conversation with Lord Frederick Campbell [1], a letter from Lord Townshend, and have seen some papers drawn up by M^r. Tisdale [2], all concerning the seals, and find to my great concern that this business calls for an immediate decision, for as I understand, the Commission is called a grievance, and will be followed by addresses, and M^r. Tisdale is of opinion that this office belongs of right to the Irish and ought not to be withheld from them, and what is still more decisive, that there is not a lawyer in England duly qualified to execute the office. It seems odd enough that his Lordship should rely upon this occasion for advice upon a gentleman, who is a principal candidate for the office. But, so it is, and Lord Townshend is so overcome by his arguments, as to adopt all his ideas, and to press the business with as much warmth as M^r. Tisdale himself.

My lord informs me further, that your Grace is brought over, and Lord Townshend assures me, that M^r. Conway is of the same way of thinking; and most probably Lord Shelburne, from his connexion with Ireland, will agree.

Now, my dear lord, I take it for granted, that M^r. Tisdale knows all this, and that the only difficulty remains with me. In this state of the business, it is no longer a subject of deliberation, but is in truth decided; for my single resistance must not stop a proceeding agreed to by the majority of the Cabinet : and indeed it is too much for me to contend against the whole kingdom of Ireland, with the Lord Lieu^t. at their head, unless your Grace was of the same opinion with me.

But, if this thing is to be done, I wish it may be done handsomely, with a proper respect and complaisance for the Irish Bar : and though it is manifestly extorted, let it seem at least not to proceed from a conviction of its being right, but to be bestowed, as a royal favour ; and give me leave to repeat again my wish, that S^r. A. Malone may be the man. M^r. Tisdale's age, giving a probability of a speedy vacancy, in my opinion is of no consideration, seeing, that after England has once yielded the point, she can never reclaim it, especially, as it has been given up upon a struggle.

My dear lord, the present state of Ireland fills my mind with anxiety. The Privy Council is so numerous, that the Lord Lieu^t. cannot command it, and they are as mutinous as the H. of Commons. This board, the guardian and enforcer of Poynings' Law, and the Lord Lieu$^{t's}$. body guard is surrendered up to the Irish, and Poynings' Law virtually repealed.

---

[1] Fourth son of John Duke of Argyll, and M.P. for Glasgow. He was now secretary to Lord Townshend.

[2] Attorney-General for Ireland, for thirty years M.P. for Dublin University.

The king's influence and all the rewards of Government alienate to men, who being first rendered independent, immediately turn ungrateful; and turn the Crown's battery against itself: and now at last the highest office of the law (the rest having been given up before) is torn away from Government by violence. For, I do assure your Grace, that M^r. Tisdale's papers breathe nothing less than defiance and opposition. In this state of things, the Lord Lieu^t. is won over to be the Irish champion; and in this critical moment uses his power to force the measure by a proceeding that is indeed inevitable.

He tells us in his letter, that this measure is the very criterion of an odious, or a popular Administration, that, if it is not granted, it will be a proof of his own insignificance, and *that it will be safest for him to confess it to all mankind.* He then descants on his own merit in accepting this office at such a time, and upon so short warning, as if it had been forced upon him against his will, and concludes with saying, that he leaves his letter with me, as a justification of his conduct, in case such events should follow as he has reason to expect.

When such language is used, there are but two things to be done; to quarrel, or to submit. The first being at this time to the last degree imprudent and dangerous, which his lordship well knows, makes the latter necessary; and therefore if there was no more in the business, but this consideration, I should resolve at once to acquiesce. But what makes me submit with more chearfulness, is your Grace's opinion, founded I am persuaded upon a full and attentive reflection of the difficulties, that would otherwise attend the Lord Lieu^{vs}. government at this time, when perhaps England is too weak to make a struggle on such a point. I am not enough acquainted with that country to be obstinate on this subject, which is more a State question, and not properly within my department.

But, my dear lord, the time must come, (I wish it was come) when a different plan of government must take place for that country. I am apt to believe, that Lord Chatham intended now to begin it, and to enable himself to contend with the powerful connexions there, proposed to establish himself upon the basis of just popularity, by granting the four favorite Bills[1]. This intended scheme has got wind, and the Irish grand juries begin to form all their addresses for the Septennial Bill, &c. What will Lord T. do with these favorite Bills? Are they to be resisted? I am afraid the Irish will think they have taken the Great Seal by storm, and will be apt to try the Lord Lieu^{vs}. metal by other attempts in the same way. How, if his lordship should give way and tell the king's

---

[1] These were a Habeas Corpus bill, and bills to make the judges irremovable at the royal pleasure, to restrain the grant of pensions, and to limit the duration of Parliament.

servants here, that, if his advice is not followed, he will declare his insignificance to *the whole world*? Or, if on the other hand, he is disposed to a firm refusal, what will become of his popularity? He that begins by yielding, will find it difficult to change his mode of proceeding.

These my remarks upon the Lord Lieu^{ts}. conduct are intrusted only to your Grace, and will, I am sure, be safely lodged in your breast. How just they are, you will judge, when I shew you his lordship's letter. In the mean time, if your Grace pleases, my language shall be, that altho' I wished very much, that a Chancellor might be sent from England, yet, since I find by the united opinions of those who understand that country, better than I do, that it would be too hazardous at this time, to disappoint the expectations of so many powerful persons there, I submit myself to better judgments. I take it for granted, that your Grace has consulted Lord President, and I hope he will concur; for, though there may be difference of opinions amongst us, as there must be sometimes, if we are honest men, yet our actions ought to be united.

I have the honor to be, with the most perfect esteem and regard, your Grace's most obed^t.

Faithful servant,
CAMDEN.

Sepr. 29th, 1767.

N.B. This letter of Lord Camden's of Sepr. 29th 1767 must not appear during the life of Lord Townshend; after this, it cannot be prejudicial to any person. The subject gave rise to a curious discussion: and I can see no reason for suppressing afterwards, observations which do credit to the head and heart of Lord Camden, tho' communicated under injunctions of secrecy at the time.

MY DEAR LORD,

I find by your Grace's letter, and one I received at the same time from Lord Shelburne, that I am called upon to name a person for the Irish Seal.—He must be eminent, and one who at this ticklish juncture would be every way fit for the office. I doubt it will be too much for me in such a dearth of men, willing to accept, to recommend one who will answer that description, nor dare I undertake it without the sanction of a Cabinet. The whole business is indeed a State question, and does not properly fall within my department: and I presume, when I left London that the nomination of a fit person would be the discussion of another Council. This consideration does in reality make part of the general question, and may of itself decide it; for, if no such person can be found here, the Irish must have their Chancellor, 'ex necessitate'; and I am persuaded at last it will end there, as I had the honor to tell your Grace in a former letter.

Mr. Justice Bathurst seems, in your Grace's judgment, not to be improper; wherein I have the pleasure of concurring; but I do not believe, that he will ever be persuaded to undertake it. M^r. Solicitor, from what I have heard, will certainly refuse: in which case, I am reduced to Aston and Hewitt: the first is thought unfit, especially at this time; the other though a good lawyer, and an honest man, will probably be thought not of sufficient eminence, to be recommended at this time. Nay perhaps it would be difficult, considering all that has passed, to prevail on any body to accept it, if he knew what we all know, with the unwillingness of Ireland to receive a Chancellor from hence.

I wish I could know your Grace's opinion upon the whole of this business, for our Council was not meant to be conclusive till that was taken.

Thus much I have ventured to say to your Grace at this distance; but, whatever be the result, it will be impossible for me to take any step till I come to London, which will be next week: for, it would be very imprudent upon many accounts to feel pulses, or make applications by letter.

I am sorry, that it does not suit your Grace, to give the little office I applied for to my friend: but the answer is a fair one: your Grace's servants have a right to be preferred to mine; but, as you have so much to give, and I so little, give me leave to trouble you, on some future occasion, when it shall not be inconvenient, in favour of M^r. Greenland.

I have the honor to be, &c. &c.

CAMDEN.

BATH, *Oct^r.* 20th, 1767.

Lord Northington's opinion concurred so fully with Lord Camden's on the disposal of the Great Seal of Ireland, that the Cabinet was persuaded not to give way to Lord Townshend's reasoning in favor of an Irish lawyer's holding it: and I am persuaded that our firmness gave more real consideration to his lordship's situation, and dignity and weight to his Government, than any yielding of his own would have effected.

Before Parliament met, M^r. Serj^t. Hewitt accepted the Seal, with every good disposition to discharge properly the great trust put into his hands: and his learning as a lawyer sanctioned our expectations from the appointment. He was a true Whig: and bore a character to which all parties gave their assent and respect; and though his speeches in Parliament were long and without eloquence, they were replete with excellent matter and knowledge of the law. His conduct in Ireland, under the peerage of Lifford, soon gained the esteem of the public.

The rapid illness and unexpected death of Mr. Chas. Townshend, who, seized with an inflammation in his bowels, died in the first days of September, distressed us much; as the filling properly up so great a chasm in our body was of the utmost importance.

After the experience His Majesty had of Lord North's disposition when he declined, in the last winter, the offer of the office from Lord Chatham, it appeared to be hopeless to apply to him now; though all our friends wished his lordship to be successor to Mr. Townshend. However, His Majesty laid his commands on me to write directly to Lord North, offering him the seal of Chancellor of the Exchequer: the choice of this nobleman was particularly satisfactory to me, as I knew him to be a man of strict honor: and he was besides the person whom Lord Chatham desired to bring to that very post. What follows is his lordship's first answer to my letter, of which I conclude I took no copy, as I do not find any.

WROXTON, Sepr. 6th.

MY LORD,

I have just received your Grace's letter, and am much shocked at the news it brings. I am greatly honored by the proposition your Grace makes to me, but it is too important a subject for me to be able to give an immediate answer to it. That, you will be so good as to permit me to defer, till I have the honor of seeing your Grace in London, which I hope to have, at the time appointed in your letter.

I am, my lord, your Grace's
Most obliged and faithful humble servt.
NORTH.

Lord North came up to London according to his intention, had a very gracious audience of His Majesty, was afterwards with me to state his reasons for declining the office, and set out directly to re-join his father at Wroxton. The seals cannot be kept vacant many hours: and in a hurrying moment, I offered them with the king's leave to Lord Barrington. His lordship accepted the offer, through duty and gratitude, to His Majesty, and expressed his hopes, that it would be only a temporary appointment, untill His Majesty could consider where better to place them. Those who knew the amiable temper of this honorable person will not be surprized at this instance of an accommodating conduct in his lordship. Having, as I thought, fixed a Chancellor of the Exchequer, I set forward with M^r. Bradshaw for Euston, where I wanted to spend a few days, but was overtaken at Woodford by a messenger, who delivered the following letter from Lord North, which I shall transcribe;

WROXTON, Sepr. 10th, 1767.

MY LORD,

    I am just arrived here, full of the warmest sense of gratitude to His Majesty, and your Grace, but very uneasy for fear that my refusal of the honorable offer lately made to me, should have given offence, or appeared to proceed from want of zeal to His Majesty, or regard for his present ministers.

    Your Grace will do me the justice to believe, that I am incapable of saying what I do not sincerely mean, and I do assure you, that in any situation, I shall be always ready to give all the assistance to Government in my power.

    Upon my return here, I find Lord Guilford astonishingly recovered [1], the cause of his illness removed, and the whole family in spirits. Mine are so much raised by it, that, if you continue to find any real difficulty in disposing of the seals, I shall be ready to obey any call from His Majesty, or your Grace, tho' I own, I am better pleased to serve on in my present office. I am, my lord, with the highest respect and gratitude, your Grace's most obliged and

Faithful servant,
NORTH.

This alteration of mind in Lord North, was received by me with much satisfaction, convinced, as I was, that I should have in him an able assistant both at the Board, and in Parliament. We turned back a little way to the house of an acquaintance, who furnished us with every thing necessary for writing. The messenger was soon dispatched back with

---

[1] Lord Guildford was born in 1704, and survived till 1790.

letters to the king, Lords Barrington and North; and we proceeded on our journey.

Lord Barrington was happy to remain in the office [1], which he worthily filled; and the accession of Lord North, as Chancellor of the Exchequer, brought great consideration to the Administration. At that particular point of time, there was much to encourage, and little to alarm any honest man, entering into a ministerial situation. It would be idle to expect that any nation can long be free from various ills; especially a country, like ours, spreading its government into so many remote branches. Yet, on the whole, the moment must be acknowledged to have been favorable.

What was then passing in Poland and between Russia and the Porte, were undoubtedly important events, and were neither overlooked nor unlamented by the British Cabinet: but the distant situations of these countries, rendered all active interference on our parts, except by our good offices, preposterous, but we were not prevented however from interesting ourselves in the warmest manner, where we might with propriety, in the cause of the dissidents [2], and His Majesty was equally desirous that his wishes in their favor, might be conveyed directly to the King of Poland.

The Duc de Choiseul and the French nobility would willingly have entered (I have no doubt) into a war, impatient to retrieve the honor and credit of their arms, which had been so frequently tarnished in the late war, both by sea and land. But the abhorrence, which Louis 15th had of war, was not to be overcome by the ambitious views of his minister. Our policy, however, was constantly to have a fleet in forwardness equal to what both houses of Bourbon could bring forth.

From America we had as yet received no account of the good effect of the Act passed for inforcing the quartering the troops in New York, nor of the ill-humour expressed by some

---

[1] Lord Barrington was Secretary at War.

[2] The dissidents were members of the Protestant and Greek Churches who were excluded from office and political rights. The grievances of the dissidents furnished an excuse for the interference of Russia.

of the colonies on the absurd taxes of the last Session. At Boston it produced violent resolutions, inviting to adopt a system of non-importation.

The principal grievance attendant on this moment was the great distress felt especially by the poorer sort, from the high price of all provisions, and particularly corn. Several successive bad crops and harvests were the real cause: and, I believe, that every thing was done by the Legislature that could be thought of for their effectual relief: though I was not forward in taking up the visionary projects which were often started in Parliament, whose interference in these matters is too often attended with pernicious consequences.

Shall I say, that all was prosperous in India, while I am persuaded that I trace the germs of our interior luxury and profligacy of manners, with a great share of our present corruptions, in various ways, to our fatal connexions with that country? It is true ; the English arms flourished, and did conquer: but, the hearts of Englishmen, were each day further reconciled to every act of oppression, extortion, and cruelty. Even to this day, I cannot bring myself fairly to rejoice, when I hear the account of a splendid victory, gained over some country power, which probably might have become, by good management, an ally: because it brings to my thoughts all the evil, which, I conceive, India, has brought to this country[1].

It was at the end of August that I received from Lady Chatham the following letter, with Lord Chatham's request, who continued to be oppressed by his most afflicting disorders.

MY LORD,

The interest your Grace is so good to take in Lord Chatham's health, makes me trust, that you will excuse my giving your Grace the trouble of these few lines, to say, that he continuing extremely ill, Doctor

---

[1] There is an anti-Imperial tone about these reflections which makes them come strangely from a follower of Chatham.

[2] This letter is printed in the *Chatham Correspondence* (ii. 282), but is dated ' September —,' apparently by the editor.

Addington is of opinion, that an immediate change of air, and a journey are indispensibly necessary. His state of weakness being such, that he is totally unable to write himself, he hopes your Grace will allow him in this manner to take the liberty of begging your Grace, to lay him with all duty at the king's feet, with his humble request, that His Majesty will be graciously pleased to permit him to go for some time into Somersetshire in hopes of his recovery.

Lord Chatham and I have enough experienced your Grace's goodness, to relie you will pardon this trouble,

I am, my lord,

Your Grace's most obed^t. humble serv^t.

H. CHATHAM.

No time was lost in laying the letter and request before the king, by whom I was commanded particularly to express His Majesty's concern to find that Lord Chatham's disorder was so afflicting, as to render it necessary for him to remove to so great distance ; that His Majesty earnestly hoped, that it would be of effectual service to his health, for the recovery of which he should eagerly look, anxiously expecting that moment, when he could again be assisted by his councils [1].

A very few days after this application of Lord Chatham's to the king, through me, M^r. Chas. Townshend died at Sudbrook, his villa near London.

Lord Shelburne, with the leading members of the Cabinet were much busied, about this time, in framing the best bill they could point out, to be offered to Parliament, for meliorating and settling the civil and ecclesiastical constitution of Canada : and I am glad to be able to transcribe a letter from the Lord President on a business full of difficulty.

9th *August*, 1767.

GRAINGE.

MY DEAR LORD,

My eyes would not permit me to write to your Grace by the last post, as I intended, with respect to the affairs of the Canada Legislation [*sic*]; and to inform you fully of my idea on that business. I must first premise, that the formation of any plan of that kind can never commence nor proceed through the office, that I now enjoy, in whatever hands it

---

[1] The letter of which the substance is given here is printed in the *Chatham Correspondence*, iii. 283.

shall be placed : because the Council cannot correspond with any of the king's officers there, to know the true state of that country, which correspondence alone resides in the Secretary of State. When such information is acquired by him, I am of opinion that, before a plan can be formed, which must necessarily have the sanction of Parliament, it is necessary to have the full sense of the king's servants upon that subject, that the measures may have the general support of Government; and not be thrown, as they were last year upon one person, not in the least responsible for them. When every information is obtained, I am certain your Grace's penetration anticipates the difficulties to be encountered, not only from the civil constitution of that province, composed of French received under a capitulation, incorporated with English intitled to a Legislature at some time, and who have been encouraged to call for it, by the proclamation, the King's commission, and other excitements. To this, as great a difficulty succeeds, with regard to a Popish hierarchy, and of course a Protestant one ; both of which are in my opinion delicate subjects : loads too heavy to be sustained by any strength, less than that of a concurring Administration. I have all along been of this opinion in different Administrations, and have been willing to lend my aid to this difficult task.

I hope to be able to be in London in about ten days, though I am very indifferent still.

Your Grace has heard the Receiver is dead : I hope my recommendation may take place, or my credit will be very low here.

I have the honour to be, &c. &c.

NORTHINGTON.

I am not aware that any particular occurrence, previous to the meeting of Parliament, is omitted, which should have been introduced into this memoir. On account of its being the last Session, the Houses were convened in November, in order, that the business might be carried sufficiently forward to allow the Parliament to be dissolved in suitable time for the election of a new one.

Without being able to make out a case on which the jarring opinions of the Rockinghams, Bedfords and Grenvilles could well agree, the Opposition was earnest to find one out at all events. The Duke of Bedford's friends were evidently the most impatient, under an exclusion of office ; and perhaps one may also say, that they were less embarrassed with scruples, on the head of measures, than the other parties, with whom they were acting. Lord Weymouth went so far as to move the House for a day in January to be fixed, to go into a Committee on *the state of the nation*. The nature of Lord Weymouth's motion surprized us; as we could not conceive any ground his lordship could stand on, where he could have the voice of the public with him, for, except the scarcity of corn, there was no grievance. However before the recess for Christmas took place, the friends of the Duke of Bedford, through the channel of Lord Ossory, opened to M^r. Meynell, an intimate and most esteemed friend of mine and member for Stafford, their desire to enter into negociation with me, in order to be received on reasonable terms into the Administration : that two seats at the Cabinet were all they did, or would expect, and that the Duke of Bedford desired to give his full support, without holding any office. As to any other favors, or situations for their friends, these were to be discussed at a meeting for such purposes. My answer was, that it would be very satisfactory to me, if we could make such a junction ; and that I should request the king's permission to hear what they would propose. In consequence of these messages, through M^r. Meynell verbally, it was settled that Lord Weymouth and Lord Ossory, M^r. Meynell and myself should meet at this gentleman's house, as if by accident in our walks. But I must observe, that the mystery attached to the meeting was not derived from any caution to be attended to on our side.

There were circumstances at this time, which contributed much to facilitate this arrangement. Lord Northington had for some time past signified his desire to retire from office, on account of his increasing infirmities : and General Conway likewise was uneasy that no means were yet found to allow his return to the service ; [where] the post of Lieu^t. General of the Ordnance, being preferred by him, to that of Secretary of State.

At the meeting for negociation, it was evident, that the two lords came with great disposition, at least, if not determination to acquiesce in what might be reasonably proposed.

Indeed, the principal points had already been understood; and, though, I doubt not; they might have been beaten down *farther* in some of their expectations, I could see no dignified reason or policy, in placing those, who were acceding to our Ministry, in situations which their interests also did not call them to maintain. Besides, the conditions, now proposed and accepted, were short of those which Lord Chatham would have agreed to ; either in the conference he had himself with the Duke of Bedford in Decr. 1766 [1], or in that I had with Lord Gower in June 1767.

The arrangement was settled and laid before His Majesty to which he agreed except in one particular. The next vacant Garter was to have been given to the Duke of Marlborough, on stating this to His Majesty he said that he had intended in his own breast, to mark by this favor, his approbation of my conduct. Thanking His Majesty for his consideration of my zeal in his service, I humbly entreated him to allow me to decline the honor, till a future moment, as it would grieve me beyond measure, to think, that I had been in the remotest manner, the cause of setting aside an accession of strength, which was so much wanted, to His Majesty's Government; and especially in the House of Lords.

I saw Lord Weymouth the next morning, and acquainted him, that His Majesty had acquiesced in the particulars we had entered into; that my colleagues had approved them, and that I should be glad to hear that the D. of Bedford was fully satisfied in order that I might proceed in the business ; which desire produced the letter following.

Thursday night, 11 o'clock.

MY LORD,

In consequence of your Grace's wishes, I have communicated to the Duke of Bedford the conversations which have passed between your

---

[1] This seems not to be quite accurate. If the terms demanded by the Bedford party are referred to (*supra*, p. 106 *n*.) it will be seen that those conceded in December, 1767, are much more liberal than those which the king regarded as extravagant in 1766.

Grace and me; and can now inform you, that the Duke of Bedford and the rest of our friends have consented to them. I think it very unnecessary in this note, to recapitulate what the terms agreed on are, as I am perfectly satisfied, that there can be no misunderstanding between your Grace and me on that head. I take this earliest opportunity of acquainting your Grace with this matter, as you desired, that you may take the steps to-morrow, which you may think necessary.

I have the honor to be, &c. &c.

WEYMOUTH.

LETTERS, 1767

Some Data on the present state of men &·cet. with a sketch of a joint letter to Lord Chatham from L^d. President and the D. of G[rafton] [1].

Supposing—

1. The impossibility of carrying on L^d. Chatham's Ad^{mn}.

2. The D. of Grafton not being willing or averse to be minister.

3. The K. wisheth to have the Session fought out in order as it is said not to be taken captive.

4. Then the D. of G. stands minister during the *Inter* P^t. to act on a 1000^d events—upon wch he will not open the P^t. as minister.

5. The D. of Gr. no resort but to form an Adm^n of the E. of B. or to be negotiating between that and R.—the ŏr parties absolute—and my op: R. will not coalite with B.[2]

6. The op^n of Court was to have supported L^d. Ch. and present Ministry but is now to try the B.[3] faction wch is to me impossible of success.

7^{ly}. Ld. Ch. hath joined with E. Bute[4] on supposition of his being the root may be true) but he is afraid to meet it.

---

[1] These *data* and the letter which follows are in Lord Northington's handwriting, are very sketchy, and not very legible.

[2] This enigmatical paragraph may be interpreted to suggest an alternative between a Ministry resting on Bute and the king's friends, and a Ministry resting on a coalition of the Rockingham and Bedford parties.

[3] Bedford.

[4] The introduction of Bute's name to practical politics suggests that they who believed in the continuance of his influence were right. At any rate, Chatham's Ministry now consisted of a few personal admirers and a number of office seekers and of king's friends.

MY LORD,

The present situation of the king's affairs relative to Adm^n. having been so untoward from the want of y^r. lp^s. great support and influence ; from the unfortunate situation of y^r. lp^s. health, on whose weight and abilities the whole was rested ab initio; and now being come to the last chrisis, and essential for the king's immediate consideration, is the occasion of this trouble. Y^r. lp^s. Ministry have during the whole Sess^n. been none—Conway, Townsend the only efficient men in the House of Commons perpetually opposite to y^r. lp^s. desires and of the majority of sentiments of the Cabinet. The divisions in the Lords, in part by force of faction are prevalent and ascendant, the last division being carried by a maj^{ty}. of 3, 2 of wch were the K's. brothers. In this state of affairs our respect for y^r. lp. confirmed by our general support of you in y^r. absence makes it essential to ask whether you have in y^r. extraordinary abilities any measures to suggest for bettering these matters and in support of y^r. own Adm^n. If not, all our powers and faculties having been tried, tho destitute of councel, we think our hon^r. requires us to inform the king, that we have not a possibility of serving His Maj^{ty}. with effect hon^r. or justice to him or the public [1].

LORD NORTHINGTON TO THE DUKE OF GRAFTON

MY DEAR LORD,

I was this morning at Court and had the honor of speaking to H. M. at the Drawing Room, but as he had no commands for me and several persons of Ministry going in, I did not trouble the Closet. But I thought it fit to signify to your Grace, that I am convinced from circumstances that it is wished by *many* to pause till after the Session is up. And I could perceive by the discourse of a noble neighbour of mine that the thing you are enquiring after is as extensive as I thought it, and too large for y^r. reception. The *many* alluded to above are not of our friends, and it being my permanent opinion that we sh^d. penetrate thro' the present cloud, I send this for y^r. better and cooler judgment. I was much surprized too to find that the noble and warm neighbor of mine, did not adopt the thing in extenso, and therefore I conclude he is of the politics of the *many* abovementioned, which tho' beyond my line to fathom, I judge are not benign to y^r. Grace's sentiments or mine.

The S. S^y.[2] was beginning a long account of the state of Am^a. [America] his having got to the mastery of it, and yesterday rec^d. gen^l. directions thereon from the K. &c. &c. But in the midst of this Hurlo-thumbo they were both called in, staid a long time in the Closet and I left there.

---

[1] This is probably the rough draft of the paper of July 2, referred to *supra*, p. 150.

[2] The Southern Secretary, Shelburne.

Now as I am most certain this 1ᵈ. knows nothing of that business, I must be persuaded it is a preparation to quit   participating his public transactions to the consideration of the co-Ministry.

My lord, the affection I bear to yʳ. Grace's sentiments honʳ. and abilities (and you know I can speak on this occasion only from truth) have induced me to suggest every material circumstance relative to yʳ. Grace's conduct in this *nice and important chrisis*, and if my friendship outruns my judgment I am confident that I shall not only receive your pardon, but thanks, for my warmth, in endeavouring to express myself
My dʳ. 1ᵈ.
Yʳ. Grace's
Most respectfull and
Obedᵗ. servᵗ.
NORTHINGTON.

11 June, 1767,
LONDON.

THOMAS BRADSHAW TO THE DUKE OF GRAFTON

GREAT GEORGE STREET,
Thursday morning, 3 o'clock.
[14ᵗʰ May, 1767.]

MY LORD,

The House of Commons sat 'til one o'clock[1], and it is with great satisfaction I have the honor to acquaint your Grace, that upon a division, it was carried for the proposition moved by Mʳ. Townshend, 180 to 98.

Mʳ. Townshend opened the business of the day with a declaration, that he was not at Council when it was resolved to lay the American papers before the House ; that it did not belong to him, in respect of his office, to take the lead in the business, but that he opened it as a member of Parliament : he stated it fairly and ably ; mentioned his duties, but refer'd the consideration of them to the Committee of Ways and Means— he also stated the intention of Government to establish a Board of Customs in America. Mʳ. Dowdeswell, prefer'd the mode of requiring the civil magistrates to billet in private houses, if the Assembly would not make provision for the troops.—Mʳ. Edwᵈ. Burke spoke with great acrimony against Government ; treated the proposition as a mark of extream imbecility ; that it threaten'd a great deal without being likely to prove effectual, as the colony could do without new laws if they chose it. Lord North supported the proposition, saying, that, if it was not

---

[1] This was the great debate of May 13, in which Townshend unfolded his scheme for taxing the colonies.   It is unreported in the *Parliamentary History*, but Walpole, *Memoirs*, iii. 28, gives a fairly full account of it.

unexceptionable, it was at least such a one, as seem'd most likely to unite different opinions.

M^r. Grenville attacked M^r. Conway with great violence upon not having transmitted to the colonies the resolution of the Lords; asked, by what authority he had said that Parliament were ready to forgive; animadverted upon his changing his department, and upon the alteration in the powers of the Board of Trade; talked of encouragement given to the colonies in their misbehavior, and that impeachments might follow the authors; he then proposed different measures, such as, to order the Treasurer of New York to pay the money; to address the king to bestow marks of favor on the persons who had suffered for their good behavior and had not been compensated; to reward the colony of Barbadoes, who acted dutifully and had been unfortunate, with a grant of £10,000; and to establish a test for Assembly men and officers in America, by requiring them to subscribe a declaration, to the effect of the declaratory Act of last year, which last measure he means to move upon the report. He stated the intended duties on wine, fruit, and oyl, as a subversion of the Act of Navigation under colour of a tax; supposed that M^r. Townshend had been diverted by influence from other more effectual taxes, and said he would propose a better tax, viz. *on paper currency*: he also attacked very violently Lord Shelburne's letter of last September to Governor Barnard[1].

M^r. Conway defended himself against M^r. Grenville's attack; lamented his misfortune in differing from his friends, but said, he thought the proposition *violent, dangerous,* and *ineffectual,* and stated the instance of disobedience as a trifling one.—M^r. Townshend applied himself particularly to answer M^r. Conway; said, that the more trifling the occasion, the more marked was the spirit of disobedience; objected to the test proposed by M^r. Grenville, as carrying universal imputation on all the colonies, whereas part only had, in this particular, misbehaved—laughed at the idea of granting public money to Barbadoes for a bare discharge of their duty—disclaimed the giving up any taxes from influence; said, that he had drop'd the salt, on conviction that it would not answer; that the scheme upon tea must depend on a settlement with the India Company; and, as to paper currency mentioned by M^r. Grenville, he had always intended, but forgot to mention it in his opening. M^r. Yorke spoke very much in support of M^r. Grenville's arguments, and adopted all his propositions.—M^r. Rigby renew'd the attack upon M^r. Conway with great vehemence; observed, upon his having mention'd lenient measures, that M^r. Conway had no business to write lenitives to America, which the Parliament did not prescribe, and that it was the apothecary's going beyond the doctor: he took notice of the frequent complaints of

[1] See Fitzmaurice, *Life of Shelburne,* ii. 27.

N

a want of permanency in the Administration; wished the gentleman (M^r. T.) who had stated that so strongly the other night, and whose performance had as much wisdom in it as it had wit, had disclosed to the House who was the former of all these short lived Administrations, and what hidden influence raised, and displaced them. Sir George Saville and Lord John Cavendish spoke against the proposition.—Col. Barré justified Lord Shelburne; wished the proceedings of the House to be as unanimous as possible, but thought the ground bad, and that the Mutiny Act was of an odious nature.

Lord Clare supported M^r. T.'s proposition; thought there was no great difference between that and the others, but wished to know, for which the majority would vote, that he might vote accordingly.

M^r. Wedderburn [1] was very personal against M^r. Conway; denied the prevalence of any hidden influence, and complained that M^r. Conway had opposed M^r. T.'s proposition, without substituting any other : this occasioned M^r. Conway's declaring, that M^r. Townshend's was the most exceptionable of all that had been made ; and that he himself was for raising the money by a local tax.

The East India Committee was at first agreed to have been fixed for to-morrow; but upon M^r. Dyson's mentioning the bill relating to the dividend, it was agreed to be postponed to Wednesday next. Sir G. Colebrooke [2] and M^r. Cust [3] wished it to be postponed, upon the expectation of further propositions—both M^r. Conway and M^r. Townshend disclaim'd any further negociation on the part of Government. M^r. T. Townshend read the papers your Grace gave him, of which the House testified their entire approbation, and agreed to defer the Committee, not in consideration of the Directors' request, but upon the single ground of the bill for limiting dividends.

M^r. Townshend will meet your Grace in Grosvenor Square, on Saturday evening at 8 o'clock. He asked me, if you seem'd to consider his resignation as decisive of the fate of Administration—I told him I had no reason to believe you did. He had seen M^r. Worsley in the morning, and told him of M^r. Conway's intended resignation : by the channel he made choice of it is easy to guess, to what place he wish'd this information to be convey'd.

I beg your Grace will pardon the hurry in which I have set down these particulars, at so late an hour, and with a violent head-ach.

I have the honor to be, with the greatest respect, &c.

THO^s. BRADSHAW.

[1] Alexander Wedderburn(1732–1805), afterwards Chancellor, Baron Loughborough and Earl of Rosslyn, was at this time a follower of Grenville. In 1771 he became a Tory.

[2] M.P. for Arundel, the father of the well-known Oriental scholar.

[3] Peregrine Cust, M.P. for Bishops Castle.

GREAT GEORGE STREET,
Saturday, 16ᵗʰ *May*, 1767.

MY LORD,

The House of Commons sat till near one o'clock this morning, upon the report of the resolutions of Wednesday last[1].

It was moved by Garth and Rose Fuller to recommit the first resolution, upon the ground of New York's not having been guilty of a *direct* disobedience to the Mutiny Act. The distinctions taken by them were exploded by the Attorney General so effectually, that that ground of recommitment was soon changed, and the debate went on, upon general objections to the whole plan of the proceedings.

Upon this general ground, Mʳ. Conway stated himself as obliged to be for the recommitment: Mʳ. Townshend opposed it firmly, and even eagerly; exposed the frivolousness of the distinctions upon which it was moved, but chiefly pressed the disgrace that would attend the House, if they should appear unable to persevere for two days together in the same opinion, upon a matter of such importance; observed, that want of sufficient efficacy was the objection to his plan, and that nothing could be so likely to render it inefficacious, as the appearance of hesitation in deciding upon it. Mʳ. Townshend spoke so ably, and with so much effect, as to leave no doubt but that all who had concurr'd in the resolutions, would adhere to them; the debate, however, continued some time longer. Mʳ. Dowdeswell and Lord Rockingham's party repeated their former objections, tho' apparently with less earnestness than formerly.—Sir Gilbert Elliot[2] spoke strongly against the recommitment; stated Mʳ. Grenville's management in the Committee as calculated for the purpose of uniting for a moment, upon a single question, opinions, and interests, so thoroughly discordant, as to be incapable of being long kept together, and advised Mʳ. G. not to venture a recommitment, least if the present propositions were laid aside, instead of a more efficacious plan, he should find himself obliged to accept of a weaker one.—Mʳ. G. proved how much he felt this speech, by the acrimony with which he answer'd it.

Mʳ. Stanly spoke against the recommitment, and by way of anticipation, objected to Mʳ. Grenville's scheme of the test: the question of recommitment passed in the negative, without a division.

Mʳ. Grenville then moved an amendment to the first resolution, by stating, that some of the colonies persisted in denying the authority of Parliament, as a foundation for a resolution which he was to move afterwards, for establishing the test. Mr. Dyson objected to this; as altogether improper, if meant to be substituted instead of the particular

---

[1] See vol. xxxi. p. 364 of the *Commons' Journals*, and vol. xvi. p. 331 of the *Parliamentary History*. There is no record of the debate except a speech of Governor Pownal not here alluded to.

[2] M.P. for Roxburghshire: father of the first Earl of Minto.

proceeding upon the province of New York, the peculiarity of whose conduct required some specific provision ; and as offered out of it's proper place, if intended merely as a collateral proceeding. Some debate ensued upon this, and the amendment was rejected by 150 to 51 : such of Lord Rockingham's friends as stay'd, were in the majority.

The three resolutions were then agreed to. M^r. Grenville moved a resolution for establishing the test, which without much debate was rejected by 141 to 42. He then moved an address that the king would bestow marks of his favor upon such governors and officers as had suffered for their loyalty &c. in America, which passed nem. con. He also moved an address for favor to Barbadoes in consideration of their having obey'd the Stamp Act, and of their late misfortunes. Rose Fuller laid in a like claim for Jamaica, in respect of their obedience, and Lord Adam Gordon for Canada ; the motion was rejected without a division.

I thought it proper to inform your Grace of these particulars, previous to your meeting this evening. I beg leave to return my sincere acknowledgments for the honor of your note, and to assure your Grace, that I shall be happy in every circumstance, which marks my zeal, and my respectful attachment to you.

I am assured from good authority, that the leaders of the last general court, have fallen upon a new plan for carrying their point, and hope to bribe Parliament into an allowance of their encreasing their dividend, by an immediate offer of a large specific sum, instead of a moiety of the surplus. I think it my duty to apprize your Grace of this intention, lest, when the offer is made, or the view of it held out, any attempt should be made to conceal from your Grace the real motive.

M^r. Townshend was so warm yesterday morning upon his treatment in being opposed by the Secretary of State[1], and that the *Secretary at War*[2] went about complaining of his American proposition, that I think he will mention these circumstances to your Grace to-night, and therefore I beg leave to state to your Grace the grounds upon which he complains of Lord Barrington.—My obligations and my affection for that lord made me see him immediately, and I stated to M^r. Townshend before he went to the House in the presence of M^r. Cooper how that matter stood.

At the meeting at M^r. Townshend's, where the plan was opened and everybody desired to give their opinion freely, Lord Barrington said he was of opinion, that the conduct of the Assembly of New York did not amount to an actual disobedience of the Mutiny Act, altho their disposition to disobey, was too evident : the day after the resolutions were moved in the committee, Lord B. sitting in the House, by M^r. Cooper, (who was also present at the meeting at Mr. Townshend's,) told him he continued of the same opinion ; Sir W. Baker came up to them and said

[1] Conway.   [2] Lord Barrington.

the same thing, to which Lord B. replied, that he had been just expressing the same opinion to M^r. Cooper[1]. Lord Barrington notwithstanding this opinion, for which he privately gives his reasons, voted with Government upon every question.

I have the honor to be, with the greatest respect,

My Lord,

Your Grace's

Most humble, and most

Obliged servant,

THO^s. BRADSHAW.

PS.—I do not recollect whether in my former letter I mentioned to your Grace, that on Wednesday night General Conway, Lord Beauchamp, the Walpoles, and L^d. Fred Campbell were in the minority, and Mr. Conway with Government.

GREAT GEORGE STREET,

20th *Oct^r*. 1767.

MY LORD,

As Lord North thinks it necessary to send a messenger to your Grace, upon the subject of the distillery, I beg leave at the same time to acquaint you, that I have seen M^r. Calcraft[2], who came to town to wait upon your Grace, in consequence of the note I wrote him in your name. He expresses great attachment to you and Lord Chatham, but considers M^r. Pitt's re-election as a matter, that may, unless it is properly understood, very much affect his interest at Wareham; that however, to show his regard to your wishes, he makes the following propositions. He will bring in M^r. Pitt at present, provided he gives it under his hand that he will not interfere at Wareham at the General Election; he will bring in any other person you recommend, and by that means make a vacancy for M^r. Pitt at another place; or he submits, whether M^r. Pitt may not enjoy the emoluments of the place of Surveyor of the Woods, without the appointment, till the end of the next session : he concluded by hoping your Grace would consider this as a matter of property, in which he was obliged to take care of his own interest.

The Solicitor General is returned from Taunton : he has no doubt of his success, but thinks the contest will be expensive, if the Lords stand their ground.

I have the honour to be, with great respect, &c.

THO^s. BRADSHAW.

[1] Secretary to the Treasury.

[2] John Calcraft (1726–1772) started in life as a follower of Henry Fox; made a fortune as an army agent; acquired a large borough influence, and from 1769 to his death was an active purveyor of political intelligence to Chatham and Temple.

A List described as

'Names taken down at the time of the negotiation, from Lords Weymouth and Ossory as persons to be noticed at the time or as soon as could be arranged.'

Lord Gower.
Weymouth.
Sandwich.
Mr. Rigby.
Vernon.
Thynne.
Lord Ch. Spencer.
Lord Bolingbroke.
Essex.

D. of Marlborough.
Mr. Brand.

Lord Eglinton.

CHAPTER V

THE Cabinet was composed of the following persons,

Lord Camden .	. .	Lord Chancellor.
Earl Gower	. .	Lord President.
Earl of Chatham	.	Lord Privy Seal.
Lord Shelburne ⎫ Lord Weymouth ⎭	.	Secretaries of State.
Duke of Grafton	.	First Commissioner of the Treasury.
Lord North	. .	Chancellor of the Exchequer.
Lord Granby .	. .	Commander in Chief.
Genl. Conway .	. .	Lieu^t. Genl. of Ordnance.
S^r. Edwd. Hawke, K.B.	.	First Commissioner of the Admiralty.

It appeared to me, that for some time His Majesty observed a shyness towards our new allies, as if he had not forgotten the treatment he had received from their party in 1765: and the king even cautioned me against allowing their advice to be too prevalent. But the engaging manners of the two lords overcame by degrees all the prejudice there might have been against the whole party, and their habits and principles of government entitled them more to Court favor, perhaps, than mine.

In the House of Lords this accession of strength was essentially felt; and damped every expectation which the other parts of Opposition might have formed to have embarrassed the Administration.

However Lord Weymouth lay open to an attack, which

was not missed, and which his lordship had expected : though
we had been obliged to adjourn over by the Xmas Recess
the day, on which Lord Weymouth had moved to summon
the House 'to consider the state of the nation,' but, the
circumstance was never treated in a serious manner.

An incident happened before the close of this year 1767
which would not have been noticed here, had it not, in its
effects, occasioned very perplexing difficulties, and given much
uneasiness to the king's servants : but it may help to shew
what then was the disposition of Lord Chatham towards the
Ministry; for it ended in his reassumption of the Privy Seal.

Lord Botetourt, much attached to Lord Bute, and considered to be wholly devoted to His Majesty, (in whose bed
chamber he ambitioned to be placed) had embarked great
part of his fortune, speculating on the expectation of vast
profits from some great manufacturing company in the west.
In the process of this affair, a *Caveat* was entered, in the
Privy Seal Office, against the scheme ; and, (as far as I now
recollect) against incorporating the Company[1]. The delay of
the cause before the Privy Seal, Lord Botetourt stated to be
ruinous to his property ; and he sometimes threatened, that
he would bring up his complaint to shew, that the public
justice was impeded by the long absence of the Lord Privy
Seal, and that he would pray for a redress of so great a
grievance.   With the assistance of some friends, we succeeded
so far, as to keep his lordship for some time tolerably calm.
But, after Christmas all our intreaties were of no avail: his
violent importunities reached Lord Chatham, and determined
him to desire leave to resign the Seal.

Whether Lord Chatham had conceived, or had it intimated
to him, that this might be a manœuvre, contrived by those,

---

[1] Lord Bottetort appears to have contemplated a fraud on his creditors by
incorporating a Company on such terms
as would save his private estates from
the creditors of the Company of which
he was a member.   Sir Denis Le Marchant in a note to Walpole, *Memoirs*,
iii. 152, states that the patent did not,
in the end, pass the Commissioners of
the Privy Seal. Lord Bottetort, as Nor-
borne Berkeley, had represented Glou-
cestershire. He was appointed Governor
of Virginia in August of this year and
died there in 1770.

who were styled the king's *friends* in order to offend him,
I know not: but, if ever he had a notion of the kind, it is
plain that he did not long retain it; as he so readily
acquiesced in the expedient, which was proposed, for the
return of the Seal into his hands.   Besides, what purpose
could have been answered by losing the credit of Lord
Chatham's name, though he was unable to assist with his
counsels? And in what situation would these nominal friends
have placed him, where his influence could have been less
formidable to them?

A letter, similar to that I received from Lord Botetourt
and probably one as abrupt; had occasioned Lord Chatham's
message to me.

I insert Lord Botetourt's to me, together with my answer.

MY LORD,

Your Grace's fair and noble manners, entitle you to notice, that
I mean to-morrow to move the House, that a day be appointed and lords
summoned, in order to take under consideration a matter of justice, and
to declare that I shall then complain of the Earl of Chatham for delay in
his office.   I have the honor to be, with the utmost respect, my lord,

Your Grace's very devoted humble ser^t.

BOTETOURT.

SUFFOLK ST.
Jan^{ry}. 19th, 1768.

GROSVENOR SQUARE,
Jan^{ry}. 19th, 1768, at night.

MY LORD,

Your lordship has surprized me by your letter, declaring your resolution to make a motion to the House of Lords, which so materially affects
Lord Chatham's present situation in the king's service.   This step is so
important in every light, to your lordship, to the king, and to the publick
that I should hope you will not precipitate the matter so suddenly, whilst
most of the king's servants are as yet unacquainted with the circumstances
of your lordship's case, and have had no possible opportunity hitherto to
take it into their consideration: nor can I think your lordship would wish
to do so before you have received His Majesty's final answer, which has
not as yet been given to your lordship; His Majesty desiring further time,
before he signified his opinion on the subject: and therefore I wish your
lordship to consider whether you can, consistent with duty to the king,
make this business publick before you have received that answer; too

important perhaps for His Majesty to choose to deliver to your lordship, before he can have consulted his principal servants.

Therefore, I would entreat your lordship, to delay it for a little time, that we may be able to turn it in our thoughts, in order to give your lordship the best satisfaction the nature of the case will admit.

I have the honor to be &c. &c.

GRAFTON.

The morning following, Lord Botetourt, by a short letter, promised me, that he would not *utter* on the subject, till he saw me.

In the audience I had of His Majesty, wherein I laid before him the letter I had prepared to be sent directly to Lord Chatham, the king not only concurred in every part of it; but likewise told me that he should express it in a letter, which he intended to write in his own hand to his lordship, on this occasion. What follows is a copy of my letter, and the answer to it.

GROSVENOR SQUARE,
Jan^{ry}. 21st, 1768.

MY DEAR LORD,

M^r. James Grenville having just left me after having communicated a message from your lordship, contained in an answer to a letter he had wrote, without the knowledge of Lord Chancellor or of myself, it puts me under the necessity of troubling your lordship with this letter. My first business must be, to assure your lordship that the hopes and expectations of your return to the head of affairs were never of more importance to the king's service than at this moment, consequently your holding the office you are in is of no less necessity. I will next add to what you owe to His Majesty and the public, the right those have to claim it from your lordship, who have remained in the king's service, and particularly myself, who came into, and remained in my present office solely at your instigation, and who have gone through difficulties inexpressible, prompted to it by my zeal for the king's service, and thinking that it might be the means of furnishing again to your lordship the opening of serving your king and country with the lustre you have done. After having expressed the obligation, (the word is not too strong), you are really under to us all, as well as the service that the king may, and does expect from your lordship's recovery, I would suggest to your lordship an expedient, as natural as it has been usual, to remove this difficulty, which the peculiar character of the noble lord who presses his grant seems to make necessary. For on one hand no persuasion has weight with him, and if threats were added, he is of a temper more likely to add it to his complaint than to

drop from thence his resolution; on the other, I dread alike the bankruptcy
of the Company he is engaged in; when, if it should happen, as certainly
as falsely the illnatured clamours of the world will lay their ruin to the
grant having been delayed and not heard before the Privy Seal.

When the Bishop of Bristol was absent long for the Peace of Utrecht
there was a Commission of Clerks of the Council &c. to hold the Privy
Seal though he enjoyed the title, and signed the treaty under the name
and in the full possession of his office. The same was done when the
Duke of Bedford went to Paris, and I am confident if the office was
searched, twenty other precedents if they were wanted might be found.
Thus, my dear lord, might this intricate matter be easily unravelled; the
grant of this unreasonable lord heard by the assessors, whom these commissioners would call in, the hope of the public of seeing your lordship
return to the head of affairs not disappointed, the only flattering side
which has given me courage to surmount so many difficulties still assisting me to persevere, and lastly His Majesty continuing to hope that he
may be aided by your lordship's counsel, certain to add glory to the
king's reign, and dignity to his government. These, my dear lord, I may
venture to assert from the truest knowledge, are also His Majesty's
wishes. They are too great for you to resist, considering from what
different quarters they spring, unless your own judgment can suggest any
more eligible expedient and such as may be capable to answer these
purposes.

I have the honor to be &c. &c.

GRAFTON.

HAYES, Friday night,

½ past 8, Jan^{ry}. 22^d, 1768.

MY LORD,

The gout not fixing, my lord is so extremely ill and weak that he is
under an absolute impossibility to write; begs your Grace will permit
him, under this most unfortunate circumstance to acknowledge by my
hand all your Grace's goodness and friendship, and in this situation,
being equal but to very few words, he desires to say only, with regard to
the Privy Seal, that, having nothing so much at heart as the king's most
gracious pleasure, and what is judged to be most for His Majesty's service,
he is all obedience with respect to the Commission, and feels in the
deepest manner the king's infinite goodness. He trusts the Duke of
Grafton is persuaded how much his Grace's wishes ever weigh with him;
and hopes the conciseness of this answer to his Grace's most obliging
letter will be pardoned by him.

I have the honor to be
with the highest esteem and respect my lord,
Your Grace's most obed^t. humble servant,

H. CHATHAM.

Thus was this business terminated, after having given many of us much trouble and concern: the caveat was duly heard by the commissioners and their assessors; and the Privy Seal returned to Lord Chatham through his friend Lord Camden.

This last session of the Parliament passed without much struggle: but ministers were not allowed long to enjoy this peaceful state. Other distressing circumstances were rising, and quickly after the dissolution, made their appearance.

A beginning, however, was made, towards a better system of government in Ireland; but, it was a beginning only, and ought to have been carried on further, gradually establishing, by equitable laws, the comforts of society in that kingdom. The Octennial Act, which now passed, paved the way; and had it been prudently followed up, might have rendered that country satisfied, and happy, and seeking no longer any other connexion, since the kind and considerate conduct of Britain became so evident towards the sister kingdom. Thirty seven years however have now elapsed; and who will say that Ireland can possibly be expected to lend its due strength to the empire, till very different modes of governing that country shall be allowed to take place?

The scarcity of corn, and the high price of provisions of every kind, had been continual for two years, and more: and its pernicious consequences were now felt through the spirit of discontent and riot which broke out in many parts of the kingdom, but was most serious in and about the metropolis; notwithstanding all had been done that could be thought capable of relieving the distress of the lower orders especially.

On the river, the outrages committed by the coal-heavers and sailors, and against each other in formidable numbers, were to a great degree alarming. Several of each body were murdered by the other party. The seamen would neither engage, nor suffer any ship to sail, till the merchants had articled to give 35s. a month to each man, alledging, that their families would be starving in their absence; and on the day of the meeting of the Parliament, they assembled in great numbers in order to come down, with some appearance of regularity, to petition the two Houses. At last, being advised by several persons to disperse quietly, they did so, after having been for some time in both palace yards.

It was extraordinary that this combination of the seamen was not foreseen by the merchants, in a case wherein they were so much interested : for, if the slightest information had reached the Admiralty, a few frigates, and light vessels brought up the river would easily have supported the civil power in preventing every outrage.

The coal-heavers were clamorous for higher pay, and incensed against the seamen, who would not allow a stroke of work to be done by any of their people towards unlading the colliers, or other ships. The trade suffered considerably by these delays; for, it was not till the month of July that the sailors took fairly to their work [1].

Artisans of almost every denomination also combined for an advance of wages, and their discontents and disobedience to the laws, led them to join often, in numbers, those mobs which the consequence of the election for Middlesex frequently produced.

Before I enter at all into the business of the Middlesex Election, which I shall dive into no deeper than the object of this memoir requires, I wish to lay all before you, that had passed between M^r. Wilkes and myself previously to that epoch.

M^r. Wilkes may have dined with me twice or thrice; and though I sometimes have met him at the Political Club, and on visits to some of my friends, my acquaintance never went so far as ever to be in a room alone with him, at any time.

---

[1] For an account of these strikes, and of the spirit of riot and disorder which prevailed, see Lecky, *History of England*, iii. 125.

Walpole, *Memoirs*, iii. 219, gives a graphic account of the siege of the house of one Green, who was obnoxious to the coalheavers. Green killed eighteen of his assailants, and escaped after a siege of nine hours; but a few days later, his sister, while giving a supper in honour of his escape, was dragged into the street and murdered. Walpole comments on such things happening 'in a vast capital —free, ungoverned, unpoliced, and indifferent to everything but its pleasures, and factions.'

In Spring 1763, returning from Newmarket, I heard that Mr. Wilkes was confined (a *close* prisoner) in the Tower, on a bailable offence. The circumstance appeared to me so very oppressive and unjustifiable, that I proposed to walk thither the next morning in order to be fully satisfied as to the fact. Lord Villiers and Ld. Middleton[1] accompanied me: and being let into the house of the Major of the Tower, we were shewn the warrant of the commitment, but were refused the liberty to see his prisoner; though the major treated us with great politeness.

Some of Mr. Wilkes's friends applied to the Court of Common Pleas for a writ of Habeas Corpus; under which he was to be brought before the Court. While this transaction was proceeding, he wrote to me the letter which follows.

Tower, *May* 3d, 1763.

My Lord,

I want words to express the gratitude of my heart to your Grace for the honor of your regards to me here. I suffer in the cause of liberty, of which your Grace has already stood forth the great protector. If it is thought adviseable for me to put in bail, in order to recover my liberty, would it be trespassing too much on your Grace's goodness to beg the sanction of your name, in conjunction with some other nobleman. Give me leave, my lord, to add that it is only a sanction, for no consideration could induce me to desert so glorious a cause, which I wish to see, I believe much more than Government itself, decided by the justice of my country.

I am to be carried down in half an hour to Westminster, where if your Grace will favour me with an answer, you will add to the obligations I have already receiv'd, and if possible, to the infinite respect, with which I have the honor to be,

My lord,
Your Grace's most obedt.
and most humble servant,
JOHN WILKES.

Tuesday, the fourth day of my imprisonment.

On the receipt of this letter, at my return home, I thought it better to write to Lord Temple, desiring his lordship to make my excuse, as soon as he saw Mr. Wilkes. My letter is here inserted.

---

[1] Henry, fifth Lord Middleton (1726–1800).

BOND ST., *May* 3ᵈ, 1763.

MY DEAR LORD,

I sit down to open my situation to your lordship with much less apprehension than I should do to most of my friends, since I have seen so many instances of your goodness, I may say partiality to me. A letter from Mʳ. Wilkes, which I enclose, came to me while I was out a riding this morning: your lordship will see the purport of it and as it is now too late to send him any answer, I flatter myself you will add this to many other obligations and that you will tell him how I stood circumstanced the first time you either see, or write to him. In short, my lord, I went as I think every acquaintance is almost bound to do, to see Mʳ. Wilkes in his confinement, to hear from himself his own story and his defence; and to shew that no influence ought to stop the means of every man's justifying himself from an accusation, even though it should be of the most heinous kind. Hearing the shyness of lawyers in general to undertake his cause, as also the manner (perhaps unwarrantable) of his confinement, I was more desirous than ever to shew, that as far as my small power could extend, no subject of this country should want my countenance against oppression. But, my lord, when I look upon myself as called in to bail, tho' it had been for the person in the world who had the most right to have asked that sort of favor from me, I must nevertheless have trod very warily on ground that seemed to come any ways under the denomination of an insult on the Crown. That, my lord, is, and always has been a rule laid down by me which I will most religiously observe, that nothing in which I engage against His Majesty's ministers, whom I disapprove, shall ever be carried on by me with the shadow of offence against his person or family.

The consistency of my character, will I hope therefore be my excuse to him, I am confident it will be to your lordship, which I most desire. I might add to this, that on talking this point over with my relations, I have given them my opinion and assured them that my meaning was only to go as far as I have represented to your lordship, to whom,

I have the honor to be &c. &c.

GRAFTON.

P.S.—I am authoriz'd to say the same motive induced Lord Villiers to accompany me to see Mʳ. W.

Lord Temple's answer was the following:

PALL MALL, *May* 3ᵈ, 1763.

MY DEAR LORD,

Having received from Mʳ. Wilkes a request similar to that which he had the honor of making to your Grace, I instantly complied with it and as I heard of his intention of applying to you, I was desirous of waiting upon your Grace this morning in order to explain to you the motives which had determined me to lend myself with pleasure to his desire. No man in the kingdom can bear a more dutiful regard than I do to the Crown, or is more full of veneration for His Majesty than myself, at the same time I hope there is not any man in the kingdom more ready to stand forth, as far as in me lies, the zealous protector of the liberty of the subject. Without entering into the question whether M^r. Wilkes be, or be not the author of the last North Briton and whether it be libellous or not, I think he has been proceeded against in a manner that ought to give a just alarm to every true friend of this Constitution; in that light I hold it an honour to be his bail, and so does the Duke of Bolton [1], who on the same principle has voluntarily offered himself. If your Grace could have seen this matter in the same way, I think an opportunity was offered to you of shewing to the world in an amiable light one of the great and amiable qualities, which are already so universally recognized in your Grace. Allow me to assure you, no man honors you more than I do, and that I am, with sincere respect,

My dear lord,

Your Grace's most obed^t.

and most humble servant,

TEMPLE [2].

I beg you will excuse this scrawl, from the extreme hurry in which I write.

M^r. Wilkes soon after went abroad, and his return was announced to me by the following letter, which surprized me much, as he was under a verdict of outlawry.

Novr. 1st, 1766.

MY LORD,

It is a very peculiar satisfaction I feel on my return to my native country, that a nobleman, of your Grace's superior talents and inflexible integrity is at the head of the most important department of the State. I have been witness of the general applause which has been given abroad to the choice His Majesty has made, and I am happy to find my own countrymen zealous and unanimous in every testimony of their approbation.

I hope, my lord, that I may congratulate myself as well as my country on your Grace's being placed in a station of so great power and importance. Though I have been cut off from the body of His Majesty's subjects by a cruel and unjust proscription, I have never entertained an

---

[1] Charles, fifth Duke of Bolton (1718–1765), he died unmarried, and with his brother who succeeded him the title expired.

[2] In the *Grenville Papers*, ii. 53, the Duke of Grafton's letter is printed, but not the reply. Lord Temple's answer was written in haste, and he kept no copy of it.

idea inconsistent with the duty of a good subject. My heart still retains all its former warmth for the dignity of England, and the glory of its Sovereign. I have not associated with the traitors to our liberties, nor made a single connection with any man who was dangerous, or even suspected by the friends of the Protestant family on the throne. I now hope that the rigour of an unmerited exile is past, and that I may be allowed to continue in the land and among the friends of liberty.

I wish, my lord, to owe this to the mercy of my Prince. I entreat you to lay me with all humility at the king's feet, with the truest assurances that I have never in any moment of my life, swerv'd from the duty and allegiance I owe to my Sovereign, and that I implore and in every thing submit to His Majesty's clemency.

Your Grace's noble manner of thinking, and the obligations I have formerly receiv'd, which are still fresh in my mind, will I hope give a full propriety to this address, and I am sure a heart glowing with the sacred zeal of liberty must have a favorable reception from the Duke of Grafton. I flatter myself that my conduct will justify your Grace's interceding with a Prince, who is distinguished by a compassionate tenderness to all his subjects.

I am, with the truest respect,

My lord, Your Grace's

Most obed^t. humble serv^t.

JOHN WILKES.

Considering it to be my duty, I both mentioned the letter I had received, and showed it to His Majesty who, as well as I recollect, read it with attention ; but made no observation upon it. Lord Chatham, on reading it remarked on the awkwardness of the business, with which it was so difficult to meddle ; and on my pressing to know what was to be done, he answered : ' the better way, I believe at present, is to take no notice of it.' And his advice I followed. The session opened in a week after; and from the hurry of weighty business, the concerns of M^r. Wilkes engaged but little the attention of Ministry, or indeed of the Court. To some of his friends, who once or twice pressed me to intercede for a pardon, I constantly replied, that I thought my shoulders were not yet equal to the business, and that I conceived the weight of Lord Chatham's name could alone effect it : though I added, that there would be no step taken from the side of Administration to molest M^r. Wilkes, or in any way disturb

O

him in his present situation; and that I hoped all other quarters might be as well disposed to favor him. So little indeed was there a desire of molesting M^r. Wilkes that I firmly believe, had he not stepped forward as the chieftain of riot and disturbance, he might have remained unnoticed, as long as he had lived.

His appearance on the hustings as a candidate for the City, at the general election, was as sudden as it was unexpected by us all. On his failure there, he offered himself for the County of Middlesex; and by the assistance of many and considerable mobs stopping up every avenue to Brentford, even at the distance of some miles, he was returned first on the poll, many of the freeholders of the other side being prevented, or intimidated from giving their votes.

You will think, that I have dwelt longer than was necessary on the particulars of my acquaintance with this gentleman: but I had a mind that you should know the extent of my knowledge of him; especially, as I have been represented as one of his intimates. I do not mean to be equally prolix on the transactions concerning him [1], either in Parliament, or in

---

[1] The position of Wilkes, now, and during the remainder of this Parliament may be shortly stated for the convenience of the reader.

In 1764 Wilkes had been expelled the House of Commons for having written and published a scandalous and seditious libel (*The North Briton*, No. 45): he was subsequently tried and convicted for reprinting the same libel, and for blasphemous and obscene libels contained in the publication of the *Essay on Woman*. He did not appear to receive sentence, and was outlawed.

In 1768 he returned to England, despite his outlawry, for the general election. He might have asked for a pardon with some chance of success, but this he refused to do. He stood for the City unsuccessfully: then for Middlesex, and was returned on March 28.

On April 20 he surrendered to his outlawry, and on the 27th Lord Mansfield held the outlawry to have been unlawful, and void.

The conviction, however, was still outstanding: he appeared to receive sentence on June 20, and was sentenced to one year's imprisonment, and a fine of £500, on each of the two charges—seditions, and obscene and blasphemous libel. Every stage of the proceedings was marked by riot and disorder.

In one of these riots Lord Weymouth, the Secretary of State, wrote to the Chairman of Quarter Sessions at Lambeth, telling him not to hesitate in calling military force to his aid. Wilkes obtained a copy of this letter, and in December, 1768, sent it to the *St. James' Chronicle*, with a note describing it as 'a hellish project, brooded over by some infernal spirits.'

The Lords asked for a conference with

the Court of King's Bench, because these are related minutely in many publications, which save me that trouble ; and I shall content myself with producing the remarks only, which the papers I have before me can furnish. If I was asked, as to my opinion on this perplexing subject, I should readily answer, that on the first step of expulsion, all dignity was gone from the house, if they could admit a person under a verdict of outlawry, to sit one hour, as a member of it. When he was returned member again and again, I cannot see why the repetition of an insult to the House of Commons should have altered the right, provided it be granted, that it had existed. The two Houses must separately be sole judges of the seats of their members. Destroy that right, and their independance is gone : for where else can it be placed ? The most just rights and powers may be abused, but it does not follow, that they are to be abolished, unless it can be shewn that they may be placed elsewhere, without injury to the Constitution. However, the frequent and repeated struggles to set aside the election of a person, though under such a stigma, gave occasion to keep alive a spirit of riot, which, becoming every day more violent, threatened to bring on a disrespect to all government and lawful authority. Whether the decision of the House of Commons, that Col. Luttrell was duly elected, who had not by a great many, the number of voices which Mr. Wilkes had was in strict justice determined, I will not take upon me to decide. But sure I am, that in the temper of those times, when the public were more than alive

the Commons, and invited them to concur in voting this publication to be a scandalous and seditious libel.

It was argued in vain that the question of libel was for the Courts, and that if there was a question of privilege it concerned the Lords. The House of Commons voted the paper to be a libel, and on February 3, 1769, Wilkes was expelled, on the motion of Lord Barrington, for being the author of the libel on Lord Weymouth, of No. 45, of the *Essay on Woman*, and for being under sentence of imprisonment.

He was re-elected in February, in March, and in April ; his election was in each case declared void, and himself incapable of sitting in that Parliament.

On April 15 the House resolved that Colonel Luttrell, whom he had defeated on the 13th by 1,143 votes to 296, ought to have been returned, and this resolution was upheld on petition on May 8.

to every constitutional question, anarchy and confusion would soon have followed, in case the repetitions of Brentford election, and votes of expulsion had not been stopped in some manner: and how they would have been terminated without greater objections, I am not able to say. Lord Mansfield afterwards in 1770, maintained, 'that a question touching the seat of a member, in the Lower House, could only be determined by that House: there was no other Court, where it could be tried, nor to which there could be an appeal[1].'

A mob, which had been so useful to M^r. Wilkes at Brentford, was soon succeeded by another, wishing to conduct him in triumph to the House of Commons from the King's Bench prison to which he had been committed: and the tumult was so great on the occasion, that the magistrates were compelled to read the Riot Act, and to call on the military to support them in so doing. The unfortunate death of a young man, whether he was an innocent spectator, or not, exasperated this mob to a high pitch against the soldiery; and added greatly to that confusion which sailors, coal-heavers, and other bodies of men had brought on, demanding generally an increase of their wages. Many persons, I am sorry to say, lost their lives in most of these risings; and many were found guilty, and several of the most desperate suffered for their crimes.

It was injuriously imagined, that there was a willing disposition in the Court, and among the members of Administration to persecute M^r. Wilkes on account of former offences. I owe it to my colleagues to give my testimony against such a calumny: and I am persuaded, that His Majesty himself would readily have approved, in this case, whatever measure his principal servants had recommended[2]. Within the Court,

---

[1] Lord Mansfield had authority on his side, for the House of Commons, in 1712, had treated Walpole as they treated Wilkes in 1769. But Chatham put the matter in its true light when he said, 'the county of Middlesex chose a gentleman *in no way incapacitated* by the law of the land' (*Parl. Hist.* xvi. 958). Expulsion marks the disapproval of the House of Commons, it does not create a legal incapacity.

[2] Lord Barrington, in moving that Wilkes should be expelled, and speaking of the conduct of Wilkes on his

there may have been, and certainly were, some individuals, who would gladly have seen the author of the North Briton smart for all the lashes he had laid on others[1]. But let not the innocent bear the reproach of faults, which cannot be justly brought to their charge.

If there was blame in our measures, it may be equally imputed to the majority of those, who composed the larger meetings which the minister of the House of Commons usually assembled to advise with, on all weighty matters. And, so little was the measure premeditated or settled, that Lord North, in sending to me, in the country, an account of the opinions of his counsellors, told me that M^r. Dyson, who was present, would draw out the minute of proceeding, as nearly as possible to embrace the way of thinking of the largest number of the members who were consulted. This, I shall hope, will satisfy you, that there was no specific mode laid down for these gentlemen to approve; or which the Ministry wished to adopt. This excellent custom of summoning, on frequent occasions, those, who composed the Boards, Privy Counsellors, Attorney and Solicitor General, and all friendly members to take part in debate, has, I understand with much concern, been dropt of late: for, in my opinion, the disuse of this salutary practice leads by degrees to accustom a majority to place a more implicit confidence in a minister, than the principles of a free government can well admit[2].

It was Lord North's first intention to have had such a general meeting of those members of Parliament, to whom

---

return to England, said, 'from the lenient character of those who serve the Crown I believe a pardon would have been granted if properly applied for: and I for one would have been glad to have it brought about' (*Cavendish Debates*, i. 151).

[1] The Ministry might have escaped much blame if the House of Commons had been left to itself in a matter which mainly concerned itself. But the vote of expulsion was moved by the Secretary at War, and the incapacitating vote by Lord Strange, a placeman and 'king's friend,' who had played an active part in embarrassing the Rockingham Ministry (*Rockingham Memoirs*, i. 300).

[2] The practice referred to seems to relieve the Leader of the House from a responsibility which properly belongs to him.

communications are usually made, and they had notices sent to them : but he afterwards thought it would be better, previously, to take the sense of the members who were of the Cabinet, together with the lawyers : and notes were sent, postponing the attendance of the other persons, who had been summoned. The meeting then consisted of M^r. Conway, Lord Granby, S^r. Edward Hawke, Master of the Rolls, Attorney and Solicitor General, Hussey, Thurlow, Moreton [1], Dyson, with the two Secretaries of the Treasury: M^r. Rigby, M^r. Townshend, and M^r. James Grenville, who did not receive the second notes, attended in consequence of the first.

Lord North very ably opened the purpose of the meeting : M^r. Dyson stated the precedents of expulsion: and the Attorney General informed the company what had passed in the Courts, and in what particular situations M^r. Wilkes might stand, at the meeting of Parliament, as an outlaw, or as suffering an infamous punishment, in consequence of his conviction. M^r. Hussey was strongly against a second expulsion for the same offence, *in being the author of a political libel*; for he said, his conviction for the poem could not be thought of in the House of Commons, without coupling it with the means used to obtain evidence against him.—In a word, the greater part of the company seemed struck with M^r. Hussey's objections; but my correspondent, who was present, says, that he thinks it might be collected, that all, except M^r. Hussey himself, will be for expelling Wilkes, upon the double ground of outlawry and conviction; and M^r. Conway declared as much before he went away.

The meeting was not called upon to declare the part they respectively meant to take, nor, were they informed that Government had come to any resolution upon the subject of Mr. Wilkes.

Lord North sent circular letters, requesting a full attendance, at the opening of the session : for, besides whatever might be determined as to the case of Wilkes, it was necessary; as

---

[1] John Moreton, Chief Justice of Chester.

there was reason to believe that an attempt would be made
to place M^r. Dowdeswell in the chair as Speaker.

On the first consultation in the Cabinet on the management
in Parliament M^r. Wilkes being chosen Member for Middlesex,
there did not appear to the Lord Chancellor, or to any of us,
the difficulties, which after arose. Lord Camden, soon after
altered his opinion, as the letters I insert from his lordship
(which are all I find on this subject) describe. It was much
to be lamented, that Administration were at so early a period
of this business, deprived of the advice of this great lawyer
whom posterity will justly rank among the most able, learned
and distinguished of our Chancellors, both in Parliament and
in the Courts of Westminster Hall.

MY DEAR LORD DUKE,

Whatever vexation and inconvenience I may feel at this unexpected
summons, which calls me from hence above a week before the time, yet
I shall without fail give my attendance at the time appointed. The
event is disagreeable, and unforeseen, for I am persuaded that no person
living, after Wilkes had been defeated in London would have thought it
possible for him to have carry'd his election for the County of Middlesex.
Sure I am, that if the Government had arrested him while he was
a candidate, that step would have secured his election, and would have
been considered as the cause of his success, if it had been taken.
I cannot pretend at this distance without further information to advise
what proceedings are now necessary to be taken, but the only subject for
consideration seems to be what measures are to be taken by the House
of Commons at the meeting of the Parliament. If the precedents and the
Constitution will warrant an expulsion that perhaps may be right.
A criminal flying his country to escape justice—a convict and an
outlaw—That such a person should in open daylight thrust himself upon
the country as a candidate, his crime unexpiated, is audacious beyond
description.

This is the light in which I consider the affair, the riot only inflaming
the business, for that does no more shew the weakness of Government
than any other election riot in the kingdom. But it would be well to
consider, what may be the consequence if W. should be reelected. That
is very serious. I take it for granted that he will surrender and sue in his
judgment in the K. Bench the first day of the term, when I suppose the
outlawry will be reversed, and he imprisoned. We expect him at this
place to-night, where I suppose he intends to remain till the term, and

this town is not a little alarmed least the same spirit of violence should follow him hither. But I trust we are not mad enough here to follow the example of the metropolis.

Whatever may be the heat of the present moment, I am persuaded it will soon subside, and this gentleman will lose his popularity in a very short time after men have recover'd their senses.

I am my dear lord with the
most perfect attachment and respect
Y^r. Grace's most obed^t. faithful
Servt. CAMDEN.

April 3rd, 1768,
BATH.

MY DEAR LORD,

I dare say you have been informed of what passed to-day in the Court of King's Bench, and that Mr. W. is still at large. His counsel however promised, that he should be forthcoming in custody, and then move to be bailed, sue out a writ of error, and reverse his outlawry : they gave notice likewise, that they intended after they had got rid of the outlawry, to move in arrest of judgement. Your Grace will be pleased to understand, that Mr. W. stands at present *convicted* only by *verdict* : and if there shall appear to be any material defect in the record, that the judgement must be stayed : in which case, he must be discharged, and he becomes a free man upon this prosecution, as much as if he had never been convicted.

I dare say your Grace will see, upon this short representation, that till judgement is finally pronounced against Mr. W. by the Court, no man has a right to pronounce him guilty, more especially, as he *appears*, and intends to object in arrest of judgement.

This appears to me a real difficulty attending the measure, which yesterday we thought so clear.

For, how can the House expel a member, either as an outlaw, or a convict, while the suit is pending, wherein he may turn out at last, to be neither the one, nor the other.

Ward[1] was expelled upon his conviction; but, I observe in looking into the Journal, that he absconded, and so it was reported to the House, upon a summons delivered at his last place of abode; so that not attending upon this summons—he was expelled—tho' judgement was not

---

[1] This must be John Ward, expelled the House in 1727 after conviction for forgery. A conviction for felony would now be a statutory disqualification, but until 1870, a person so convicted would be regarded as not 'fit and proper' within the meaning of the writ addressed to the sheriff. Lord Camden takes no account of the fact that Ward was convicted of felony, Wilkes of misdemeanour.

pronounced at that time.   I am afraid, considering the necessary delay in
courts of law, it will be impossible for the King's Bench to give judgement before the Parliament meets ; and therefore, it deserves the most
serious consideration, whether the proposed measure should be pursued,
while this obstacle stands in the way.

Your Grace will be pleased to observe, that Mr. W. was expelled not
for the crime of the libel, but for having slandered the Parliament.

I have the honor to be, with the truest zeal and
attachment your Grace's most obed^t. faithful ser^t.

CAMDEN.

April 20th, 1768.

MY DEAR LORD,

I have the honour of your Grace's letter, and will certainly attend the
meeting of the king's servants on Wednesday morn^g. next.   I do wish
most heartily that the present time could be eased of the difficulties that
Mr. W.'s business has brought upon Government: a fatality has attended
it from the beginning, and it grows more serious every day.   Your Grace
and I have unfortunately differ'd.   I wish it had been otherwise.   It is
a hydra multiplying by resistance and gathering strength by every
attempt to subdue it.   As the times are, I had rather pardon W. than
punish him.   This is a political opinion independant of the merits of the
cause.

I am very glad to hear the holydays have given your Grace so happy
a respite.   They have been to me a perfect paradise, as I have employ'd
my whole time in studying the Douglas cause, and my mind has been
totally vacant from political vexation.

I have the honour to be
with the greatest sincerity
Y^r. Grace's most obed^t.
Faithful serv^t.

CAMDEN.

Jan^{ry}. 9th, 1769,
CAMDEN PLACE.

Late at night April 26th M^r. Wilkes gave notice to the
Attorney General, that he would surrender the next morning ;
and he accordingly delivered himself into the custody of one
of the Sheriff's officers, and was brought into Court, when the
writ of error was granted upon his outlawry : his Council
then moved that he might be bailed under the Statute of
King William, which was argued till past 6 o'clock, and the
Court determined that an outlawry after conviction was not

bailable by that Statute, and that he had not made out a case which entitled him to be admitted to bail, under the discretionary powers vested in the Court: he was therefore ordered to be committed to the King's Bench prison, and as he was going there in a coach, a mob took off the horses, turned the marshall of the prison out of the coach, and drew M^r. Wilkes in triumph to Spital-fields, from whence it was supposed, the mob had been collected.   However, as soon as he could effect it, M^r. Wilkes came alone in a hackney coach to the prison.

The disposition to riot and disorder, encouraging a resistance to all legal authority even among the seamen, not being sufficiently subsided, it was not thought adviseable to prorogue the Parliament, but, by adjourning only, to have the means of assembling it shortly on any emergency.

On the 2nd of June, M^r. Bradshaw [1], one of the Secretaries of the Treasury, on the occasion, writes thus to me, who was in the country;

'Lord North went to the king this morning, and received his commands for adjourning Parliament to the 21st instant, which His Majesty very much approved: Lord Chancellor had proposed yesterday, the adjournment for one week only; at the end of which, he hoped there might have been a prorogation: I waited on him, late last night, at Lord North's desire, and informed him of your Grace's opinion, in which Lord North entirely agreed, and he approved of Lord North's seeing the king, and obtaining his consent for an adjournment of three weeks— Lord Chancellor's wishes for a speedy prorogation arise, not only from the dislike of Wilkes's business being brought to Parliament, after the decision of the Court of King's Bench : but, that suits may be carried on against members, which the long continuance of privilege has prevented for four terms.

The petition from the merchants was, by the interest of M^r. Maitland, and some other friends, laid aside for the present; but S^r. Joseph Mawbey [2] had a petition for a free and general importation of provisions, signed by the principal traders in the borough : however, Lord North came early to the House, and signified His Majesty's pleasure, that they should adjourn to the 21st before S^r. Joseph had brought his petition : the House of Lords was also adjourned; and nothing passed in either

---

[1] Bradshaw had been a clerk in the War Office, he was now private Secretary to the Duke, and appears to have in-   curred the special animosity of Junius.
[2] M.P. for Southwark.

House. Lord Chancellor told me, he had mentioned the North Briton to the king, and that His Majesty had desired him to give directions for the printer's being prosecuted: in consequence of which, he had spoken to Lord Shelburne to have a case prepared, for the opinion of the Attorney and Solicitor General; and I understand from Nuthall, that they are to give their opinion on Saturday.

I have the satisfaction to inform your Grace, that the seamen remain quiet, and by a note from Cockburne, I find, that the ships that were stopt have got their men again, and are preparing to sail.

Mr. Nuthall (Solicitor of the Treasury) assures me, he will spare no pains to discover the promoters of these riots; and he has people employed to find means, if possible, of bringing the authors of the late murders to punishment.

I have the honor to be &c. &c.

THO^s. BRADSHAW.

From this adjournment, the Parliament was prorogued to November; as every thing appeared to be returning to their usual courses.

At the beginning of the present reign, and soon after the resignation of M^r. Pitt, a proclamation issued, from what motive I know not, by which the insurgents in Corsica were to be considered by us as rebels to their lawful sovereign, the Republic of Genoa [1]. The Genoese profited but little from their assistance from us: for unable to suppress Paoli and his patriots, they were treating with the Duc de Choiseul for the surrender of the sovereignty of the island to France. This accession to the territories of the rival kingdom could not be palatable to our Government, nor to the nation; tho' I never could think that the possession of Corsica would add to the crown of France, the degree of advantage, which many were industriously giving out. And though, on his side, the French minister may have been rash, or wicked enough, to plunge his country into the horrors of war, through a restless ambition, our consciences would never have allowed us to advise, on this occasion, a re-commencement of hostilities.

[1] Corsica had been for long in a chronic state of rebellion against the Republic. Genoa now determined to sell its unruly possession to France. For a full account of the action of our ministers see Fitzmaurice, *Life of Shelburne*, ii. ch. 1.

However, short of a direct declaration, 'that war would be the inevitable consequence of the rashness of the French minister,' no measure was neglected to put him off from the plan he had formed. Lord Rochford who was the British Ambassador at Paris had received the fullest instructions; and his lordship conducted himself with dignified firmness and discretion throughout the business. At one time, he was confident that he should have succeeded, and wrote over, that the Duc de Choiseul's language had so much softened, that his lordship had every hope, that the French minister would not risk the attempt. In the audience of the next week, Lord Rochford found to his great surprize the former tone taken up: and in a private letter to me, he accounted for the strange change in the duke, to the imprudent declaration of a great law lord, then at Paris, at one of the minister's tables, 'that the English Ministry were too weak, and the nation too wise to support them in entering on a war for the sake of Corsica [1].'

This declaration might contribute more than any thing to reconcile Louis the 15th to his minister's project. The business was growing each day more serious. In the mean time, our surprize was great, that we had not one word of information, or application for assistance of any kind from General Paoli. On conversing in private with the Sardinian and Dutch ministers, we discovered that Paoli's silence could only be ascribed to the weight given to the above-mentioned proclamation, which had damped all his hopes of succour from Great Britain.

From these ministers I also learnt, that the cause of the insurgents had received some pecuniary assistance from their respective States; but, that Paoli stood in the greatest need of arms in particular, as well as money.

The gentleman dispatched from Lord Shelburne [2] to know

---

[1] This statement, made by Lord Mansfield, coupled with the language of Shelburne's opponents in the Cabinet, as reported to Choiseul by Châtelet the French minister in England, confirmed the French in their confidence that England would not fight for Corsica.

[2] Mr. John Stewart: his instructions from Lord Shelburne were to ascertain how far the French were prepared for

from the general himself the wants of the Corsicans, had been
directed to stop at more than one place in his way. The
Cabinet heard this account with much disappointment ; seeing
that it would probably frustrate their intentions of supplying
in time, every article that Paoli could wish for, excepting
a naval or military force : provided, that with such assistance,
he could make it appear that he could hold out any reasonable time.

Much vexed with the conduct of the business, as were my
colleagues who were enquiring earnestly for the speediest
communications with Paoli, I ventured to propose to them
to allow me their authority, in sending off the day following
an old acquaintance of mine, in whose honor I could confide,
and who should go through France by the shortest route.

The person I had in view to entrust with this message, was
Capitaine Dunant a Genévois, who had served with distinction
in the Swiss troops in the pay of the King of Sardinia. I saw
him the morning after our meeting, and had particular satisfaction in giving him his instructions, as he readily comprehended the commission entrusted to his management. A
testimony, that he was employed by me, in order to give him
credit with our *naval* officers in the Mediterranean, to whom
he might apply for assistance, was, from consideration for his
safety, nearly all that was delivered to him in writing. What
follows, is from a rough draft of the paper delivered to him.

MONSIEUR,

    Il convient aux affaires du roi mon maître, d'être informé au juste
de la disposition du Général P—— à l'égard de ce nouvel événement de
la cession que les Génois viennent de faire à la France des places & du
reste de l'Isle de Corse. L'amitié que j'ai pour vous & la connoissance
que j'ai eu de votre caractère depuis douze ans passés me fait penser qu'il
n'y a personne, par laquelle je puisse avoir cette information nécessaire
si bien qu'en vous chargeant de faire ce voyage. Je souhaite que vous
témoigniez à ce général que cette cour-ci ne peut regarder qu'avec
déplaisir cette démarche de la France, et en lui faisant voir cette lettre,

war, as well as the capacity of the Cor-   till the first week in August. His report
sicans for resistance. He left England   is to be found in Fitzmaurice, *Life of
in May, 1768, and did not reach Corsica   Shelburne*, ii. 141.

ce général ne pourra hésiter de vous parler sur les moyens qu'il a de
résister actuellement pour conserver la liberté de ces compatriotes puis
qu'elle montre la confiance que j'ai en vous.

J'ai l'honneur d'être &c. &c.

GRAFTON.

After a long conversation, necessary for explaining fully to
him the views of His Majesty and his servants, Capt. Dunant
set off that night. He posted through France : and finding
difficulty from Marseilles, to get over to the part of Corsica
occupied by the insurgents, he turned for Nice and Genoa,
and was fortunate in finding my relation, Captain, now
Admiral Cosby, at the latter place, who, immediately, as he
saw that Dunant was sent on a commission of mine, sailed
with him that very evening for Corsica.

On the night following, two Corsican captains came aboard
the Montreal, lying off Isola Rossa, who, understanding that
Captain Dunant wished to be introduced to the commandant,
offered to present him. Lieutenant Stanhope, one of the
officers of the Montreal went on shore with them ; and with
the commandant of Isola Rossa himself, they proceeded for
Corte. Captain Dunant found no difficulty in making it
evident, that he was really deputed from the British Court :
and though the Corsican chiefs were very mistrustful of all
strangers ; yet General Paoli received our Commissioner with
great frankness, civility, and joyful attention. He next
morning gave Captain Dunant a long audience, and at the
end of it permitted them to take down in writing the result,
dictating to him the following words.

Corte ce 24 de Juillet 1768. entre 11 heures et midi dans les apparte-
ments du Général Paoli.

Voici la réponse dictée par le même Général Paoli au Capitaine
Dunant ;

Le Général Paoli sera à la tête de sa nation : il combattra jusques au
dernier soupir, pour défendre et conserver la liberté de sa patrie.

Son peuple, animé du même sentiment, témoigne de l'empressement
d'en venir aux prises avec les François, qu'ils supposent alliés avec les
Génois, et avoir pris de concert des mesures, pour envahir leur liberté.
Lé Général a de la peine d'arrêter l'ardeur de la nation.

Dans la *Consulta Generale* de la nation Corse, le peuple s'est taxé lui-même, en contributions extraordinaires, de 4 (   ) pour mille livres de fonds: afin que le Général Paoli puisse augmenter le nombre de ses soldats payés ; pour pouvoir les maintenir toujours postés, vis-à-vis des François, dont ils sont aujourd'hui à la portée du pistolet ; pour empêcher qu'ils ne passent les limites.

Le Gén : Paoli a disposé un corps de 400 hommes, qui observe les troupes, qui occupent Ajaccio, et 100 autres la Pievo di Brando : Il a fait établir un cordon de troupes, depuis Brando à Patrimonio, pour couvrir le Capo Corso, dont on menace de couper la communication, et de l'envahir.

Les troupes Françaises, au nombre de 16 bataillons, et la Légion Royale, occupent la Bastia, Bonifacio, Ajaccio, Cabri, et San Fiorenzo ; où ils ont arboré leur pavillon.

En conséquence, les Corses sont postés à Feriano, Patrimonio, Bar-baggio, Tarinola, Olmeta, & Nonga. À la pointe du Cap, il y a des troupes Corses en avant, & elles occupent encore les hauteurs en face de S'. Fiorenzo, *ditte le Strette di Patrimonio*. En général l'isle est gardée par la nation Corse, dans tout son contour, par des compagnies de milice ; Et, dans chaque porte principale, le chef, ou commandant, par le moyen du signal de 2 coups de canon, peut rassembler 3, 4, à 5 mille hommes. Tout ce qui peut porter les armes dans toute la nation est prêt à se sacrifier, et n'a devant les yeux que la liberté, ou la mort.

Le Général Paoli étoit assuré, que la Cour d'Angleterre n'ignoroit point ses intentions, informé par celle de Turin, par ses Ministres aux Cours étrangères, & par le canal de plusieurs gentils-hommes Anglois, qui sont venus dans l'Isle de Corse, et qui sont en relation avec ce Général.

Le Général Paoli a besoin de tout ; d'argent, d'artillerie, et surtout de bâtimens armés, qui puissent en imposer à ceux des Français, qui croisent dans les bords de l'isle. De plus, il lui seroit important d'avoir d'une Espèce de petites pièces de campagne portatives sur des mulets ; et leur Dotte, d'être pourvu aussi d'un nombre suffisant de fusils, armés d'une bayonnette, tels que ceux de l'Infanterie Angloise.

With the preceding report, Cap^tn. Dunant delivered to me a Letter from the General, which is here added.

Corte 24 Luglio 1768.

ECCELLENZA,

Il Signor Capitano Dunant, che approdò l'altro jeri sopra fregata Inglese al nostro scalo dell' Isola rossa, giunse qui jeri accompagnato dal Sig^r Stanhope. tenente di detta fregata. Sebbene egli non mi abbia portata alcuna lettera dell' Eccellenza vostra a me diretta, mi ha però manifestata la lettera di credenza che lo autorizza a portarsi in Corsica, ed a trattar meco sulle circostanze presenti di quest' isola. Egli ha compita onorevolmente e con lodevole zelo la sua commissione, ed ho luogo a sperare che con altretanta fedeltà adempirà egualmente all incarico di ragguagliare l' Eccellenza vostra dello stato attuale degli affari di questa nazione sopra i quali abbiamo a lungo conferito, del costante mio impegno, non meno che di tutti questi popoli di sostenere e difendere con ogni possibile sforzo i diritti della commune libertà, e di contestarle nel tempo stesso i sentimenti della più grata riconoscenza per il generoso interesse che cotesta Corte si compiace di prendere a questo oggetto, unitamente a quelli della più perfetta rispettosa stima con cui ho l'onore di essere

Di vostra Eccellenza,

Devo^mo. obbiend^o. ser^te.

PASQUALI DI PAOLI.

There was nothing in Paoli's conference with Captain Dunant, which marked the smallest indication of dejection. He was confident of the attachment, and general support of his nation : and he made no doubt, that, with the succour of arms furnished to him, and the other articles he had mentioned, he should be able to defend himself for a considerable time ; at least for 18 months.

In the mean time, many of us had begun to entertain doubts, whether the Order of Council, before alluded to, must not necessarily be repealed. It was desirable to avoid that step, as it would be a publication of our intentions to send the assistance which Paoli asked for, our object being to effect it in such a manner, as should least risk a breach with France. The opinion of Lord Chancellor was clear, that the necessity no longer existed, and that, from the change of circumstances which had befallen the Corsicans, and had altered their condition without our privity or consent, the Order of Council was no longer to be regarded as in force. A moment was not lost in supplying most of the articles requested by the Corsicans ; and indeed many thousand stand of arms, under the good management of M^r. Boddington were so furnished from the stock in the Tower, as to give no indication that they were sent from our Government.

At the moment, however, we were enjoying the expectation

of seeing France baffled in her scheme, and her ambitious attempt, we had the vexation to find General Paoli himself obliged to give way, after several severe blows and losses, through the backwardness of his followers, and perhaps also the treachery of some, in whom he had too much confided. Compelled by these circumstances, Paoli got off soon to Leghorn ; and afterwards retired to England [1].

LETTER, 1768

GREAT GEORGE STREET,
31ˢᵗ *May*, 1768.

MY LORD,

I was very sorry to hear this morning from M^r. Cokburne, that the seamen assembled again last night ; they began with a streightsman, worth upwards of £90,000, out of which they took all the men by force, cut her tackle, and declared that no ship should sail, unless her seamen had 35^s. a month wages ; they afterwards served several other vessells in the same manner. It is much to be lamented that a sufficient force was not kept in the river, to prevent what has happen'd. The Admiralty are now sensible that such a force is necessary, and they have this day ordered nine cutters, two sloops, and two frigates in addition to the yachts, to be stationed between Gravesend, and Limehouse.

I waited upon Lord Weymouth, who desired me to acquaint your Grace, that he did not think it necessary to call you to town, before the time you intend to return ; he had heard of the rising of the seamen. I mentioned to him, that you thought a reward should be offer'd for the persons who committed the horrid murder of the sailor, but he seem'd to

---

[1] The Corsican affair showed the weakness of the Ministry, and the opportunities which their divided counsels offered to our enemies.

We might have treated the matter as one with which we were not concerned, and then we should not have suffered in prestige. We might, and Chatham certainly would, have told the French that we should treat the occupation of Corsica as a *casus belli*, and the weakness of the French navy at this time would almost certainly have caused the French to give way.

Shelburne was for a bold policy : the Bedford party was for peace at any price. Grafton adopted a half-and-half but wholly indefensible line of action, inquiring as to the fighting capabilities of Corsicans and French, supplying the rebels with arms, and thus showing at once his wishes and his powerlessness.

think the seamen had sufficiently revenged themselves upon the coal-heavers, many of whom they have put to death; and indeed Cokburne knows, from one of the men concerned, that four coalheavers were carried by the seamen to the middle of the river, and drowned, in revenge for the murder of their companion. Surely my lord, examples should be made of both parties, if sufficient proof can be obtained against them.

Lord North tells me, that the Speaker is very desirous Parliament should be prorogued, and not adjourn'd, on Thursday; his reason is, an apprehension, that, if the House meets after Wilkes's outlawry is decided in the Courts, it will be impossible to avoid taking up that matter, whatever the decision may be. I cannot but take the liberty of saying, that while his Parliamentary situation remains in doubt, the attempts to intimidate Administration, and to inflame the minds of the people, by the most infamous publications, will continue; and if the House is to meet for any business whatever, it seems to me every hour more desirable, that M^r. Wilkes's business should come under their consideration. Lord North intirely agrees with your Grace, that things are not yet sufficiently quiet, for a prorogation; a petition for the free importation of all species of provisions, from all parts of the world, is intended to be presented by a number of people on Thursday, which is certainly meant to distress Government, by obliging them to pass such a bill, at a time when all the country gentlemen are gone home; or to put a negative upon a measure, which holds out an appearance, tho a false one, of relief to the poor; Lord North will endeavour to stop the petition, but I have little hopes of his succeeding; if it is received and ordered to lie upon the table, that will be understood as a negative. Lord North says many persons, and some in Government, are for passing such a bill, not from a belief that any real advantage will be derived from it, but to satisfy the people that every possible step has been taken for their benefit; if this should be resolved on, Lord North is of opinion, that when the petition is received, it should be refer'd to a committee for the day after the next meeting, which in that case should be fixed at the distance of three weeks, and notice should be sent to every member, that such a bill was intended to be brought in; he has desired me to represent all this to your Grace, and to send my letter by a messenger, wishing to know your Grace's opinion, as early to-morrow as possible, what may be most advisable to be done upon this occasion.

It is very disagreeable to me to disturb your Grace in your retirement, with what I know must be very unpleasing to you, but I really think it my duty to send you a paper which has been published, of so dangerous a nature, that it seems to me necessary that it should be taken notice of immediately: if your Grace should be of that opinion, I humbly submit, whether, the Attorney General should not be ordered to prosecute

the printer as soon as possible. I have order'd M^r. Francis [1] to secure
evidence of the publication, in the usual manner.

I beg your Grace will accept my best thanks for the happy days
I passed at Wakefield Lodge, and allow me to assure you of the sincere
respect, with which I have the honour to be

My lord
Your Grace's
most humble and most
obliged servant
THO^s. BRADSHAW.

I request your Grace will present my best compliments to M^{rs}.
Haughton [2]; I hope she continues as well, as I had the pleasure of seeing
her. I have this moment received a note from M^r. Cokburne that the
seamen are quiet at present, but the ships are still detained.

M^r. Selwyn is in the country, and therefore I shall not venture to move
Lord Garlies's writt, unless M^r. Selwyn should be with your Grace, and
that you inform me he has no objection : his servants do not know
where he is.

---

[1] It is difficult to say why Francis
should have been chosen to find evidence for a prosecution in respect of
this paper, unless it were one especially
connected with the War Office. If so,
the paper in question may be the letter
ascribed to Junius, signed 'Fiat Jus-
titia,' which appeared in the *Public
Advertiser* on the 19th of May—a vehement attack on the Secretary at War
(Lord Barrington) for addressing a com-
mendatory letter to the troops who had
taken part against the rioters in St.
George's Fields. If Francis were Junius
there is some irony in these instructions.

[2] Mrs. Haughton or Nancy Parsons,
married in 1776 to Viscount Maynard.
She died in France in the winter of
1814-15. By the kindness of Mr. Oman
I have been supplied with an account of
her funeral from Mrs. Williams' *Narrative of Events in France*, p. 93. Speaking of the tolerance of Louis XVIII,
the writer describes a Protestant funeral
which took place in a Roman Catholic
church some leagues distant from Paris,
where 'the funeral sermon was preached
by the Protestant President from the
pulpit of a Catholic church to a numerous Catholic audience, and with
Catholic priests present. The deceased
was an English lady of some renown
about the middle of the last century.
Her misfortunes and errors (for which
the tears shed over her grave by the poor
are a sure proof that she had atoned)
have been recorded by the celebrated
Junius, under the name of Miss Ann or
Nancy Parsons.'

CHAPTER VI

REMOVAL OF SHELBURNE AND RETIREMENT OF CHATHAM

ABOUT this time an incidental occurrence gave rise to such a torrent of invective against the Administration, that I think fit to state the real fact.

The Assembly of Virginia had voted a salary for the Governor of their province. The government had, for many years back, been given (like the military governments in this country) to a general officer, and the practice (though not strictly proper as applied to Virginia) had till then never been complained of.

It was the unanimous desire of the Cabinet to put an immediate end to this unjustifiable abuse of the appointment : and Sʳ. Jeffery Amherst (the then Governor) was immediately informed, that His Majesty, by the advice of his ministers, intended to send over a resident Governor, and grant to Sʳ. Jeffery an adequate pension, until a suitable honor, or appointment could be found for him.

Sʳ. Jeffery[1], whom I saw more than once on the occasion, would never be persuaded, that the mode proposed would in fact both satisfy the colony, and stop the obloquy to which he was exposed, from holding a post paid by the colony for a different purpose. But it was in vain to argue with Sʳ. Jeffery,—adding every assurance of the desire of His Majesty and of his servants of seizing all opportunities of testifying that regard which they were fully sensible was his due,—as

---

[1] Amherst seems to have made great difficulties over this transaction, and demanded exorbitant terms. See Walpole, *Memoirs*, iii. 240.

he persevered in refusing every compensation : on our side, we lamented, that the measure was seen in so false a light : but, being convinced of the rectitude of it, we could not give way to S^r. Jeffery Amherst's ill-humour, or the suggestions of his friends. Another reason for introducing this occurrence here arises from Ld. Chatham afterwards making a grievance of it; though I am convinced, that he was not apprized of the fund out of which it was paid, nor had heard that the Virginians had made a special complaint, that their salary to a Governor was perverted to a *sinecure* place.

In the interesting and most important conversation I had with L^d. Chatham on the king's birth day 1767, I stated to him my doubts, how far Lord Shelburne, considering the little cordiality shewn by his lordship towards myself, and other members of the Cabinet of late, could be expected to draw at all with us. And I scrupled not to say, that if he persevered in his present temper and conduct he could not be allowed to continue in his office. Lord Chatham expressed his concern on hearing the account ; and though he acknowledged that it would be a great disappointment to himself, he acquiesced, that the case might be such as to make it necessary. Having premised this, I shall enter on a transaction, which was attended with very unpleasant consequences, and such as were most important to the public, as well as to myself. It is needless to relate the particulars of the many differences of opinion between L^d. Shelburne and myself[1] : suffice it to say, that the coolness, which had taken place from the time of the fatal illness of L^d. Chatham in 1766 kept encreasing to a degree, to become at length almost a state of hostility between us. This was our situation: and

[1] The difficulties which Grafton experienced in dealing with Shelburne were common to all who had to do with a man who seems to have been almost universally mistrusted. But just now the king and the Bedford party were anxious to get rid of him, for though the colonies had been taken from his department by the creation of a third Secretaryship filled by Lord Hillsborough, he still continued to urge a conciliatory policy on the Government.

He resigned on October 20, 1768, a few days after Chatham.

though I had many conversations with Lord Camden on a point so very distressful to him, on account of his friendship to us both, I had not finally determined to take the step of removing him from his office, until I wrote the letter, to which the following is the answer: however I might foresee that it would inevitably happen. I am concerned that I have no copy of my own letter; but I seldom, if ever, kept one of any I wrote to Lord Camden.

MY DEAR LORD,

I was in bed and asleep, when your Grace's letter arrived last night, and by no means so well recovered, as to be able, on my first being waked, to answer it: this morning I am much better, and hope that my letter may arrive, before your Grace leaves London.

I understand your Grace's plan is fixt; and I saw plainly, the last time I was in town, that Lord S——s removal was determined. What can I say to it my dear lord? It is unlucky.

The Administration, since L^d. Chatham's illness, is almost entirely altered, without being changed; and I find myself surrounded with persons, to whom I am scarce known, and with whom I have no connection. L^d. Chatham is at Hayes, brooding over his own suspicions and discontents. His return to business almost desperate; inaccessible to every body, but under a persuasion (as I have some reason to conjecture) that he is given up and abandoned. This measure for aught I know, may fix his opinion, and bring him to a resolution of resigning. If that should happen I should be under the greatest difficulty.

I am truly my dear lord, distressed: I have seen so much of Courts, that I am heartily tired of my employment; and should be happy to retire upon a scanty income, if an honorable opportunity offered to justify my retreat to the king, and your Grace: but that step I will never take without your consent; till I find I have lost the king's favor, and your confidence: unless I should be forced by something more compelling than the Earl of S——'s removal.

After all, though your Grace is so good as to relieve me from any opinion on this subject, yet the case being stated, as it is, that either your Grace or the earl must quit, my opinion is clear, in a moment, that your Grace must remain.

I am my dear lord,
With the truest zeal and attachment
Your Grace's &c. &c.
CAMDEN.

Sepr. 29th, 1768,
CAMDEN PLACE.

Lord Camden's distress on this occasion added much to my own : and my perplexity also was not a little encreased by the instigations to remove L^d. Shelburne, which fell daily from His Majesty, and my new allies. Lord Chatham being inaccessible to every body, after another full consideration of the business, I saw no better mode of approaching his lordship, than by a letter to Lady Chatham ; and I addressed that to her ladyship, which I propose to insert, directly below one which I received from Lord Camden about that time.

BATH, *Oct^r.* 4th, 1768.

MY DEAR LORD,

I should have answered your Grace's letter sooner, if I could have procured a safe conveyance, not caring to trust it to the common post. I am to return your Grace thanks for the obliging manner in which you are pleased to receive my poor sentiments, which, however undeserving, in other respects, shall always have the merit of sincerity and plain-dealing.

Lord S——s situation is unpleasant enough : but by no means so alarming, as the clouds that are gathering in France and N. America. With respect to the first, your Grace is perfectly apprized of my sentiments ; I shall only say on that subject, it does behove his lordship, either to be cordially reconciled, or to resign : for it is neither just nor honorable to confound, much less to betray an Administration, while he remains a member of it. I should wish the first on many accounts ; and yet I fear that can hardly be expected, considering what has passed, especially the last affront, in setting aside his lordship's nomination to Turin [1].

As to N. America, before a speech can be sketched upon the subject, it is necessary to know what measures the king's ministers mean to pursue : for the Speech and the Address must mark the outlines of these measures.

I was a long time in hopes, that Massachuset's Bay would have been the only disobedient colony [2]: it would have been no difficult measure to

---

[1] Shelburne proposed to send Lord Tankerville to Turin, but Grafton, at the instance of the Bedford party, took the matter out of Shelburne's hands and recommended Mr. Lynch to the king.

[2] The colonies began to make agreements among themselves not to import English manufactures. The Assembly of Massachusetts took a leading part in denouncing Townshend's revenue laws, and calling on the other colonies to resist them. In June, 1768, there was a serious riot in Boston, consequent on the seizure by the Custom House authorities of a sloop containing smuggled goods. Troops were sent to maintain order, and it was evident that the latent disloyalty of Massachusetts needed firm and delicate handling. The rash measures of Townshend had fanned the spark into a flame.

have dealt with them, if the others had sit still, and remained passive :
but I am deceived in that expectation : for it is now manifest, that the
whole continent will unite and make it a common cause. We are shifted,
by I know not what fatality, upon M^r. Grenville's ground ; and being
pressed on the one hand by the Declaratory Law, and on the other by the
colony's resolute denial of Parliamentary authority, that the issue is now
joined upon the right, which in my apprehension, is the most untoward
ground of dispute that could have been started : fatal to Great Britain,
if she miscarries : unprofitable if she succeeds. For it is (as I believe
your Grace thinks with me, it is) inexpedient to tax the colonies, as we
maintained, when the Stamp Act was repealed. After both sides are half
ruined in the contest, we shall at last establish a right, which ought never
to be exerted.

If the Americans are able to practise so much self-denial, as to subsist
only for one twelve-month without British commodities, I do very much
fear that they will carry their point, without striking a blow. Patience
and perseverance in this one measure will ruin us. And I am more apt
to dread this event, because it seems to me, that the colonies are more
sober, and consequently, more determined in their present opposition,
than they were upon the Stamp-Act. For, except only the riots at Boston,
I see nothing like active rebellion in the other provinces. If it should
happen, the merchants and manufacturers here at home will be clamourous ;
and half our own people will be added to the American party.

Your Grace will ask upon this representation of things ; What is to be
done ? Indeed, my dear lord, I do not know what is best to advise.

The Parliament, I presume, while the Declaratory Law stands will not
endure an avowal of the American principle ; consequently cannot repeal
the Act in question : because that would admit the American principle to
be right, and their own doctrine erroneous. Therefore, I conclude the
Parliament will not repeal ; consequently must execute the law : and this
of course must be the language of the Speech.

The method, how to execute it, is the next consideration : and here
I am much at a loss. There is no pretence for violence any where but at
Boston : that is the ringleading province ; and if any country is to be
chastised, the punishment ought to be levelled there.

I have been sometimes thinking, that, if the Act was repealed in favor
of the other provinces, excepting Massachuset's Bay, and there executed
with proper rigour, that such a measure might not be unsuccessful : but
I am aware that no man perhaps but myself could be brought to relish
such a measure of concession ; as almost every body else holds the
Declaratory Law to be a sacred fundamental, never to be departed from.

I submit to the Declaratory Law, and have thought it my duty upon
that ground, as a minister, to exert every constitutional power, to carry the
Duty Act into execution. But, as a member of the Legislature, I cannot

bring myself to advise violent measures to support a plan so inexpedient and so impolitic. And I am very much afraid (I speak this confidentially to your Grace) that if a motion should be made to repeal the Act, I should be under a necessity to vote for it. But, there are so few in my way of thinking, that such a motion is not to be expected.

I am very sensible, that a difference of opinion on a subject so serious and important may be prejudicial to the Administration; and I lament the occasion, being persuaded that a most perfect union amongst us is essential, and I will labor to effect *it* with my best endeavors : but I do fear most exceedingly that upon the American question the Bedfords and myself will be too far asunder to meet. I must maintain my own ground : the public knows my opinion, and knows theirs. Neither of us can be inconsistent with ourselves.

This letter is to your Grace only. You are my Pole Star, Lord Chatham being eclipsed. I had rather see your Grace at the head of Government, than any other man in this kingdom, and therefore, I have disclosed to you my whole heart upon this ill-fated business ; though I am sensible that my sentiments do not altogether coincide with your Grace's opinion.

There is nothing I dread so much as a war with America. I shall be very happy to know your councils in town upon this subject.

Corsica is rather a delicate, than a difficult business. Might not the king say, that foreign affairs do not wear quite so promising and favourable an aspect, as they did. That however desirous he is to maintain the public tranquility, to attain which desirable end, he will use his utmost endeavors, yet he is determined to preserve the dignity of his Crown, and the rights of his subjects inviolable. I don't give your Grace the words: I only mark the idea, and I do it in obedience to your Grace's commands.

I return your Grace a thousand thanks for your kind enquiry after mine and my son's health. I am tolerably well, and begin to drink the waters with success : and I hope my son is recovered.

I have the honor to be most truly, with

the most perfect attachment to your Grace

Your &c. &c.

CAMDEN.

I hope, that by stating the particulars of the letter, I have not committed a breach of trust, towards Lord Camden ; as 37 years are now elapsed, which have carried to the grave every one of the parties, and as the publication of the sentiments on the American occurrences show a disinterested consistency, which do him so much credit. To have suppressed it here, I should have considered to be very blameable; though but a small part of the letter relates to the matter now before us, yet every part of it tends to shew the circumstances of the time.

In consequence of what I have already mentioned to be my design; I wrote to Lady Chatham as follows;

NEWMARKET, Octr. 5th, 1768.

MADAM,

It would give me the most cordial satisfaction to be able to have the honor of seeing your ladyship for one quarter of an hour, at any day, or hour, after Saturday next, that you shall be pleased to command me to wait on you at Hayes. It is so long since Lord Chatham's health has allowed his lordship to see me, that struggling in a most arduous career, where friendship to him could alone bring me from a. life much more pleasing to my own mind, I think, I am entitled from this circumstance to claim the favor I beg of your ladyship, in order to disburthen my mind on some particular subjects; and that your ladyship may know, at least, that my whole conduct has not, nor shall have, any other bias, than that which brought me forward into my present situation. I shall be in London on Saturday, and hope to find the favor of a line from your ladyship, to whom

I have the honor to be, with the truest esteem
and the most profound respect,

Madam &c. &c.
GRAFTON.

Countess of Chatham.

On arriving in London I found the following letter—

HAYES, Friday night,
Octr. 7th, 1768.

MY LORD,

I was honored this morning with your Grace's most obliging letter, received by the post. Your Grace will, I hope, believe that I must, at all times, feel myself much flattered in receiving a visit from you: but I should think myself inexcusable, if I suffered your Grace to have the trouble of coming to Hayes, without first apprizing you, that the very weak state of my lord's health renders it impossible for me to convey to him the communication of any business. I beg further to add, that being conscious, how unequal I am to judge of political matters, I should feel happy to be allowed to express by this letter, *the whole* of what I can have to say to your Grace; my real good wishes for the honour of His Majesty, and for the success of his affairs, which are in your Grace's hands. If your Grace should notwithstanding continue in the intention of doing me the honor of a visit, I shall hope for the favor of seeing you about noon, on Sunday next.

I have the honor to be with the highest
esteem, and greatest respect &c. &c.

H. CHATHAM.

In the interview of some length, which I had with her ladyship, I understood that Lord Chatham continued in that weak state, which rendered him still incapable of all business, and unfit to have his mind turned to any. Thus, precluded from all hope of bringing back any distinct account of his sentiments, on what was so much on my own head and heart, I had no other means left, than to lay before Lady Chatham the great difficulties in which the Ministry was involved, desiring her ladyship to take the proper moment to let his lordship be acquainted with them. Her ladyship was so good as to assure me, that she would communicate the purport of my visit : provided, it was left to her to judge the suitable moment. I began my discourse by assuring Lady Chatham, that, notwithstanding the king had now for so long a time, by Lord Chatham's dreadful illnesses, been deprived of all assistance from him in his Councils, His Majesty did not despair of seeing soon his return to the head of affairs, which I was expressly commanded to deliver, as the king's particular hope and expectation. I ventured to add my own declaration, namely of being ready and anxious to return to him that lead in administration, to which his experience and ability had just claim, and which had been imposed on me, at his lordship's earnest request : and was considered by myself as a painful and temporary possession. I added, that every man, whom Lord Chatham had left in the Cabinet, desired as earnestly, as I did, his return to power : and, that I had taken care, in bringing those into Ministry, whom his lordship had more especially pointed out as the most desirable acces-sion to support it, to have it plainly understood by them[1],

---

[1] Whatever Grafton may have in-tended, it is clear that those members of the Bedford party who joined the Ministry had no idea of waiting with impatience for the return of Chatham. Grafton was misled by the efforts which

that His Majesty and his ministers, were looking out with impatience for the day, on which Lord Chatham could again take the lead in the king's Councils.

I endeavored next to explain the nature of the supposed grievance complained of by S^r. Jeffrey Amherst; and, that it never was the intention of the king's servants to remove him, without securing to him a more eligible situation. Possibly, I did not succeed in explaining sufficiently the circumstances attending this affair; as Lord Chatham afterwards laid so much stress on it.

On the principal point, on which we were so earnest to know Lord Chatham's sentiments, I could no longer expect to receive satisfaction. I confined therefore, my discourse, to what I had communicated to Lord Chatham in 1767, concerning Lord Shelburne, whose want of cordiality to me, and the continuation of his unfriendly conduct laid me under the necessity of now proposing his removal from office: I added, that Lord Chatham would recollect my acquainting him, at that time, that it was likely, that I should be driven to that most unpleasant measure. Lady Chatham listened with the greatest attention to the whole of the information, which I delivered with entire frankness; and then, after some civil enquiries, I took my leave. It will appear singular ; but I do not recollect, that we ever discoursed on this event, when a few years after I lived in long and friendly intimacy with Lord Shelburne, and had regained the confidence of Lord Chatham.

His Majesty was anxiously expecting my return from Hayes; and listened with great attention to my report, doing me the honor of approving the manner in which I had conducted the business. The king was also anxious that, as

Chatham had made in 1766 to effect a junction with the Bedford party, and by the advice which he had given in May, 1767, that the Ministry should try to gain strength from this quarter.

These recruits were eager to accept and to retain office. Grafton was fond of amusement, had no love for official life, and was ill-supported by Camden and Conway. It is no wonder that he was overpowered by his new allies before he had realized the situation.

Lord Shelburne was to be removed, it should be done in the least hostile manner possible.

To this state of things, I cannot do better, than to add the subsequent letters, which point out correctly, what was passing. As Lord Chatham was represented to me, to be *brooding over his discontent*, I was not surprized at the tenor of his letter, which is here transcribed ; tho', from the representation of his state of health, I could not have expected so soon to have heard from him. The two last lines were in Lord Chatham's own hand, and well written.

HAYES, Wednesday, Octr. 12th, 1768.

MY LORD,

My extremely weak and broken state of health continuing to render me entirely useless to the king's service, I beg your Grace would have the goodness to lay me, with the utmost duty, at His Majesty's feet, together with my humble request that His Majesty will be graciously pleased to grant me his royal permission to resign the Privy Seal. May I be allowed, at the same time to offer to His Majesty my deepest sense of His Majesty's long, most humane, and most gracious indulgence towards me, and to express my ardent prayers for His Majesty.

Tho' unable to enter into business, give me leave, my lord, not to conclude without expressing to your Grace, that I cannot enough lament the removal of S^r. Jeffrey Amherst, and that of Lord Shelburne.

I will add no more to your Grace's present trouble, than to desire your Grace will accept my sincerest acknowledgments of all your goodness to me. I beg your Grace to believe me, with the highest esteem and most perfect respect

Your Grace's most faithful and most obedient
humble servant,
CHATHAM.

Without much hope of being successful in my attempt, I wrote the answer which follows, being desirous, that nothing should be left untried, that could induce Lord Chatham not to adhere to this resolution; and His Majesty deigning to honor the Earl with a letter from himself the next day, did every thing that we could desire. The king did me the honor of transcribing, with his own hand, the answer His Majesty received from Lord Chatham which I was commanded to communicate to the Lord Chancellor immediately. Lord

Chatham rested in this letter his desire of resigning entirely on the weak and broken state of his health without the mention of any public measure[1].

My letter to Lord Chatham was written in haste; and I transcribe it from a very rough draft, taken at the time.

GROSVENOR SQUARE, Oct[r]. 12th,
1768.

MY LORD,

I feel too much concern on the idea of any circumstance, that can induce your lordship to retire from your situation in the king's service, from the prejudice it must bring on His Majesty's affairs, that if I had no other reason, I should, even on this consideration, beg leave to represent my sentiments on an event so unhappy for this country. But, my lord, having myself given way some time ago to your entreaties to me, to remain in my present post, when your health was at least as bad as it now is, I have some right to claim from you a return of the same conduct, when I see, as your lordship was pleased then to say, that nothing could be so truly serviceable to His Majesty's affairs. Give me leave to recall this conversation and assurance from your lordship to your recollection, and on the ground of it to entreat your lordship not to deprive His Majesty of that support, which even the hope of your recovery gives to his Government.

Your lordship's letter also laments a circumstance, which I mentioned to Lady Chatham, as one, appearing to me to be necessary, and on which I intended humbly to submit my opinion to His Majesty.

I lament it also, as Lord Shelburne was recommended by your lordship: but, give me leave to say, that, in the same situation your lordship would have given the same advice as that which my honor, as well as my duty to the king, will call me to give.

I could heartily have wished to have had an opportunity of explaining to your lordship many important subjects, and amongst them, how much S[r]. Jeffrey Amherst misconstrued the intention of His Majesty and his servants towards him. But your lordship's health depriving me of that

---

[1] When Chatham recovered his health and returned to the House of Lords, he used language which was not justified by the circumstances of his resignation. He said, 'I soon found that there was no original Administration to be suffered in this country. The same secret invisible influence still prevailed which had put an end to all the successive Administrations as soon as they opposed or declined to act under it.' Grafton might be pardoned for replying that these words were 'the effects of a disordered mind brooding over its own discontents' (*Chatham Corresp.* iii. 422).

satisfaction [1], I could only impart to Lady Chatham in general the earnest wish I shall ever have for your recovery, and that I have ever been and shall always remain with the truest attachment, esteem, and respect,

Your lordship's &c. &c.

GRAFTON.

P.S. Your lordship will observe, that I must postpone the obedience I owe to your commands, in hopes of seeing that what I have said in this letter has had some weight with your lordship.

The day following this second letter came to me from Chatham, the few latter words of his own hand writing.

HAYES, Thursday, $Oct^r.$ 13th, 1768.

MY LORD,

I am truly sensible how real an honor your Grace does me in the wish you are so good as to express, with regard to the letter with which I took the liberty to trouble your Grace yesterday. It must ever be a great grief to me to be reduced to a necessity of doing any thing contrary to your Grace's wish; but, unfortunately the necessity which compelled me to trouble your Grace upon this painful subject, obliges me again to ask the same favor of your Grace; to lay at His Majesty's feet my most humble request contained in my letter of yesterday. Give me leave, my lord, to renew to your Grace the sincere assurances that I shall ever retain, with pleasure, the fullest sense of all your Grace's goodness towards me. I am with the highest respect,

and attachment, my lord
Your Grace's &c. &c.

CHATHAM [2].

His Majesty, on seeing this second letter from Lord Chatham, determined to write to his lordship, and my answer, as under, was sent by the same messenger as the king's.

GROSVENOR SQUARE, Oct. 14th,
1768.

MY LORD,

It was with the most real regret that I found myself obliged by your lordship's second letter, to lay your request before the king. The manner,

---

[1] It is noticeable that Chatham never saw Grafton between the interview in May, 1767, and their meeting at the *levée* in July, 1769, and that he never gave the Duke a chance of defending or explaining a policy which he attacked as being not only misguided, but treacherous to himself.

[2] These letters appear in the *Chatham Correspondence*, ii. 340 *et seq.* Their tone does not suggest the dissatisfaction which Chatham expressed in the House of Lords on March 2, 1770 (*Chatham Correspondence*, iii. 423).

in which His Majesty received this unwelcome news better proved to me, than I can describe to your lordship, the sense His Majesty has of the prejudice that this step of your lordship's will bring to his affairs. Tho' every representation of mine has not availed : yet, I must flatter myself, that the king, whose sincere wish for your lordship's return to conduct his affairs I have been a witness to, will be able to persuade, where, from this ground alone, he has so good a right.

I have the honor to be with every sentiment of the most perfect esteem, honor, and respect,

My lord &c. &c.
GRAFTON.

By the return of the messenger, an answer was brought to His Majesty's letter; and this note for me.

Octr. 14th, 1768.

Lord Chatham presents his best compliments to the Duke of Grafton, and hopes his Grace will pardon his not answering the honor of his Grace's letter, having made an effort, greatly beyond his strength by renewing, with his own hand, his humble supplication to His Majesty.

The day following I received the letter which I transcribe from Lord Camden.

My DEAR LORD,

My concern upon the intelligence contained in your Grace's letter is inexpressible, and tho' I was apprehensive that Lord Shelburne's dismission would make a deep impression upon Lord Chatham's mind, yet I did not expect this sudden resignation. I will still live in hope that His Majesty's letter may produce an alteration ; because there is a possibility, tho' at the same time I do not flatter myself with any sanguine expectations. Your Grace and I feel for each other. To me I fear the blow is fatal, yet I shall come to no determination. If I can find out what is fit for me to do in this most distressed situation, that I must do, but the difficulty lies in forming a true judgment. Whatever my decision may be, I will never resign my active endeavors to support the king's service, or my unchangeable attachment to your Grace. This most unfortunate event will throw the king's affairs into a state of utter distraction. Perhaps order may spring up out of this confusion. I do assure your Grace that my mind is at present in too great an agitation to be soon settled, and therefore I do not give myself leave to form any opinion concerning my own conduct. I shall wait with impatience to hear the conclusion, and am with the truest zeal and attachment

Your Grace's most ob^t. and faithful servant
CAMDEN.

BATH, Octr. 14th, 1768.

I insert two more letters from Lord Camden, as they relate to our present subject.

BATH, *Oct*^{r}. 16th, 1768.

MY DEAR LORD,

Your Grace's intelligence does not surprize me, I expected it, and had predetermined my own journey to London, before I had the honor of your Grace's letter. Unfortunately, one of my children is so ill, that I must wait a day or two, before I set out, in order to see what turn her distemper will take. I propose however to be in town on Wednesday next, or Thursday at the latest.

Nothing could give me so much satisfaction as to join with your Grace in one line of conduct; and yet I see plainly, that our situations are different, and the same honour, duty to the king, and regard to the public, operating upon two minds equally aiming at the same end, may possibly draw us different ways: but I dare say your Grace will believe me in all events and circumstances, what I really am, with all respect and unfeigned attachment &c. &c.

CAMDEN.

On the 4th of November I received the short letter which I likewise transcribe.

MY DEAR LORD,

I sat late in Court, and have but just dined. I intended to have sent a line to your Grace, tho' I had not received the honour of your letter. M^r. Dunning stays in his office at *my request*.

I am &c. &c.

CAMDEN.

Friday Eveng.

I shall ever consider Lord Chatham's long illness, together with his resignation, as the most unhappy event that could have befallen our political state. Without entering into many other consequences at that time, which called for his assistance; I must think that the separation from America might have been avoided: for in the following spring Lord Chatham was sufficiently recovered to have given his effectual support in the Cabinet to Lords Camden and Granby and Genl. Conway, with myself, who were over-ruled in our best endeavors to include the article of teas with the other duties intended to be repealed. There can be no doubt, that the favor would have been gladly received by the colonies; especially, if it was held out to them, that their former con-

stitutions, with their different charters, were no longer suited
to their condition ; and that Great Britain was ready to confer
with them on establishing a free Government, dependent on
the mother country, and exclusively possessed of the full right
of taxing themselves.   When I advance these sentiments with
so much confidence to be my belief, I assure you that it is
the result of mature deliberation.   Is there a man in the
kingdom left, who does not now deplore the bad policy
which was adopted ; and feel the infatuation of so large a
part of the nation, urging on measures which were so evidently pernicious, and which ended with our loss of America,
when a contrary conduct might possibly have cemented the
colonies to us by a firm union, calculated for the happiness
of both countries ?   But what a reverse ! !

'Animus meminisse horret; luctuque refugit.'

I do not know that I could have stated this important
transaction of Lord Chatham's resignation, followed by that
of Lord Shelburne, with the exactness and perspicuity which
may be deduced from the letters cited above.   To your judgment, and that of others they are committed, and in my
opinion, this correspondence is most capable of determining
it : and I have more satisfaction that the business should
stand on the testimony of these letters, than on any thing
I could add.——I must not omit, that Lord Bristol became
Privy Seal, without a seat at the Cabinet[1], and that Lord
Rochford succeeded to Lord Shelburne[2].   Hoping that Lord

[1] George William, second Earl of
Bristol (1721-1775), had been our ambassador to Spain 1758-1761, and was
appointed by Chatham, Lord-Lieut.
of Ireland.   Chatham was consulted by
him as to accepting the Privy Seal, but
declined to give an opinion.

[2] The Earl of Rochford (1717-1781)
had been ambassador in Paris 1766-
1768.   He did not now succeed Shelburne, but took the Northern department, while Weymouth moved into
Shelburne's place.   Junius criticized

the arrangement.   'Lord Rochford
was acquainted with the affairs and
temper of the Southern courts—Lord
Weymouth was equally qualified for
either department.   By what unaccountable caprice has it happened that the
latter, who pretends to no experience
whatever, is removed to the most important of the two departments, and
the former by preference placed in an
office, where his experience can be of
no use to him ?'

Northington might have considered himself still equal in health
to the business of the Privy Seal, His Majesty in the first
instance made the offer to his lordship, but this he declined
on reasons which were very satisfactory to the king.   Parliament met a short time after; the interesting points for consideration were too important not to render the early meeting
necessary.   It has not come into the place of this memoir
to enter into the particulars of debates, and occurrences in
Parliament; as they are so well known : and indeed in this
place, I should not have it in my power, as I find few letters,
or other documents, that could assist my memory.   The
majorities were great on all the principal measures brought
forward in this Session.   If Lord North did not rise in popularity, without doors, he rose greatly in the estimation of
those who were the best judges of distinguished parliamentary
abilities.   At the Treasury, his talents for business in finance
were eminently superior to any thing we had seen in M^r. C.
Townshend.

Some time after the opening of the Session, when it was
debated, in what manner the House should proceed in the
business of M^r. Wilkes ; the Solicitor General (M^r. Dunning)[1]
differed in opinion with most of the king's servants, as to the
mode of conducting the accusation.   This offended Lord
North much more than it need have done : he complained
to me the next day most bitterly; and entreated me to desire
Lord Camden to see M^r. Dunning upon it : which I did,
tho' very reluctantly, seeing that Lord North was so much
affected.

I insert the letter, which I received in consequence of my
visit.

My dear Lord,

    I had an opportunity, after I saw your Grace yesterday, of hearing
an account of what passed in the House of Commons, and I find the
debate turned upon this ; whether they should vote the paper a libel,

---

[1] John Dunning (1731–1783), Solicitor-
General 1767–1770, created Lord Ashburton 1782 and Chancellor of the Duchy.
He was a follower of Shelburne, and
sat for his borough of Calne.

before Wilkes was heard in his defence; and that this was no question on the merits; but only discourse upon the mode of proceeding: that the Solicitor General thought if M^r. Wilkes was to be heard, he ought regularly to be at liberty to speak to the nature and quality of the paper, as well as to the fact of writing and publishing. And, indeed, my dear lord, I am of the same opinion: and I do verily believe, that no lawyer can hold a different language. The Solicitor said, that, difficult as the task would be for M^r. W. to maintain in argument that the paper was no libel, yet he ought not to be precluded from that argument, which he would be, if the House determined it to be a libel. Moreton seemed to be in the same way of thinking: and if the House should proceed on the business by calling upon Wilkes to make his defence, I do not see how they can, consistent with the terms of justice, pronounce the paper to be a libel, till they have heard him. We had a right to call it a libel, because the author could not be on his defence before us: but if the author had been called to our Bar, we should most certainly have heard him, before we had voted the paper to be a libel.

Now, my dear lord, give me leave to say, that Lord North should not be quite so much offended with M^r. Dunning, because the matter, before the House, was rather a discourse upon the method of proceeding, than a measure of administration.

Upon these grounds, after much consideration, I thought it most prudent, I dare say, your Grace will agree with me, not to send to M^r. D.: at least, till I have seen your Grace again: for it is too disrespectful a proceeding to expostulate with any gentleman for his conduct, before you have some serious objection to his behaviour. I do not believe M^r. D. will be so base, as to remain in office, and not to be hearty in the support of administration. I have the honor &c. &c.

CAMDEN.

Decr. 18th, 1768,
  LINCOLN'S INN FIELDS.

The prejudice of Lord North against M^r. Dunning was not removed by this explanation of ours, nor could he be brought to treat him with that confidence which the situation of the other had a right to expect from the minister of the House of Commons; and M^r. Dunning was too high minded to submit to any indignity. Not long after, he resigned his office, and was succeeded by Thurlow, a bold and able lawyer[1], and

---

[1] Edward, first Lord Thurlow (1732–1806), Solicitor-General 1770, Attorney-General 1771, Chancellor 1778-1783 and again 1783-1792. He was distinguished in his profession by a vigorous intellect, rather than by wide learning or subtlety of reasoning. In politics his bold, imperious manner created an impression

a speaker of the first rate, as well in Parliament as at the
Bar.—His principles leaned to high Prerogative : and I fear
his councils brought no advantage to the king or to the
nation. M[r]. Dunning's colleague, Col. Barré, much attached
to Lord Shelburne, had resigned a lucrative office when his
lordship quitted. He was a man of an upright and honorable
character ; he came to me at the time, expressing his concern
that we were to part ; and I flatter myself that I possessed
his regard to the end of his life.

The steps in general, taken by the House in the business
of Mr. Wilkes's four elections for Middlesex were very
unpopular without doors. But the rage did not spread forth
into the breasts of so large a part of the nation until Colonel
Luttrell, who had only 296 votes to Mr. Wilkes's 1143, was
declared by the House, on his petition, to be *duly elected*.
How this decision could have been avoided, or a better
substituted I cannot well pronounce ; but, it was generally
thought that the occasion could not justify the violence
diffused into so many counties of the kingdom. Meetings
were held, and petitions were drawn up and signed in many
parts—those of Yorkshire and Westminster went directly to
pray for a dissolution of Parliament : most of the others
implied the like desire. A few counties, I think rejected the
petition which was proposed to them ; but these were not
numerous. The vote of the Commons was on the third of
March 1769 ; and Parliament was prorogued on the 9th of May.

The internal state of the country was really alarming : and
from my situation I had more cause to feel it than any other
man. But a measure, at this time adopted by a majority
of the king's servants, gave me still more apprehension, considering it to be big with more mischief : for, contrary to my
proposal of including the articles of Teas, together with all
the other trifling objects of Taxation, to be repealed on the
opening of the next session, it was decided that the Teas
were still to remain taxed as before, tho' contrary to the

of straightforwardness of which his con-　is an evil figure in the history of the time,
temporaries were soon disabused. He　coarse and dishonest.

declared opinions of Lord Camden, Lord Granby, General Conway and myself. S^r. Edward Hawke was absent through illness: otherwise I think he would have agreed with those, who voted for including the Teas in the repeal. But, this was not all: and considering what important consequences this very decision led to ; there is no minute part of it, on which you should not be informed. When we had delivered *seriatim* our opinions, the minute, as is usual, was taken down by Lord Hillsborough [1]; and in that part, where the intentions of the king's servants were to be communicated by a circular letter to all the governors in America, the majority allowed the first penned minute of Lord Hillsborough to be amended by words as kind and lenient as could be proposed by some of us, and not without encouraging expressions, which were too evidently displeasing to his lordship.—The quick departure of the packet carried off Lord Hillsborough's circular letter, before it had got into circulation, and we were persuaded on reading the dispatch attentively, that it was not in the words, nor form, of the last correction agreed to by the Cabinet. Thus, it was evident to us, who were over-ruled in the Cabinet, that the parts of the minute, which might be soothing to the colonies were wholly omitted. Lord Camden in particular, much offended at this proceeding, mentioned the circumstance to me, and immediately charged Lord Hillsborough with the omission, and insisted on seeing the minute ; from which the circular letter ought to have been drawn. Lord Hillsborough expressed his sorrow that the packet was sailed: but, that he was certain, that the circular was drawn conformably to the minute. The present Lord Camden gave me leave to copy the following papers, which passed between his father and Lord Hillsborough on this occasion, and which I had

[1] Wills Hill, second Viscount and first Earl of Hillsborough, was appointed Secretary of State for the Colonies in January, 1768. This was one cause of disagreement between Grafton and Shelburne from whose department the colonies were thus taken. Hillsborough held this office until 1772, and was re-appointed Secretary of State in 1779. He retired in 1782 and died in 1793. He is known in our history as a ' king's friend' who helped to lose the American colonies.

particularly desired his lordship to search from among his father's papers.

Copy.—from Lord Chancellor (Camden) to the Earl of Hillsborough, Secretary for the American Department.

Lord Chancellor presents his compliments to Lord Hillsborough and begs leave to know, whether the circular letter to the governors in America, explaining the conduct of the king's servants in respect to the dispute between Great Britain and the colonies is dispatched, or not : because Lord Chancellor has material objections to the draught which came first to his hands the day before yesterday. ·

June 9th, 1769,
   LINCOLN'S INN FIELDS.

Copy.

Lord Hillsborough presents his compliments to Lord Chancellor, and is sorry the circular letter has been long dispatched. He wrote and sent it immediately after the Cabinet, nor can he conceive what can be his lordship's objections to it, as it is exactly conformable to the Minute, and as near as possible in the same words.

HANOVER SQUARE,
   June 9th, 1769.

Copy.

Lord Hillsborough conceiving that Lord Chancellor means to have the rough draft of the minute of Cabinet, taken the 1st of May, he spent half the day in looking for it, and cannot find it, altho' he supposes he still has it,—but having the fair draught which he communicated to his lordship and the other lords, and laid before the king, and which is conformable to the rough draught, he has not attended to the preservation of the latter. Enclosed he has the honor to send a copy of the Minute No. 1—and also a copy of the Circular Letter No. 2—which he hopes L^d. Ch. upon reconsideration will approve.

HANOVER SQUARE,
   Saturday night.

Copy.—L^d. Chancellor to Lord Hillsborough.—No date—but either a day or two after the preceding *necessarily*.

MY LORD,
   I had the honor of receiving your lordship's note with copies of the Minute and the Circular Letter, and am very sorry to say that I cannot bring myself to approve the letter, though I have considered and reconsidered it, with the utmost attention.

I wish your lordship had not mislaid the original minute, because I do not remember the first sentence of the fair draught to have been part of that original, and so I told your lordship when you was pleased to shew me the draught a day or two after the meeting. All that I mean to observe to your lordship upon that subject is, that this sentence was not a part of the original minute, nor in my poor judgment necessary to have been made a part of it.

But the principal objection wherein I possibly may be mistaken, is to the letter, which ought to have been founded on the minute, and it is this, that the letter does not communicate that opinion, which is expressed in the second paragraph of the minute, and which the Secretary of State is authorized to impart both by his conversation and correspondence.

The communication of that opinion was the measure; if that has not been made, the measure has not been pursued, and therefore your lordship will forgive me for saying that though I am responsible for the minute as it was taken down, I am not for the letter. I confess that I do not expect this letter will give much satisfaction to America, perhaps the minute might : but as the opportunity of trying what effect that might have produced, is lost, I can only say, that I am sorry it was not in my power to submit my sentiments to your lordship before the letter was sent.—

Copy. N⁰. 1.

At a meeting of the king's servants at Lord Weymouth's office—
1ˢᵗ May, 1769.

Present

Lᵈ. Chancellor.	Lᵈ. President.
Duke of Grafton.	Lᵈ. Granby.
Lᵈ. Rochford.	Lᵈ. Weymouth.
Lᵈ. North.	Genˡ. Conway.
	Lᵈ. Hillsborough.

It is the unanimous opinion of the lords present to submit to His Majesty as their advice that no measure should be taken which can any way derogate from the legislative authority of Great Britain over the colonies. But that the Secretary of State in his correspondence and conversation be permitted to state it as the opinion of the king's servants that it is by no means the intention of Administration nor do they think it expedient or for the interest of Great Britain or America to propose or consent to the laying any further taxes upon America for the purpose of raising a revenue, and that it is at present their intention to propose in the next session of Parliament to take off the duties upon paper, glass, and colours, imported into America, upon consideration of such duties having been laid contrary to the true principles of commerce.

WHITEHALL, *May* 13th, 1769.

Copy.   No. 2.
Circular.
SIR,

Inclosed I send you the gracious speech made by the king to his Parliament at the close of the session on Tuesday last.

What His Majesty is pleased to say, in relation to the measures which have been pursued in North America will not escape your notice, as the satisfaction His Majesty expresses in the approbation his Parliament has given to them, and the assurances of their firm support in the prosecution of them, together with his royal opinion of the great advantages that will probably accrue from the concurrence of every branch of the legislature, in the resolution of maintaining a due execution of the laws, cannot fail to produce the most salutary effects. From hence it will be understood that the whole legislature concur in the opinion adopted by His Majesty's servants, that no measure ought to be taken which can any way derogate from the legislative authority of Great Britain over the colonies; but I can take upon me to assure you notwithstanding insinuations to the contrary from men with factious and seditious views, that His Majesty's present Administration have at no time entertained a design to propose to Parliament to lay any further taxes upon America for the purpose of raising a revenue, and that it is at present their intention to propose in the next session of Parliament : to take off the duties upon glass, paper and colours upon consideration of such duties having been laid contrary to the true principles of commerce.

These, sir, have always been and still are the sentiments of His Majesty's present servants, and the principles by which their conduct in respect to America have been governed, and His Majesty relies upon your prudence and fidelity for such an explanation of his measures, as may tend to remove the prejudices which have been excited by the misrepresentations of those who are enemies to the peace and prosperity of Great Britain and her colonies, and to reestablish that mutual confidence and affection upon which the safety and glory of the British Empire depend.

I am &c.

(Signed)   HILLSBOROUGH.

This unfortunate and unwarrantable letter, (to give it no harsher epithet) of Lord Hillsborough to the governors in the different colonies, was many years after the subject of discourse between Lord Camden and myself. This circular was calculated to do all mischief, when our real minute might have paved the way to some good. Beside many other objectionable points, how could Lord Hillsborough venture to assert in the first line of this letter the word *unanimous*? For he could not have so soon forgotten that there was but one single voice for the measure, more than was the number of those who were against it?

You will readily imagine, that on this defeat in the Cabinet I considered myself no longer possessed of that weight which had been allowed to me before in these meetings, especially, as the proposal was on a matter of finance, more particularly belonging to my department. My resolution was soon taken to withdraw myself from my office, which was become very uncomfortable and irksome to me, on the first favorable opportunity that offered. The resistance to any further steps calculated to alienate the colonies would probably have furnished good ground for my retreat : but, while I remained in office, none was proposed. I had occasion, however, to look about me, and to tread my way with more wary steps than I had hitherto done. It led me plainly to perceive that from the time of Lord Camden's altercation with Lord Hillsborough, the former minister had sunk much in the royal estimation. As to myself, there was no alteration in His Majesty's condescending goodness ; but though this was not diminished, I was sensible that His Majesty was more forward to dictate his will to me than to enquire first my opinion on any measure that was to be considered, as had been his usual practice. My tame submission to be over-ruled in Cabinet might give the king's friends an idea that I might be more pliant, and rest my favor on their support. But they knew me little who thus judged of my temper; nor did they imagine that an honorable liberation from the Treasury was of all others the thought on which I indulged my hope[1].

---

[1] It is often forgotten, when Grafton's action is condemned, that a Prime Minister, as we understand the term, was not recognized in the eighteenth century. We are apt to speak of the First Lord of the Treasury of those days as though he chose his colleagues and determined their policy. But the Treasury, though it furnished the means of keeping a party together, did not necessarily give to the First Lord a controlling voice in the choosing of colleagues and of a policy. Grafton in 1783 (*infra*, p. 361) told Shelburne that

To have offered to resign, while the spirit of petitioning was so violent in many counties, would have been highly blameable in me: for the petitions were directed against the Administration, and the Parliament which had supported us. Other causes brought forward my resignation, and at a time when the sting of these petitions was no longer so much to be feared.

On the 24th of June 1769, I married Elizabeth[1], third daughter of S[r]. Richard and Lady Mary Wrottesley, whose merit as a wife, tenderness and affection as mother of a numerous family, and exemplary conduct thro' life, need not be related to you. In a week, or ten days after, I went from Woburn, accompanied by the Duke of Bedford, to the Installation at Cambridge[2], where in the preceding year, on the death of the Duke of Newcastle, the University had done me the honor of electing me as Chancellor, to succeed to his Grace.

he would regard him not as a Prime Minister, but as *holding the principal office* in the Ministry; and such was evidently the view which he took of his own position.

[1] The Duke was divorced at the beginning of the year from the first Duchess of Grafton, who thereupon married Lord Ossory. He seems to have broken with Mrs. Horton in the winter or spring. His political anxieties at this time were certainly crossed by domestic distractions.

[2] For this Installation, Gray wrote his 'Ode for Music.'

CHAPTER VII

THAT ceremony being over, I returned to London, where I first heard that Lord Chatham was so well recovered as to be expected to attend the king's next levée. Lord Camden had seen him, and I think, the day before his appearing mentioned to me Lord Chatham's intention. Lord Camden informed me, that he was far from being well pleased, but did not enter into particulars: except, that he considered my marriage to be quite political; and it was without effect that Lord Chancellor labored to assure him, that it was otherwise, and that he could answer, that I was as desirous as ever of seeing his lordship again taking the lead in the king's Administration. This neglect on the part of Lord Chatham piqued me much: I had surely a claim to some notice, on his recovery, when at his earnest solicitation I embarked in an arduous post, when he was incapable of business of any sort: and if Lord Chatham had wished to receive the state of political matters, I hope that it is not saying too much, that he ought to have requested it of me. He chose the contrary; and even in the king's outer room, where we met, before the levée, when I went up to him with civility and ease, he received me with cold politeness; and from S^t. James's called and left his name at my door.

On my returning home, I took down a minute of this occurrence of the day, which I have preserved. It runs thus;

7th July 1769. Lord Chatham waited on the king for the first time, since his long confinement, was graciously received at the levée, and was desired to stay, after it was over; when the king sent for him into the Closet.—His Majesty took the opportunity of assuring him, how much he was concerned, that the ill state of his health had been the occasion of his quitting the king's service. His lordship answered, that His Majesty must feel, that in his infirm state he must have stood under the most embarrassing difficulties, holding an office of such consequence, and unable to give his approbation to measures that he thought salutary, or his dissent to those, which appeared to him to have another tendency; that he was unwilling to go into particulars; yet he could not think, that one, especially, had been managed in the manner it might have been : for, if it had been despised thoroughly at the outset, it never could have been attended with the disagreeable consequences which have happened, but that it was now too late to look back [1].

The Indian transaction was also found fault with [2]. His lordship besides observed, that their general courts were got upon the worst of footings, exercising the conduct of little Parliaments; that he wondered, that the inspectors were not sent to three different places. There were also other observations on the head of India. His lordship added, that he doubted, whether his health would ever again allow him to attend Parliament : but, if it did, and if he should give his dissent to any measure, that His Majesty would be indulgent enough to believe that it would not arise from any personal consideration : for he protested to His Majesty, as Lord Chatham, he had not a tittle to find fault with in the conduct of any one individual, and that His Majesty might be assured that it could not arise from ambition, as he felt so strongly the weak state from which he was recovering, and which might daily threaten him, that office, therefore, of any sort, could no longer be desireable to him.

---

[1] This must be the Wilkes affair.   [2] *Supra*, p. 125.

From this time until the meeting of Parliament I saw no more of Lord Chatham. His suspicions of me were probably too firmly rooted to be removed by Lord Camden's assurances that they were groundless. His lordship desired no further interview, and I had such a sense of the unkindness and injustice of such a treatment, where I thought that I had a claim for the most friendly, that I was not disposed to seek any explanation.

Lord Camden and myself, unfortunately, saw less of each other, than in other summers; both of us profiting, by a retreat into the country, of the leisure which a recess from Chancery and Treasury business offered. The affair of petitions was becoming every day more serious, encreasing in number; the consequences were ever uppermost in my thoughts. M^r. Stonhewer and a few friends were with us at Wakefield Lodge; with them I conversed much on all that I foresaw of mischief from these intemperate petitions [1]; and I shall lay before you the copy, which I have in M^r. Stonhewer's hand writing of the letter which I wrote, wishing to consult Lord Camden, the lawyer, as well, as the friend, from whom I might expect the soundest advice: well convinced, that his to me came on all occasions from the sincerity of his heart.

WAKEFIELD LODGE, *Aug^t.* 29th, 1769.

MY DEAR LORD,

I have made use of the leisure which the Treasury holidays have given me to revolve over here in quiet such points as our duty seem'd to call upon as publick men most to give attention to. The petitions, I must say, have greatly engrossed and puzzled my thoughts; indeed the conduct on this strange occasion, which has been stirred up by the envy and malice of opposition without a single thought on its pernicious consequences hereafter, appears to me to be most delicate indeed. I am alarmed, I own to your lordship, at the mischief that may, from this source, before it is long, arise to this Constitution which those who are now in office, will heartily, I am convinced, join in endeavours to deliver

---

[1] These were petitions from different parts of the country demanding the dissolution of Parliament, and arguing in some cases, that the presence of Luttrell in the House, when Wilkes had received a majority of votes for Middlesex, invalidated every act of the existing Parliament.

down to their successors as pure as they received it. No trouble will stop us in this purpose, and most essential part of our duty, nor shall we be afraid to wade thro' the rage of popular clamour for the moment, if on consideration any effort of that sort shall appear to be necessary. I am not easy in my mind nor can I be so until I know at bottom what are the penalties these gentlemen who have been the promoters of these steps have made themselves liable to, or how far they are criminal. When we have this from authority, the king's servants will consider the *State part* of it, how far the petitions themselves can be allowed to sleep without some notice, having been delivered to, and of course known to the Crown, especially as the matter of these petitions is defamatory of Parliament itself, and may perhaps prove to be a violation of the Constitution. I profess to your lordship openly, that I do not see how they can lye wholly lock'd up in an office, and no farther produced or mentioned. My thoughts have been running on this business both day and night. I wish but to do right ; and shall never be afraid to meet difficulty on *good ground*: and some there must be if an active measure is resolved upon ; but believe me that great part of that vanishes when a measure of itself right, is known to be cordially approved of and determined by the king's principal servants. If nothing is to be done, and that it shall be thought most judicious to let the consideration wholly drop, for God's sake, let it not be before every point relating to it shall have been maturely weighed by us. Let it not be said that innovations of a dangerous tendency, injurious to Parliament, and dangerous to the Constitution, have been established in these times, because the ministers have not attended to the nature of them, or have been too inactive to resist such wicked measures. This subject is too much and too closely connected with the laws and indeed with the very being, in my opinion of this Constitution for me not to want the advice and assistance of those who love it as much as myself, and who know it so infinitely more. It was a disappointment to me not to meet your lordship during the four days of last week which I passed in London. My mind was too full for me not to trouble you with this letter. Be so good to give me your thoughts on the *present state* of this weighty business ; they will greatly relieve mine, altho' they can only be your thoughts on the *present* state of it, as I felt that it is not prepared nor digested enough to be yet decided upon. The Middlesex and the City Petitions your lordship had seen ; Surrey has now gone to the grievances only of the right of election violated as they complain. One will come from Worcester and in Wiltshire the *Pardon of the Chairman* is added ; the petition mostly encouraged by our old friends Popham and Beckford ; others will probably come.

The opinion in form of the king's servants will of course be taken, if any proceeding is to be entered upon. I have desired in my case, a person under me to be collecting the different facts and proofs: if not wanted by them, they will be satisfactory to myself.

You know the difficulties we have had about the Board of Trade Council; I will submit this arrangement to you, and if your lordship approves of it, I think that I can bring the *whole* about if I have your leave to *try*. M^r. Justice Clive's infirmities render it indispensable for the king to make him the usual provision on retiring, he might even be told that some gentlemen who have felt the inconvenience of it have determined to move in Parliament what would be most disagreeable to him and would in fact reflect on us. Indeed my dear lord, I hear from all quarters the necessity of this. Moreton might succeed him. Thurlow to him; and our friend Jackson come to the post of all others I most wish to see him in. Will you allow me to set about it? It requires some management, but I think if left to myself, I shall succeed. I have already made this too long a letter to trouble your lordship with further particulars on this second subject.

I have the honor to be &c.

GRAFTON.

P.S.—I shall be sincerely rejoiced to hear the little man is recovered.

Though I have inserted this letter of mine, I should certainly now wish to correct some sentiments therein expressed. You will partake in my disappointment, I am confident, when I acquaint you, that I have no opinion to lay before you, from this eminent and constitutional lawyer, whose sentiments on so peculiar a state of things, as well as his advice how to proceed upon them, would have been so satisfactory to myself at the time; and to the world in every age. But to deliver on recollection only the sentiments of a man, of his high character and authority on so serious a subject, would be in me arrogant, and little suited to that respect I shall ever attach to the memory of my friend.

Lord Camden's answer to my letter was in these words;

MY DEAR LORD,

I have the honour of your Grace's letter, which I have read over, and considered with my best attention: but the subject, being new and unexpected, I am not able at present to form any opinion, till I have given it a further consideration: and I should be unwilling to commit my crude thoughts to paper, which indeed would not be worth your Grace's perusal; and which perhaps I might change myself upon second thoughts. As I am not honored with any intercourse with any of the king's servants, except now and then with your Grace, I should be very glad to have a personal interview with your Grace, when we should both be able to explain ourselves with more freedom and confidence than can be uttered or communicated by letter. I go to-day to Camden Place, and, except a short excursion or two to Deal, and into Sussex, shall remain there till the 10ᵗʰ, the day for proroguing the Parliament. So that if your Grace will honour me with an appointment, I will wait on you in London, at your own time and place : when I shall be ready to communicate my poor opinion to your Grace as well on the main article of your letter, as the law arrangement, which your Grace is pleased to propose.

I have the honor to be &c.

CAMDEN.

Sepʳ. 1ˢᵗ, 1769.

I am much obliged to your Grace for inquiring after my little boy. He is most fortunately recovered.

The only remark I shall make on this letter is, that it was less cordial than any Lord Camden ever wrote to me either before, or since. The coolness between Lord Chatham and myself gave him much vexation[1] and the general posture of affairs encreased his uneasiness. We met in London about the middle of September : and after a long and general consideration of all that appertained to the petitions, and how far they gave necessary ground for more special notice, we agreed that in the disposition of the nation, it would be wise to avoid, if possible, every step that could irritate; and that to leave the spirit to evaporate, as there were hopes that it might, would be the most expedient measure to adopt.

His Majesty had been graciously pleased at this time to summon a Chapter of the Garter, in order to invest me with the Insignia of the Order; and the king did me the honor to observe, that he was pleased to have the greater satisfaction in conferring that favor, as I was one of the very few who had received it unsolicited. The Order of the Garter is a

---

[1] Camden's relations with Chatham do him little credit. When Chatham was well, Camden was childishly afraid of him and forgetful of what he owed to himself and his colleagues in his anxiety to propitiate the great man. When Chatham was ill, Camden was 'the harshest interpreter of his long sickness and of his late conduct in every particular' (*Grenville Papers*, iv. 64). When Chatham died, Camden considered his death 'a fortunate event' (*Rockingham Memoirs*, ii. 357).

high distinction still; tho' certainly it is somewhat dropped from its ancient celebrity by the addition that was made to the number of the knights some years after this.

In this month, we were involved in a very serious and delicate business, which appeared at one time to be big with alarming consequences. A French frigate had come into the Downs, without paying the compliment to His Majesty's ships which the general instructions from the Admiralty to all commanders of ships direct them to require; but with which no nation except the Dutch ever complied; and they, in consequence of a treaty. An officer from a king's ship went on board the French frigate remonstrating with the commander on his conduct, and assuring him, that he must insist on the compliment; but, meeting with no satisfactory answer, the lieutenant of our ship soon fired his first shot ahead of the French ship, and on perceiving no notice to be taken of his gun, he fired into the Frenchman with ball; and, as it was said, killed one of the men.

The proceeding was warmly resented by the Court of France, who required the fullest satisfaction for the affront, together with the dismissal, *from the service*, of *the officer*, who had presumed, in time of perfect peace, to fire into a frigate belonging to the French king. Office papers were ransacked for precedents to justify the claim : few were found, and the paucity of these did not assist our cause. From the reign of Charles 2^d when a long and serious altercation took place on a similar occasion, and which may be found in the memoirs of Mon^r. d'Estrades[1], and of his embassy here, one single instance (except the present) was found. This instance fell out while the Duke of Newcastle was Secretary of State, who had on the complaint of the French Court, recommended to his late Majesty to break Lieut^t. (afterwards Admiral) Smith : as soon as the Ambassador had acquainted his Court, M^r. Smith was restored to rank, and quickly promoted.

---

[1] Godefroi, Conte d'Estrades (1607–1686), was engaged in much diplomatic business, and arranged the sale of Dun-kirk. His memoirs were published in 1743.

Finding that there was so little ground on precedent, it
became our duty, as ministers of the Crown, to get rid of this
unpleasant incident, in the best manner we were able ; provided
the national honor, and that of the flag should not suffer in the
explanation.   Lord Weymouth reported to the Cabinet, that
in the audience which he gave Mon^r. de Chatêlet, his reply
upon every memorial, and his language every day became
more resolute, by insisting on a suitable satisfaction for the
affront which had been done to the king his master's dignity.
It was Lord Weymouth's opinion also, that if we could find
out some expedient at the same time to save our own credit,
the ambassador would close with it.   Lord Weymouth
thought, from my knowledge of Mon^r. de Chatêlet, that
I might *unofficially* hold with him a language tending to
bring about an arrangement, which might save the honor of
both parties.   At the desire of Cabinet, I undertook it, hoping
that S^r. Ed^d. Hawke would call on me the next morning, and
state fully to me what in his opinion would, and would not
save the honor of the Navy, and the lustre of the British flag.
In point of justice, not one word can be said : but it may be
a question whether the ideal sovereignty of the narrow seas
be not essential in elevating the enthusiastic courage of our
seamen : tho' they have now in the year I am writing, and
I hope, will ever have the best of pleas, from their own incredible superiority in skill and bravery over those of any
other country.   The morning after the meeting of the king's
servants, S^r. Edward called on me early, and in a long conversation, we discussed every means that could be devised to
answer the present purpose : and at length agreed upon one
expedient of which I made successful use in my visit to the
French ambassador; on whom I called directly ; and began
by stating to him the object of my visit, namely, to endeavour
by a frank and open conversation with him, to hit off some
means of preventing a breach between our two countries:
and in the course of our interview, I desired him particularly
not to allow himself to be led away with false notions of the
disposition of our country, from the specimen he had observed

of the disposition to riot and disorder ; and to give me credit .
when I assured him that all these would vanish on the
breaking out of a war, especially on ground so popular as
that of the honor of the flag ; to carry which on with spirit,
every Englishman would part with his last shilling. He
replied, that peace was the object of his wish, as much as
I had professed it to be mine. Besides, recapitulating all that
had passed with Lord Weymouth, he would impart this to
me, as Duke of Grafton ; 'that nothing could urge Lewis 15th
into another war, except where his honor was concerned ;
and, that he personally felt the present affront most sensibly :
he added that Mon^r. de Choiseul's interest would suffer
greatly by a war, and that he would shew his disposition to
avoid it, if such did present itself.' The ambassador proposed
various schemes for reconciliation : but none of them came
within my own notions of what might have been admissible
by the nation. Those, which I first mentioned met with no
better reception from Mon^r. de Chatêlet : and after a long
parley of two hours, we were near parting, when I thought
I might lay before him, as the only means, the very proposal
I had settled with S^r. E^d. Hawke. It was this, that the
answer to the French king's complaint, should be to say,
that His Majesty could not do so great an injustice to
a lieutenant in his service, as to punish him without hearing
his account of this unfortunate transaction ; and that the
officer having now sailed to the East Indies, such an account
could not be obtained till the return of the lieutenant. I added
to Mon^r. de Chatêlet that his return would not be expected
for three years ; when the affair might be supposed to have
slipped into oblivion. The ambassador, after a little consideration, told me that he liked the proposal ; and would
do his endeavors to make it palatable to the Duc de Choiseul.
This arrangement succeeded so fully, that we have never
heard one word more of the business : since the expedient
was accepted. I do not know that I was ever so much elated
as in my walk home, turning in my thoughts the effects of
my visit, and reflecting on the misery which probably would

be warded off from the heads of so many individuals and families. I cannot give too full testimony of the candour and zeal with which the ambassador took up the business, and recommended the expedient to his Court: his influence prevailed, and the recollection of this conduct encreased my concern on hearing of the horrid death of him and his amiable lady upon a scaffold, during the frenzy of the Revolutions in France.

You recollect, my dear Euston, the resolution I had formed of retiring from my situation, whenever I could find the moment favorable; as also my remark on the visible and rapid decline of my friend Lord Camden's favor at St. James's. This latter circumstance served to confirm me strongly in the former. For, I was not so blinded, as not to feel the ground around me to be treacherous and unsafe; though the Closet was still favorable, and afforded all apparent support; yet, I probably owed it to those to whom my principles could never be quite congenial, and who might, on some occasion, where we differed, shew to me my presumption and my insignificance: particularly as they expressed their attachment strongly, because *I was emancipated from the chains of Lord Chatham, and the burthen of Lord Camden.*

Parliament was to meet on the 9th of January 1770. The necessity of having a Chancellor to vindicate the law authority of the Cabinet was dinned into my ears in most companies I frequented; and it was particularly remarked, that Mr. Charles Yorke had taken no part in the whole business of the Middlesex Election, that need preclude him from joining in opinion with the decisions of the Commons. Such insinuations were very irksome to me: and about the Court I was still harassed with them. At last, when I was passing a few Christmas holidays at Euston, Lords Gower and Weymouth came down on a visit. They informed me, that the king, on hearing their intention of going to Euston, had expressly directed them to say, that the continuance of the Lord Chancellor in his office could not be justified; and that the Government would be too much lowered by the Great

Seal appearing in opposition: and His Majesty hoped, that I should assent to his removal, and approve of an offer being made to Mr. Yorke. My answer, as well as I recollect was; that, tho' it did not become me to argue against His Majesty's remarks on the present peculiar state of the Great Seal, I must humbly request, that I might be in no way instrumental in dismissing Lord Camden.

In a few days, after my arrival in London, the session opened: when the Lord Chancellor spoke warmly[1] in support of Lord Chatham's opposition to the address; and while we were in the House, Lord Camden told me that he was sensible that the Seal must be taken from him, though he had no intention to resign it. At St. James's, it was at once decided, that the seal should be demanded; but at my request, Lord Camden held it on for some days merely for the convenience of Government, during the negociation for a respectable successor. No person will deny, that M^r. Charles Yorke, S^r. Eardley Wilmot[2], and M^r. De Grey would any of them have filled the high office of Lord Chancellor, with the full approbation of Westminster Hall. They were all three thought of for it: though S^r. Eardley's impaired state of health, accompanied by an humble diffidence of himself, which had been a distinguishing mark in his character through life, forbad all hopes of his acceptance.

While I continued in office it was my duty as well as desire, to exert myself in endeavouring to render the king's Administration as respectable as I was able. Though I lamented, and felt grievously the loss of Lord Camden's support, from which I derived so much comfort and assistance: yet, I was satisfied that the lawyers I have mentioned were

---

[1] This was the speech in which Camden said 'he had for some time beheld with a silent indignation the arbitrary measures which were pursuing by the Ministry; that he had often drooped and hung his head in Council, and disapproved by his looks those steps which he knew his avowed opposition could not prevent.'

[2] Sir John Eardley Wilmot was Judge of the King's Bench 1755-1766, and Chief Justice of the Common Pleas 1766-1771. His learning, abilities, and self-distrust are often mentioned in the memoirs of the time.

men equal to discharge the duties of a Chancellor. I therefore received the king's commands to write to Mr. Yorke directly. I saw him the next day. He received the offer of the Great Seal with much gratitude to His Majesty, but hoped, that he should be allowed to return his answer, when he should have given it a day's consideration. M^r. Charles Yorke remained with me between two and three hours ; dwelling much on the whole of his own political thoughts and conduct, together with a comment on the principal public occurrences of the present reign. When he came to make remarks on the actual state of things, after speaking with much regard of many in Administration, he said, that it was essential to him to be informed from me, whether I was open to a negociation for extending the Administration so as to comprehend those with whom I had formerly, and he constantly, wished to agree. My answer was, that he could not desire more earnestly than myself, to see an Administration as comprehensive as possible ; and that this object could only be brought about by the re-union of the Whigs[1], adding, that I should be happy to have his assistance to effect it. M^r. Yorke appeared to be pleased with this answer ; and after many civilities on both sides, we parted. On his return to me the next day, I found him a quite altered man ; for his mind was then made up to decline the offer from His Majesty, and that so decidedly, that I did not attempt to say any thing further on the subject. He expressed, however, a wish to be allowed an audience of His Majesty. This was granted, and at the conclusion of it the king, with the utmost concern, wrote to acquaint me that M^r. Yorke had declined the Seal. On his appearing soon after at the Levee, His Majesty called him into his Closet immediately after it was over. What passed there I know not ; but nothing could exceed my astonishment when Lord Hillsborough came into my dressing room, in order to tell

---

[1] Grafton seems strangely blind to the divergence of opinion which existed among the so-called Whigs. It was not likely that the Rockingham party would follow Yorke into the Ministry, or that, if they did so, they would work with Weymouth and Sandwich.

me that M^r. Yorke was in my parlour, and that he was Lord
Chancellor, through the persuasion of the king himself in his
Closet.   M^r. Yorke corroborated to me what I had heard
from Lord Hillsborough, and I received the same account
from His Majesty, as soon as I could get down to St. James's.
M^r. Yorke staid but a little time with me: but his language
gave me new hopes, that an Administration might shortly be
produced which the nation would approve.   How soon did
this plausible hope vanish into a visionary expectation only,
from the death of M^r. Yorke, before he became Lord Morden,
or we could have any preliminary discourse on the measure
he earnestly desired to forward.   I had long been acquainted
with Mr. Yorke, and held him in high esteem.   He certainly
appeared less easy and communicative with me, from the time
of his acceptance to his death, than I might expect: but it
was natural to imagine that he would be more agitated than
usual when arduous and intricate business was rushing at once
upon him.   I had not the least conception of any degree of
agitation, that could bring him to his sad and tragical end:
nor will I presume to conjecture what motives in his own
breast or anger in that of others had driven him to repent
of the step he had just taken[1].   By his own appointment,
I went to his house about 9 o'clock in the evening two days,
as I believe, after M^r. Yorke had been sworn in at a council
board summoned for that purpose at the queen's house.
Being shewn into his library below, I waited a longer time,
than I supposed M^r. Yorke would have kept me without
some extraordinary cause.   After above half an hour waiting
D^r. Watson his physician came into the room: he appeared
somewhat confused, sat himself down for a few minutes, letting
me know, that M^r. Yorke was much indisposed with an attack
of colic.   D^r. Watson soon retired; and I was ruminating on

---

[1] Walpole, *Memoirs*, iv. 52, states
some facts which tend to show that
the reproaches of Rockingham and
Hardwicke drove Yorke to suicide.
He describes the desire shown by Burke
to throw the blame on the king for
having constrained Yorke to enter his
service, and concluded not unreasonably from Burke's agitation 'that they
wanted to disculpate Lord Hardwicke
and Lord Rockingham of having given
occasion to Mr. Yorke's despair.'

the untowardness of the circumstance, never suspecting the fatal event which had occurred nor the still more lamentable cause ascribed for it by the world and as I fear upon too just ground. I rang the bell, and acquainted one of the servants, that M^r. Yorke was probably too ill to see me, and that I should postpone the business on which I came, to a more favorable moment. M^r. Yorke, I believe, was a religious man : it is rare to hear of such a person being guilty of an action so highly criminal. It must therefore in him have been a degree of passionate frenzy bearing down every atom of his reason : you will not wonder, that I cannot think on the subject without much horror still.

Here I stood again under more perplexing difficulties than ever : and without any expectation of additional strength, but what would arise alone from the appointment of an able Chancellor. Lord Chief Justice Wilmot, after M^r. Yorke's death, declined the acceptance of the Great Seal from the causes I have already assigned. Under these unpromising circumstances, I still persisted in endeavoring to fill up the vacant Chancellor's post, by an efficient and respected character. By the king's commands, I saw M^r. de Grey, a most able and upright lawyer, and as perfect a gentleman ; and who afterwards became Lord Chief Justice of the Common Pleas. In a long conference we had at his house, he appeared inclined to undertake the situation, in spite of his frequent attacks of gout. But on entering something further into particulars, he put this question to me ; ' Are you determined yourself to remain a certain time in your present post ? '— My answer decided him at once to decline : for I told him, that I thought of retiring, as soon as I could reconcile it to my own heart : and that I foresaw this might be very near at hand indeed : for I assured him, that I should not seek for any other Chancellor, if he refused the offer of the Great Seal.

You will feel for me in this distressing dilemma : you will perceive that I had left nothing untried to bring the vessel to tolerable trim : and when you consider, that quitted by Lord

Camden, and at the same time by Lord Granby [1], I had no reliance in the Cabinet, but on General Conway alone [2], I trust you will think that, under such circumstances, I could not proceed, and be of service to the king, or to the country; and recollect that the hopes of co-operation with M[r]. Yorke to bring about an essential addition of right principle, credit, and support, vanished of course with himself. I laid before His Majesty directly my difficulties, and observed that they were such, as compelled me to retire from my office, though it would be my full desire to give all assistance to His Majesty's Government. As it would be thoroughly ungrateful to pass over entirely the concern His Majesty manifested on this occasion, I am induced to observe, that the king's earnestness with me, to alter my resolution, far surpassed every thing, which my poor services could possibly have merited [3].

[1] The seals were taken from Camden on January 17, though he received notice on the 13th of the intention to remove him. Granby resigned on the same day, after great pressure had been brought to bear on him by Chatham and his following (*Chatham Corresp.* iii. 370-376).

[2] Walpole, *Memoirs*, iv. 66, says that Grafton was betrayed by the Bedford party and even by his secretary Bradshaw, and that he complained of this to Conway. The charge against Bradshaw is doubtful: at least he recovered and retained the confidence of the Duke: but Rigby and Weymouth almost certainly regarded their nominal Premier as a disturbing element in the Cabinet.

[3] The resignation took place on Jan. 27. A letter from the king fixes the date.

'Duke of Grafton, in consequence of what you said last night I have convinced Lord North of the necessity of my consenting to your acquainting your friends to-morrow of your intention of retiring, among whom I hope you will see the Duke of Newcastle.

Queen's House, *Jan.* 28, 1770,
ꟛ p[t]. 8 p.m.'

CHAPTER VIII

TOWARDS the end of January 1770, I left the Treasury; but continued to give the Administration under Lord North what support I was able. The number of independent gentlemen members chiefly of the House of Commons, who came to meet me at this juncture, expressing their desire of taking their part with me, both surprised and flattered me: for many of the number were little known to me. I returned them many thanks for the honor they did me by this proof of their good opinion, which I should never forget; though my mind was made up, as I told them to keep myself as single and independent as a political man could be.

At this time Lord Chatham's virulence seemed to be directed against myself: he persisted for some days in the intention of charging me, in Parliament, with having advised the removal of Lord Camden, on account of his vote in the House: nor was he dissuaded from this, till Lord Camden had assured him that he knew so perfectly that the advice did not came from me, that he should, if his lordship made the motion, think it incumbent on him to rise in his place, and declare that he well knew it was not from my advice. This idea was wholly dropt in our House, on this declaration from Lord Camden; but I think that some member of the House of Commons made a motion of the same tendency, but met with no support.

In the last days of January, Lord Rockingham moved for a day to be fixed, when he should enter upon the consideration of the state of the nation. Lord Chatham meant to be the seconder; but I started up myself to second Lord Rockingham, and to profess my readiness and wish to go into any enquiry that the House should approve [1]. On the day fixed, the Marquis made his motion, which related wholly to the rights of the Commons on judicial authority in matters of election. In debate, arguments went further: and in particular Lord Chatham condemned the conduct of the Commons, with much asperity, in a speech which betrayed no want of mental or bodily powers. A great majority supported the ministers, and Lord Marchmont [2] made the following motion which was not only approved, but said to be penned by Lord Mansfield himself, who gave it his fullest support, in a very brilliant speech; 'That any resolution of this House, directly or indirectly impeaching a judgment of the House of Commons, in a matter, where their jurisdiction is competent, final and conclusive, would be a violation of the constitutional right of the Commons, tends to make a breach between the two Houses of Parliament, and leads to a general confusion.' This motion was, as I thought, highly necessary, and it received my fullest support. Lord Chatham continued, for two months together, in a more active opposition to the Ministry than I had ever known in his lordship: and after many motions, which were all negatived, he moved an address to His Majesty to dissolve the Parliament, on the ground, that the people had no confidence in the House of Commons, at a time when the discontents in England, Ireland and America were threatening to a high degree. This motion was rejected, as you may imagine, without much debate: and by Administration, with little attention [3].

Lord North, become principal minister, brought in the repeal of all the port duties, except that on teas: and as

[1] For an account of this debate see *Parl. Hist.* xvi. 745.

[2] Hugh Hume, third and last Earl of Marchmont. His eldest son, called to the Upper House as Lord Hume of Berwick, died in 1781, and he in 1794.

[3] The debate is to be found in vol. xvi. of the *Parliamentary History*. The motion was rejected by 85 to 37.

I had been greatly hurt when I could not carry the point in Cabinet, to have the teas also exempt, it was some satisfaction to think that I was no longer in Administration, nor, a sharer in a measure so ill-fated and unwise. If there had been temper in the nation to have considered the interests of the two countries; and wisdom enough in the Ministry to have proposed a full and total repeal, much, I shall ever think, might have been done.

I shall now turn to another new event; it is well known, that the great European Powers had for ages back, too much acquiesced in the preposterous claim of the Spaniards to the whole of South America, except the possessions of the Portuguese at the Brazils, and of the Dutch at Surinam. Frezier in his voyage[1], relates, that the Falkland Islands were first discovered and taken possession of by the English: they lie directly east from the entrance of the Streights of Magellan and at a certain distance from the continent. Under M^r. Grenville's Ministry, it was determined, that at Port Egmont, a station should be established where ships steering for the South Seas might be provided with refreshment, water, and some repair. On our coming into office with Lord Rockingham, Lord Egmont, First Lord of the Admiralty, had our authority to proceed in the scheme, and a block house fort was carried out from hence to be put together at Port Egmont; as we could not imagine that the Spaniards, though jealous to an extreme of all that tended to lay open the South Sea trade, should venture to bring these islands within their presumptive limits. The French indeed, had erected a fort on another of these islands, but relinquished it on the representation of Spain, by whom it was called Port Solidad.

The Tamer sloop, Captain Hunt, fell in with a small Spanish vessel, belonging to Port Solidad, as he was cruizing near to Port Egmont, and he ordered it to depart from those coasts. The Spaniard obeyed; but as it was probable, that his orders were

---

[1] Frezier wrote *A Voyage to the   and Peru*, 1712–1714. London, 1717. *South Sea and along the Coasts of Chili*

to report what the English had of force on the island, the vessel sailed off for Buenos Ayres, from whence the Governor (Bucarelli) returned the same charge to Captain Hunt to abandon his design of a settlement on those islands, which as he stated belonged to the Crown of Spain. Many warm messages passed in consequence of these notices; and neither side being disposed to give way, Captain Hunt thought it right to sail for England, before any act of hostility should be committed; and report the state of all matters, respecting the new settlement: and he arrived in the month of June 1770.

Bucarelli soon after this ordered a considerable sea force against Port Egmont, where a miserable block house fort, and two small vessels were called upon to capitulate; it could not be refused: but it was followed by one of the most outrageous insults ever offered from one nation to another. The rudders of the Favorite and her consort were taken off, and were not restored till such time, as the Spanish commander should please to allow our vessels to sail. The indignation of the nation was such as became a great Power grossly insulted : England felt at the same time the means she possessed to resent the affront; and was ready in every way to support the Ministry in obtaining just satisfaction. A respectable fleet was soon assembled at Spithead, and I never heard that the language held to the Spanish Court was not suitable to what the dignity of the Crown, and the national honor required. The Court of Spain, after much altercation and doubts, gave way at last, and stipulated to restore Port Egmont to our possession. So far was publickly known; tho' it was believed not to have been an entire surrender of the island to us; but the concession was said to be clogged with a humiliating promise on our part of abandoning it, after a short possession[1]. Lord Weymouth, quitting his office at this moment, it was

---

[1] This was not so We did not promise to give up the islands, nor did Spain abandon any claim of right. For an account of the islands when reclaimed by us in 1833, see Darwin's *Naturalist's* *Voyage round the World*, p. 180. The islands are now governed under the provisions of the British Settlements Act, 1887.

thought to have been occasioned by an unwillingness to put the seals to a stipulation unworthy of the British name. The reparation for the insult was not sufficient for an offence unheard of; and I should have been also of opinion that the concession was very inadequate.

I shall conclude the account of this serious transaction, with a curious anecdote I learnt afterwards from the best authority; and which will serve to shew the complete ascendancy the French Cabinet had at that time over the Court of Spain.

The restless disposition of the Duc de Choiseul, prompted him to consider the moment favorable for forwarding his favorite purpose of reducing the power of Great Britain. With this view, through the channel of Grimaldi, he did every thing to foment the commencing quarrel with England; and, as I believe, trusting that he should be able to shew to his royal master that if called on by Spain for troops or ships, under the Pacte de Famille, these might be duly furnished, as an auxiliary, and not as a principal in the contest. Choiseul's design, however, was so veiled over, as to be kept away from the knowledge of the French king; and the rivals of Choiseul's power did not fail to improve the advantages they had obtained. The French king with much anger charged his minister to take care, that there should be no rupture between Spain and England; well knowing that Spain would acquiesce, when France was firmly decided. At this moment a courier arrives with such dispatches, to Prince Masserano, the Spanish Ambassador to our Court, as would at once have plunged the two countries into an inevitable war: the messenger brought also other letters, communicating to their Ambassador at Paris the directions sent to Masserano. Immediately on Choiseul's reading the letters, he saw but one way left by which he could obey his master, and hope to preserve his own power, he dispatched a courier to Monsieur Francés, left Chargé des Affaires at London; where the two couriers arrived the same morning. Francés flew directly to the Spanish Ambassador, whom he found on the point of setting out for an audience of the Secretary of State, on the subject of the dispatches he had just received. The Duc de Choiseul's letter was given to Masserano to read ; wherein he ventured to intreat him not to enter on the orders he had received from his own Court ; as he might be assured, that he would receive instructions of a different nature, as soon as time would allow them to come from Madrid. Masserano having read his own dispatches over again, as also those addressed to Francés, with some difficulty was brought to comply with the advice of the latter : for he was undoubtedly not ignorant, that the weight of French councils would preponderate at his Court : therefore he submitted. I was well acquainted with Mon^r. Francés, while he was with Mon^r. de Chatêlet in England. After the American war, he passed over into this country to visit all those from whom he had received civilities : I saw him a great deal, and we had many interesting conversations ; and from him, in one of these, I had the anecdote above related.

The prevention of a war, though with a change of conduct, was now not able to maintain Choiseul in his master's favor : and his rivals seeing his credit thus weakened, easily succeeded by various means to bring it to the ground. He was banished to one of his country seats (Chanteloup) and was succeeded in his ministerial employment by the Duc d'Aiguillon.

This dispute and negotiation with Spain, took place during the prorogation of 1770, and Parliament meeting in November, the king stated, in the speech from the throne, the gross insult against the British flag ; and both Houses rebounded [sic] with the unanimous resolution of obtaining just and suitable satisfaction.

Being released from business, and from an office which was peculiarly irksome to me, tho' the power annexed to it is, and will ever remain, the object of so many men's ambition, I took with more eagerness than ever to my hunting, and other idle, but less creditable dissipations ; I was not however inattentive to what was passing, and my friends kept me well informed of the measures which were in agitation.

I had not been for some time past satisfied with the management of the navy : S^r. Edward Hawke had for many months been in a state of health that took off from his usual exertions in the business of his office. Through the Comptroller of the Navy, Cap^n. Cockburne, I was acquainted, before I quitted my office, with every particular I wanted, and the knowledge of this compelled me to draw Lord North's attention to this essential service, before it should suffer in any branch. By letters to M^r. Bradshaw, who staid a short time, as Secretary of the Treasury, with Lord North, at my request; I thought that I should best succeed in my object : as M^r. B. would not fail to renew to his lordship a subject which I had so much at heart : in case he perceived that it was in any shape overlooked. About six weeks from my resignation, I received the following letter from M^r. Bradshaw, on this subject. It is docketted March the 4th, 1770.

LINCOLNS INN FIELDS, Sunday,
4 o'clock.

MY LORD,

I have had an opportunity of talking to Lord North upon the subject of the navy. He does not seem alarmed at the situation of France and Spain, but he thinks it necessary, that not only the intelligence from abroad but the situation of our fleet, should be taken into consideration, and he intends to call a Cabinet for that purpose. I did not fail to urge, that no time was to be lost, as the Trade would sail in the course of this month, and that it would then be difficult, at any expence or by any means, to get men.

He disapproves either an address, or a vote of credit, on account of the alarm that would be occasioned thereby : but he thinks an augmentation might be made in the same manner suggested to your Grace, and if there was any danger of wanting money, a sum might be voted for discharging the debt of the navy, and applied to the purpose of the augmentation. Upon the whole, he desired me to acquaint your Grace that he will take this important matter into immediate consideration.

I have the honor to be &c.

THO^s. BRADSHAW.

The account from Falkland's Islands arrived about three months afterwards; and in September Lord Gower undertook to come down to Wakefield Lodge, to communicate to me the state of things, which he did very openly, and acquainted me also, that Parliament was to meet on the 13th of November.

The vigor of our preparations to meet a war was the best means, by which the negociation then pending could end honorably for this country. Instead of which my letters stated to me that the Admiralty mismanaged through tardiness, and likewise by a want of secrecy, the measures on which they were occupied.

In October, the Spaniards were arming: but there did not appear to be any particular stir in the French ports; tho' Monr. de la Borde, the confidential banker of the Court, certainly ordered all his stock in our Funds to be sold.

It was the general observation of all concerned that the seamen entered voluntarily in much greater numbers than was ever known; which circumstance might have given a wonderful advantage, in fitting out a great fleet with more expedition: the consequence of which might have been evident to the king's servants.

There was a strong belief about this time that I was to be invited to become First Lord of the Admiralty; and in the opinion of many, it was thought that I was particularly desirous of holding that office. A few days previously to Mr. Rigby's setting off to make me a visit at Euston, he asked Mr. Bradshaw, if there was any reason to believe, that I *would* come to the Head of the Admiralty: Mr. Bradshaw's answer was, that he had often heard me talk of that situation, as one that was of the utmost importance to the country, and where a great deal of good might be done; and that his private opinion was, that, if I could be prevailed on to take any office, the Admiralty was more likely than any other. Having gone so far I will not close the subject, (very uninteresting to any but to my own friends) without mentioning my real sentiments. I was always strongly of opinion, that a naval officer should preside at the head of the Admiralty. Any other could never know enough to give an answer satisfactorily to the incessant questions which must necessarily be put to him by a Cabinet composed of land-men. In such cases what can the First Lord do, but run out to get the information from others, who, in consequence, must be let into the secret of what is passing, the knowledge of which ought to be confined as much as possible to the Cabinet alone. Admiral Keppel and Lord Howe[1] were both as men and officers well qualified for the station, though probably Mr. Keppel would have declined it as he was much connected with Lord Rockingham, and his friends who were hostile to the Ministry. Had I been assured, that Lord Howe would not be allowed to succeed Sr. Edward Hawke, and that Lord Sandwich was otherwise to be undoubtedly the First Lord, I do not know whether I might not have been induced on that consideration, to take the charge upon me. Admiral Pigot[2], in that case, I should have wished to have been my right hand man, and it would have been my endeavor to collect in, and around, the Board those men whose ability and characters stood highest in the navy: and we should have taken care that every officer we wished to employ should with confidence have relied on the liberal and honorable conduct they were to expect from us: and the country would have profited by the services of all our best naval officers, an advantage which Lord Sandwich's Admiralty could never gain. If such a measure had taken place, we should have felt an essential loss in Capn. Cockburne, who had been chosen just before Member for Hull:

---

[1] Richard, fourth Viscount and first Earl Howe (1725-1799), he was First Lord of the Admiralty in the Administrations of Shelburne and Pitt, and was the victor in the battle of June 1, 1794. He and Keppel, 'Black Dick and Little Keppel,' at this time commanded the confidence of the navy to a remarkable degree (*Rockingham Memoirs,* ii. 365). Captain Mahan would seem to rate Howe above Keppel as a commander (*Sea Power,* 352, 364).

[2] Hugh Pigot (1721-1792), a Lord of the Admiralty in the Rockingham and Shelburne Ministries.

and probably became a victim to the hurry and festivity of the Election there. But after all the offer was never made: Lord Sandwich was appointed; and you may not be displeased to see the following letters, which give not only some particulars on the subject, but serve to shew on what footing I stood with those who had been my colleagues in the king's service.

LINCOLNS INN FIELDS, 5ᵗʰ *Janʳʸ*. 1771.

MY LORD,

Lord North wrote to me to call upon him early this morning. He asked me, if I had ever heard you express an inclination to be at the head of the Admiralty. I answered, that I had repeatedly heard you say, when at the head of the Treasury, that you thought the Admiralty a most important department, and one, in which a person properly qualified, might do the most essential service to this country, and I added that you formed that opinion, from being perfectly acquainted with the department, and the manner in which it had been administered for some years past. He then asked me, if I thought you would accept it, if it was vacant; I told him, that I knew you would not withhold your assistance from the king, and the country, whenever you thought you could really be of use to either. That you could most certainly be of the most essential service to the country at this time by taking the Admiralty, which in its present situation required both personal weight, and ability, in the person who was to direct it; and therefore, that I had no doubt, if that department was properly offered to you, but that you would accept it: provided you thought you could put the navy on the footing that it ought to be; and that it was the wish of His Majesty and his Administration. Lord North only said; that not knowing any thing of your sentiments, he had, on his first coming into office, promised to mention Lord Sandwich to the king, whenever the Admiralty shall be vacant. He asked more than once, when you would be in town; and then changed the subject, which I did not appear earnest to renew. I enquired of his lordship, how Sʳ. Edward Hawke was: he told me, he did not know. But I *know*: he is very ill, and that Lord North has now a letter from him to Lord Rochford, in his possession, in which the poor old man tells him, that he finds himself unable to attend Cabinets, or Sᵗ. James's; and that, if he does not very soon find an alteration in his health for the better, he shall endeavour to creep once more to Sᵗ. James's, and there thanking the king for all his kindnesses to him, lay his office at his feet.

The law and all other arrangements are at an end for the present. Masserano declares, that he expects daily orders from his Court to give us the satisfaction we demand; but, that knowing, as he now does, that

Mr. Harris is recalled, he cannot venture to execute any orders he receives, without fresh instructions when his Court is informed of Mr. Harris's departure. Lord North hopes to remove this difficulty, if Masserano should receive the orders to make the satisfaction, by naming an ambassador the very day the satisfaction is received.

His lordship is still sangwine for peace; and yet it is certain, that Buccarelli is appointed Lieut. Governor of Arragon.

I have the honor &c.

THO^s. BRADSHAW.

LINCOLNS INN FIELDS, 10th *Jan.* 1771.

MY LORD,

I find S^r. Edward Hawke resigned the Admiralty yesterday to His Majesty. I was with Lord North till he went to Court, and he did not say a word to me on that subject, tho' part of our conversation naturally led to it. Lord H. being in the country, I am without any information of what is intended, but I have this moment received a note from Lord Rochford, desiring to see me to-morrow morning. I have the honor to be &c.

THO^s. BRADSHAW.

With the insertion of this one other letter from M^r. Bradshaw, I shall put an end to this topic, which will be interesting to my friends only; and which has already run into too much length.

LINCOLNS INN FIELDS, 11th *Jan^{ry}*. 1771.

MY LORD,

Lord Rochford began by telling me, that he wished to talk confidentially to me with regard to the arrangement that was made *yesterday*, which he took for granted I had heard of. I told him I had not. He then informed me that S^r. Edward Hawke had resigned, and that Lord Sandwich *was* first Lord of the Admiralty. He took a great deal of pains to assure me, that what he was going to say to me, was entirely from himself, arising from his personal attachment to your Grace, and his duty to the king; but I am convinced he had the same *reason* for sending for *me*, which induced him to write to *you* some time ago. After this, he told me, that though he was far from thinking you would accept of the Admiralty upon the eve of a war, yet that, as you had been much talked of for that department, and as when he received the king's commands for the appointment of Lord Sandwich, he could perceive there was *something upon His Majesty's mind*, he wished to consult me as a *private friend* whether any thing could be done, to mark His Majesty's high estimation of your Grace, or to prevent your feeling, that there had been any want of attention to you upon this occasion. He expressed his gratitude and his attachment to you; declared his opinion that the department should have been offered to you, by His Majesty, *at all events*, and repeatedly wished me to remember, and at a proper opportunity to state to your Grace, that he neither had, nor could have, from his situation any share in this transaction; and here I am bound in justice to Lord Rochford, to assure your Grace, that I am convinced his declarations in that particular are strictly true; and that he sincerely wishes you at the head of the Admiralty.

I told Lord Rochford that I would begin by reminding him, of my having some time ago given him my opinion, in conversation, that your Grace would accept of the Admiralty if it was the wish of the king, and of his ministers, that you should be there; because the eve of a war was a time when much was to be done, and consequently much good might be done in that department, which I well knew was the only consideration that would induce you to accept of an office; that with regard to your Grace's feelings, upon the present occasion, the not being in office, I was sure would not give you any unpleasant feelings; but as his lordship had mentioned that His Majesty had *something upon his mind*, I could easily conceive, that if any thing had passed between His Majesty and your Grace (of which I was totally ignorant) at any time upon this subject, the disposal of that department, without any notice being taken of you, could not but be *felt* by your Grace, as such a conduct could only be accounted for by a change in His Majesty's sentiments and wishes; or from the king being *overborne* by his minister—that with regard to the latter, tho' your Grace had no ministerial information, you was not ignorant that His Majesty, differing in opinion from Lord North in the manner of bringing about a very important arrangement in the law, had absolutely refused to make S^r. F. Norton a peer—that as to Lord North your Grace could have no *feelings* with respect to his lordship. You was not a person wishing or soliciting for office, and if his lordship did not think that such an acquisition as your Grace in an important department was a most desirable object, and worth his utmost endeavors to obtain, he was certainly master of his own conduct—that I was indeed not a little surprized that his lordship (Lord North) should consult me on Saturday morning last, whether I thought your Grace would accept of the Admiralty, when he was resolved to give it to another; as in my opinion he had better have done, without my sentiments on that head; and as his lordship (Lord Rochford) had been very frank with me, I would fairly tell him, that I had wrote you my conversations with Lord North, which Lord North must be certain I would do; I concluded with saying, that as to an opinion what could be done to prevent your Grace's thinking you had been neglected I could form none, not being master of the whole subject: that the delicacy of the *whole* depended upon what had passed with your Grace in the Closet, of which I was entirely uninformed, and

should not have suspected that any thing had passed there, but from
what had dropt from his lordship (for he told me he feared something
had passed there, tho' he did not know what). That I should sincerely
lament on His Majesty's account, if you had any cause to think yourself
neglected; for tho' I knew your noble principles, and your resolution to
combat faction, and support Government as long as it could be supported,
yet it was, if his lordship's fears were just, but a bad return for your
conduct, and a bad encouragement to others to follow your example.
I have been obliged to write your Grace a very long letter, but
I thought it proper that you should know every circumstance of my
conversation with Lord Rochford who thinks as he ought with regard to
your Grace; and laments very sincerely for the sake of the king, and the
public that you are not in office. I have not heard a word from Lord
North. I find Lord Suffolk is to be offered the seals, which indeed I had
no doubt of, when I heard they were vacant. I have the honor to be
with the greatest respect my lord

Your Grace's most obliged and faithful servant,

THO^s. BRADSHAW.

P.S.—I beg your Grace will present my best respects to the Duchess.
It gives me unspeakable satisfaction, that you, to whom I have the
greatest obligation, and the most sincere attachment are not dependent
for your happiness upon kings or courts. Almost 12 o'clock. Lord North
has just been *here* for two hours, and what is astonishing, he has never
once mentioned Admiralty, S^r. Edward Hawke, or Lord Sandwich.

Lest any doubt should arise in the breast of any person,
to His Majesty's disadvantage on some expressions in the
foregoing letter, I feel it incumbent on me to assure you,
that nothing had passed between the king and myself, on
this subject, which could occasion to His Majesty any uneasy
sentiment: but Lord Rochford and M^r. Bradshaw were not
probably informed, as I was, of the king's strong dislike to
place Lord Sandwich, whose character he disapproved, in any
elevated post [1].

About this time, Lord Rochford received the king's commands to keep me informed of all business of any consequence,
that was in agitation: a distinction, which tho' honorable
to myself, was not without some inconveniences: and I

---

[1] Sandwich succeeded Weymouth as
Secretary of State in December, 1770,
and within two months was moved to
the Admiralty. Lord Halifax took his
place, Lord Suffolk being Privy Seal.
Halifax died in the following June, and
Suffolk became Secretary of State.

believe that it was pretty well observed untill the time when His Majesty thought proper to make me the offer, through Lord North, of the Privy Seal. I heard that there were many about Court who wished it to be filled by Lord Weymouth: but, His Majesty was pleased to say that he would not hear of a competition. The offer certainly came to me in the most flattering manner possible, and I accepted the office with every sense of duty, stipulating only, that I should be considered as holding the office, without being summoned to any Cabinet. This stipulation was the only prudent part, in my accepting the Privy Seal at all: for, if I had given it due consideration, I should have felt that the reasons which made me avoid the Cabinet, namely, the little confidence I had in the principles of many members of it, ought equally to have shewn me, that I was not likely long to support their measures. I give a letter, which I received from Lord North, on my appointment, as it confirms the avowal of the condition, under which I accepted the Privy Seal.

Downing St. Tuesday,
7 o'clock.

My dear Lord,

I should have answered your obliging letter as soon as I received it, had I not been engaged at a board which lasted till dinner. The expressions contained in your letter, and the conversation I had with Bradshaw concerning it, made me most sincerely happy. I wait to have some discourse with your Grace in which I may more fully express to you the satisfaction I receive from every instance of your friendship. I am not acquainted with your Grace's former opinion respecting the Confidential Cabinet, but you will consider, that it is not near so numerous now, as it was when Lord Bristol[1] was appointed Keeper of the Privy Seal. Your Grace may however be assured that the king means to offer you the Privy Seal, in the manner the most agreeable to you, and I know that I may equally depend upon your advice and assistance, whether you are nominally of the Cabinet or no. I write in a hurry, and I am informed that your Grace is in a greater hurry in expectation of

---

[1] The king, writing to Lord North, mentions that Grafton 'had ever thought the confidential Cabinet too numerous,' and had on that account desired that when Lord Bristol was Privy Seal he should not attend those meetings (*Letters of George III to Lord North*, i. 26).

a christening this evening, so I will trouble you no longer, especially as I shall see you to-morrow at S'. James's.

I am my dear lord with great truth and respect
Your most faithful humble serv^t.
NORTH.

The friendly letter from Lord Camden on my return to office, was so gratifying, that I cannot resist the temptation of introducing it here; as it will help to shew our constant attachment, in every scene of life.

MY DEAR LORD,

Tho' my private and retired situation makes me look upon all Court changes with indifference, yet I am in hopes the public may reap considerable advantage by your Grace's return to power: and therefore I take the liberty of adding my private congratulations to those your Grace will of course receive from a thousand humble servants, the friends of your present fortune. Your Grace will remember in what manner we parted, when I was dismissed from my office. That I wished, even in that discontented minute, to separate our private from our public characters; and to preserve a friendship between us independent of politicks; and that your Grace met me with reciprocal professions of cordiality and personal esteem. My wishes and inclinations continue so much the same, that I see no reason why your Grace's promotion should make any alteration in my sentiments. From being free from all political attachments, I am determined to live and converse as I like, without regarding the dislike of any man, though perhaps I may alarm his jealousy, or provoke his suspicions; and therefore if I was not more afraid of public calumny than I am of any private or particular displeasure, I should certainly as I intended pay my respects to your Grace next week, which your Grace must now excuse me from doing, because that would look more like courting your fortune, than seeking your friendship. Notwithstanding which I shall still hold myself engaged, if you please, to spend a day with your Grace at Wakefield Lodge some time in the summer. And when every body sees, as they will in a month or two, that I am neither partaking your good fortune, nor paying homage to it in the moment of your preferment, I shall set at nought every other suspicion that jealousy or malevolence may raise against my conduct. Your Grace will accept of this apology in lieu of a visit and believe me with the most perfect sincerity and esteem,

Your Grace's most obed^t.
Faithful servant,
CAMDEN.

June 14, 1771,
CAMDEN PLACE.

Among the various and some important Acts passed in the next and subsequent sessions, there was nothing done, or even attempted, that could soothe the discontented minds of our American brethren. If there was nothing done to conciliate there was much done to aggravate their grievances: and an opportunity of sending teas, free from taxation, to the American market (which might have been done on the fair pretext of relieving the East India Company's affairs by a great extension of this trade) was unfortunately omitted. Bad management of the Company's affairs, both at home and abroad having brought them to a very necessitous condition; the directors came to Parliament with an ample confession of their humbled state together with entreaties for assistance and relief, and particularly praying, in their petition, that leave might be given to export teas free of all duties to America and to foreign ports. Would not the sagacious minister have availed himself of this fortuitous or rather providential occurrence, and have built on it the future good understanding of every part of the Empire?

Had this leave been granted to America only, exclusive of the other great salutary considerations, no one will hesitate in allowing that it would have been an excellent commercial regulation. Then, if the effect be considered, which it must have had throughout the coast of America, who is there now who would have wished that so beneficial expedient had not been tried? For it will be recollected, that the attempt to land the teas charged with a duty, gave occasion to the first great insurrection in America; which, in the other case, would never have existed.—It may be said, that the small duty upon tea was but the pretence, while the dread of the Declaratory Act was the real sore point: the truth of which I admit to a great degree. Still let it be remembered, that the repeal of the Stamp Act, 1766, was most gratefully received by the colonies, notwithstanding it was accompanied by this famous Act.

Among the king's more confidential servants, Lord Dartmouth[1], who was at the head of the American department, was the only one, who had a true desire to see lenient measures adopted towards the colonies: wherefore he was the only minister with whom I could converse with comfort. I often brought him to coincide in opinion: and I recollect, that once calling on him in St. James's Square, where a meditated joint address was to be settled that morning by the Cabinet, he promised that he would offer my amendments to them, with his own wishes that they might be admitted.

His lordship had scarce finished his words, when Lord Mansfield's chariot driving up to the door, Lord Dartmouth said, most seriously to me; 'There, Duke of Grafton, is the man; who will prevent your wished for alterations from taking place.' The event accorded with Lord D.'s apprehensions.

At a time, when all bodies of men were disposed to be weighing their rights, and stating their grievances, it was not strange, that the clergy of the established church should produce their ground, on which they considered themselves in their consciences to be much aggrieved. Thus, from the obligation of signing the thirty nine Articles, they prayed for relief. A matter of such serious concern merited to be well attended to: and the following part of that petition, which was presented to the House of Commons, marks well the distresses of their minds.

It is therein said,

'Your petitioners apprehend themselves to have certain rights and privileges, which they hold of God alone—of this kind, is the exercise of their own reason and judgment. They conceive they are also warranted, by those original principles of reformation from popery, on which the Church of England is constituted, to judge in searching the Scriptures, each man for himself, what may, or may not be proved thereby. They

---

[1] William, second Earl of Dartmouth, Secretary of State for the Colonies 1772–1775, Lord Privy Seal 1775–1782. George III welcomed him to his service as 'a man of excellent personal character.' He had been a member of the Opposition, and his appointment was regarded as a step towards conciliating the colonies.

find themselves however in a great measure precluded the enjoyment of this invaluable privilege, by the laws relative to subscription whereby your petitioners are required to acknowledge certain articles and confessions of faith and doctrine, drawn up by fallible men, to be all, and every one of them agreeable to the said Scriptures. Your petitioners therefore pray, that they may be relieved from such an imposition on their judgments, and be restored to their undoubted rights as Protestants, of interpreting Scripture for themselves, without being bound by any human explanation thereof. Holy Scripture being acknowledged certain and sufficient for salvation.'

In another place they scruple not to declare, that the imposition of subscription, was an encroachment on their rights, both as men, and as members of a Protestant establishment.

The conduct of these respectable petitioners was perfectly suitable to their station, and I shall ever lament, that they were not successful in their application to Parliament.

They were united on the ground of their grievance; and differed only in the mode of introducing their conscientious sufferings to Parliament: the meeting at the Feather's Tavern, which consisted of some hundreds, preferring to petition the House of Commons directly: and that part, which met at Tennison's Library with M^r. Wollaston of Chiselhurst, thinking it to be more proper to address the Bishops, to bring the business before Parliament. From the Archbishop (Cornwallis [1]) Mr. Wollaston met with a gracious reception, though no answer was given to him. But from his Grace, with the Bishop of Peterborough [2] and some other of the Bishops, we, who most interested ourselves for reasonable relief to the clergy, received the fullest expectations, from their declaration and assurance that the Bench itself would take the matter under consideration, trusting that they might be able to bring about the object desired in that manner which was thought to be most judicious in a civil and religious view.

I acknowledge, that my judgement had led me to expect

[1] Frederick, seventh son of the fourth Lord Cornwallis (1713-1783), Bishop of Lichfield 1749-1768, Archbishop of Canterbury 1768-1783.

[2] Hinchcliffe.

a good issue to the business, provided the bishops had engaged in it liberally, in the following session, as some of them had professed to be willing to do. This last mode of proceeding would have appeared the most decorous to many; and I still think, that the minds of men, enlightened by the reading of the *Confessional*[1], the *two letters* by a *Christian Whig*[2], the *queries*, relating to the Book of Common Prayer, &c., would have inclined them to receive the measure, so proposed, with much satisfaction. May the day soon arrive, when all that is not scriptural shall cease to be supported by the sanction of fallible men[3]! I am credibly informed that Bishop Lowth famed both for the great learning he possessed, as also for his moderation and liberality, had undertaken to review these articles, and having reduced them by discharging the offensive parts, had the mortification to see his amendment and reductions set aside, and as it was said, by high authority.

On my return from Bath, where I had been sent for recovery from a violent stomach attack; and where I had been passing some time, I heard the account of the affair of Lexington, a commencement of avowed hostilities against the Americans, with the deepest concern: and all the information I could collect, tended only to prove to me, that Government, in regard to America, projected no plans, except such, as I from my heart disapproved.

[1] Written by Francis Blackburne, rector of Richmond and Archdeacon of Cleveland. The treatise was 'An inquiry into the right of establishing systematical confessions of faith and doctrine in Protestant churches.'

[2] Written by Richard Watson, then Regius Professor of Divinity at Cambridge, afterwards Bishop of Llandaff. See Abbey and Overton, *English Church in the Eighteenth Century*, vol. ii.

pp. 22, 27, and Leslie Stephen, *English Thought in the Eighteenth Century*, vol. i. pp. 454–458.

[3] For an account of the interest which Grafton took in religious questions, of his secession from the Church of England and of his acceptance of the Unitarian faith, see *Uncorrupted Christianity unpatronized by the Great*, a sermon preached on the occasion of his decease, by Thomas Belsham, Lond. 1811.

CHAPTER IX

GRAFTON IN OPPOSITION

BEFORE I quitted the office I held, it was understood that Mr. Penn had come over from Philadelphia, charged with a petition from Congress to the king: and it was added that no notice would be taken of it by His Majesty's principal servants[1]. It was evident to all considerate men, that the connection of the two countries hung on the decision; for it was stated to many, that on the vote for Independence, Mr. Dickenson[2] and his party had the ascendancy in favour of dependence on this country: and besides, it was equally well known, that a compromise had taken place in order to render the petition unanimous, by the promise of a declaration for Independency from the majority, in case of the rejection of this final application.

I had met with nothing encouraging in the efforts I had made, with the hopes of softening the temper of those measures which appeared to me to be calculated to widen the breach between Great Britain and her colonies: nor had I any longer much expectation, that good could arise from any advice of mine. Yet it will be found, that most men are now of opinion that, long after this period, at various times, a reconciliation might have been easily managed, which would have restored a certain union between the two countries: and a candid consideration of the important evidence delivered by Mr. Penn at the bar of the House, ought to have laid the

[1] *Infra*, p. 282, *note*.　　　　　[2] Author of the *Farmer's Letters*.

foundation of the preliminaries. With hopes much damped by the accounts from America; and by the observation of the manner in which they were considered, I was still anxious for the success of my endeavors; and with that view, I wrote what follows to Lord North, to which his answer is affixed.

WAKEFIELD LODGE, *Aug*. 31st, 1775.

MY DEAR LORD,

I am totally uninformed, in what manner His Majesty's servants mean to proceed in the next session, respecting the unhappy state of American affairs. But the object itself is so great, and the consequences so alarming, that I should be undeserving of that goodness which your lordship has so frequently shewn to me, if I concealed from you my thoughts on the subject; and I hope that you will receive them with that friendly disposition, which this letter intends to convey. For, I can protest to you, that my constant views in a political life are to shew my dutiful and grateful attachment to His Majesty, together with my zealous desire of seeing his Government flourish under your lordship's Administration. I earnestly wish to model my conduct on all occasions, conformably to these two ends. My opinion on our present situation is the result of much serious reflection, and so convincing to my own mind, that I cannot see the subject in any light capable of drawing me from it. I am sensible, how much more easy it is to determine what should not be done, than to lay down the exact measures that ought to be followed: but, I am so anxious to see a speedy end put to our unfortunate differences with the American colonies, that I will acknowledge, I would go great lengths to bring about such a reconciliation as might promise some degree of stability. The inclination, in general, of men of property in this country, and some of the declarations held forth even by the leaders of the Congress in America differing little more than in words, I cannot consider such a reconciliation to be impracticable: and in the present desperate state of things, it appears to me to be very adviseable to attempt it at any rate. A petition, indeed, from persons styling themselves the deputies of the United Colonies, met in Congress, may be inadmissible by His Majesty, as no such body can be acknowledged by the king; yet, may there not be sufficient matter in the contents to encourage individuals to come and state to the whole legislature the wishes and expectations of the different colonies in order that harmony may be restored again?

Some intercourse between two parties, certainly nearer in purposes than each conceives of the other, might thus be opened: the want of which has been our principal misfortune from the first, and must be the cause still of protracting all accomodation. Your lordship may not know that many persons hearty friends to Government have altered their opinions by the events of this year. Their expectation of a strong party in America ready to stand forth under the protection of a regular military force is at an end: they foresee the inefficacy of doubling this force, being now convinced that the Americans can, and will increase theirs accordingly. The training of their men during the winter cannot fail to form them into better troops, and their behavior already has far surpassed the expectation of every one. In short, my lord, many consider the event for us not only to be hopeless, but bringing on certain disgrace and ruin; many see that the expences that must attend such measures will lay a burthen upon this country which in our situation, nothing can justify but an insult from a foreign enemy. If what I have said at large should be different from your lordship's purposes, I cannot flatter myself that it can have any weight; yet let me intreat you to enquire after the opinions also of those independent friends from whom you have received and do expect support in a measure of this magnitude, as I apprehend that you will find many of them who see this business in a different light since the trial, from what it appeared to them before. If Parliament meets early, might not the two Houses address His Majesty that orders should be given to his general to communicate to the rebel army that from various motives of tenderness, affection and humanity, no hostile steps should be taken until the issue should be known, in case the colonies would depute persons to state to Parliament their wishes and expectations. Then a long adjournment might give time for such an application from them, which if declined would prove to the provincials the reluctance which Great Britain has to a civil war, and would give a spirit here (which there is not now) to proceed in it: or, if accepted, might be still in time to restore quiet and a good understanding.

I am so well here since my return from Bath, that I am tempted to set out in a few days to drink the waters again for a fortnight; otherwise I should have come to London, and desired to have the honor of conversing with your lordship rather than to have troubled you with so long and tedious a letter, but this is now impossible as it is the only fortnight I can lay hold of for Bath.

I have the honor to be &c.

GRAFTON.

To this letter I received no answer for seven weeks: after which the following came.

DOWNING STREET, Oct'. 20, 1775.

MY DEAR LORD,

I deferred answering your Grace's very obliging and friendly letter till I could with a tolerable degree of certainty convey to you the general outline of our American plan. For that purpose I take the liberty of

inclosing a draught of the king's speech which is now so nearly com-
pleted, that it will, I believe undergo very few alterations, before it is
delivered in Parliament. It is longer and fuller than speeches at the
opening of sessions have usually been; because it was intended to give
a general plan of the measures to be pursued against the American
rebels. Your humble servant, and I believe I may add His Majesty's
other counsellors still remain ready to agree with any province in
America upon the footing of the resolution of the House of Commons of
the 27th of February last[1]: but the leaders of the rebellion in the colonies
plainly declare themselves not satisfied with those conditions and manifestly aim at a total Independence. Against this we propose to exert
ourselves using every species of force to reduce them; but authorising at
the same time either the Commander in Chief or some other Commissioner,
to proclaim immediately peace and pardon, and to restore all the privileges
of trade to any colony upon its submission. Authority will likewise be
given to settle the question of taxation for the future upon the plan held
forth last year; and to put every other matter now in dispute between
them and this country in a course of accommodation. Till the provinces
have made some submission, it will be in vain to hope that they will come
into any reasonable terms, and I am afraid, that declaring a cessation of
arms at this time would establish that independence which the leaders
of the faction in America have always intended, and which they now
almost openly avow. I beg pardon of your Grace for touching on these
matters so slightly and superficially but I shall be glad of an opportunity
of going into the business more largely when your Grace comes to town.
In the mean while I must desire you not to communicate the inclosed
speech to any one, as it is not yet entirely perfect, and has not been
finally settled in the Cabinet.

I have the honor to be with the greatest respect
My dear lord,
Your most faithful humble ser[t].
NORTH.

The contents of the speech which Lord North inclosed in
his letter left me no room for doubt: and on my arrival in
London, I obtained an audience of the king who received me
in the same gracious manner which I had ever met with from
His Majesty[2]. I ventured however to state to him my appre-

---

[1] This resolution was to the effect
that when any colony should engage to
make provision for the common defence
and the support of the civil government
and administration of justice it will be

proper to forbear levying any duty, tax,
or assessment, except for the regulation
of commerce, such duty to be carried to
the account of such colony.

[2] Nevertheless the king never forgave

T

hensions for the country from the injudicious measures into which we were plunged, through the violence of his ministers, who were not aware of the impracticability of their schemes from a want of knowledge of the resources of the colonies. I added that, deluded themselves, his ministers were deluding His Majesty. The king vouchsafed to debate the business much at large; and appeared to be astonished, when I answered earnestly, to his information that a large body of German troops was to join our forces, that His Majesty would find too late that twice that number would only increase the disgrace[1]: and never effect his purpose.

On coming out of the Closet, I related to the Archbishop Cornwallis, my friend, what I had done; as I did to two or three of my acquaintances I saw at Court. His Grace expressed much sorrow; and I believe, was much concerned that we were to part in politics. It struck me, that Mr. Rigby was the only one, who appeared apprehensive lest my opinions should draw with them many to opposition. But his judgment here was as erroneous, as it often proved.

In a day or two after, I supported warmly the amendment moved on the address[2], and entirely on public ground. In the course of my speech, I gave much into the belief, that could this nation bring itself to restore the colonies to the condition, in which they stood in 1763, peace would be quickly established. The rest was directed to prove the pernicious and fatal consequence, that could not but be foreseen from a continuation of a war so circumstanced. On the following day I was ordered to bring the Privy Seal with me to St. James's; where His Majesty gave me a second patient hearing, on what I foreboded regarding our contest with America. The Seal, which I left with His Majesty, was

---

what he regarded as desertion on the part of Grafton. In his letters to Lord North there occur frequent exhortations to North not to desert him as Grafton had done.

[1] The hiring of German troops, from the petty German powers, to help to subdue our English colonies was the final step towards their alienation.

[2] Grafton spoke vigorously against the address, though still in office. He urged the repeal of every Act passed since 1763 relative to America.

immediately given to Lord Dartmouth[1]. Lord Rockingham's difference from me, with that also of his friends, having been only on political points; we readily renewed our intimacy, when the cause of misunderstanding was removed.

On occasion of the Prohibitory Bill[2], as it was called, I received at Euston the following letters.

MY LORD,

I imagine that your Grace is fully apprized of the purport of the bill, which has now passed the House of Commons, and which was brought up yesterday to the House of Lords where it was read a *first* time yesterday, is ordered to be printed and will be read a *second* time on Friday next. It is to be lamented that the Ministry chuse to push such a measure as this is, at a time when there are but few lords in town. The ministers speak of this act as decisive. I fear it may be so, but not according to their opinion for they conceive that it will intimidate the colonies, while I indeed can only conceive, that it will drive them to greater degrees of passion and exasperation.

I will not now take the liberty of troubling your Grace with the variety of objections which may be made to this bill. At all events, it appears a measure that ought to have a very serious consideration.

I had a letter from the Duke of Manchester yesterday and I have received one this evening from the Duke of Richmond, they will be in town for Friday. Lord Shelburne is in London, I took the liberty of writing a note to his lordship this evening, but I have not an answer as yet.

Having understood that your Grace had expressed a wish of knowing when this bill would be debated, it has encouraged me, to venture to send your Grace the information by express that Friday will be the day in the House of Lords. If your Grace should be inclined, and should come, your presence in the House of Lords would be of great service towards setting the merits of the bill in a proper light, and it would undoubtedly give great satisfaction and encouragement to the friends of peace and conciliation.

I have the honor to be &c.

ROCKINGHAM.

GROSV^r. SQ. *Dec^r*. 12, 1775.

[1] Lord Dartmouth was unwilling to leave his post of Colonial Secretary, and there was a good deal of expense to the country. Lord George Sackville, now Lord G. Germaine, took Dartmouth's place to help North in the Commons. Weymouth became Secretary of State instead of Rochford, who received as a consolation a pension of £2,500 a year. *Letters of George III to Lord North*, i. 286–292.

[2] A bill to prohibit trade and intercourse with the rebellious colonies, introduced by North on Nov. 20, 1775.

M^r. Fox's two letters were also written on the same subject as the foregoing.

MY DEAR LORD,

As your Grace seemed to wish to be informed of any thing of moment, that might be going forward, during your absence, I think it right to inclose you the bill which has been read a second time in our House, and which we are to have in the committee to-morrow. Upon reading this bill you will see in a moment, that it contains the whole of the business of the session ; and therefore I own, I think it ought not to go through the House of Lords without any remarks upon it. It puts us in a state of complete war with America, and by the plunder it encourages. it seems to sow the seeds of perpetual enmity with those, with whom all parties propose friendship and intercourse. The two last provisions of it avowedly contain all that Parliament is to do with respect to the commissioners : so that you see how little we are to know of the destinations or instructions of those, to whom the whole power of this country is entrusted.

It certainly cannot come into the House of Lords before the beginning of next week, and what opposition is intended to it there, I really do not know ; but clearly think there ought to be some. There are many objections I have not touched upon, particularly that of giving the whole trade into the power of the West India Governors.

We do not yet know, who are intended to be sent as commissioners. The report is, that Lord Howe is to be one. I thought it necessary my dear lord to write to you upon this subject early, because I should imagine that with regard to the opposition in the House of Lords much would depend upon your opinion, which I should be very glad to know.

Though I wrote this letter merely with a view of acquainting you with the state of this bill, I cannot let this opportunity go by, of assuring you how very happy I feel to be of opinion on public affairs, with a person, with whom I have always wished to agree ; and with whom I should act with more pleasure, in any possible situation, than with any one I have been acquainted with.

There is a report of an engagement at Bunker's Hill, in which the provincials are said to have had an advantage ; but I believe it to be without foundation.

I am yours ever &c.

C. J. FOX.

LONDON, *Dec.* 4th, 1775.

MY DEAR LORD,

As you expressed a wish to know the day, on which the *Prohibitory Bill*, as it is called, was to be debated, Lord Rockingham is just going to send to you for that purpose: and he seems to wish me to write at the

same time. I have really but little to add to what I wrote your Grace
upon that subject before. I will only observe, that if you read the bill
attentively, you will find there are some circumstances in it, that are
rather new, particularly the confounding of all West Indian and even
British property, with American, if happening to be on board an American
vessel.

The Duke of Richmond will certainly be in town, and I suppose the
Duke of Manchester[1]. With regard to the other lords of the description
you allude to, I really know nothing : but, I should suppose Lord Shelburne
will be there ; as he is in town. Upon all these circumstances, your
Grace must judge of the propriety of coming or staying : I will only say,
that whatever part you take, I for one shall never attribute it to any want
of *zeal* in a cause which, the moment it is seen in the light in which we
see it, must appear to be the greatest that ever engaged any men.

I shall certainly do myself the honor of paying my respects to your
Grace at Euston during the recess : but Harbinger has been so ill, that
I am afraid I cannot assist you in making a sweepstake.

I am, my dear lord your's ever very sincerely

C. J. Fox.

London, *Dec*. 12, 1775.

The light in which the business appeared to us was partly
this, that if a cordial reconciliation was not *speedily* effected
with the colonies, to lose America entirely would be a lesser
evil than to hold her by a military force, as a conquered
country : and that the consequences of holding that dominion
by an army only, must inevitably terminate in the downfal of
the constitution, and liberties of Britain. Thus, success itself
would be dreadful. To prevent these threatening consequences, the Opposition was most honorably engaged : and
it was with the most hearty concurrence with the principal
men who composed it, that I added my little aid : having
fully opened our minds to each other, and found little difference in our opinions.

The mercantile part of the country were more concerned,
and therefore felt serious alarm on the measures of government. These men were chiefly with us : but the landed

---

[1] George, fourth Duke of Manchester
(1737–1788). He is described in the
Rockingham Memoirs, ii. 431, as 'a
Whig with a strong leaning towards
the prerogative.'

gentlemen were not enlightened, at that time, sufficiently to feel the impending danger: a great majority of them were not only abettors of the pernicious measures of the Ministry; but were so uncandid as to brand us as the most wicked of statesmen, and as the cause of the failure of the minister's plans, which were in fact too unwisely drawn to hold out any prospect of success. Our cause, however, though not honored with the support of the largest portion of the landed interest, had to boast of that share of it, which comprehended the most respectable characters of the nation.

I did not aim at any particular knowledge of Lord Shelburne's opinions, as I had heard from Lord Camden that they tallied, to a great degree, with our own. But, I was however much pleased with the following paragraph of a letter which dated Nov. 4th, 1775, I received from Lord Camden; 'The mention of the last lord's (Shelburne's) name gives me an opportunity of acquainting your Grace, that I was desired by him to deliver a handsome and a frank message to your Grace, which I could not well do then, nor indeed can I now; because I cannot venture to recollect the words, and I am afraid of going too far. Thus much I can safely say, that he will fairly open his mind, and tell your Grace very frankly how far he will go, and where he will stop: and in my opinion, he, and his friends Barré and Dunning have a manly and explicit way of proceeding that pleases me.'

After some conversation with Lord Shelburne on public affairs, in consequence of the above message, we became good political friends, and remained so, with the exception of a few immaterial squabbles, to the end of his life.

Lord Chatham's state of health was so very bad, as to prevent him from appearing at all during this session. But, it is but justice due to the eminent personages who composed this opposition to say, that there never existed, at any time, such another in purity of intention towards the public, to whose benefit and welfare their measures were solely directed.

On the plan of this memoir you are not to expect the history of the war, nor more than the documents in my possession can furnish; tho' it will be my desire from these and my own memory to relate what I may think will be acceptable to you. Letters from principal men, on important subjects, however, have the first title to our attention: and I mean to lay them before you in preference to any thing I can bring forward in a different manner.

Proceeding thus, the letters following from Lord Camden find their place:

MY DEAR LORD,

As your letter came to London under a cover, I did not receive it till yesterday morning. It made me very happy, in the good account it gave of your Grace's health. When I was at Bath, I made some acquaintance with D^r. Delacour, who is persuaded your Grace may, if you please, be restored to a state of perfect health. I am much the better for my journey, and am so satisfied with the efficacy of Bath for my constitution, that I am determined to make it another visit next spring; nor shall any consideration of politics restrain me; for indeed my dear lord, the chance of doing good is at an end. So many circumstances have combined, like so many fatalities, to overturn this mighty empire, that all attempts to support are weak and ineffectual. Who could have imagined, that the Ministry could have become popular by forcing this country into a destructive war, and advancing the power of the Crown to a state of despotism? And yet, that is the fact; and we of the minority suffer under the odium, due only to the ministers, without the consolation either of pay or power.

America is lost, and the war a foot[1]. There is an end of advising preventive measures; and peace will be more difficult to make, than the war was: for your Grace justly observes, that the claims of the Americans, if they are successful, will grow too big for concession; and no man here will venture to be responsible for such a treaty. For, I am persuaded it will be the fate of England to stoop, though I don't know the minister to apply so humiliating a remedy. Shall we ever condescend to make that country a satisfaction for damages? and yet, she will never treat without it. What then must be our conduct in Parliament? I am at a loss to advise. I thought, from the beginning of the year, secession was the only measure left, I still think the same: but I will enter the lists of a more active opposition, if that shall be thought best. I wish it were

---

[1] The battles of Lexington and Bunker's Hill had taken place on April 19 and June 16, 1775, and in May the Congress of the thirteen colonies had taken measures for armed resistance, and had appointed Washington Commander-in-Chief.

possible for the whole body to unite; but union is only understood and practised on the other side of the Atlantick. That would be respectable, and perhaps formidable: but, I do not expect to see it. Absence would look more like union to the public, and might perhaps join us at last into a confederacy.

If motions are to be made, they should be in concert, and we ought to protect and defend each other from attacks, like real friends: else like other broken forces we shall be put to the rout. We must, however, my dear lord, wait till we meet, and the field before us will furnish measures. I have been now two months absent from the scene of business, and during the whole time, have not received a line from a creature living upon the subject of politicks. So little are we together upon any joint plan: I am however in good health and spirits, and please myself with the expectation of enjoying your Grace's company during the remainder of the session.

Euston is too far, and my own house full at present; else, knowing by Wakefield what I should meet with in Suffolk, I should fly to your Grace's family immediately. I have the honor to be &c.

CAMDEN.

Lord Chatham continues in the same melancholy way: and the house is so shut up that his sons are not permitted to receive visitors.

Jan^{ry}. 4th, 1776. CAMDEN PLACE.

MY DEAR LORD,

I had the honor of your Grace's note this morning, and am not surprized at your postponing your London journey till the 28th. I shall not be in town many days before, and I presume, that nothing of any moment can start before your Grace's arrival; without whom I do not mean to join in any business respecting America. I shall persist to the last, in giving my testimony against this pernicious war, tho' I neither expect success, nor popular applause. But it will be no inconsiderable consolation, to hear my name joined to your Grace's, let the event turn out as it may.

I beg your Grace will present my respects, with the compt^s. of the season to the Duchess, and

Believe me to be &c.
CAMDEN.

Jan. 7th, 1776.

I hope your Grace has received my last.

MY DEAR LORD,

Upon looking carefully into the Act, passed before Xtmas [1], to give the property of the prizes to the captors; and more especially into the last

---

[1] 16 Geo. III. c. 5, the Prohibitory Act, the introduction of which is referred to on p. 275.

clause, I find the bill has given the king a full power, not barely to suspend, but finally to stop the operation of the Act, by a positive repeal, whenever *he shall think* the provinces are *disposed* to return to their duty. His power therefore is absolute not only to suspend, but to put an end to the Capture Bill, even for the sake of opening a treaty. For, a proposal of terms, such as His Majesty may think do manifest a disposition to return &c., being a ground according to the Act of Parliament to justify a total cessation of hostility by sea, will, a fortiori, give him authority to suspend the same for a time.

Your Grace will observe, that the condition, upon which the king is authorized to issue his proclamation, is not *an actual return to their duty*, which (if the Act was so penned) could mean nothing short of an *unconditional submission*, but a *disposition* to return; of which *disposition*, the Crown being the judge—any plan of peace, which His Majesty may conceive reasonable, and likely to be adopted by Parliament, may fairly be construed into a *disposition*, &c.

This Act therefore does in effect put the very terms and conditions of the peace into the hands of the Crown: for altho' he cannot by his own authority repeal any of the bills, now enacted against America, yet upon a sketch of a treaty, he may engage to propose any such plan to Parliament, and will be pretty sure to carry his point there, more especially if he changes his Administration.

If my reasoning is just upon this bill, which I submit to your Grace's better judgment, then the very ground of the motion fails, and it must not be made.

I have lodged this at your Grace's house, to be delivered to you the moment you come to town, and will be ready to wait on your Grace the moment I hear you are arrived.

I have the honor to be &c.

CAMDEN.

Tuesday, *Feb.* 20, 1776. DUKE St.

A disposition to return &c. is not properly a *condition* to warrant the proclamation, as I have expressed it in the former part of my letter, but *the encouragement of the well affected*, and *the speedy protection of such as are well disposed*, are no other than the motives and reasons for the Parliament giving the king a full and unlimited power to repeal the bill, for he is the sole judge, when it will be proper to give to them *encouragement* and *protection*; and what kind of behaviour ought to be deemed a *disposition* &c.

This therefore is the language of the Act. Your Majesty shall be at liberty to repeal the bill, whenever you shall think it expedient to encourage or protect those, that you shall be satisfied are well affected or *disposed* to return to their duty.

These words *disposed &c.*, which we did not much attend to, are very deeply considered, and give the key to the whole clause.

The evidence delivered by M^r. Penn[1] was more particularly attended to, than falls, in general, to the lot of witnesses examined at our Bar. His character for veracity and honor was universally acknowledged, and the very ample powers and authority he had to express what he delivered on the disposition of the colonies, as well as of the Congress in particular, drew from his audience an uncommon interest. But it availed little; and Lord Mansfield scrupled not to pronounce, 'that M^r. Penn was speaking under influence, and that consequently his whole evidence, must, in toto, be set aside.'

Indeed his lordship had no other resource to get rid of an invincible chain of evidence: and the House was sufficiently pliant to support his lordship in a position so ill-founded and unjust.

This disposition shewn by Parliament, to agree in every proposal from Administration at a moment of danger so very critical, damped every hope of future success in the cause, however well chosen the ground might be. Disheartening as the circumstances stood, we would not be dismayed; and among others, who had more weight, I framed, with the concurrence and assistance of those with whom I acted, a motion, to which the attention of the colonies, I attempted to prove, might be drawn, though it never would, nor could be to the powers given, under the Act, to the Commissioners. The object of the motion, which I made in the House of Lords, about the middle of March [2], was to take off, if possible, the impression which the Act lately past gave of *unconditional*

---

[1] Richard Penn brought over a petition from Congress voted in July, and presented on September 1. The petition, though somewhat vague in its terms, seemed to show a desire for a friendly adjustment of difficulties. It was received in silence by the Secretary of State (Dartmouth), who wrote a few days later to inform Penn that no answer would be made. The petition, the examination of Penn, and the debates, which arose thereon, are to be found in the *Parliamentary History*, vol. xviii. pp. 896-935.

[2] On March 14, *Parliamentary History*, xviii. 1247.

submission, and which the language of His Majesty's ministers too plainly conveyed. The substance of it was, 'that an humble address be presented to His Majesty, that in order to prevent the further effusion of blood, a proclamation might be issued, declaring, that if the colonies shall present a petition to the Commissioners, appointed under the late Act, setting forth what they consider to be their just rights and real grievances, that, in such a case, His Majesty will consent to a suspension of arms ; and that, assurance shall be given them, that their petition shall be received, considered, and answered.' The measure appeared to me likewise to inculcate the idea that there might be terms and conditions implying mutual concessions, on which a satisfactory and permanent accomodation might be founded, and a constitution suitable to their situation fixt and established : and all this, I maintain'd, was still within reach without the necessity of a separation from the mother country.

I stated repeatedly, that the mere mention of the words, 'unconditional submission,' was destructive of every hope, and rendered all reconciliation impracticable : therefore the necessity of this or a similar measure was indispensable. I dwelt much also on the disadvantages under which this country was contending with America ; and that the resources and spirit of the colonies would be found far to exceed what they were represented to be. In the course of this speech, I informed the House, and warned the ministers, that I knew, from unquestionable authority, that two French gentlemen had been presented by General Washington to many leading men in the Congress ; and who knew the object of their mission. Thus, we were convinced, that a direct interference from foreign powers had taken place, as to our civil contentions : and from a formidable quarter, which attempt required to be instantly counter-acted.

The motion was ably supported by many on our side : and the speeches on the other were ingenious, but miserably mistaken in all that the speakers presumed to prognosticate. Besides, the doctrine of unconditional submission being vindicated throughout, they ridiculed the possibility of an effectual resistance from America; and they declared their firm disbelief of any interference on the part of France or any other foreign power: for as they had colonies of their own, they could never be stirring up revolt, among those of other nations. The debate was long; but the motion was rejected by a majority of 91 against 31.

A respectable historian of the present day observes on this event; that 'What had been hitherto perfectly easy and feasible, now became by a change of circumstances desperate and hopeless.' It had that appearance I confess; yet, when it is considered, that the peace was not made till the end of the year 1782, I must think that an earlier change of Ministry, would have seized many opportunities of establishing a more beneficial connexion and intercourse with America, before that country had leagued itself too far with France.

Another historian of credit states that, 'this day will perhaps hereafter be considered, as one of the most important in the English history. It deeply fixed a new colour upon our public affairs. It was decisive on this side of the Atlantic with respect to America; and may possibly hereafter be compared with, and considered as preliminary to that, on which, unhappily, in a few months after, the independence of that continent, was declared on the other.'

Some months after, I received from a quarter, which I could depend upon (with nearly the same confidence, as if I had been present at the transactions), intelligence so essential to the concerns of this country, that notwithstanding the ungracious reception which my former communication had met with from Administration I could not resist the desire I had of discharging my duty, by communicating the contents of it to the Secretary of State. I accordingly waited on Lord Weymouth: introducing my business, with saying to his lordship, that though he was at liberty to give what credit he thought fit to my information, I should consider myself to be impardonable, if I did not in confidence relate the following circumstances to his lordship, in order that the

king's servants might make the proper use of them: that
I had received my intelligence through a channel which had
never deceived me: that his lordship well knew the delicacy
of communications of this kind, and could not expect any
further particulars, relating to it. except that I did not attain
the intelligence at His Majesty's expence: that the Duke of
Bridgewater [1] well knew, that my information, regarding the
decision of the French Cabinet, on the business of Falkland's
Islands was more accurate than that of Administration: and
I might add, that the Cabinet of France had since verified in
every point the informations which I had before received: on
which grounds I gave perfect confidence to that, which the
same channel now brought to me.

Having thus introduced my business with Lord Weymouth,
I proceeded, saying, that I concluded his lordship must have
heard from our ambassador, that Silas Deane arrived at Paris
in July: tho' he might not be apprized, that this gentleman
had frequent conferences at Versailles with Mon^r. de Vergennes;
that Silas Deane [2] had been traced to a Monsieur Dubourg's
where he had met more than once Girard [3], who was considered
as one of the ablest Secrétaires de Bureau, and much in the
confidence of the minister; and that there was full ground
for belief, that Vergennes [4] had himself been present at these
meetings; but was conveyed to them in a carriage, borrowed
for the occasion. I added, that his lordship ought to be
informed, that 10,000 stand of arms were sent, or ordered
down to Nantes, consigned to the address of a Mon^r. Pinet
there: that cannon had been cast in the royal founderies, and

[1] Francis, third and last Duke of
Bridgewater (1736–1803), the celebrated
promoter of inland navigation. How
he was concerned in the matter referred
to I do not know. At the time of the
affair of the Falkland Isles he was busy
completing the canal between Manchester and Liverpool: nor can I ascertain that he ever held political office.

[2] Silas Deane came over to Paris in
July, 1776, as a secret agent, to ascertain
the feeling of the French Court. Later
in the year he was appointed with Frank-
lin and Lee a commissioner to negotiate
with the European powers. He deserted
the American cause with Arnold.

[3] Gerard de Rayneval, vide infra,
p. 346.

[4] Vergennes was at this time Foreign
Minister to Louis XVI.

which had not the arms of France impressed upon them in
the customary way; the workmen from thence knowing that
they were ordered, and in haste, for some foreign service.
I observed to Lord Weymouth, that some of these points
might without difficulty be soon ascertained by our ambassador; particularly whether M^r. Deane was generally
considered by those about Court as an agent from America ;
and whether, among the numberless officers who had petitioned
to go over to join Genl. Washington, there were not some who
had obtained leave.

I observed to his lordship that it was impossible for me to
imagine that Lord Stormont[1] had not acquainted him, that
American ships were received and protected in the ports of
France, where their cargoes of every description were unloaded;
when they openly took in arms and ammunition as their
returning lading.

The ambassador could not have omitted to inform his
lordship, that the preparations making in all the French
ports gave serious ground for alarm, and indicated plainly the
hostile disposition of the French Court.

In addition to all these matters, I ventured solemnly to
assure his lordship that I had it from authority, on which
I confidently relied, that the Cabinet of France had been
unanimous in their determinations, that the moment was too
inviting to be passed by, and that France must seize the
favorable opening of taking part with the Americans against
Great Britain.

If Lord Weymouth wished to bring the matter to issue;
he had only to apply to the French Court for the removal of
Silas Deane out of France, when he would receive for answer
a refusal: for the Court of France felt the advantage they
should derive from the bad policy which had already entangled
us in a ruinous war, and was determined to avail itself of it.
I cannot say, that I expected much open communication from

---

[1] David, fifth Earl of Stormont, in
the peerage of Scotland, was ambassador
at Paris, 1772-1778, and Secretary of
State, 1779-1782. He succeeded his
uncle, the first Earl of Mansfield, in
1793, and died in 1796.

my old friend, in return for mine: nor was I disappointed, when from a man of his well known closeness of character, though endowed with many excellent qualities, I was coldly thanked for my attention, and dismissed without being questioned on any one particular.

It is a great relief to my mind, especially at the period now before us that I have not undertaken to give the accounts of the successes, or of the disgraces, which befell the British troops: as they are already before the public, and appear to be with accuracy reported.

To those persons, who were well acquainted with the characters and dispositions of our rulers, it was not strange that ill success should generally attend their plans and measures. Lord North in private life was an upright honorable man; and his talents were unquestioned: but he neither had the peculiar talent himself of conducting extensive war operations; nor was the ability and judgment of his co-adjutors sufficient to make up the deficiency.

Lord Sandwich at the Admiralty was very unpopular with the highest order of the naval officers, many of whom declined serving under him, after the court martial on Admiral Keppel[1]; alledging that they did not consider their characters to be safe in his hands: nor was the confidence in the Cabinet much improved by the choice of Lord George Germaine, as the War Minister.

The session, which terminated on May the 23^d, 1776, had produced no measure, by which the minds of men of judgment could be turned to any comfortable expectations. Whatever attempt the Opposition made towards reconciliation with the colonies, was each day treated more and more with asperity: and, indeed, it was dispiriting to find so large a majority in both Houses, still supporting the impolitic counsels of the Ministry. Thus disheartened and with slender hope of moderating the current of the tide, we in the Opposition had nothing left, but to retire to our country seats; and there

[1] This took place after the quarrel between Keppel and Palliser, arising out of the conduct of the latter in the indecisive battle off Ushant in 1778.

meditate, if we could, on every means that might be employed, to bring Great Britain to see, how much she was acting against her true interests.

It was a great misfortune, and loss to the country, that Lord Chatham was still in that condition of health, as to be incapable of giving his assistance in Parliament, which, I firmly believe, would have had an effect which no other could.

Lord Camden passed over to Ireland, on a visit to his daughter, married to Mr. Stewart, now become Earl of Londonderry: and I have often since indulged in the idea of the happiness my old friend would have enjoyed had he lived to see the marriage of his amiable grandaughter to my worthy son Charles[1] take place.

Before Lord Camden left Ireland, I received the letter, of which the following is a copy:

MY DEAR LORD,

It is now near a month, since I had a letter from Walpole, dated at Wakefield, intimating that your Grace wished to hear my sentiments upon the present state of affairs. This letter reached me at Santry, Lord Chancellor's house, within 2 miles of Dublin, where, after I had for some days been occupied with sights and dinners, a fit of the gout laid hold of me, and kept me confined, till by making an effort to return back hither, I ventured into a post chaise, before the fit was well spent, and got home safe (for in Ireland, I call this house my home) and now, my dear lord, why have I so long delayed to comply with your wishes? Why, besides my own unworthiness to give an opinion to your Grace which I am fitter to receive, the difficulty of forming one, at a time like this, where a man's conduct may depend upon the issue of American events, has withheld me hitherto, from committing my thoughts to paper, more especially as the times grow dangerous, and words must be well measured before they are spoken. The colonies have now declared their independence[2]: *they are enemies in war, and friends in peace*; and the two countries are fairly rent asunder. What then are we? mere friends or enemies to America. Friends to their rights and privileges, as fellow subjects, but not friends to their independence.

This event does not surprize me; I foresaw it. The ministers drove it on, with a view of converting a tyrannical and oppressive invasion into

---

[1] Lord Charles Fitz-Roy, the youngest son of the Duke by his first wife. He served in the army, and sat in several Parliaments for Bury St. Edmunds. He married Lady Frances Stewart in 1799.

[2] July 4, 1776.

a national and necessary war; and they have succeeded too well: and now I expect the Opposition will be called upon to join with them in one cause; and we shall be summoned as Englishmen to unanimity.

But, if your Grace should see a French war to grow out of this civil dispute, which I expect and believe to be unavoidable, our provinces will then be leagued with our enemies, in. an offensive war against Great Britain. In such a situation, a private man may retire and lament the calamities, which he endeavored fruitlessly to prevent. But, how can he give an active opposition to measures that self preservation will then stamp with necessity? I have but one line to pursue, if I am to bear any part, and that is, a reunion with America, almost at any rate. 'Si possis recte: si non quocunque modo.' But I do not expect the Ministry, the Parliament, or the nation will adopt any such system. So that, what with the general fear in some of incurring the popular odium, and in others of seizing this opportunity to make their fortunes, by shifting their position according to Lord Suffolk's phrase, the minority next winter will dwindle to nothing. And now, my dear lord, is such a letter as this worth the postage? and yet this is even all that I can say uninformed as I am, and so distant from the scene of business. Your Grace however will be the first person with whom I shall wish to confer upon my return, which I am now meditating, as I propose in about a fortnight to set out for England; when I hope to find your Grace's health established. Mine continues very tolerable, because I continue in the same abstemious regimen. My journey to Ireland in some respects has answered, in others, been disappointed, but that is the chequered condition of all our pursuits: and I am philosopher enough to be content while my stomach is at ease: and if we sleep a little sound with our ill success in politicks, I can still find comfort enough in your Grace's friendship, as a private man, if you will permit me, to compensate all my public disappointments.

I am &c.

CAMDEN.

Augt. 29, 1776. BANGOR.

Your Grace will be so good to give my respects to the Dutchess and Lady Georgiana.

Since I wrote the above, the Gazette account of S^r. P. Parker's repulse from Charlestown[1] arrived—a miserable tale of loss, disappointment, and disgrace; and wherein the demeanor of the land army is concealed under a pretended ignorance of the depth of the ford, which is very strange.

---

[1] General Clinton attacked Charlestown on June 28, 1776, supported by the fleet under Sir Peter Parker. The attack was repulsed with the loss of an English frigate.

For how could it be, that Clinton should remain ignorant of that important fact, who had then been encamped upon Long Island from the 8th to the 28th and might have tried the sounding of the ford, whenever he pleased. This business grows every day worse and worse : the attack of New York [1] will be pretty decisive one way or other. Some success on our side may give an opening for reconciliation. If we are repulsed there too—'actum est'—the colonies are gone for ever: England has made its last effort, and must retire.

Parliament met on the 31st of October, 1776, soon after the account of the successes of the king's troops at Long Island and New York. These gave an opening to expressions of triumph, which were but of short duration. The Opposition abated nothing of their former zeal for reconciliation, but it did not appear that any fresh strength in Parliament supported their attempts.

I here insert some more letters received from Lord Camden about this time :

MY DEAR LORD,

I am very sorry I cannot contrive so, as to accept your Grace's obliging invitation to Euston. But, unluckily Mr. Pratt is under a necessity to pay a visit this week to a relation, before he goes to Cambridge : and I shall be obliged to return immediately, in order to prepare for my Bath journey.

These engagements will take me of course from Parliament till after Xtmas, and I presume your Grace has no intention at present to trouble that assembly sooner.

Lord Rockingham, I understand with his friends, will likewise retire into the country [2] : but if your Grace should call upon me, before I go to Bath, to join in any public business, I will be forth-coming, and postpone my Bath journey. If however, in the mean time, I should have the honor of seeing you at Camden Place on Tuesday, which may possibly happen to suit with your Grace's inclination, we might settle our political plan with more certainty.

I have the honor &c.

CAMDEN.

*Nov*r. 3d, 1776. CAMDEN PLACE.

---

[1] New York was captured by General Howe on Sept. 15, 1776.
[2] The Rockingham party proposed to secede from public business at the close of 1776, but the secession was not united or complete and it proved a failure (*Rockingham Memoirs*, ii. 307, 317).

MY DEAR LORD,

I hope M^r. Stonhewer made my apology to your Grace, for running back to Camden Place when I was within 30 miles of Euston, which mortified me much more than it could disappoint your Grace.

I am here perfectly idle, and at ease, nor do I expect any call to Parliament, before Christmas ; and therefore propose in about ten days to set out for Bath. I should not have troubled your Grace with this letter, which conveys nothing in the way of intelligence worth sending ; but for the sake of the inclosure, which I received this morning from Hayes, and I dare say, your Grace will be pleased to see it from the best authority, in the very words it was penned, tho' your Grace as well as myself had heard of such a declaration but very imperfectly represented, as most things are that are circulated by verbal reports.

Lord Chatham is certainly better, and I believe, if he could recover strength enough to crawl down to the House of Lords, tho' but for one day, he will go, and make a solemn declaration of his opinion.

Your Grace's occupation, I hope, is in the field, following your hounds, an admirable exercize, if not over done—mine is likewise in the field, tho' in a gentler way. I am covering my ground with shell marle, in good health. I recommend to your Grace moderate exercize and temperate diet : and with my respectful compt^s. to the Duchess and Lady Georgiana beg leave &c.

CAMDEN.

Novr. 22^d, 1776. CAMDEN PLACE.

MY DEAR LORD,

You made me happy by the honour of your letter this morning to find your Grace has not entirely forgot your poor friend at Camden Place : to say the truth I never expected your Grace, as the weather has proved so very uncomfortable, for except one week, when I was in Essex upon a visit, there has been hardly a day to tempt your Grace abroad, though I will not even yet despair. I beg leave to congratulate your Grace upon the increase of your family, and hope the Duchess is as fortunate in her recovery as my own daughter, who is likewise at this very time in the same condition : your Grace will be so good as to present my best respects to her. I have read the account of our two sons in the papers this morning at the Edinburgh Theatre and am excessively happy to observe a growing friendship between the two young men, and hope the world will always find them together when they come hereafter to act a part in the great theatre of the world. I have seen my great neighbour but once since I came into the country. He was then well and in high spirits, and promised to return the visit.

As Lady Camden goes to town to-morrow, she will send this to your Grace's house, and bring back to me at night any answer you think fit to send, if you think it worth while to send any. Your Grace's intelligence has stolen into the papers, but it is much more satisfactory to hear it confirmed by your letter, since the newspapers are so poisoned with falsehood, that I find it utterly impossible to distinguish the truth. Your Grace who is nearer the scene, and in the way of private intelligence, seems to think some change must take place. I despair so far, as to think even that without hope. But, if it should, where is that man, who will undertake at this crisis to save England? No regular physician will engage a cure: and no quack can accomplish it. America is gone for ever: and nothing remains now, but a treaty with her as an independent state, which we must not propose, and the ministers dare not attempt. And yet, I think if an able Administration was formed, and ground given for its stability and continuance, I could venture as one to join in such a measure, and run the hazard of it: we must not go to war with France, if it can possibly be avoided, tho' the ministers are now, as it should seem, endeavoring to provoke the people, to a clamour for that measure, in order to silence all censure upon their own misconduct, in the general calamity of such a distressful situation: not, that any thing can prevent it, but a peace with America. Your Grace's letters have recalled me into the political world, from whence I have been perfectly retired, since I left London, and have been better employed, in looking after my farm, and studying my health. I have read Cornaro's [1] treatise upon health and long life, and find it so rational, that I am determined to pursue it. Indeed I had nearly adopted his regimen, before I saw his book, which is the most rational plan I ever met with on this subject. I wish your Grace would read it with some attention [2].

If your Grace will not come to Camden Place, I will come and see you in town, tho' I should like the first better than the second. I am disengaged all the mornings this week, and the days except Wednesday, Friday, and Saturday.

I have the honor &c.

CAMDEN.

July 27, 1777. CAMDEN PLACE.

Since I wrote this, I have received a melancholy account of a stroke received to day by Lord Chatham as he was riding. He fell from his

---

[1] Cornaro was an Italian who, having broken down in health at the age of forty, framed for himself a rule of diet under which he lived to be a centenarian. He died in the latter part of the sixteenth century.

[2] Grafton, though a man of active habits and attached to outdoor sports, seems to have been somewhat of a *malade imaginaire.*

In *Moore's Diary,* v. 204, are some quaint anecdotes, told to Moore by the second Lord Lansdowne, concerning the care of the Duke about the cooking of his daily dinner of mutton, and how he had to explain his movements, during an interview with a colleague, as needed to make up his daily modicum of bodily exercise.

horse, and lay senseless for ten minutes. The message to-night is, that he is very much recovered. Whether this was apoplectic, paralytic, or gout in the stomach, I cannot learn. I wish it may not prove fatal! The public has lost him and I fear he and England will perish together.

MY DEAR LORD,

Though perhaps I ought according to the forms of good breeding, to have thanked your Grace much sooner for your obliging present of game, yet, I thought it better to wait till I could give you some satisfactory account of my neighbour Lord Chatham's health, and his intentions at the opening of Parliament ; and so send your Grace a letter better worth reading, than a mere card of thanks. If your Grace thinks, as I do, that the Earl's recovery, may, upon some possible event, give a new turn to publick affairs, you will not be sorry to hear that he is now (tho' it seems almost miraculous) in bodily health, and in mental vigour, as equal to a strenuous exertion of his faculties, as I have known him these seven years. His intention is to oppose the address, and declare his opinion very directly against the war, and to advise the recalling the troops, and then propose terms of accomodation, wherein he would be very liberal and indulgent, with only one reserve and exception, viz., that of subjection to the mother country : for, that he never could bring himself to subscribe to the independence of America. This, in general, will be the line, and this he will pursue, if he is alone. I should imagine your Grace would have no objection to concur with this plan, tho' it is certain beforehand that all the breath will be wasted, and the advice over-ruled by numbers. Yet it would be right to stand firm upon the same ground, and not depart an inch from our steady purpose of opposing this war for ever. L^d. C. does not mean to have any meeting, or conference with the heads of parties, in which I agree with him, and your Grace will not disapprove : thus much I thought it my duty to impart to your Grace : for my own part I still continue in the same state of despondency, hoping nothing, and fearing everything. So that all my serious thoughts are employed about my own health, and my little domestick concerns, wherein I receive the satisfaction of seeing my endeavors prosper. I hope to hear as good an account of your Grace's health, as I am able to give you of mine : which I so improved by abstinence, that I sometimes forget my age—My son is gone to Cambridge this day; but he does not expect to meet Lord Euston till the 2^d week in Novr. Nothing gives me so much pleasure as to observe a growing friendship between the two young men, which will probably be lasting : because it is contracted by themselves, and is merely voluntary on both sides. Your Grace will be so good, as to present my most respectful comp^{ts}. to the Duchess.

I am my dear lord,

with the utmost &c.

Oct. 29, 1777. CAMDEN PLACE.   CAMDEN.

The health of Lord Chatham had been so greatly mending during the last summer, as to allow him, tho' wrapped in flannel, to come down to the House of Lords, on the 30th of May, 1777, when he moved, 'That an humble address be presented to His Majesty most humbly to advise His Majesty to take the most speedy and effectual measures for putting a stop to the present unnatural war against the colonies, upon the only just and solid foundation namely, the removal of accumulated grievances[1].'

He spake with his usual spirit, and appeared to want no force of reasoning in recommending his measure. On this occasion, it was particularly grateful to me to perceive, that Lord Chatham was disposed to treat me with all the attention and confidence I could wish, in consequence of some conversations I understood Lord Camden and his lordship had on the whole of my conduct.

Without a word said on the past, I found him perfectly open, and communicative to me directly: and so we remained towards each other as long as Lord Chatham lived.

Previously to the meeting of Parliament, Oct. 1777, on my coming to London, I received the note following from Lord Chatham, which I give with more satisfaction, as it completely demonstrates (contrary to the insinuations of many) that there subsisted an established good understanding between us.

Lord Chatham presents his respects to the Duke of Grafton, and begs leave to trouble his Grace with the inclosed motion intended for the first day in the House of Lords. If fears for the public, and unfeigned respect for the Duke of Grafton, may be an apology, this liberty will find pardon.

HAYES, Nov[r]. 18th, 1777. Tuesday night.

His Grace will perceive the motion is simple[2], and avoids all entanglement of detail.

---

[1] For particulars of this debate see *Parliamentary History*, xix. 316.

[2] The motion consisted in an amendment to the Address, urging the cessation of hostilities in America, see *Parl. Hist.* xix. 395. In a note on p. 360 is given Boyd's report of Chatham's speech, and his outburst of indignation at Lord Suffolk's defence of the employment of the Indians in our war with the colonists.

It would be useless to attempt to describe to you the brilliancy of Lord Chatham's powers, as an orator, on this memorable occasion: for no relation can give more than a faint idea of what he really displayed. In this debate he exceeded all that I had ever admired in his speaking. Nothing could be more eloquent and striking, than the arguments and language of his lordship's first speech, on moving the amendment proposed; or which might be properly called a new address. But, in Lord Chatham's reply to Lord Suffolk's inhuman position, 'that besides the policy and necessity of employing Indian savages in the war, the measure also was allowable on principle, as it was perfectly justifiable to use every means, that God and Nature had put into our hands.' On which Lord Chatham started up with a degree of indignation, that added to the force of the sudden and unexampled burst of eloquence, which must have affected any audience: and which appeared to me to surpass all that we have heard of the celebrated orators of Greece or Rome.

The presence of Lord Chatham, and in so good a state of body and mind, as to give expectation of material assistance from him, instilled fresh spirit into the Opposition; and to that part of the nation who thought as they did. Still, the majority, both in and out of Parliament, continued in a blind support of the measures of Administration. Even the great disgrace and total surrender of Genl. Burgoyne's army at Saratoga, was not sufficient to awaken them from their follies. The day, however did come at last; but so late, that it was no longer possible to bring the two countries into such an union as would best have secured the welfare and safety of both.

Some few days after M^r. Fox moved for an inquiry into the state of the nation; to which Lord North gave his full assent. But, the minister with warmth refused to lay certain papers before the House, tho' he was informed, that, on the same motion being made by myself, they had been granted that day to the Lords. Thus it was curious to see, under these circumstances, the ductility of the majority, for they decided,

on a strong division, not to have those papers, which the
House of Lords had obtained [1]. From hence, it will not
appear strange, that many motions from M[r]. Fox, Col. Barré,
M[r]. Burke and others, in this committee of inquiry met with
the like fate.

On the day following, certain accounts were received from
Genl. Burgoyne, of his total discomfiture, at Saratoga, and
that he had been under the necessity of surrendering to the
enemy [2] together with his whole army. The last letters, tho'
not flattering, had not led to expect an issue so disastrous
as this. The amazement of the whole nation was equalled
only by the consternation they felt: while the judicious
observer saw the cause of the calamity to have originated
from the unskilful planning of such an expedition.

On the 5th of December, Lord Chatham attended the
House of Lords, and moved, 'an address to His Majesty, to
cause the proper officer to lay before the House, copies of all
orders and instructions to Gen[l]. Burgoyne relative to the late
expedition from Canada.'

On the failure of this first motion of L[d]. Chatham, he
moved, 'that all orders and treaties relative to the employment of the Indian savages be laid before the House.'

The debates on these important subjects were, as you may
imagine, very interesting: Lord Chatham, in both, did ample
justice to his cause; and was ably supported by Lord Camden,
Lord Shelburne, and others. In the course of these debates,
an opportunity somehow offered, to give room for a strong
censure on the conduct of the Archbishop of York, as well
as on his principles, who had dared to stigmatize the fair
character of the Marquis of Rockingham (for his meaning in
a late charge could not be mistaken) and his adherents, as
traitors to their country [3]: and I availed myself of the opening

---

[1] *Parl. Hist.* xix. 513.

[2] The surrender of Burgoyne at Saratoga, which took place on October 17,
1777, was the turning-point in the war.
In February, 1778, the alliance between
France and the States was formally executed, and thenceforward we had a great
naval power constantly threatening our
communications with America.

[3] *Parl. Hist.* xix. 513 *et sq.*

to the extent of my wishes. But Lord Shelburne in his speech spared his Grace still less: and Lord Chatham, learning at the moment only the circumstance from me, exceeded us both, in the strength of his attack on the archbishop, who, by any person acquainted with the publication, must be deemed to have deserved it from us. Lord Chatham attended, and joined us also, in deprecating the idea of extending the adjournment, in the present critical situation of the country, to so distant a day as the 20th of January.

I shall here insert for your inspection two letters I received from M^r. Fox soon after I got down to Euston.

MY DEAR LORD,

You have long before this heard of Burgoyne's surrender, with all the circumstances attending it : you will easily guess the effect produced here by such an event, upon the public. But the manner and conduct of His Majesty's principal servants would I believe astonish you. Lord Suffolk chose but yesterday to talk in a high tone of the *vagrant congress* as he called it : and though Lord North hinted at terms to be now offered to America, yet he affected to talk language of great firmness, with respect to himself, and gave very strong assurances to his friends, that he would not quit his situation. To corroborate the language and to hold out to the public, that no negociation would be attempted with any part of opposition, Lord Jersey and Hopkins are turned out, and their places filled as you will see by the papers. This is their idea of firmness, and the preliminary step they take towards conciliation with the colonies, is to shew a determined spirit of persecution against all, who ever entertained an idea of that sort, before they were beat into it. To do the public justice, I do really believe, that the ministers are held in the most universal contempt both by friends and enemies : but I do not yet see so much mixture of indignation with that contempt as I expected.

I hope to do myself the honor of waiting upon you in the course of next week, and of talking over more at large the very singular and critical state of this country.

I am &c.

Yours ever sincerely

C. J. FOX.

LONDON, *Dec*^{br}. 12th, 1777.

MY DEAR LORD,

As the Gazette of to-night is not likely to come out time enough to go by the post, I write this to let you know (what you probably will have heard from others) that an officer arrived last night from Burgoyne by way of Quebec. He brings letters from Burgoyne dated Oct[r]. 20th, Albany, confirming all we had before heard. These letters are to be printed out at length by the particular desire of the General and his friends here, though I understand there are passages in them, which our governors will not much like to make public: for if I am not mistaken, the orders given for advancing at all hazards, will be stated to have been so peremptory, that the General did not think himself at liberty even to call a council of war, upon the subject of retreating.

Lord Petersham[1] is expected daily with a duplicate of these despatches by way of New York. He is spoken of in the highest terms in all Burgoyne's.

Pray remember me to Vernon[2], if he is with you. I was extremely sorry to hear he has been ill: I am afraid it will not be in my power to wait upon your Grace this week, as I intended ; but it shall not be long before I have that honor.

I am &c.
C. J. Fox.

London, Dec[r]. 16th, 1777.

I inclose in another cover a letter I have received from a friend at Bristol, which was printed in a hurry there, from a Boston newspaper, and some manuscripts, which my friend has good reason to think authentic.

The debates during this session were unusually frequent and warm; and began to occupy every day more the attention of the nation.

During the course of the session, an unexpected circumstance came to light: it was first brought to me, through the same channel of intelligence, in which I had so great reason to confide. I was acquainted by it, that a treaty of alliance &c. was signed between France and America, on the very evening before that of the departure of my information. The particulars were circumstantial as to the place, at which it was signed, and as to the persons present. The same mail had brought also that morning letters from Lord Stormont, without the slightest suspicion of such a connexion.

I received my account, just as I was going down to the

---

[1] Afterwards the third Earl of Harrington (1753-1829).
[2] A sporting friend of the Duke

(Walpole, *Memoirs*, iii. 119); he married the youngest daughter of the first Earl Gower.

House of Lords, where no business was particularly appointed, though a debate on American business was expected in that of the Commons. M[r]. Fox to whom I communicated the particulars of my intelligence[1], gave me full credit, on the assurance I gave him of my full belief; and in his speech, on that day, he called on the minister either to acknowledge this serious notification, or to confess that the Administration was shamefully ignorant on these essential points, on which it was incumbent on them to have the best information: in proof of which an unsuspected treaty of alliance &c. between France and America attested their unfitness for their situations. In the House of Lords, I begged their lordships' attention, while I communicated an event, of great importance, and which I defied the king's ministers to gainsay, namely, that treaties of amity, commerce and alliance, had been entered into between France and America. The ministers, and Lord Weymouth in particular, protested that nothing of the sort had ever come to their knowledge; nor could they imagine that such a measure was in contemplation. They acknowledged, that the letters, that very morning received from Lord Stormont, were silent on the subject: but on my repeating, that I rested my character on the fact, they begged to consider it as a more serious business, and I was at last, in private desired by these lords, to acquaint them with what I knew, in which I readily acquiesced accordingly. At the end of a week or little more, this event came officially to the knowledge of ministers, and indeed to every one. After the declaration they had made, of disbelief, 'that any alliance of the sort was in existence, or even in contemplation,' it must have been humiliating to be necessitated, Lord North in the

---

[1] This intelligence was given to Grafton by Mr. T. Walpole in order that it might be communicated to Fox and to no other member of the Whig party (*Life and Times of C. J. Fox*, i. 176). Fox raised the question in the Commons on February 17, but without stating the source of his information. North said that 'it was possible, nay too probable; but not authenticated by our ambassador.'

Grafton's speech was on March 5, and he is made to cite Fox as his authority (*Parl. Hist.* xix. 834). He must have been misrepresented, as Fox derived his information from the Duke.

House of Commons, and Lord Weymouth in ours, to bring down from His Majesty a message to both houses, informing them, 'that a rescript had been delivered by the ambassador of His Most Christian Majesty, containing a direct avowal of a treaty of amity, commerce, and alliance, recently concluded with America': in consequence of which offensive communication, on the part of the Court of France, His Majesty had sent orders to his own ambassador to with-draw from that Court.

Here, a new scene opens, and fresh difficulties arise, without any cheering prospect of a better management of the military force of this country. The great committee of inquiry into the state of the nation was drawing to a conclusion, when the Duke of Richmond moved the House of Lords to present in consequence an address to His Majesty, and in his speech maintained the necessity of an immediate recognition of the independence of America. Lord Chatham was apprized of his Grace's purpose, and was much grieved, when he heard, that attending the assembly of the militia in Suffolk, I had no intention to come up for that day's debate. Indeed by this decision, it happened, that I avoided a scene, as shocking as can well be conceived. Lord Chatham more fit to have been in his bed, than in the House of Parliament, would not be stopped by his infirmities, from attending on that day: and as Lord Camden favored me with the relation of this great man's and I will add illustrious patriot's last efforts to save his sinking country, I will give it to you in his own words, preferably to every other.

MY DEAR LORD,

I cannot help considering the little illness which prevented your Grace from attending the House of Lords last Tuesday to have been a piece of good fortune as it kept you back from a scene that would have overwhelmed you with grief and melancholy as it did me, and many others that were present: I mean Lord Chatham's fit that seized him as he was attempting to rise and reply to the Duke of Richmond; he fell back upon his seat and was to all appearance in the agonies of death. This threw the whole house into confusion: every person was upon his legs in a moment hurrying from one place to another, some sending for assistance, others producing salts, and others reviving spirits: many crowding about the earl to observe his countenance—all affected—most part really concerned, and even those who might have felt a secret pleasure at the accident yet put the appearance of distress, except only the *Earl of M.*: who sat still almost as much unmoved as the senseless body itself. D[r]. Brocklesby was the first physician that came but D[r]. Addington in about an hour was brought to him. He was carried into the prince's chamber, and laid upon the table supported by pillows. The first motion of life that appeared was an endeavor to vomit, and after he had discharged the load from his stomach that probably brought on the seizure, he revived fast. M[r]. Strutt prepared an apartment for him at his house where he was carried as soon as he could with safety be removed. He slept remarkably well, and was quite recovered yesterday, though he continued in bed. I have not heard how he is to day, but will keep my letter open till the evening that your Grace may be informed how he goes on; I saw him in the prince's chamber before he went into the house, and conversed a little with him, but such was the feeble state of his body, and indeed the distempered agitation of his mind, that I did forebode that his strength would certainly fail him before he had finished his speech. In truth he was not in a condition to go abroad, and he was earnestly requested not to make the attempt; but your Grace knows how obstinate he is when he is resolved. He had a similar fit to this in the summer, like it in all respects: in the seizure, the reaching, and the recovery; and after that fit, as if it had been the crisis of the disorder, he recovered fast, and grew to be in better health than I had known him for many years: pray heaven, this may be attended with no worse consequences. The earl spoke, but was not like himself; his speech faltered, his sentences broken, and his mind not master of itself. He made shift with difficulty to declare his opinion, but was not able to enforce it by argument. His words were shreds of unconnected eloquence, and flashes of the same fire which he Prometheus like had stole from heaven, and were then returning to the place from whence they were taken. Your Grace sees even I who am a mere prose man am tempted to be poetical, while I am discoursing of this extraordinary man's genius. The Duke of Richmond answered him, and I cannot help giving his Grace the commendation he deserved for his candour, courtesy, and liberal treatment of his illustrious adversary. The debate was adjourned till yesterday, and then the former subject was taken up by Lord Shelburne in a speech of one hour and 3 quarters[1]. The Duke of Richmond answered, Shelburne replied, and the duke who enjoys the privilege of the last word in that house, closed the business. No other lord except our friend Lord Ravensworth speaking one word. The two

---

[1] For this debate see *Parl. Hist.* xix. 1032.

other noble lords consumed between three and four hours. And now my dear lord, you must with me lament this fatal accident : I fear it is *fatal*, and this great man is now lost for ever to the public, for after such a public and notorious an exposure of his decline, no man will look up to him even if he should recover, France will no longer fear him, nor the King of England court him—and the present set of ministers will finish the ruin of the country, because he being in effect superannuated, the public will call for no other men. This is my melancholy reflection. The opposition however is not broken and the difference of opinion will wear off: so far at least the prospect is favorable. I think I shall not sign the protest, though in other respects I shall be very friendly. I have troubled your Grace with a deal of stuff, but the importance of the subject will excuse me. Jack will have the honor of spending his Easter at Euston. Is Lord Euston to have a commission in the militia ? I have endeavored to dissuade my son. I thank your Grace for the plover's eggs, it is plain you think me an epicure. I have hardly room to present my respectful compliments to the duchess &c. and to subscribe myself as I ought with perfect esteem and respect

Your Grace's &c.
CAMDEN.

Ap : 1778. N. B. STREET.

PS. I understand the earl has slept well last night and is to be removed to M^r. Sargent's to-day in Downing Street. He would have gone into the country, but Addington thinks he is too weak.

Thus passed the last effort of this eminent and patriotic statesman. Lord Chatham had recovered from a similar fit in the preceding summer : but this proved fatal, and he died a few days after he had been removed to Hayes.

From this time till the middle of November, I passed, with the West Suffolk Reg^t. of Militia, in camp at Coxheath, and under the command of Lieut : Genl. Keppel [1], who had the merit of forming many raw corps, into a well disciplined, and formidable army. The small regular force left in Great Britain, as well as in Ireland, rendered the militia service most essential and we had the satisfaction to see it improving to an effectual defence.

---

[1] William, a son of the second Earl of Albemarle. He greatly distinguished himself in the attack on the Havana in 1762.

CHAPTER X

IF any person would at this time sit down deliberately and dispassionately to follow up the steps taken on both sides, during the contest with America, I am persuaded that he would rise with a conviction, that the opportunities were numerous, when a more temperate and conciliatory conduct might have terminated the struggle, and saved the dismemberment of so large and powerful a portion of the British Empire. He will perceive, I think that while the affairs of the Americans were directed by wonderful ability, wisdom, and fortitude, our Ministry were only acting on the spur of the occasion, without plan and without system. Lord North's abilities, though great, did not mark him as a character suited to the management and direction of great military operations. His lordship was formed for the enjoyment of domestic comforts, and to shine in the most elegant societies: his knowledge, however, was very extensive, as was his wit; but he became confused, when he was agitated by the great scenes of active life [1]. Whatever was done by the Ministry, was either ill planned, or ill timed, the terms which might have produced peace the preceding year, were offered, when the moment was past, and the Administration, blinded by the

---

[1] The correspondence of George III and Lord North, at this time, shows how anxious North was to retire, and how completely he had become the mere instrument of the king, who now interfered in all the details of departmental business.

credit given to the loyalists, could never be brought to see things in their true light, nor did they know the real resources of the enemy.

The Toulon fleet, under the command of Count D'Estaing, was ordered to the coast of America, with troops on board, while a considerable squadron was getting ready in the harbour of Brest. D'Estaing was for some weeks baffled in his attempts to get through the Streights of Gibraltar, notwithstanding which delay, (incredible as it may appear) Lord Howe had not the least intimation from the Admiralty, that a French fleet might be expected in the North American seas; though the forwardness of this fleet for sailing was known throughout Europe; and not a sloop or cutter dispatched with this necessary information to Lord Howe: nor did he know any thing of his danger, until a frigate of his own was driven into his fleet by two French ships. This anecdote may be depended upon, as I heard it more than once from Lord Howe himself. His superior skill saved him from being obliged to fight d'Estaing, on terms so inferior as to allow no possible hope of a victory[1]. Lord Howe's ships were all small; until he was joined by the shattered ships of Admiral Byron, which dropt in piece-meal as a reinforcement. It proved to be a material one, though our fleet was still inferior to the French, for Lord Howe stretched every nerve, and with wonderful professional skill and activity appeared again at sea, in a time so short as to astonish every one. But the confidence of his fleet in him gave new life to all his exertions. The two fleets were in sight of each other soon after; and a bloody contest would probably have followed; had not a most uncommon storm separated the two fleets, on the point of engaging. Both fleets suffered much, but the enemy's the most by this tremendous storm; and D'Estaing after

[1] Lord Howe had moved from the Delaware to New York, where he was for a time blockaded by d'Estaing. The American land forces under Sullivan and the French fleet combined for the destruction of the British troops on Rhode Island. Sullivan had landed there in numbers superior to the British, but the storm referred to in the text caused the withdrawal of d'Estaing, and consequently the retreat of Sullivan, which was not effected without difficulty.

some attempts in conjunction with General Sullivan, in which he was thwarted, sailed first to the West Indies, and then for France, disappointed in the object of his mission.

Lord Howe also, after a campaign in which he had added to his consideration as a great naval officer, returned in the beginning of winter to England, fully determined never to serve again under that Board of Admiralty, who had risked so unaccountably their country's safety, and his own honor, by a most culpable neglect.

On the first alarm from the expectation of a war with France, Admiral Keppel was the officer whom the nation wished to see appointed to the command of the channel fleet; and the admiral was destined to it, by His Majesty, who offered that command to him in the most gracious and flattering manner. Admiral Keppel called on me soon after, desirous that I should know what had passed in the Closet. He spoke to me in the most grateful style on the reception he had met with, and only expressed his disappointment in not having Vice Admiral Pigot with him. The king perceiving it said, you cannot object to Palliser [1], to which Keppel answered according to his generous nature 'No, Sire, Palliser, tho' there has been some little coolness between us of late, is a brave and good officer, and he will do his duty.'

Admiral Keppel finding His Majesty so bent to have Palliser, as the Vice Admiral of the fleet, which was fitting out, pressed the appointment of Pigot no further, but observed that the officers, as well as their ships, would want relief from time to time, when the next would be the turn of Pigot to serve, though he had much wished to have had him now with him. The want of information at the Admiralty was conspicuous on the present occasion; and Admiral Keppel sailed with the expectation of meeting a fleet of the enemy, not very superior to his own either in number, or in rate:

---

[1] Sir Hugh Palliser (1723–1796) had served with the distinction in our previous wars, and was at this time a Lord of the Admiralty; his conduct in the sea fight of July 27, 1778, is not easily explicable.

but at sea he picked up undoubted intelligence, that the French had ready to come out of Brest, a fleet much stronger than the Admiralty was apprized of. On this he returned to port for a reinforcement, with which he sailed again immediately. On the 27th of July he brought the French fleet to action, and had greatly the advantage in the fight, in spite of the untoward circumstances which ended in a court martial on both admirals; to the honorable acquittal of Keppel, and with a slight stigma on Admiral Palliser[1]. The conduct of the Admiralty was highly and very universally blamed: and it gave rise to the indisposition that appeared in the most distinguished of our naval officers to serve: the consequences of which were very severely felt by the nation on many occasions.

M[r]. Fox moved a censure on the First Lord of the Admiralty, for having ordered out Admiral Keppel with twenty ships of the line, when it might have been known, that the French had thirty-two ready at Brest, besides a great superiority of frigates, thereby risking the safety of the country which had been drained of its regular force. Addresses to the king for the removal of his lordship were proposed in each House of Parliament, which tho' over-ruled, were supported by respectable minorities.

Late in the session which sat till the 3[d] of July 1779, the rescript from the Spanish Ambassador was sent down as a message from His Majesty, announcing to us, that another great power was added to the number of our enemies.

During these various, unhappy and serious occurrences, Lord North was well known by his friends, and indeed by some of us, to be very uneasy in his situation, and at intervals very anxious to quit it. Two applications[2] came to myself

---

[1] Palliser applied for a court martial against Keppel, and when Keppel was acquitted, demanded a court martial on himself. The serious charges against him were dismissed, but he was censured for not having informed the Admiral in command that his ships had become disabled in the battle.

[2] The second of these applications must be the negotiation referred to in the letters of George III to Lord North of February 1 and 4, 1779, vol. ii.

from His Majesty, and as I understood with Lord North's knowledge and assent: but as one proposed only a desire to admit Lord Camden and myself into such offices as should please us best, this overture took but little time in consideration; tho' it shewed how ill informed they were of our manner of thinking and of acting. The second proposition, being conveyed through Lord Hertford, the Lord Chamberlain, and with intimation at the same time to me, that Lord North was very willing to make room, and give facility in forming a new arrangement without him; the application called for further attention. I saw in the evening at Lord Gower's by appointment, Lord Chancellor and Lord Weymouth: the latter lord took the principal part. It was confirmed by his lordship, that Lord North both knew, and approved of, this meeting; that we might discuss the business as if he was already out of office; and that Lords Camden and Shelburne would find greater facility in His Majesty towards forming an Administration, than they would expect. I only replied, that as His Majesty allowed me to consult the Lords Shelburne and Camden, I should be unwilling to risk an answer on a point so important, without the sanction of their concurrence. I found them waiting for my return from the meeting, and we sent an answer that very evening, Feb^{ry}. 3^d, 1779, in these *precise* words to Lord Weymouth, as they had been drawn up jointly by Lords Camden, Shelburne, and myself.

'That it is impossible to give an answer to Lord Weymouth, till such time as a proper application can be made to Lord Rockingham, and the Duke of Richmond, to know their sentiments.'

On hearing nothing further from ministers, we concluded that the answer of us three had closed the business: by which

pp. 224, 225. Of the first I can find no trace in those letters.

Two serious attempts to form a coalition were made in 1778, one before and one after the death of Chatham (*Life and Times of C. J. Fox*, i. 179, 193). Two more were made in 1779, one in February, described in the text, and one in December (*Letters of George III to Lord North*, ii. 296, 302). These last were confined to the Whigs of the Chatham section, Shelburne, Grafton, and Camden; the overtures of 1778 were wider in scope.

it was apparent, that the Court were not yet disposed to trust the reins of government into the hands of the whole Opposition, or to adopt a change of systems, and of measures.

We derived, however, one essential advantage from the opportunity it gave of shewing to Lord Rockingham, the Cavendishes, M^r. Fox, and their principal friends, that we would not stir, except in conjunction with them. This circumstance cemented the Opposition into a more solid body and furnished the means that Lord Camden and I improved by persuading Lord Shelburne not to contest with Lord Rockingham the Treasury, in case a new Administration was to be formed. Lord Shelburne yielded the point with a better grace than I had expected, and it must be considered as of consequence, since nothing could be more generally circulated by the ministerial party, or more universally, credited than the impossibility of such a compliance ever existing between the leaders of Opposition.

Two letters from Lord Camden will find here their proper place.

My dear Lord,

I did not receive the honor of your Grace's letter till yesterday, upon my return from a little excursion to Sussex; and should in obedience to your commands, have repaired to the camp to-morrow or next day; but a letter from Ireland this morning bids me expect M^r. Stewart in a day or two; so that I am obliged to put off my intended visit to Warley till next week, and your Grace will be sure of seeing me long enough before you go into Suffolk. A conversation with your Grace upon the state of the kingdom at present will give me as much satisfaction as I am capable of receiving upon so hopeless a subject. If your Grace can suggest any plan of proceeding for the Opposition, likely to change the Court system, or animate the public, I shall be happy to adopt, as well as to promote it : for my own part, I confess fairly my own opinion, that the opposition to the Court is contracted to a handfull of men, within the walls of Parliament; and that the people without doors are either indifferent, or hostile to any opposition at all. Whether this singular and unexampled state of the country is owing to a consciousness among the people, that they are as much to blame as the ministers, and are ashamed to confess their own error; or whether in truth they hold the Opposition so cheap as to think the kingdom would suffer instead of mending by the exchange, or from a combination of all these motives chuse to suffer patiently rather than encounter the troubles that are apt to follow upon a general disturbance : whatever is the cause of that slavish resignation, that is predominant at present; the fact is they do not desire a change. What then is to be done, in order to obtain some degree of popularity?

I shall make a simple answer by saying *nothing*, and yet perhaps that *nothing* if well conducted might have a stronger operation than the vain repetition of those feeble efforts, that have hitherto been made in Parliament, by perpetual wrangles, personal animosity, abuse, and bad language; for this attack has been returned two fold upon us, and has set the parties against each other, like a couple of prize fighters combating for the entertainment of the gazing public, who are greatly diverted at a blow soundly given, or dextrously parry'd, without a wish for the victory of either of the combatants. This has been the conduct of opposition hitherto. If on the other hand, a firm and temperate opposition, in short speeches, a few debates without rancour, could be established, such a course might probably restore us to the good opinion of the public, and then the distress of the times might work them into an opinion that the Opposition mean really the good of the whole. This or any idea may serve to talk of, but to say the truth, I have no hopes left for the publick, the whole people have betrayed themselves, and are not worth fighting for. I have the honor to be with the most perfect regard and attachment your Grace's most obedient

Faithful servant
CAMDEN.

Sepr. 16th, 1779.   CAMDEN PLACE.

MY DEAR LORD,

As it is very possible your Grace among a thousand serious matters that occupy your mind may possibly forget your obliging promise of a couple of peach trees, I beg leave to remind your Grace of it, least the season should be lost, which will make the difference of a year ; a period which, in my life is equivalent to about 20 in your Grace's. I understand by my son that your Grace is not in camp, but expected there soon, so I direct this to Euston.

I set out for Bath to-morrow, and intend to call upon Lord Shelburne in my way, and will communicate your Grace's idea to him : we may talk of publick matters when we meet, but I see no likelihood of any co-operation upon a system. Chance will direct this session as it did the last, till at last the Constitution will be undermined, or the country conquered. Men are either rous'd or tam'd by oppression; England is more dispos'd to the last, than the first. And yet we are noisy enough upon an election. Witness Middlesex : how must the Court laugh to see two patriots at loggerheads for the representation of this county? The disappointed party revolts of course. I shall be back in a fortnight, by which time I should hope the camp would be broke up, and I may have the pleasure of seeing your Grace in town. I am my dear lord with the greatest respect and attachment,

Your Grace's most obedient faithful ser[t].

CAMDEN.

Oct. 17th, 1779.   CAMDEN PLACE.

Your Grace will be so good to present my respectful compliments to the Duchess.

About this time, some of the ministers began to feel themselves most uncomfortable in their situations, and in particular Lord Gower, to whose good sense the danger of the country and the incompetency of the Ministry could not but be apparent. On the meeting of Parliament, Nov[r]. 25, 1779, Lord Gower, then President of the Council, declared his apprehensions publicly, saying 'that no man of honor, or conscience could remain, and see such things pass, as he had done, and that sincerity and activity in our councils could alone restore energy to the Government.' This profession proceeded from his lordship in his speech on a spirited amendment which Lord Rockingham moved to the address, and which was supported by the largest minority we had lately seen in that House; for the lords in opposition to the address were forty-one. These encreasing numbers may be attributed to a sense of danger which appears more menacing, in proportion as it is in sight ; and here we had the mortification to see S[r]. Charles Hardy's[1] fleet retreating up the Channel, with the combined fleet pursuing them. I know it from the best authority, that it was by accident alone, that a real and great invasion did not take place; for Mon[r]. Rochambeau with 60,000, chosen troops had every thing ready for embarking, fully determined to attempt Plymouth, as their first object, when the Spanish Admiral communicated to the French commandants at sea, and land, that his crews were dying so fast of a malignant disorder, as to make it necessary that he should return without a moment's loss of time to Spain, being unfit for the present service. The Duc de Lian-

---

[1] Appointed on the resignation of Keppel.

court was a Maréchal de Camp (Major General) on this staff, much in the knowledge of the measures of his Government, and with him I have often discoursed on this project of the French.   They were accurately acquainted with the place, and its environs, and there was no competent judge, who did not see that the little preparation for the defence of Plymouth (now rendered more defensible), was then a pleasing temptation to the enemy.

I shall add nothing on the appointment of Lord George Germaine to the office of Secretary of State, nor of the peerage conferred on him afterwards, when he was compelled to withdraw from the public odium, which was falling fast upon him.   It is difficult to deem it an honor conferred, when he left one House, under virulent and just reproach, and came into the other, little disposed to receive him among them, and insulting him in the words of their protest[1].

It may be collected, that the country gentleman, whether convinced or ashamed of his error, but certainly feeling the pressure on his purse, which the great contributions for carrying on this destructive war had considerably encreased ; began to remonstrate against the burdens which he was called upon to support.   Economy became the general cry through the kingdom, and representations for the necessity of effectual measures to prevent and correct abuses in the expenditure of public money, which had been so liberally granted, flowed in by petitions from every quarter.   The county of York had the honor of taking the lead in this patriotic and constitutional business : and their petition was put into the hands of the upright and respectable S^r. George Saville, their representative in Parliament.

The influence of the Crown, encreased beyond all measures of constitutional reckoning, was now generally felt as the great means by which the Ministry still drew forth such majorities.   Debates on this head became very frequent in

---

[1] The protest was made on Feb. 18, 1782, when Lord George Germaine became a peer under the title of Lord Sackville (Rogers, *Protests of the House of Lords*, ii. 212).

Parliament, and the members in both Houses who were in opposition to these ministers were daily encreasing; and this operated so much, that on the 6th of April, 1780, when M^r. Dunning made his famous motion, namely, 'That the influence of the Crown had encreased, was encreasing, and ought to be diminished,' he carried his point by eighteen voices. On the 10th other motions were carried on the same ground by the Opposition; the Administration not daring to divide. Every thing seemed to bespeak an overthrow of Ministry; when unluckily S^r. Fletcher Norton the Speaker was taken so ill, as to make it adviseable to adjourn to the 24th of April [1]. During this interval, ministerial engines were at work to bring over converts, and I much fear, that many who had declared that the influence of the Crown ought to be diminished, now drank of its temptations: and it may be said, that to this circumstance materially the Ministry owed their continuance in power.

To these events succeeded a formidable proof of the lengths to which popular licentiousness can reach if not checked by firmness and moderation in its beginning. The riots which became so alarming, commenced at the chapel near Lincoln's Inn Fields, which belonged to the Sardinian minister. The cry of *No Popery* was the catch word, and brought forth with all the old persecuting spirit which was still to be found at the end of the eighteenth century: and there were some persons, to whom the rioters more particularly looked up: for it was not the Act for moderation towards the Catholics which affected these leaders, who cared little for religion; it was only made by them a pretext for their violent and frantic projects, which the timidity and indecision of the ministers allowed the rabble to a great extent to perpetrate. The event was disgraceful to the utmost degree to the country, although it was evident to most persons, that the sedition might have been suppressed, on the second day at furthest.

---

[1] The king thought that the Speaker feigned illness in the interest of the Whigs, because some of that party wished to attend the Newmarket races (*George III to Lord North*, ii. 316). If so the device failed to serve its purpose.

But how could that be expected, when the Secretary of State's servants wore in their hats, as a passport, the cockades of the rioters? But here no resolution appeared; all spirit and shew of firmness possessed by our rulers, were reserved to be displayed on the other side of the Atlantic: while, by a strange pusillanimity, this riot was left to increase to a length of many days; and to be quelled at last by the effusion of much blood. These riots, however, disgraceful as they were to the nation, served to prop up for a time a feeble Administration, and the dread of any thing like to anarchy, would have driven the men of property to support any Government, and to look up to a military force alone for their protection. The pains taken, and the stories propagated, in order to insinuate that the riots were a deep scheme laid by the Opposition, would hardly now be credited; though such vile reports did then meet with belief, from men, who ought to have been ashamed of such credulity[1].

In the beginning of the year 1781, the Dutch were added to the list of our enemies[2], and letters of marque and general reprisal issued against them. The debates in both Houses were considerable, though the addresses to His Majesty on the occasion were carried by large majorities.

M[r]. Burke's Reform Bill was revived, but rejected, though 190 voted for it[3].

This unhappy year did not close, without intelligence being brought hither, that Lord Cornwallis with a second royal army had been compelled to lay down their arms, and capitulate at York town: surrendering to the allied army of

---

[1] For an account of the Gordon riots which lasted from the 2nd to the 9th of June, 1780, see Lecky, *Hist. of England*, iii. 500-523. The French as well as the Opposition got the credit of the riots.

[2] War with Holland had been declared in December, 1780, on the discovery of proposals for a treaty between Holland and the revolted colonies which the Dutch Government refused to disavow (Lecky, iv. 158-162).

[3] Burke's scheme for regulating the civil list was something more than an economical reform. It would have prevented the king from spending large sums on Parliamentary corruption. How large were the sums thus spent we learn from the letters of George III and Lord North, ii. 425, 426. Thus Burke's scheme was 'a Reform Bill' in more senses than one.

Americans and French, commanded by Washington, made Marshal of France[1]. A sense of past error, and a conviction that the American War might terminate in further destruction to our armies, began from this time rapidly to insinuate itself into the minds of men. Their discourse was quite changed, though the majorities in Parliament were still ready to support the American War, while all the world was representing it to be the heighth of madness and folly. The defections from the minister, especially in the Commons, with encreasing minorities, must have made the minister sensible of his falling state. He persevered on, however, under the bitterest attacks and threatenings, sometimes defeated, at others well supported, till towards the end of March 1782, when as the Earl of Surrey[2] rose to make a motion, Lord North, guessing its tendency, said, that he would save the House the trouble of a debate, by acquainting them, that His Majesty had come to a resolution to make an entire change in his Administration.

There was no member of the House more looked up to, both for talents, probity, military knowledge, and experience than General Conway. Some little time before, he had made two motions much to his honor; the last of which was carried by 234 to 215 in a full House[3]. An address in consequence was drawn up, and voted to be carried up to the king by the whole House. The words of the motion were as follows:

'That it is the opinion of this House that a further prosecu-

---

[1] The surrender of Cornwallis, rendered inevitable by the superiority of the French naval force to our own, took place on Oct. 19, 1781.

[2] Charles, Earl of Surrey, who succeeded his father as eleventh Duke of Norfolk in 1786, was at this time M.P. for Carlisle. The dexterous way in which North managed to announce his resignation is told in the *Life and Times of C. J. Fox*, i. 275.

[3] Conway's two motions were both of the same tenour. The first, brought forward on Feb. 22, was lost by one vote; the numbers were 194 to 193. The second was carried, as described on Feb. 27. The king returned an ambiguous answer. Thereupon direct votes of censure were moved by Lord John Cavendish on March 8, by Sir John Rous on the 15th, and lost on each occasion by ten votes. Lord Surrey's motion, which was about to be introduced on March 20, was anticipated by North's announcement of his resignation.

tion of offensive war against America, would under present circumstances be the means of weakening the efforts of this country against her European enemies and tend to increase the mutual enmity so fatal to the interests both of Great Britain and America.'

After this the struggle was at an end.

CHAPTER XI

HIS Majesty's first step was to send for Lord Shelburne, who much to his honor and credit, expressly desired of the · king, that not he, but Lord Rockingham should be placed at the Treasury, and primarily consulted on the forming of an Administration. His Majesty graciously acquiesced; and it would probably have been a happiness to the country, if it had pleased the Almighty to have extended Lord Rockingham's valuable life to a more distant day. The arrangement took no long time in forming: and I believe in none was there less struggle for offices. The Cabinet at first consisted of Lord Thurlow as Chancellor, Lord Camden as President, myself as Privy Seal, Lord Rockingham as First Lord of the Treasury, Lord Shelburne and M^r. Fox as Secretaries of State, Lord Keppel as First Lord of the Admiralty, and of Genl. Conway as Commander in Chief. Mr. Dunning and S^r. Fletcher Norton were soon added as members of our Cabinet by Lords Rockingham and Shelburne, when they were both made peers, by the titles of Ashburton and Grantley. The Duke of Portland went over to Ireland, as Lord Lieutenant, Col. Barré became Treasurer of the Navy; and M^r. Burke was made Paymaster. These changes were well received by the nation, who had lately become heartily sick of the American War, and dreaded the thoughts of a continuance of that pernicious system. Peace was the ardent wish of all; yet the means of soon obtaining a fair and honorable termination of the war appeared still to be at a distance. Those who were the most rigid to keep up some sort of dependency of the colonies on this country had given up every hope of this kind; for they saw the indissoluble union which subsisted between our formidable foes. The nation however also discerned a spirit and activity in every department, which had not been observed of late; and the low state of the fleet at home, lower by much than the retiring Ministry had told us that we should find it, was raised through zeal and alertness to a pitch, which ordinary exertions could never have effected.

During the short time M^r. Fox remained in office, the famous Irish Declaratory Act, known commonly under the title of 'Poynings' Law,' was repealed on his motion [1]. M^r. Burke's Reform Bill was again introduced, and passed [2]. The Irish were so highly pleased, with this favor granted, or this justice done to their nation, that they instantly decided to raise 20,000 seamen for His Majesty's service. Other salutary laws, besides these had been proposed to His Majesty, and approved of, as necessary to be enacted.

It may not be amiss to observe here, that all the resolutions on Wilkes's election for Middlesex were ordered to be expunged from the journals, after some length of debate.

Soon after this, M^r. Pitt stepped forward with his desire of entering into the state of the representation of the people, and moved for the appointment of a committee to enquire into it: a measure of the sort was at that time thought to be most necessary: and many well attended meetings throughout the kingdom shewed their zeal and desire to forward the business, though the mode of fixing it was various, beyond what could

---

[1] This is a somewhat vague description of the process of granting legislative independence to Ireland. The Declaratory Act, 6 Geo. I, c. 5 (1720), established the legislative sovereignty of the British Parliament over Ireland; Poynings' Law (1495) limited the powers of the Irish Parliament to the acceptance or rejection of bills approved by the Crown in Council. The Declaratory Act was repealed in 1782; and the king, in compliance with an address of the British Parliament, assented to bills of the Irish Parliament which removed all restrictions save the royal veto.

[2] The progress of Burke's bill served to show the dissensions in the Cabinet, and that Shelburne and Thurlow were alone in the confidence of the king (*Memorials of C. J. Fox*, i. 314).

have been imagined. However the necessity did not so forcibly speak to the members of the House: for M^r. Pitt's motion, though supported warmly by M^r. Fox, was rejected by twenty voices [1].

Matters were bearing a better aspect, till the unexpected and fatal death of Lord Rockingham, brought back a gloom, and almost a despondency for the public welfare, into every patriotic breast.

He dyed July 1st, 1782.

Soon after this lamentable event, M^r. Fox retired from office; in an affecting speech he did ample justice to the character and sound principles of his late friend: but M^r. Fox insinuated that dissentions were arising where Lord Rockingham's influence and example would have been probably able to prevent disunion.

I find from a kind of short diary, taken down at the time, that M^r. Fox's advice, previously to Lord Rockingham's death, prevailed less often than would be expected from talents so superior.

M^r. Oswald [2] had been the person first pitched on to see and communicate with D^r. Franklyn on the subject of pacification. On this gentleman's return it was M^r. Fox's wish to have placed the whole negociation with any of the Powers at war into the hands of M^r. Grenville [3]: but, the Cabinet decided, that, as the doctor desired M^r. Oswald's return, to whom he had spoken with openness, and freedom, it would be impolitic not to comply with a request of this nature. Besides it was not yet fully known in what light our offers

---

[1] The adverse majority was made up of Rockingham Whigs and the followers of North.

[2] Richard Oswald, a Scotch merchant, who owned property in America. He had no diplomatic experience and was most unduly ready to accept any terms which the Americans might be pleased to offer (Lecky, iv. 230; Fitzmaurice, *Life of Shelburne*, iii. 175 *et seqq.*).

[3] Thomas Grenville, third son of George Grenville. He was twenty-six years of age, had been in the army, and, since 1779, had sat in the House of Commons for Buckinghamshire.

A more extraordinary pair to conduct a difficult negotiation it is hard to conceive than the inexperienced ex-guardsman who represented the views of Fox, and the effusive merchant who was the spokesman of Shelburne.

to treat might be received by the French Ministry.   The line of our proposals was independence for America, and the restitution of matters to the state in which they stood on the Treaty of Paris; and these were to be considered as the basis of the negociation.   M^r. Thos. Grenville was soon after sent over to Paris to treat, according to M^r. Fox's plan, with all, or any of the belligerent Powers.

In the mean time, I had the satisfaction to see very efficacious measures, for offence, as well as defence, set forward, and with success, Genl. Conway's department and the Duke of Richmond's, as well as the Admiralty exhibited an activity which had not been witnessed in any of these of late.   On the other hand, it was grievous to me to remark the daily jealousies, which even reached often to altercation, between M^r. Fox and Lord Shelburne: the latter I think, differed more from system and dislike: the other with an honest warmth could not brook such constant aggressions.   My endeavor was to conciliate all sides; and with Lord Camden, we entreated Lord Shelburne, for the sake of the public, to bear as well as he could, the resistance of which he complained.   But it was evident to me at the time, as it must have been to any one of the least observation, that constituted as it was, the system could be but of short duration.   Every day confirmed my conjectures: and in proportion as divisions encreased, Lord Shelburne was more earnest to put every means at work to attach to him Lord Camden and myself: whose characters he much mistook; thinking perhaps, as he had seen us once look up to Lord Chatham, we might submit in a good degree to be guided by him.   But he soon found, that our views were for the public, while his own were too much directed to personal ambition.

May 2^d, 1782.   After a tedious debate on the Cricklade bill[1], Lord Camden and myself went to dinner together at Lord Shelburne's; where we had much political discussion on the state of the Cabinet: but from Lord Shelburne

---

[1] A bill for disfranchising Cricklade on account of its notorious corruption.   Thurlow on this occasion, as on others, vehemently opposed his colleagues.

nothing like cordiality towards Lord Rockingham's Ministry. On the 5th at my house the same conversation was renewed; when no better disposition appeared: on the contrary Lord Shelburne expressed with much warmth his dissatisfaction, that Lord Camden should doubt the purity and soundness of the ground on which Lord Shelburne stood at S^t. James's, as also whether he had reason to place so great confidence in the Chancellor. On the 8th at my house, after dinner the same topick of political discussion naturally arose. We agreed in our opinions on the state of the Cabinet: but we both of us entreated Lord Shelburne that for the benefit of the public, as well as in honor towards individuals embarked with us, we were compelled, he and all of us, to exert ourselves to keep the present system fast. We did not allow that the hasty mode of proceeding which he complained of in M^r. Fox together with the little practicability of the Duke of Richmond in business made this so difficult. We added our earnest entreaties to Lord Shelburne, to undergo any thing rather than to have a separation from Lord Rockingham's friends: saying, that if a breach did happen, it should be clear to all mankind where the fault lay.

I noticed, however, that every engine was set to work, to bring from Lord Camden a declaration, that he would go on with Lord Shelburne, in case of such a separation. No artifice could prevail on Lord Camden to acquiesce, though Lord Shelburne pressed him in a manner which appeared to me to be by much too warm. On my part, I gave his lordship no expectation, that he could depend on my assistance on such a juncture. Indeed my language might have been such, as to prevent his putting directly such a question to me.

About this time I was very ill and confined from a most violent attack of S^t. Anthony's fire. It was a full fortnight before I was equal to serious business; and when I was, my colleagues were so obliging as to meet at my house. This illness did not prevent me from fully enjoying the account of the great victory obtained by S^r. George Rodney over the French fleet, off Dominica, which I received from Lord

Keppel at breakfast on the 18th of May. This glorious victory was of infinite consequence in various ways, when we consider the whole situation of our affairs : but that it might have been rendered more complete by Lord Rodney's permitting the division under Lord Hood to have pursued the crippled ships of the enemy cannot be called in question by any one who reflects upon the situation of the two fleets at the end of the action [1]. Lord Hood's relation to me of the fight strongly confirms this opinion to have been well founded : Still Lord Rodney's exertions were very great, and we must ever remember his merits with gratitude.

On the 26th of June a Cabinet was assembled in the morning at my house : when on intelligence received of the combined fleet having sailed from Cadiz, with a large convoy, Lord Howe was ordered to proceed with his own fleet, strengthened by some ships from those commanded by S[r]. Lockhart Ross, in-hopes that his lordship would find a favorable opportunity of attacking the enemy. Contrary winds and bad weather obliged Lord Howe to return to port, without effecting this purpose. At another Council in the evening of the same day, it was agreed that, with every testimony of our earnest desire of acting with the Empress of Russia, in the closest connexion, yet, that the *armed neutrality* cannot be *formally* admitted. It was also here again explained, that independence to America was offered, in order to obtain peace, or to separate the Americans from their allies. The little prospect we then saw of succeeding in the French negociation, occasioned us to desire as earnestly to bring it to a short issue, as the Court of Versailles was endeavoring to protract it.

Lord Rockingham was considered on this day to be in very great danger.

---

[1] De Grasse was defeated by Rodney on April 12, 1782. Five French ships of the line were taken, including the Admiral's flagship, and two others with two smaller ships on the 18th. If pursuit had been prompt Hood believed that twenty ships might have been taken. Captain Mahan says 'this cautious failure is a serious blot on Rodney's military reputation' (*Influence of Sea Power on History*, pp. 484-498).

On Friday the 28th M^r. Fox called on me in the evening; when naturally and with much frankness, he entered upon his awkward situation at Council; complaining of the *decided* opinions against every thing proposed by him; and added that it would be impossible to go on in such a way: and that he could not proceed to write to M^r. Grenville, till he had laid the matter before another Cabinet. In answer to this I endeavored to assure him that he ought to be more candid and just towards his colleagues, whose opinion, I was convinced, arose from their sincere thought, and not from any unworthy motive. I begged him to consider where the public had to look, in case there should unfortunately be a breach among us. My humble advice and earnest wish was, that he together with Lord Shelburne, and Lord Rockingham would have one meeting, bringing thither a full disposition to endeavor to put an end to all doubts and *jealousies*: and I added that without some step of this nature, I plainly saw that we should break and undo what we had been labouring for years to establish:—a Whig Administration. For if this system was broken, the purposes of the Court would be completely answered, and from thence would proceed a Ministry actuated by the same principles as the last. Mr. Fox replied, that he saw too plainly that the present could not last, and grounded his argument, on his considering Lord Shelburne to be as fully devoted to the views of the Court, as Lord North ever had been. In the sequel, I was convinced of my error in thinking otherwise, but at that time, I maintained Lord Shelburne's intentions to be pure, and regardful to the public. I represented that there were really no grounds for such suspicions, and on the contrary, added assurances, that had I the smallest idea of Lord Shelburne's deviating from the line we were pursuing, the confidence I now had in him would cease. Having my concurrence, that there should be another Cabinet before his letter to M^r. Thos. Grenville was dispatched, M^r. Fox left me, to ruminate on this most untoward and unfortunate turn, which our political affairs had inevitably to undergo. Lord

Keppel I saw afterwards, and with him had much private conversation on all the consequences that were to be dreaded. He told me how sore he had just found M^r. Fox, on the contradictions he was daily meeting with at Council. I endeavored to argue with him also, that no one ought to impute to persons so respectable, as they were who composed the Cabinet, the desire of obstructing M^r. Fox's plans, while in fact, they might only be sincerely delivering their opinions. Lord Keppel was not so partial to Lord Shelburne; but he still thought with me that should Lord Rockingham live, matters had not gone so far, as to preclude a better understanding; altho' Lord Shelburne's jealousy of M^r. Fox was daily more observeable. At a Cabinet held on the 30th, the day previous to that on which Lord Rockingham died, M^r. Fox pressed us earnestly to give separately our opinion on the same point he had urged on Wednesday, relatively to the independence of America being freely granted, even without a treaty for a peace [1]. The majority was for a treaty accompanying the *surrender* of the *claim*: but that it was also adviseable that independence should in the first instance be allowed, as the *basis* to treat on. This decision not coming up to M^r. Fox's ideas: he declared with much regret, that his part was taken to quit his office, which the illness alone of Lord Rockingham occasioned him for the present to hold. Such was the state of the Cabinet when the country had to deplore the loss of this most amiable man and upright minister.

As no information can arise from a more exact and authentic source I shall continue to make use of the diary as far as it will carry me. Staggered as most of us were, on the consideration of the consequences of the death of Lord Rockingham, for which we were not prepared, there was

[1] Such a recognition of the independence of the colonies would have greatly simplified the relations of Fox and Shelburne.

Shelburne's department of the Secretariat embraced what are now the duties of the Home Office, the Irish Office, and the Colonial Office. If the colonies were an independent power the dealings with them would fall to Fox as Foreign Secretary.

a moment, when I was in hopes, that even M^r. Fox and
Lord John Cavendish might have been induced to form a
part, though the latter would not have held the Chancellorship of the Exchequer, under any first lord, the Duke of
Portland and M^r. Fox excepted : so great was the desire of
avoiding another disunion among the Whigs. But it was
otherwise ordained, and the Earl of Shelburne, authorized by
His Majesty, communicated to us, that he was to be placed
at the head of the Treasury, which arrangement, if harmony
had been the general object, ought to have proceeded from
the recommendation of the king's principal servants to His
Majesty, called to a Council [1]. This communication was made
in the morning subsequent to the Marquis's death ; and was
received with the respect due to the quarter it came from,
though neither the manner, nor the contents could be palate-
able. Lord Shelburne was to meet Lord Rockingham's friends
at night. Lord Shelburne with Lords Camden and Ashburton
dined that day, en famille with me ; the former informed us,
that he had received two letters from the king, to say, that
His Majesty should place the Treasury in his hands; adding,
as Lord Shelburne said, that he would have no other there.
He told us also, that he had seen M^r. Fox and others of the
Cabinet ; and that, though M^r. Fox was the most difficult,
yet he was not without hopes, that they might still concur.
By the Duke of Richmond's language to Lord Shelburne,
and M^r. Fox's to me that morning, I flattered myself with
the hopes that matters were not without the reach of reasonable adjustment. We all then pressed Lord Shelburne, who
was going to meet these gentlemen again that evening, to
give them every fair latitude, short of the possession of the
Treasury, in order to make it satisfactory to them; being
convinced that it was from our joint efforts alone, that good

[1] This was the assumption of the
Whig party as reconstituted by Rockingham and Burke. The leaders were to
choose the Prime Minister. The king
was to have no initiative. The theory
was not reasonable, nor warranted by
the needs of constitutional government.
The king's choice of ministers is limited
by the wishes of the people as represented
in Parliament, not by the inclinations of
a few magnates.

at this time could be expected, Lord Shelburne gave us the strongest assurances, that he should attend to our advice. In his turn, he was earnest that we should promise not to leave him in the lurch, in case M^r. Fox and his friends should quit their situation: but Lord Shelburne was unable to get Lord Camden to say more, and even that with much difficulty, than that he would remain in office for three months. As to my stay in office, I considered it as due in some measure to Lord Shelburne; at least for a short time, on account of his lordship's having given way to Lord Camden and myself in our remonstrances against Lord Shelburne's disputing the Treasury with Lord Rockingham. This was a cogent reason with Lord Camden and myself; for we neither of us were approving the state of affairs, nor the arrangements which were proposed. However we received every assurance, that on public ground only his lordship would stand; and that the principles, on which we had engaged, should be the guide of his conduct. This declaration was immediately rendered of little effect, when to our astonishment Lord Shelburne told us that Bishop Hinchcliffe was not to be translated to Salisbury: though we had considered the bishop's promotion fixed: but a promise to Bishop Barrington from the king was to over-rule the appointment of the other, altho' Bishop Barrington had been an earnest supporter of the American War. It was in vain that we argued against his lordship's giving way, stating the just reflexion he would bring on himself. Nothing would avail—Lord Shelburne persisted, and hoped to lessen our anger, by acquainting us that D^r. Watson was to be bishop of Landaff, in which insignificant see, so little adequate to his eminent virtues and character, he has been suffered to this day to be lost, much to the discredit of the Government of the country.

At Euston, to which place I went to recover my strength, I was acquainted by letter from Lord Shelburne, that M^r. Fox had actually resigned. On Saturday the 6th I received early a letter from Genl. Conway, pressing me strongly to come up

directly to London. But the country air, which I much
wished to enjoy a few days longer, was my excuse for
delaying my stay till the Wednesday following. On my
arrival in London, I heard of the filling up of most of the
offices, many of those who filled them were unknown to me,
as was the intention in regard to others. On this day, by an
injudicious speech in the House Lord Shelburne gave great
umbrage to many of the friends to the *new* system, as it seemed
calculated to create much distrust among the Americans[1].
M^r. Fox on the other hand, was said to have exceeded himself in oratorical powers.

After a long absence of my own from S^t. James's, on the
11th of July, I was able to pay my court to their majesties.
In the evening Lord Camden called on me, when we had
much conversation on the unexpected arrangement for the
see of Salisbury, where Bishop Hinchcliffe's just pretensions
were set aside, in a manner which was highly discreditable
at the outset of a new system. This disappointment did not
tend to make us relish the more our public situation, or to
hope much better things from what was to come. I may
also say from the testimony of Lord J. Cavendish, that Lord
Rockingham had declared to him, that he would sooner
have seen the conclusion of his Administration, than that he
could consent to have it disgraced, through such an injustice
done to the worthy bishop, my intimate and respected friend[2].

I had soon after a very friendly communication of all that
had passed among Lord Rockingham's principal friends from
Lord Keppel, who kept nothing back from me, as far as he
was informed of their intention of continuing with the Ministry,
or of quitting us. By the whole of which it appeared to me,
that M^r. Fox was decided to give no facility to the new
arrangement; though he was once brought by the Duke of

---

[1] This must be the speech of July 9,
in which he dwelt much on his regret at
the necessity of recognizing the independence of the colonies, and declined to
state the purport of the despatches on
the subject (*Parl. Hist.* xxiii. 188-196).

[2] Hinchcliffe was already Bishop of
Peterborough and Master of Trinity, so
one might think that he had no great
cause of complaint: but Grafton was
very faithful to his friends.

Richmond and Lord Keppel to say to them, that if Lord John Cavendish would take the Seals, he would remain his colleague. Lord John was for a moment in doubt: but on the first of his hesitating, Fox waited not an instant; but decided his own resignation. Lord Keppel acknowledged that the share of power offered by Lord Shelburne was all that M^r. Fox could desire, to assist his management of the House of Commons, and was equal to any thing that could in justice be required, or with propriety granted. The distress of Lord Keppel's mind was great: but the sense of what was due to the country, to the fleet in general, and to the officers he had himself sent on different commands prevailed over all other considerations. In return for this frankness, I could not but lay open to him my own situation and intentions, which were to look up to the public solely: and that with the strictest honor, and unprejudiced goodwill to those who still composed the broken Cabinet. His lordship was pleased with my declaration; this he much approved; and I added, that if unfortunately any calamity befell the country, and in which he might be blamed, while he was acting on such generous ground for his country's service, that there was no man, whose support he might more confidently rely on, than mine. This declaration, together with an avowal of my principles, and that I was an independent man in the Cabinet were listened to by Lord Keppel with great attention and satisfaction. The conversation was so far pleasing to me, as I thought it gave some what of a better prospect of good being derived from it.

On the next day I had an unpleasant conversation with Lord Shelburne, on the subject of Bishop Hinchcliffe, who from the part he had taken with us in Parliament, had a right to expect to be translated to Salisbury, in preference to Bishop Barrington, who had regularly supported the American War.

At a Cabinet held this same day, it was resolved on the suggestion of Lord Keppel to order Lord Howe out again, on his arrival back at S^t. Helens, where he would receive his reinforcement, with directions to offer battle to the combined

fleet, or to cruize off Brest long enough to give the India
men a free and safe passage out of the reach of the enemy.
We had no expectation of Lord Howe's having already
engaged the combined fleet; as credible information was
brought by a Swede, that he had spoken with the combined
fleet on the 8th and with Lord Howe's on the 9th to the
westward of the Start. By this intelligence, it was much to
be wished, that the ships ready in Brest Harbour, might not
be able from contrary winds, or other causes to make a
junction with the enemy's fleet then at sea; and on our side,
nothing was omitted by Lord Keppel, that could give every
possible information to Lord Howe in this most critical and
very anxious moment.

CHAPTER XII

THE SHELBURNE MINISTRY

I HAD a long conversation the next day with M^r. Fox, whose natural character was to be open, and who was always particularly so to me. He laid great stress on what he felt, on finding that he had been so principal an instrument to make that very man minister, whom he most disliked. He also plainly told me, that he never should have sided with the Duke of Richmond, to prevail on Lord Rockingham to come in, if he had not thought, that the Cabinet formation, as delivered in, would not have been accepted by the king ; and a new scheme offered, that might encourage the public to expect more unanimity. Then we soon turned naturally to the topic of the Church preferment, on the subject of which he had often talked with Lord Rockingham, who was quite decided that Bishops Shipley [1] and Hinchcliffe should have the offer of any opening that presented itself : and we both lamented that our friend had not lived long enough to have tried in the Closet his strength on the point. Among other matter, M^r. Fox here repeated, that in his opinion, Lord Shelburne was more the minister suited to the purposes of the Court, than ever Lord North had been.

M^r. Fox might be hurt, that so few of his friends marked their approbation of his conduct by following his example [2] : but I am now satisfied, that Lord Shelburne and M^r. Fox

---

[1] Jonathan Shipley (1714-1788) had been made Bishop of Llandaff by Grafton in 1769, and in the same year translated to St. Asaph. His political opinions were those of an advanced Whig, but in the care of his diocese he followed the ways of the time, and seldom resided at St. Asaph.

[2] The important resignations besides Fox were the Duke of Portland, Lord-

were too different in character and principles to have acted
at all together: and the latter had the sagacity plainly to
perceive it, though I had better expectation [1].

On the 14th, an officer came up from Plymouth with an
account that the Vigilant and another ship had been chaced
in by the combined fleet, which in number they could not lay
at more than twenty-nine of the line. The Vigilant was
steering to join Lord Howe. On receiving the next day no
account of his lordship, our anxiety was as great as possible :
for the cloud was become more black, from intelligence being
brought, that the Dutch fleet also was at sea. Orders in
consequence were issued to every port to get every thing
possible out, that could assist or be a reinforcement or assistance to the channel fleet, in case of an action with that of the
enemy.

Each day seemed to add to our ground for anxiety, and
indeed alarm for Lord Howe and his fleet. Add to all, that
just at this moment of time the trade from the east and
west was expected daily to arrive, and was possibly at the
mouth of the channel: so that dangers of every kind surrounded us; though we had the satisfaction to feel that we
could not well have amended the orders, which had been
given. Notwithstanding the inferiority of numbers, we looked
up with a degree of confidence on the spirit and skill of our
navy, when commanded by our greatest seamen; and from
a naval victory alone, could we expect to be delivered from a
situation so distressing and threatening.

It was at this time, that we felt with indignation the sad
effects of that wretched policy, by which we became enemies
to the States General. At dinner at my house this subject

Lieutenant of Ireland, Lord John Cavendish, Chancellor of the Exchequer, and
the rest of the Treasury Board, Burke,
Sheridan, and Lee, the Solicitor-General.

[1] There were many reasons why Fox
and Shelburne should quarrel. Fox had
probably not forgotten his father's
grievances, and the ' pious fraud '; there
was the long-standing difference between
the followers of Chatham and those of
Rockingham as well as the recent dispute over the spheres of their respective
departments. But in truth Shelburne
could work with few men, and his nature
and that of Fox were peculiarly anti-
pathetic.

became the general topic of discourse, and nothing could exceed the anxiety and uneasiness of Lord Keppel and M^r. Conway, on the state of things; as well as my own: tho' they declared, that their consolation was great, when they saw the spirit every where, which brought forward so great a naval force, infinitely sooner than it could have been expected. Lord Keppel's own spirits were raised, when he talked of this, as well as of the ability and professional skill of most of the commanders; and he owned that he was led from thence, as well as from Lord Howe's knowledge and resources, to expect more would be done than so inferior a force could otherwise promise.

The promptitude, with which ships were every day made ready to get out to reinforce Lord Howe was unparalleled: and these were sent out as single ships, but under peculiar orders of vigilance and every precaution to avoid danger: which measure was persisted in even after the arrival of Lord Howe's letters, on the 17th from the contents of which we derived little satisfaction, beside that of knowing that the fleet was well, in good order and spirits, and prepared for action, whenever a favorable opportunity could be seized. His lordship stated that falling in with the combined fleet, double almost in number to his own, in the wide part of the channel, he endeavored under an easy sail to draw the enemy to follow him between Scilly and the Land's End. In which object, had he succeeded, Lord Howe would have tacked, and began a most serious fight. But the enemy were too wise to fall into such a mistake, where their superior numbers would no longer have availed. Lord Howe informed us, that his position was to the westward of the enemy, which he chose in hope of covering the Jamaica fleet, or of having an opportunity of attacking the combined fleet at some favorable moment. The consequence was so great to have his lordship's fleet reinforced, that Lord Keppel easily convinced us, that under skilful commanders, and a good look out, the risk to single ships was much less than any of us imagined. Letters were also dispatched to inform Lord Howe, stating officially that the king's principal servants desired to express the fullest approbation of his conduct in not risking an attack on the combined fleet which was so very superior to that which he commanded.

The reasons M[r]. Fox had given for his retreat from office awakened a jealousy of Lord Shelburne's disposition, in the breast of D[r]. Franklyn, but this was soon cleared up by a particular friend of the doctor's voluntarily going over to Paris on that purpose.

At a Cabinet, Lord Grantham[1] was directed to communicate to the Russian Envoy the fair state of the negociation, and confidentially to consult him on the ostensible answer to the *insinuation verbale* of the two joint imperial mediators: telling him at the same time, that the putting it now in motion was undesireable, till the Paris business took its turn: and that this Court would much wish to join the King of Prussia in the mediation, unless such a step was displeasing to the empress, who had much the appearance of being disposed in our favour. The variations, in Mon[r]. de Vergennes' answer, on the Treaty of Paris, were so little particularized, that it was evident that delay was intended by that Court, and that these were purposely undefined.

I left London for the summer soon after this, with no great confidence in any thing like stability in the Cabinet, formed as it then was. In one of my latest interviews with Lord Camden, I found that we agreed, that Lord Shelburne did not seem duely to feel the consequences of the retreat of the Duke of Portland, nor of the probability of Lord Keppel's retiring some time hence. Our opinion also was, that the advice of Lord Ashburton had no longer the weight which we hoped he still possessed. We noticed that Lord Shelburne received with coldness my advice that the honors of the late Marquis of Rockingham should be offered to Lord Fitzwilliam, altho' he twice entreated to know my thoughts upon the subject.   .

---

[1] Thomas Robinson, the second Lord Grantham (1738-1786), had been Ambassador in Spain 1771-1779. He succeeded Fox as Secretary of State.

I was always ready to go up to any council to which I might be summoned : though with my own situation I was much displeased, and could not refrain from writing the letter which follows to my good friend Lord Camden.

WAKEFIELD LODGE, *July* 28th, 1782.

MY DEAR LORD,

I begin to feel now, what I have thought often before, and that is, that a Lord Privy Seal, who is not known and understood to be *confidentially trusted* and *consulted* by the principal minister, cuts but a silly figure at a Cabinet. If he is wholly silent, and tacitly comes in to all that is brought there, he becomes insignificant, as he does officious and troublesome, if his opinions urge to take a more active part than his office appears to call from him. I have too much warmth and zeal in my disposition not to be drawn into the latter and, my spirit revolting at the former, I find that I must make my retreat, if I find my suspicions should be realised, and that the Earl of Shelburne circumscribed his confidence towards me within the bounds of great *civility* and *appearance* of communication. No one knows better than your lordship the sincere disposition that I brought into the king's service to promote that system under which we embarked, and with a hearty and disinterested friendship, particularly towards him, which made me not scruple to take the most decided part, when the unfortunate moment came when the Whigs were once more *to be broken* asunder, and to declare my full intention to give him my assistance and support. But your lordship can never know with what pains I laboured, and with success to prevent that disunion being wider ; and which would have taken off much from the credit, as well as from the solidity of the Administration. The sentiments which I brought into Administration still remain and ever will ; and my personal good wishes to the Earl of Shelburne for the honor and success of his Administration are not altered by his withdrawing that openness of conduct, that he at first held towards me. But my dear lord, if I perceive that my conjectures are founded, and that his lordship continues to with-hold those communications and schemes for the king's Government, which I am vain enough to think I am entitled to receive from any minister, and particularly from him, I assure your lordship that no consideration shall stop me from withdrawing from a situation, which I consider to be unbecoming me to hold on such a footing. I will repeat again the word *vain*, for I was vain enough to think that my experience in the place he holds would have enabled me to have given often useful opinions, and which the friendship and honesty that would have attended them might have rendered desirable to the wisest. This must however take its chance. I had once resolved from a dislike to suspense to have told him all I thought and felt on the subject: but it is knowing too little of mankind to think that opinions or *real* confidence can be forced: you may as well force love, and I was, and I think that I shall remain silent. However it has eased my mind to some degree, to have opened my design to your lordship. We have moved so much on the same principle, that I cannot help wishing to hear what you say about me. My case is particular: recollect the situation I have been in, and that, thank God! I have nothing I want, nor nothing I fear from any minister, and above all that my domestic peace and happiness ought to be, and is most the object of my wishes and pursuits, and then say, my dear lord, if I am not right.

As much as we wish to see Miss Pratt and your lordship, you must not set out till I hear whether a village at a little distance is *perfectly* free from the small-pox. Be assured, &c.

GRAFTON.

What follows is the answer I received from his lordship.

MY DEAR LORD,

I have hardly thought on any other subject since I was honored with your Grace's letter: for as your Grace has been pleased in some sort to consult me, or to wish at least to be acquainted with my sentiments, I determined not to send a hasty answer or in forming my own opinion, to suffer my wishes to interfere, but to consider your Grace's situation merely, as it stands connected with the public: which last, I am persuaded is your Grace's main object; as I flatter myself, it is mine.

I have seen, and observed with infinite concern, that Lord S. has by no means treated your Grace with that confidence I expected, after you had so earnestly laboured to support his new Administration, not only by taking so important a post in it yourself, but by keeping others steady who were wavering at that critical moment. I am myself an instance and a proof of your Grace's endeavors, for your persuasion had more force with me, than any other motive to remain in my present office. I was therefore disappointed at seeing the Earl of S. so negligent in his attention to your Grace; as if, when his Administration was settled, he had no further occasion for those, to whom he was indebted for the credit of his situation. Your Grace's real importance demanded the openest communication ; and your friendship the most confidential return: and therefore I cannot be wholly without suspicion that his lordship means to take a line, and pursue a system, not likely to meet with your Grace's approbation ; and if he does, I am not surprized at his reserve: for where there is a fundamental difference of opinion in the system, there can be no confidence. However I will not suffer my suspicions to operate with me as facts, till I have such demonstration by facts of such intention. Lord S. continues to make professions of adhering to those principles we all avowed upon the first change; and he has pledged himself publicly to support them: in which respect, it is but reasonable to wait some time for the performance of his promises. At the same time I do readily admit your Grace's dignity, rank, and former situation require something more, and you ought not as Duke of Grafton to be so under a part with the Earl of Shelburne, as to be Privy Seal without confidence.

But considering the perilous condition of the public at this conjuncture, I should be much concerned, if your Grace was to take a hasty resolution of retiring just now, because your retreat could certainly be followed by other resignations and would totally un-Whig the Administration, if I may use this expression; and this second breach following so quick upon the first, would throw the nation into a ferment. It will not be possible when the Parliament meets, for Lord S. to conceal or disguise his real sentiments, and if it should then appear, that the Government in his hands is to be rebuilt upon the old bottom of influence, your Grace will soon have an opportunity of making your retreat on better grounds than private disgust. I am not more fortunate than your Grace in sharing his lordship's confidence, yet though I am bound only for 3 months, and have the fair excuse of age to plead, I would not willingly risk the chance of any disturbance at this time by an abrupt resignation, but would rather wish, if such a measure should hereafter become necessary, to take it in conjunction with others upon public ground. I am besides but too apprehensive, that more than one of us will be ripe for it, perhaps before the session. Lord K. I know from certainty will quit after the campaign: the D. of R's discontent is marked in his countenance; and if the Whigs should desert, neither G. C. nor M^r. Pitt, nor even M^r. T. would have the courage to remain behind[1]. I do not my dear lord conceive it possible, that a Cabinet composed as ours is, can be of long duration, especially if Lord S. confines his confidence to one or two of those possibly obnoxious to the others. I have had a long friendship for the earl, and cannot easily be brought over to act a hostile part against him, and for that as well as other reasons, cannot help expressing my own wishes, that your Grace may wait a while; at least till you have received most evident conviction of his indifference to your opinion and assistance. I shall be very happy to have an opportunity of conferring with your Grace upon this subject, which in reality is too serious and extensive for a letter: and am much obliged to your Grace for forbidding my visit till the small pox had left your neighbourhood. I am at present

---

[1] Lord K. and the D. of R. are of course Keppel and Richmond. G. C. must be General Conway, and Mr. T. Mr. Thomas Townshend, Secretary of State for Home and Colonial affairs.

banished for the same cause from Chiselhurst, and am now paying the necessary visits to my relations.

I am, my dear lord &c.

Aug^t*. 1*st*, 1782.*   CAMDEN.
    NB. S^r.

Your Grace will be so good to present mine and Miss Pratt's compliments to the Duchess.

Lord Camden's advice prevailed, and I readily acquiesced to his opinion on this occasion, as I was always inclined to, on most others. However I wrote the following letter to Lord Shelburne, sending by the same post the copy to Lord Camden, who approved what I had written.

WAKEFIELD LODGE, *Aug*^t*. 6, 1782.*

MY DEAR LORD,

I return you many thanks for the communication of your lordship's having settled afresh M^r. Pennington's[1] business with the L^d. Lieutenant.

Your letter relieved my mind very much, not on the business itself, for I was convinced, that, having been empowered from such authority to convey His Majesty's assurances, and which were made known to so many members of the Cabinet, it was impossible to suppose, that it was to meet with further obstructions. But, I must acknowledge to your lordship that I was much hurt, that you, who so well knew how much my ease, and even honor were concerned, had not stated the circumstance to Lord Temple so early, as to have made it unnecessary for me to solicit it. Perhaps I am more sensible of even an appearance of indifference in my friends towards my interests and concerns, knowing the zeal and warmth with which I take up theirs: but your letter has satisfied me on this head.

Recollect, my dear lord, that I was induced, to take a part in Administration, again, solely on the hopes of co-operating with you and Lord Camden towards the public good; and that the professions of friendship and confidence you made to me, alone determined me: and as I can truly say, on my part, that I both have, and do return them ever in the fullest manner, so, on the other hand, allow me to say, tho' my opinions may not be guided by the ability which many possess, whom your lordship has the opportunity of consulting, yet they will always be directed disinterestedly, and with the most honest intentions towards public good, as well as to your honor and welfare.

[1] John Pennington, eldest son of Sir Joseph Pennington (1737–1813), created Lord Muncaster in the Irish peerage in 1783. He sat in the House of Commons for many years, and supported Wilberforce in his efforts to abolish the slave-trade.

I am anxious beyond measure to hear from Lord Howe, and that he has been joined with so large a reinforcement. Your lordship makes me happy in what you say concerning the north. I do think that great good may be expected from that quarter: but still it requires much nicety and circumspection in conducting what is to be brought about.

Be assured &c.

GRAFTON.

The letter I have been transcribing was written in consequence of a more cordial one, which I had received in the mean time from Lord Shelburne. I shall add a letter in reply, which I received a few days after from Lord Camden, as also Lord Shelburne's answer to mine, as they tend to shew, that from some cause or other, Lord Shelburne was disposed to shew me more attention and civility.

MY DEAR LORD,

I luckily came to town to-day time enough to receive your Grace's letter and answer it by this night's post. I am not sorry your former letter was kept back, as the earl has given you a satisfactory answer about Pennington.

Your Grace's answer is just what it should be, and if Lord S. does not take the hint, it will be evident your systems do not correspond. I saw him twice last week. The first time his reception was cool enough; but the next morning, when he sent for me to consult about some private business of his own, he was more open. I took an opportunity to observe to him, that your Grace was gone into the country for the summer, and asked if he had heard from you, and when he said he had received a letter about M^r. Pennington, I said, I hoped you corresponded on matters of more consequence—that your Grace in every light was a person in whom he ought to place the most implicit confidence: to which he assented, adding that your conduct towards him had been so obliging, and in all respects so friendly and so handsome, that it deserved the highest return of respect on his part. There were other parts of this conversation worth your knowing, but which I shall defer till I have the honor of seeing your Grace at Wakefield. That visit, which I should be happy to make this minute, must in spite of my inclination be postponed. For, in the first place, my brother lies dangerously ill of a fever, which will keep me within a reasonable distance of London, till the distemper arrives at its crisis. Then I expect one of my daughters and her husband from Ireland, in about a week's time: so that till they are a little settled, it will not be possible for me to make any excursion: and I hardly think I shall be able to see your Grace before the beginning of Sepr. but you may depend on me before the end of the summer. The Cabinet has caught me: for I found a summons upon my table for this evening, as soon as I got to London; so I am obliged to conclude with respects to the Duchess.

I am &c.

CAMDEN.

Augt. 7th, 1782.
    NB. S^t——.

SHELBURNE HOUSE, 10th *Aug^t*., 1782.

MY DEAR DUKE,

It was my intention to write to your Grace a long letter; but I have been prevented. I will however do it, and shall have great pleasure in delivering my mind to your Grace in whose friendship and principles I have a most perfect confidence. But it is impossible to describe to you how provokingly my time is taken up with the nonsense of M^r. Burke's bill. It was both framed and carried through, without the least regard to *facts*[1]: and penned so that every line required the opinion of the Attorney General. The only extravagance I have, or shall be guilty of, is in favour of Lord Jersey. In the mean time, I want to know your Grace's opinion about Suffolk. It is of the utmost consequence to our negociation, to shew that there is some spirit remaining with the publick. And, if our negociation fails, our existence must depend upon its coming forth. I am not without hopes, that the example might catch—and if it goes on, could wish it upon the broadest ground possible.

I am going to Wycombe for a day, and will not therefore, as I am very late, trouble your Grace with more, than to assure you that I am with the most decided attachment, your Grace's obliged

and faithful servant

SHELBURNE.

NB. The *Suffolk* measure, alluded to in this letter, related to the landowners of that county subscribing to the building of a line of battle ship; a measure proposed by other counties also, and would have taken place, had the war unfortunately continued.

On my return to Wakefield Lodge from an attendance on the Cabinet, where all business had been agitated with much harmony and pleasing communication, I wrote the following letter to Lord Shelburne: indeed, these letters are the whole, that I have to produce on the occurrences of this summer beside what is well known to all.

---

[1] This is referred to by Shelburne in a memorandum set out in Fitzmaurice's *Life*, iii. 330. He complains that the Act was drawn by 'men totally unacquainted with office.'

WAKEFIELD LODGE, *Aug^t*. 31, 1782.

MY DEAR LORD,

I trust that our decisions on Thursday night if they fail in bringing peace, will both set us clear with the American Commissioners, and prevent the splitting of our system at home [1]. To this wholesome end I see how much your lordship has sacrificed your own opinions : necessity has required the sacrifice : and in the manly manner you have done so, surely you will have rivetted, as they ought to be, those, to whose ideas you have given way.

However, my dear lord, it is right also, in every political view : for after what you told me, I see plainly, that it would have been done in Parliament, in spite of every thing, and so done when it was too late to be attended with the good consequences, which may now follow : and, if this system under you should be dissolved, from whence is any redemption for the country to be expected?   The dread of greater evils made you give way : you have a right to expect a cordial return, and I trust you will meet with it.   If the East India Company are to have their loan, I am persuaded, your lordship, on every account will prefer the mode by draft. Excuse me for saying, that some stipulation for lowering the dividend, till the money is repaid, should be required ; for it is a large sum as demanded, particularly when we know that bad management has produced their distress ; and that great sums drawn by the oppressive rapacity of their governors, have been the cause, if that country is exhausted.

A very particular, and very old friend of mine, has a *very small* place under the Master of the Horse, which would give me much concern if he should lose it.   His name is Charles Fyshe Palmer.   I understand that M^r. Gilbert has that office under consideration.   I am afraid, if he was to fall, I should be obliged to become solicitor to your lordship for something else for him, and I assure you, that no one wishes to put off being troublesome to you so much as myself,

who have the honor &c.

GRAFTON.

A few days previous to this last letter, I received the communication, that confidence was perfectly re-established between those employed by us at Paris and the American Commissioners ; which had been interrupted by the apparent difference of opinion between Lord Shelburne and M^r. Fox on the point of directly acknowledging the independence of America : the former became sensible of the necessity of this

[1] The chief of these decisions was to recognize, if need be, the independence of the United Colonies, as a basis of negotiation : see Fitzmaurice, *Life of Shelburne*, iii. 255.

concession, without which peace could not have been made at that time. We had also to lament that America, whatever should be our proposals, would not treat without France, and their whole plan was not readily to be penetrated.

News, came however, that Mon^r. de Vergennes had undertaken to specify the alterations he should require to be made in a new treaty, from those Articles of the Treaty of Paris.

The Austrian Court was eager to *mediate* between the belligerent Powers; and we hoped, that Russia would also step forward [1]; but her disposition was not so decidedly for us, though it was supposed, that Simolin had orders to second Belgioso's proposals. But the Court of Petersburgh, would not hear of the great Frederick being included in the mediation: which plainly demonstrated, how much Catherine at this period preferred the Court of Vienna to any connexion with his Prussian Majesty.

It may be right to mention here that the disturbances among the Tartars encreased daily, and were of a very serious nature [2].

On the side of Ireland, Lord Shelburne assured me, that with good management that kingdom would be quiet, whatever I might have heard of to the contrary.

And I had satisfaction also in hearing from him, that according to my humble advice, he had taken care to have some of the leading men, among the dissenters, written to, in order that they might not misconstrue any declaration he had made, as meaning a continuation of the American War; for so his opinion had been received by many.

The brilliant and illustrious victory obtained by Lord Rodney over the Comte de Grasse was followed, before the

---

[1] The relations of this country and Russia, and of that Court with Austria and Prussia, may be collected from the *Malmesbury Correspondence*, i. pp. 433–484.

Lord North's Ministry, as unfortunate in diplomacy as in other things, had alienated the Empress of Russia. Austria was less unfriendly, but from the commencement of the Rockingham Ministry our relations with Russia and Prussia improved, while those with Austria changed for the worse (p. 473). Nevertheless the substitution of Frederick for the Emperor as joint mediator with Catherine was not acceptable to the Russian Court.

[2] These disturbances were merely an excuse for the invasion of the Crimea, and for a quarrel with Turkey.

end of this year, by the more compleat military atchievements displayed in the skilful and resolute defence of Gibraltar, and in the gallant relief of that place in the face of the combined fleet of France and Spain ; greatly superior in numbers to that commanded by Lord Howe. All these memorable services will never cease to redound to the honor of those great officers who conducted our arms by sea and land, as long as the search after military prowess is valued by posterity : and I will venture to assert, that the expectation of no man was carried to the extent of what was performed.

Great, indeed, was the anxiety of the public on the perilous state of Gibraltar, against which a force so very formidable had been collected, both by sea and land. The enemy thought that they were marching down to certain conquest, and the French princes of the blood came, in order to be eye-witnesses of the downfal of this mighty fortress, of which we have proudly kept possession, ever since it was taken during the war for the succession to the throne of Spain. At Paris nothing could be admitted as fashionable, which was not 'à la Gibraltar'; the ladies dresses were entirely so ; and their very fans represented on one side 'Gibraltar comme il etoit,' on the other they were so constructed as to fall to pieces in order to represent 'Gibraltar, comme il est.' At home the danger was seen with all its consequences, and every thing thought of and prepared, which could support and relieve the place. Many circumstances rendered the attempt difficult : but still it was deemed to be necessary; and we trusted that the military skill and enterprize of our forces by sea and land, would even surmount these dis-advantages. Before the arrival of Genl. Eliot's [1] account of the glorious defence of Gibraltar, of the well conducted and successful *sortie,* and of the entire destruction of Monsieur D'Arçon's ingenious floating batteries, a Cabinet was sum-

---

[1] George Augustus Eliott (1717–1790), fourth son of Sir Gilbert Eliott, of Stobbs in Roxburghshire, served in Germany, and at the Havannah in the previous war, and was created Baron Heathfield for his gallant defence of Gibraltar. He neither ate meat nor drank wine.

moned to take particularly into consideration the most
effectual means for the relief of that important fortress,
together with other matters equally pressing. I was alone
with Lord Keppel sometime, when he opened to me the plan
of operations he had prepared, and which appeared to me to
be entitled to great applause: for none could be more rational
or simple or better calculated to answer the different services;
and I may say that whenever I have related the detail of this
business, it always conveyed to those present a high idea of
Lord Keppel's naval character, with a strong conviction of
the great utility of placing a seaman at the head of the
Admiralty.

On Lord Thurlow's coming into the room where we were
all assembled, in his blunt manner he asked where was the
man who could point out the means to save Gibraltar? Lord
Keppel answered to the Chancellor and to us, that he certainly
had a plan prepared for our consideration and approval, which
he would proceed to open to the Cabinet. But he expressed
his concern, that he was obliged to state to them another
service as pressing, and equally necessary as the relief required
for Gibraltar, namely, to get the Baltic fleet safe into our
ports. The convoy of this fleet having been informed of the
force of the Dutch, in the Texel, had put into a port of
Norway, I think Bergen, for safety.

Lord Keppel plainly told us, that the king's yards were so
destitute of naval stores, that our dependence for the means
of continuing another campaign rested on the safe arrival of
these ships, which were laden with all that was wanted for
our Navy. His Lordship added that neither service could be
neglected or deferred; and that he hoped to be able to point
out the means by which both objects might be effected. The
Duke of Richmond, said Lord Keppel, acquaints me, that two
transports to be laden with ordnance stores cannot be ready
to sail with the fleet in less time than a fortnight. The wind,
says he, is now at west, which will keep Lord Howe's fleet at
Spithead from going down Channel, as well as the Dutch from
coming out of harbour.

My plan is this, says his lordship, and it waits your con-currence: for everything else is prepared. Under the sanction of your authority, I would, before I went to bed, send Lord Howe orders to detach Vice-Admiral Milbanke with fourteen ships of the line: the Dutch from the best and surest information cannot muster more than eleven of the line fit for sea. I have too good an opinion of the wisdom of my old friends as to suppose they would be so rash as to risk their fleet out against one superior to theirs, both in number and size of the ships. To Admiral Milbanke, Lord Keppel said, that further orders should go to direct him on the instant of the wind turning to the east to sail back again to rejoin Lord Howe, who on descrying the return of this part of his fleet would get under way and join at sea, in order to proceed on their voyage. Your lordships in the meantime, said Lord Keppel, need be under no apprehensions of the Dutch coming out of port hastily on the disappearance of our ships: for they will naturally conclude that they are blown by the easterly winds into the Downs: and they are too cautious to put to sea, until they have by some scouts ascertained this point. To effectuate this will necessarily cause a delay of forty-eight hours at least: during which time every ship of the Baltic fleet may get with security into some of our ports. For I propose, says he, to send the most positive orders to the officer commanding the convoy at Bergen, without a moment's delay, as soon as the wind is at east, to run with his convoy over to any British port he can easiest reach. With these orders he will be instructed that by an exact adherence to them, his fleet is secure, and that he would run much risk by a deviation from them.

We were all so well pleased with the relief which Lord Keppel had given to our minds, that after a few questions to indulge the curiosity of us landmen, we assured him that we concurred most cordially with every part of his scheme. He then acquainted us that M^r. Stephens with two Lords of the Admiralty were waiting to sign the instructions which should go into no other hands, in order for greater secrecy. We undertook to answer to His Majesty the absolute necessity there was for his service, that the whole plan should be put into motion instantly.

The wisest of human schemes are under superior controul; and the present well digested plan must have been deferred at least, had the wind come about too soon: but all was propitious; and gave just time to the officer commanding at Bergen, to receive his orders and to execute them instantly with success. Admiral Milbanke with equal promptitude followed his instructions, and fell in with Lord Howe on the back of the Isle of Wight. The passage of the fleet with so large a convoy was much impeded by contrary winds. On their entrance into the Streights, they saw the whole combined fleet drawn up, near upon the Spanish coast. The *Latona*, commanded by Cap[t]. Hugh Conway (since known by the name of Lord Hugh Seymour[1]), led in, and some way ahead, with letters to the governor, who on seeing the *Latona* making for the harbour, sent to him to get back to apprize Lord Howe of his danger: but Cap[t]. Conway answered, that his admiral was well apprized of the strength and position of the enemy, and notwithstanding, he should be able to effect the object of his mission, by succouring and supplying the citadel. Accordingly, Lord Howe passed the French and Spanish fleets, covered the store ships and victuallers while they were unlading, received little or no interruption in performing this service. This effected, Lord Howe sailed through the Streights, and in the Mediterranean drew up in line, prepared if the enemy had chosen to attack him. But this was not their design as appeared soon after; for the two fleets had a kind of running fight when the English fleet had repassed the Streights.

The enemy was so numerous[2], that nothing could justify

---

[1] Lord Hugh Conway (1759–1803) was the fifth son of the first Marquis of Hertford, after whose death in 1794 the family resumed the name of Seymour, which their ancestor, Francis Seymour, afterwards Lord Conway, had changed when he succeeded to the property of his cousin Edward, Earl of Conway, who died in 1683.

[2] The allied ships were 49 in number,

Lord Howe, who had answered his great object, to bring on unnecessarily an unequal contest : and his orders to detach twelve or fourteen ships of the line, to reinforce Admiral Pigot in the West Indies would have been frustrated, had the fleet much suffered in such a contest : wherefore the gallant admiral having once more drawn up to offer them battle, aimed at nothing further at that time; but dispatched Vice-Admiral King with the freshest of his ships to the West Indies.

Not long after the decision of the Cabinet, we received the pleasing accounts of the signal successes of the garrison itself, in a well conducted and effectual sortie, as also of the distinguished manner, in which the formidable attack of the enemy's floating batteries were repulsed with an entire destruction of those famous vessels.

The succour of the place being completely effected by the fleet under Lord Howe, cut off all hopes which the enemy could form ; and the siege was raised, to the great mortification of the Duc de Crillon [1], and the army he commanded.

Lord Shelburne felt every day more and more the necessity of peace, and had great merit in forwarding this desirable object with firmness and activity.   Mon[r]. de Grasse was allowed on his parole to return to France.   By him Lord Shelburne made overtures to Mon[r]. de Vergennes proposing to open a negociation for a general pacification.   The Americans, Dutch, and Spaniards had so linked themselves with France, that we could hope for no success should a separate negociation be attempted.   However his lordship was obliged to some of us in the Cabinet, who equally anxious for peace, yet were unwilling to come into many points of concession which were demanded, and which Lord Shelburne would not have stood out upon, if he had not seen

the English 34. The great attack on Gibraltar was made on the 13th of September : this relief by Lord Howe was effected between the 13th and 19th of October.

[1] De Crillon had assumed the command early in 1782, after a successful siege of Port Mahon, which surrendered on February 5.

particularly Lord Camden, Gen[l]. Conway, and myself in opinion against him, on several points.

The negociation took place, and on my arrival in London, Nov[r]. 24th, I found that the Parliament was prorogued on that account.

I resume again my journal, in which there had been a chasm from September to that time: but I have so strong a recollection of the events, that I equally depend on my memory. On the day after my arrival in town, I received by my good old servant, Schaller, a verbal message from Lord Shelburne, that he came to London almost on purpose to see me, and that he should be with me at four o'clock next day. I had not yet seen any of the ministers, when his lordship called upon me according to his message. The measure of proroguing the meeting of Parliament, he told me, stood on the ground of a firm persuasion, that the Court of France was in earnest, and intended to bring forward through Mon[r]. de Regneval[1], who had returned to Paris, such answers, before the 5th of Dec[r]., as might be considered as an ultimatum, on which peace, or a continuation of the war was to be decided.

Lord Shelburne then expatiated on the little hope that could be entertained from a continuance of the war, in which opinion I perfectly agreed with him ; though I differed widely on the little consequence he gave to the cession of Gibraltar. On finding this difference in our sentiments, I said that I was sorry to hear this from him : on which Lord Shelburne observed, that I never had wished that the cession of that place should stand in the way of a peace, provided an equivalent was found, such as *Porto Rico.* I replied, understand me right, I shall always part with Gibraltar with the greatest reluctance, though I am still free to acknowledge, that I think

---

[1] This was Gerard de Rayneval, the Secretary of Vergennes. His mission was kept secret from the American envoys in Paris. There was at this time a wide divergence of interests between the French and American negotiators (Fitz- maurice, *Life of Shelburne,* iii. 254– 268). Rayneval's name seems to have been found difficult. Grafton calls him Regneval. Fitzpatrick speaks of him as ' Rennervalle or whatever his name is' (*Memorials of Fox*, ii. 9).

that a proper peace ought not to hang on this one point, in case a fair equivalent offered: but I said that I did not know sufficiently the value and circumstance of the island to say, that I considered Porto Rico to be such an equivalent as would satisfy me. To this his lordship replied, that I might be assured, that on the fullest enquiry, I should find, as he had, that the value would exceed my expectations[1].

Before he left me Lord Shelburne desired me to turn in my thoughts what would be the properest method of rewarding Gen¹. Elliot.

On the following day I wrote to Lord Shelburne expressing my hopes that an Irish peerage would not be fixed on as a reward for Gen¹. Elliot as in my opinion that honor was inadequate to his services. Afterwards I employed myself in reading over with particular attention the French correspondence, also that with Russia, Berlin, and Vienna.

About this time the Bishop of Landaff had prepared for publication his well-known letter to the Archbishop of Canterbury, on the subject of a suitable provision, &c., for the inferior clergy. His lordship approved, on reading them over, of the alterations I had presumed to make at his desire. Sure I am that every fair thinking man will admire the letter and the drift of his design.

On the same day I dined *en famille* with Lord Shelburne, when after many confidential communications regarding the present disposition of the Closet, he naturally took up the essential point of the negociation. He told me that he was persuaded from the eagerness of the French Court, that peace will be the result of Mon^r. de Regneval's journey, that Guadeloupe or (I think he said) Martinique might be the substitute to Porto Rico. His lordship also said that an Irish peerage would not be the reward for Gen¹. Elliot's services.

Lord Shelburne, who had read the letter to the archbishop,

---

[1] Grafton is described by Lord Rosebery (*Life of Pitt*, p. 37) as representing, with Shelburne and the king, the party in the Ministry who desired to cede Gibraltar. This does not seem to have been the case: yet as too often happened he might have allowed his opinion to be over-ruled.

was much alarmed on the idea of the reform proposed by the Bishop of Landaff's letter. On his pressing me much to dissuade the bishop from bringing the business forward, I endeavored in vain to convince him of the benefit the country in my opinion would reap from a measure so well considered and digested : and I left him to settle the point with the bishop himself.

On the next day advices were received of the two drawn battles in the East Indies between the French fleet commanded by Suffrein and ours [1].

With Gen[l]. Conway to whom I went purposely to talk over all the delicate points, on which the impending treaty might turn, there was but little difference of opinion ; and I received from him some pleasing accounts of military preparations which I could not but much approve.

I must here mention that the Bishop of Landaff dropt for the present the thoughts of publishing his letter [2], at Lord Shelburne's particular request, and on his positive assurance that something should be done on that line and soon. I understood from the bishop that he should print only two copies somewhat amended, one of them for himself, the other was entrusted to me.

On the 1st of December Lord Keppel called on me, we discoursed over the probable difficulties towards a peace, and I had the satisfaction to find that hitherto we differed little in opinion. He confirmed to me the pleasing communications on the naval and military preparations which I had received from Gen[l]. Conway.

On the following morning Mon[r]. de Regneval returned and with him Mon[r]. de Vergennes' son. I heard nothing that day from any of the ministers : but with Lord Camden I conversed much alone on the subjects naturally to be discussed

---

[1] These must be the first two of the five battles fought between Suffren and Admiral Hughes on Feb. 17 and April 12. The other three were fought on July 6, and Sept. 3, 1782, and June 20, 1783 : see Mahan, *Influence of Sea Power on History*, ch. xii.

[2] The letter appeared soon after : it contained a scheme for equalizing the incomes of bishops and clergy. It was published (3rd ed.) in the *Pamphleteer*, viii. 574 (1816).

next day. I told him that I saw Lord Shelburne was decided
for peace at any rate, and I conceived that he would stand or
fall by the acquisition of it. I stated to Lord Camden how
preferable in every consideration the possession of Gibraltar
was over Mahon; and in the point particularly when Lord
Camden supposed they both would become useless without
a superior fleet, in the Mediterranean, Gibraltar had an
advantage over the other which could not be called in
question: for that fortress had proved that she can stand
with an occasional relief against the greatest force: whereas
Mahon must fall if vigorously attacked. I think I drew over
Lord Camden to see this in its proper light.

On the next day Lord Shelburne sent to me to call upon
him before the meeting of the Cabinet: he acquainted me in
much hurry with the heads of the Spanish answer and
exchanges offered: he showed me also the draft for the
king's speech; then excusing himself from leaving me so
abruptly to go to the Duke of Richmond, I went down to
the Cabinet which sat discussing the several points from
eleven till half past seven: a minute was drawn at last of
advice upon the Spanish article[1]: but with an intention that
it should again come before us.

Lord Shelburne, as I observed, was particularly vexed at
what I had held out on the Spanish business, and on the
various equivalents proposed for the cession of Gibraltar.
A message from him the next morning did not surprize me,
and as he desired to see me, as soon as possible, I went to
him as soon as I had breakfasted, with a firm resolution to
maintain my ground. He, in the first place, enquired of me
where I had taken up the notion that a barren, uninhabited
island was equal or more valuable than West Florida; and
afterwards whether I still continued in the same opinion.
My answer was, that I was clear from the best information

---

[1] For this minute, see Fitzmaurice,
Life of Shelburne, iii. 305.

    Spain was to restore Minorca and the
Bahamas, and to allow an establishment
on the coast of Honduras. Gibraltar
was to be exchanged for Guadaloupe,
and West Florida to be retained by
Spain if Trinidad were ceded to us.

on the subject, that the greatest advantages both for trade and power might be derived from the possession of Trinidad ; and that I professed an indignation that Spain should succeed in having her great object, Gibraltar, conceded to her, without giving up Trinidad to be in addition to any cession she had proposed to us. I added further, and very deliberately, that friend to peace as I anxiously was, sooner than I would sign the treaty on such terms as seemed now to be intended, I could answer it to my conscience, and to my country, to advise the continuance of the war, until better terms could be obtained. After much difference of opinion on what related to the negociation, and many warm observations on the factions by which the country was distracted, he said to me : ' Duke of Grafton, I will fairly tell you that as to Lord Keppel I should be happy to see him away from his board: the Duke of Richmond also must take the part he judges proper ; I shall see it with indifference. But though it would be very unpleasant to me, and give me great concern to differ from you, yet I must bear it : for I am resolved to stand by the king.' My answer was delivered mildly and coolly : ' I trust that we are all equally resolved to do so in a constitutional manner. I will fairly tell your lordship, said I, that I came into office, meaning, as I still mean, to give you sincere support : but it must be with honor and comfort to myself, and on points of magnitude like the present you must not wonder if I do not, nor cannot give up my opinions, but defend them as strenuously as I am able.' I added, 'as to office, that day would always be the happiest of my life when I could retire from it with credit to myself.' To which he replied, that he believed me, as I was always of an *anxious* turn of mind. Lord Shelburne appeared disappointed, that I had not yielded to the arguments he used, and quitted me to go to Mon^r. de Regneval ; but not till after we had much conversed on the contested articles. In doing which, I had pressed again my advice for the retaining Gibraltar, unless such an exchange was given, as would satisfy the country : a point by no means attainable with ease.

I should here observe that the advances towards a general pacification had already made some way by the signing of a provisional article for a treaty with America on the 30th of last Nov[r]., wherein the Independence of the States was formally declared.   On my return home, I expressed in a short letter to Lord Grantham that I both hoped and understood that the essential points in dispute among us were to have another revision, before M[r]. Fitzherbert [1] was authorized to sign.   His lordship's answer to me was 'that the terms of peace with Spain would never be determined, much less signed, without the fullest reconsideration by the Cabinet.'

Lord Shelburne at the meeting at night renewed ineffectually his endeavours to get me to give way in the opinions I had given.   They were too deliberately adopted to be so easily relinquished.   Afterwards he acknowledged that since our morning discourse he had obtained some intelligence from well informed persons which greatly lowered the value of the possession of West Florida in his mind.

Thursday, Dec[r]. 5th.   The Parliament met: His Majesty's speech was well approved, and the addresses passed with little or no opposition ; but the language of many in both Houses showed that Ministry was to expect a great deal on the articles of the future treaties.   In the House of Lords it was admitted that the campaign had been *glorious* and successful ; and that in consequence it was reasonable to expect that the treaty of peace should be *fair, honorable*, and concluded on *equal* terms.

Much dissatisfied as I remained on the disposition of the Cabinet at their last meeting on the terms to be settled with Spain, I wrote early in the morning to Lord Shelburne to entreat him that a matter of such magnitude should come once again for revision before the king's servants ; especially as further objections were in my mind to the state of that

---

[1] Fitzherbert had been our minister at Brussels, and succeeded Thomas Grenville as our envoy for the negotiations in Paris.

negociation. By his answer I was told that his lordship was persuaded that he could satisfy me, if I would call on him. I went directly to Shelburne House. After some little introduction, he acquainted me that he had seen Mon^r. de Regneval on Wednesday, and had told him fairly and explicitly, that such an equivalent as would be expected to answer the public opinion must be found, if Gibraltar was to be exchanged ; and that nothing short of Trinidad or S^t. Lucia would do, in addition to what had been proposed : and Lord Shelburne added that a messenger was dispatched that night with instructions in consequence. He begged also that this information should be communicated no further as yet. Lord Grantham at Court this day informed me that he had written to M^r. Fitzherbert last night by a messenger, telling him of the general concurrence and declarations of all parties of men to give every means of exertion to the Government, towards continuing the war, in case our enemies refused to listen to *fair*, *honorable*, and *equal* terms of peace. The secretary added that these declarations must tend to strengthen his demands, and give him less inclination to recede from any. As his lordship said nothing of the instructions on the last minute of Council, I trusted that they were postponed, and that they would wait for the answer to the communications between Mon^r. de Regneval and Lord Shelburne upon the subject ; concluding this to be the case I did not put the direct question.

With Lord Camden I had much conversation, he appeared to me to lean now considerably to the opinion that Gibraltar is of more consequence to this kingdom, and that the views of its ministers ought in future to look to the possession of it as an object of more value than he at first imagined, as likewise that the cession of it, even on good terms, would be grating to the feelings of the nation.

The rising of the stocks this day and yesterday indicated to me that it is known either on the French side, or somewhere on ours, that there is to be a facility in framing the articles of peace. I trust however that from our side no facility is to be shewn except on terms which can be justified by the most wise and honest part of the community.

From this time the negociation proceeded forward at great strides. The Administration had great reason to approve the conduct of M^r. Fitzherbert, whose discernment and ability contributed very much to conclude it with all the satisfaction which our situation at war with so many Powers, and having the goodwill of none, could possibly expect. I was made happy at last by finding that Gibraltar was to be retained by England.

This point being now carried, the preliminaries adjusted for peace between Great Britain, France and Spain, to which His Majesty was advised to send his notification directly, I took the opportunity to pass a few days in the country, where I heard of Lord Keppel's and the Duke of Richmond's actual resignation[1] with sincere concern: but they were not satisfied with all the articles on which peace was to be concluded.

While these negociations for peace with our enemies were daily appearing more likely to terminate in success: the struggles at home for power disgraced our statesmen on all sides. Lord Shelburne, instigated I believe by the Court, would gladly have received Lord North and his friends to strengthen his Administration. Others I doubt not were equally disgusted with such an idea; but I owe it to my friend Lord Camden as well as to myself, to say that we both frankly told Lord Shelburne, that we would never listen to a measure, so disgraceful in itself and revolting to our minds. With those who had been driven and those who had retired from office, there was not the same delicacy; and we saw with astonishment approaches made, and friendships at last declared between the great oppugner of the American War, and the minister to whom he had imputed every evil, under

[1] Keppel resigned on Jan. 24. Richmond told the king that he would attend no more at Cabinet meetings, but would continue to preside over his department, the Ordnance, with a view to carrying out some changes which he had in hand.

which the country groaned. The debate in the House of Commons afterwards on the preliminaries was the most extraordinary that can be conceived: and the public was there informed of a connexion which both sides appeared to glory in while the nation could not with-hold the expressions of its abhorrence. With most considerate men, the terms of the peace were so much better than were expected that they scrupled not to give that attestation of their opinion: even the mercantile part of the nation felt that the kingdom wanted rest.

After an absence of ten days in the country, I returned on the 5th of Febry 1783 to London. Lord Keppel called on me on that day: but nothing particular passed between us. I was truly concerned, as I told him, that he quitted his office: for besides losing him there, I saw the unhappy breach, which was daily becoming more wide among those whom I wished to see conducting the public affairs.

Though my good and excellent friend Lord Howe had every requisite for the discharge of that difficult post; yet I shall bear ever my testimony, that no man could ever shew more zeal, assiduity and knowledge in that situation, than Lord Keppel. He had a noble mind, incapable of injustice, or of one ungenerous thought.

On the Saturday following Lord Shelburne called on me; his conversation was open as I thought mine was to him: his discourse ran on subjects of delicate political engagements, and he appeared to trust me confidentially with the schemes then working in his mind. I concealed from him none of my thoughts relative to what he had opened to me: stating clearly and distinctly that no arrangement but a fair union with those friends, who had come in with us, and since divided from us, could possibly satisfy me: at the same time begging him in case he inclined to a different arrangement to consider my office as no impediment to his views.

I liked Lord Shelburne's language this day better than for a long time past: I lamented, therefore more that he had treated of late the Duke of Richmond and Lord Keppel in a manner calculated to render a junction with them more difficult.

M^r. Fox called on me the following day, when we had a long and candid discourse upon the state of men and upon the country. My wishes he had long known, and I had no occasion to repeat them, for they were known likewise to all my friends. The Duke of Richmond's, he told me, were precisely the same as mine, and Lord Keppel's also. Much of my reasoning on public matters he allowed to be just: but still he dwelt on the necessity of the Cabinet proposing the head of the Treasury[1]; and that nothing could move him and his friends from this point; he professed, that he was totally at a loss to guess how affairs would turn out; he owned that he felt the greatest objections to join Lord North and his friends; and yet perhaps it was best, though he agreed it could not be lasting.

From the whole of this conversation with M^r. Fox I conceived but little hope of being gratified with my principal wish, namely, of seeing the Whigs once more united and co-operating to retrieve a country cruelly governed for years past, and that stood in need of every aid, as did likewise a constitution shaken on every side to its very foundation.

Two days after my last discourse with Lord Shelburne, his lordship obtained the king's leave to form a solid junction with M^r. Fox and those of his friends who had separated from us in July or since. The Duke of Richmond was previously assured by his lordship, that there should be no insincerity in the negociation. M^r. Pitt met M^r. Fox in consequence for this purpose in the evening[2]: and I understood that M^r. Fox was extremely unwilling to converse, and

---

[1] This contention of the Whigs might have been reasonable enough if the Cabinet had been the choice of the people. But to the followers of Rockingham it meant that the king was to put the conduct of affairs into the hands of a group of Whig peers and landowners, and that these should settle who were to hold the offices of State. To limit the powers of the Crown was the main object of the Rockingham Whigs.

[2] Pitt asked Fox 'if there were any terms on which he would come in.' Fox replied, 'None while Shelburne remains': and so it ended (*Buckingham Papers*, i. 149).

declared that neither he nor any of his friends would think of such a junction, unless the nomination to the Treasury was to be opened to them.

In a conversation between M^r. Secretary Townshend [1] and M^r. Frederick Montague the next morning, there was, as I heard no better hope of such a reunion, after which Lord Shelburne immediately desired to see me; he began by relating the substance of what passed at the above two interviews; and having stated that a reunion was hopeless his lordship said, that he was now brought to opt between a voluntary resignation, or holding out to be beaten in Parliament, or to strengthen himself by a junction with Lord North's friends: he therefore wished to know my thoughts, as he should be unwilling to decide the part he should take without having my opinion with those of Lord Camden, M^r. Townshend, Lord Howe and M^r. Pitt. My answer was nearly this, that no one could lament more sincerely the present dilemma than myself, but that under it I had no scruple of avowing that what I dreaded most for the country was an Administration composed of M^r. Fox's and Lord North's adherents; that a junction of Lord Shelburne with Lord North was the circumstance that would next displease me most: for either of these would tend to divide more and more those who had acted together, and I confessed that badly as the Government in the old hands would probably be administered, I had rather see them undertake it, because the Whigs now disunited would probably then get together, and while in opposition, might be instrumental to the country's benefit. This declaration seemed much to displease his lordship and I plainly saw that it ran clearly against his wishes; and thwarted to some degree his plan; the remainder of our conversation became cold, and he appeared to wish me to be gone.

[1] Thomas Townshend, afterwards Viscount Sydney, who had been Secretary at War under Rockingham, became Secretary of State for the Home and Colonial departments under Shelburne. He held the same post in Pitt's Ministry till 1789.

However, as I was taking my leave, he told me, that he had reason to think, that the friends of Lord North would not be unreasonable[1]; and Lord Shelburne added, and I will ask this question; on a supposition that none of them were to form a part of the Cabinet, what should you think of such an addition of strength? To which I replied 'that I must reserve myself to form an opinion until I could see the whole laid before me; when I should judge what it became me to do: it is possible also, that I might cordially support such a formation, though I might not chuse to bear a part in it: therefore I could not well resolve his lordship's enquiry.'

I understand that Lord Shelburne spoke that night of this discourse with me, and complained of my closeness. I conclude that he could only mean in the last declaration: for nothing could be more frank than all the rest.

A narrative taken from a journal so closely as this I fear will appear tedious; but it cannot be so deemed with propriety, if it lets us often into the ways of thinking, dispositions and manners of men, whose characters we wish to know. I shall therefore with this hope, continue the method with less scruple; even lamenting that it reaches no farther down than my own resignation: from which date, I have mislaid, or lost some notes beyond that period.

But to proceed; the Duke of Rutland[2] accepted the offer that had been made to his Grace of the Lord Steward's staff: the Duke of Marlborough after some consideration having declined it.

In the evening of the following day, Feb^ry. 13th we met at Lord Shelburne's in order to settle the address on the peace:

---

[1] Before the application made to Fox, and again, after the conversation here recorded, some approaches appear to have been made to North through Dundas (Fitzmaurice, *Life of Shelburne*, iii. 341, 344; *Memorials of Fox*, ii. 21), and again through Rigby (*Memorials of Fox*, ii. 39). Dundas seems to have mismanaged the overtures, and Rigby came too late.

[2] Charles, fourth Duke of Rutland (1754–1787), son of the popular Marquis of Granby. He succeeded his grandfather in 1779. He went out of office with Shelburne, but when Pitt came in he became Lord-Lieutenant of Ireland, and died while holding that office.

all agreed that no triumphant words could be carried, or ought to be proposed : those which pleased most, were the most moderate, and such were adopted. Lord Howe and Gen[1]. Conway, on asking some previous questions relative to disarming, were desired to lay soon before us their plans for that purpose. Having had in a corner of the room this night some disagreeable discourse with Lord Shelburne regarding Lord Jersey[1] and M[r]. Woodley, I was uneasy till I could open my mind more fully on these matters to his lordship, as well as on my own situation, I therefore called upon him the next morning before breakfast, told him the concern I felt on his language regarding both my friends ; and I expressed my wish fairly to know from him what I was to say to Lord Jersey, whom of all men, I wished to speak to without reserve ; and who ought not to be led by me into the most distant expectations, unless I saw that they were well grounded. After much discourse not necessary to be noticed on the subject, he said that though he would be tyed down by nothing specific I might say, that on proper openings, his pretensions would be weighed with the additional circum-stance on its being known that I had his interest much at heart. On Lord Shelburne's observing that I must be sensible of the readiness with which he had fulfilled my wishes on every occasion, I could not help starting, and desiring to know what offices or favors I had either asked or received for any of my friends ; and on my declaring that there had been positively none, he took me up quickly saying, do you reckon that which has been done for M[r]. Stonhewer nothing? I replied, that obliged as I was for settling his business, yet that it was only justice obtained for M[r]. Stonhewer and no favor granted to him. His lordship contending still that nothing had ever caused him more trouble in bringing about, nor equalled the odium he had undergone on that account.

In the course of this conversation I repeatedly observed to him, that I conceived when we came into office, and his

---

[1] See p. 96 note. Lord Jersey was at this time Master of the Buckhounds.

declaration had confirmed me in the belief that it was to be upon the footing of the most perfect confidence and communication; at the Cabinet, and particularly so at all times between him and me; that we had given assurances to each other, that we would fairly speak out when we imagined it to be otherwise: therefore I did, beg to declare to him, that with his lordship or any other minister I would not hold the Privy Seal except on a confidential footing. I shall observe to you that a compensation for two patent places given to M^r. Stonhewer by my grandfather as Lord Chamberlain, was the favor said to be granted to M^r. Stonhewer.

On the 15th many of the peers who take part in the debates together with Lords Pembroke and Rodney the mover and seconder dined with Lord Shelburne in order to consult on the most judicious ground on which the address should be supported: we were then informed, that at a meeting of Lord North's friends a resolution was taken to join with M^r. Fox and his party in opposing the terms of the peace.

The following day it was said, though unknown to, and disbelieved by Lord Camden and myself, that the Duke of Rutland having the Lord Steward's wand, was to have a seat at the Cabinet.

Under this conception, I went early the next morning, to ascertain the fact, from M^r. Secretary Townshend himself; when to my greatest astonishment, I found that the Duke of Rutland was actually of the Cabinet. I started so much on this information, that he said 'Surely it was within etiquette, that a Cabinet might be changed or added to, without the concurrence of the other members of it.' I replied that I could not admit this position; for I was confident, that it ought to be otherwise: and I was sorry to add moreover, that this measure was decisive of my situation. However as a friend to the Duke of Rutland, I wished to express to him that the bare appearance of any objection to his Grace was the only point that could give me any embarrassment in the business: for that the duke was a man whom I not only valued highly but was one to whom I had some obligations.

From Mͬ. Townshend's I walked up to Lord Camden's, in order to relate to his lordship, what had passed. We agreed in thinking, that I should immediately go to inform Lord Shelburne of my determination. On finding the last mentioned lord at home, I began with expressing my surprize at the information which Mͬ. Townshend had just given me: and I complained that such a proceeding little agreed with that confidence which I had been assured, I should find from his lordship when we both embarked in the Ministry; and which had been repeated on the death of Lord Rockingham. I then plainly declared to Lord Shelburne that no consideration should induce me to act so insignificant a part, or submit to be so little considered, under any Administration whatsoever. His lordship first wished to excuse himself, by saying, that he had no opportunity to impart to me his intention: but on my reminding him of the particular conversation I had with him on Friday morning last, his lordship replied, that the king's pleasure had not at that time been taken. Lord Shelburne then said, that as much as he should be sorry to be deprived of any one's assistance, he would deprecate no man (be his consequence what it would) from taking the part, which he thought to be becoming his station: however he added in a milder tone that he did not know whether it was actually done; that he must write to Mͬ. Pitt, to enquire how the matter stood: and how it was understood by the Duke of Rutland himself; and that he would let me know.

He observed, that Mͬ. Townshend was new in office; and happened to say, 'was one of the Cabinet'; when he rather ought to have said 'that it was intended that his Grace should be called to it.'

Lord Shelburne's language so thoroughly convinced me, that he expected to be the sole adviser to the king, of measures of this sort, that I became, if possible more determined to quit my office. With a declaration to this effect I left his house saying also, that as the part I should take was known fully to him, I was ready to resign at such

moment as His Majesty should approve. However, on re-
viewing in my mind what had passed in this conversation,
I was not quite satisfied with the footing on which my
decision was left; I therefore turned back to Lord Shelburne's fully determined, that whatever was the answer of
M^r. Pitt, concerning what had been said to the Duke
of Rutland, it would not keep me in my situation; for
it was a demonstration that it would be, as abetting
Lord Shelburne's views of becoming *Prime* Minister, which
were so apparent: whereas I would never consider his lordship but as holding the principal office in the Cabinet[1].
I told him that on considering again, that the king's pleasure
was taken, that it was known to the duke himself, by which
the matter was in fact determined, and no longer open to
consideration, these circumstances together with the whole
tenor of his lordship's discourse determined me to take the
earliest opportunity of desiring the king to allow me to
retire from my office: but that I should leave His Majesty
to decide when it suited best with his affairs. I acquainted
Lord Shelburne likewise that I should no longer attend any
Cabinet.

The debate on the preliminaries in the House of Lords
lasted till 4 o'clock the next morning, the numbers for our
address were 69; for the amendment, or rather against our
address, 55. That of the Commons was four hours longer:
the amendment, a gentle one, was carried by sixteen votes
against the Administration. Our debate was a very good
one: Lord Chancellor and Lord Shelburne spoke very ably[2]:
Lord Loughborough with much eloquence, but with a vehe-

---

[1] It is difficult to understand the constitutional aspect of the Cabinet as conceived by the Whigs of 1783. Fox
maintained that the Cabinet was to
choose the Prime Minister. Grafton
seems to think that a Prime Minister
might be dispensed with, but that the
Cabinet should be consulted before any
addition was made to its numbers.
How the Cabinet was to be chosen in
the first instance does not appear.

A Prime Minister in our modern sense
of the term seems hardly to have been
a recognized necessity until the time of
William Pitt. See Stanhope, *Life of
Pitt*, iv. 24.

[2] Walpole, *Journals*, ii. 584, says,
'The Duke of Grafton, though highly
dissatisfied with Shelburne, handsomely
defended him.'

mence of gesture, and a forced manner and affected exertion of voice, such as I have never met with from a British orator. For some days afterwards it was held forth that the parties were only joined to pull down Lord Shelburne on account of personal dislike and distrust. However others saw plainly that his Administration was drawing to an end; and various were the speculative opinions of the public, on the probable issue of this State anarchy, into which the king and nation had been brought. From this time therefore you may consider the Opposition as one compact body [1], though they did not yet avow their readiness to coalesce.

[1] The parties of Fox and North were not yet agreed on anything except that Shelburne should be turned out (*Buckingham Papers*, i. 158; *Memorials of C. J. Fox*, ii. 12). Fox and North met for the first time on February 14. The debate took place on the 17th, when Shelburne had a majority of fourteen in the Lords, but was beaten by sixteen in the Commons. On the 21st a direct censure on the peace was carried in the Commons by a majority of seventeen. There was some difficulty in inducing the followers of North and the Whigs to act together, but Eden worked upon the Tories while Burke influenced the Rockingham Whigs and Fitzpatrick the immediate followers of Fox (*Memorials of Fox*, ii. 23).

CHAPTER XIII

THE COALITION

ON the 19ᵗʰ of February I went to the king's dressing, was present at the receiving the address, and though I asked an audience early, it was 4 o'clock before I was admitted into the Closet. I had frankly told Lord Shelburne, on what ground I proposed to lay before the king the cause of my retiring: but on his explaining a part of it away, I agreed to narrow it; and indeed in stating my complaints to the king, I did not even come up to the line on which his lordship and I had met.

I informed His Majesty, that on a disagreeable explanation with Lord Shelburne, I had found, that the degree of confidence which I had experienced of late from his lordship was all that in future I was to expect: and that the whole tenor of his conduct towards me was much on too high a tone for me to subscribe to. I further said to the king that I came in to serve His Majesty, with every reason to expect fair communication and confidence both from Lord Rockingham and Lord Shelburne, and that I need not remark to His Majesty, that a Lord Privy Seal, having no department, and at the head of no profession, could be at the Cabinet with becoming dignity, only with the fair confidence of the principal minister. I then stated that it being evident to me, that the contrary was now the case, and therefore without presuming to look how far Lord Shelburne was aiming to break through that system of *general Cabinet advice*, which had been understood by us all, I humbly begged His Majesty's leave to resign the Seal, which I could no longer retain with honor and comfort. If I had not brought the

Seal, it was solely owing to my desire of having my retreat appear the most respectful to His Majesty, whose commands I should obey when he should be pleased to deliver it to a successor.

The king treated me undoubtedly with his usual civility : but I could perceive no sign either of surprize, or of concern. However I thought it right to say that I retired from his service as a man perfectly unconnected : and that on any favors, for which in future, I might have occasion to apply, I should presume to address myself to His Majesty himself, as well as to his minister.   However the king made me very easy on the subject of M^r. Pennington, of whom he said, using an expression which I do not recollect having ever heard to drop from him before : ' Duke of Grafton, I am ready to say, *upon my word and honor*, that there can be no Irish peers made, without M^r. Pennington's being included among the first.'   Accordingly, this gentleman was soon after created Lord Muncaster.

Previously to my going to S^t. James's, Lord Camden called on me, and imparted all that he found himself at liberty to say of a very serious conversation he had that morning with the Earl of Shelburne; who had sent for Lord Camden, as he now and then did, when he found himself in difficulties, and on this occasion, to consult Lord Camden on the part it became the earl to take.   The substance of Lord Camden's advice was decisive, and nearly this—that he advised Lord Shelburne to retire, as unfortunately it plainly appeared that the personal dislike was too strong for him to attempt to stem, with any hope of credit to himself, advantage to the king, or benefit to the country; that he had it in his power to retire now with credit, and the approbation of the world ; for, whatever the arts and powers of united parties had expressed by votes in Parliament, &c., still the nation felt themselves obliged to him, for having put an end to such a war, by a peace which exceeded the expectation of all moderate fair judging men.   Lord Camden further said to his lordship, that he might add lustre to his retreat, by prevailing on the king to call on the body of the Whigs to form an Administration as comprehensive as could be. Lord Camden went further by saying, that if Lord Shelburne could not be prevailed on to take either of the steps which would give him most credit with the world, and that he was still from engagement or inclination instigated to stand as minister, he had nothing better to advise, than that his lordship should, with manly courage, avow a close junction with Lord North's party, if he could so manage it. This indeed, might enable his lordship to carry on Administration, which a middle way and a partial junction never would effect. Lord Camden added, that he thought the last scheme to be that which ought if possible to be avoided. I observed to Lord Camden that I was clear notwithstanding the advice, that Lord Shelburne preferred it to all the others and that such would be his decision. The object of sending for Lord Camden, I believe, was with the hopes to draw him into his opinion, if he was able, and by no means to take his advice : unless it could be made to coincide with the part he was decided to take ; though he did not perceive that it was now too late for his plan to succeed. Lord Camden fairly acquainted Lord Shelburne, that he could not remain at any rate, that the whole was new modelled, and that he must claim his right of retiring at three months end, which had been stipulated at Lord Rockingham's death. Lord Camden urged to him strongly the propriety of his coming to his decision before two days were expired : the other inclined to see the event of as many months.

At night I had much conversation with General Conway, whose situation, at the head of a great profession, differed so essentially from mine, that I did not hesitate to urge him not to quit it, on account of inattentions which, in my judgment, he was not called upon to put on the same footing as those to which I was daily subject.

I had the satisfaction to find the next day, that my friends, from different quarters, congratulated me on the step I had resolved on, by retiring from a post I held on such a footing ;

and they assured me, that the world did justice to my motives.

I was this day informed from the best authority that M^r. Pitt was advised to go, from many of the most independent and respectable members of the House of Commons, to advise, and even press Lord Shelburne to withdraw. His lordship however, was not persuaded to take the advice; but determined to wait and see the event of the next day's debate. My reflection at the time was, that this ill timed resolution could tend to no other end, than disgrace to himself, though the parties formed against him would find from it a further facility to join: and thus it became the cause of greater difficulty to those, who wished to see a Ministry so formed as would have satisfied the nation.

On the 21st Lord Camden called on me in the morning, and after much lamentation on the alarming state of public matters, he told me that he was fully determined to quit his office, but that he should take every precaution to make it particularly clear that his resignation should not be interwoven with Lord Shelburne's retreat: he was anxious that his lordship's conduct on the present occasion should neither guide his in reality, nor in appearance. Lord Camden's decision pleased me much, as I told him: for his character entitled him to take his own part, whenever he thought the ground good, and honorable, without being actuated by the decision of any person whatever.

On the motion of censure, even on the preliminaries, the Opposition carried the question by seventeen. It was universally agreed that M^r. Pitt's speech on this occasion was a most wonderful performance, and justified the high opinion which the world had conceived of his abilities. The few who blamed it, as much too long, acknowledged its excellence in every other light.

From the best information I could pick up that morning, I was assured that Lord North and M^r. Fox had so far agreed, as to desire that the Duke of Portland should be the person to confer with His Majesty, if either of them was called on for his advice. It was added that they expected carte blanche.

It would be difficult to describe the resentment shewn by the independent part of the nation on the expectation of a junction, which brought discredit on the leaders; nor were those without just reproach, who had been considered as supporters, on principle, of the measures of these differing parties.

On the 23rd of February the Duke of Richmond called on me; in the whole of our discourse on public matters, I do not know that we differed on any: for we had none on his Grace's idea of equal representation [1], indeed our wishes for the public benefit coincided more than the prospect of obtaining the object was flattering.

At night Lord Shelburne summoned those who were in office, and who were brought in since the overthrow of Lord North's Ministry; where he very handsomely thanked them for their support, stating that he desired to bias no longer their future conduct; that he had taken his own determination; for he should acquaint His Majesty the following day that he should give up his employment.

He was accordingly at Court: but what passed between His Majesty and his lordship is merely conjectural. The House of Commons were ready and able to carry any personal vote against him: and appeared only to give him decent time to make his retreat. In a conversation which I had at St. James's with Lord Gower, I could see no inclination in his lordship to take in this juncture an active part: though his rage against the factions of the day and the disgraceful leagues which were forming was truly well founded.

However, a report was strongly current the next day at the House of Commons particularly and indeed generally in

[1] The Duke of Richmond had expected to succeed Rockingham as leader of the Whig party, and certainly had stronger claims than the Duke of Portland. But he was a Parliamentary reformer before his time, and was too advanced a Liberal to suit the Rockingham Whigs. They only sought to curtail the power of the Crown, and in this respect the Chathamite Whigs, Grafton, Shelburne, and Camden, had more genuinely popular views.

the world that His Majesty with the Chancellor, Lord Gower and Lord Stormont were patching up an Administration [1]. I could not believe from what I knew of Lord Gower's good sense that he would in such days risk himself at the Treasury, and I am more certain that nothing should have induced me to take a part in it, and though my name was included in the supposed arrangement I did not hear of it till I was acquainted with it at night by Mr. Fox: my assurance to him that I was ignorant of such a plan made him directly distrust the probability of the whole. I am sorry that I did not inform him that it was my determination to have no share in any Ministry which did not proceed on the desire of once more reuniting the Whigs. I thought that the present opportunity afforded the means of effecting such a work: and that if it was not made use of for such a purpose, would be a reproach for ever to those who had the means in their power and neglected them.

General Conway having been for some days confined to his room had heard no more than myself of what was passing, except by report. He told me, that the Duke of Richmond who had just left him was no better informed. We discoursed much on our particular situations; I entreated him who was at the head of so great a profession to precipitate nothing: that awkward as circumstances were, still his line was very different from mine, that being at the Cabinet as Commander in Chief, he had a distinct situation and that when a formation took place it would then be time enough to consider whether he liked the Cabinet well enough for him to become a part: as he might still with the greatest credit continue his command and attend on the business of the army only. I admitted that this plan could only be adopted on a supposition of the Ministry being so constituted as to have his general approbation, without any material objection to its measures. I said this in consequence of the General's pressing me for an opinion: and he assured me, that he would follow

[1] Such a Ministry was, for a moment, in contemplation (*Memorials of C. J. Fox*, ii. 42).

my advice so far as not to take any step without having first my opinion upon it.

It was now reported and credited that Mr. Pitt was to become the minister, persuaded to it by the Earl of Shelburne, and as such recommended by his lordship to the king. My reflection at the time was, that so young a man, though endowed with every talent that ever was the share of mortal to possess, could not, with his inexperience, suit that situation. I am sorry for it if it proves true, for his own sake, as well as for that of the country. I could hear nothing on the subject the next morning from any authority ; which strongly induced me to believe, that there was nothing settled : for I thought, that there would have been a desire expressed to know my opinion, at least on the arrangement, had it been at all advanced. However, at night, it appeared, that there had been a strong desire to place M^r. Pitt at the Treasury ; for his friends declared that they were empowerd to say, that he had declined the situation, after having been much pressed to accept it. The good judgment of so young a man, who not void of ambition, on this trying occasion, could refuse this splendid offer, adds much to the lustre of the character he had acquired : for it was a temptation sufficient to have over-set the resolution of most men.

After the failure of this attempt, I was at a loss to guess what scheme would be devised by the Court. The king's unwillingness to have a solid and firm Administration is wonderful : and the narrow policy of St. James's continued still : and perhaps it is the source from whence have flowed those misfortunes and sufferings, which Europe is enduring. Past errors have not to this day awakened them to see the cause of all; though from the pertinacity of the American War, the whole may be traced.

The present transaction was however cleared up to me the next morning February 28th by Lord Camden. I found from his lordship that M^r. Pitt did actually alter his decision, from the morning of yesterday. Lord Camden also acquainted me with the language he had held to M^r. Pitt and with the

most friendly and salutary advice which he had given
him. M^r. Pitt acknowledged to him that no one else had
spoken to him in that open manner, or flung such light on
his situation.

His young friends M^r. Pitt said had indeed said everything to dissuade him from taking a step so hazardous; but
their inexperience could not open the whole to his eyes in
the manner Lord Camden had done: he further owned that
the ground on which he was to tread was rotten, and he felt
plainly that the Court on which he was to depend for support
could withdraw it at a nod. By all this it appeared to me
that Lord Camden's fair and judicious advice went as far or
farther than any thing besides to cause him to change his
resolution.

M^r. Pitt probably was not apprized that Lord Camden
and myself might still withdraw, as the Ministry would no
longer be reckoned to be the body of the Whigs called up to
administer the king's Government. Lord Camden however
in this conversation fully cleared up this point to him, namely,
giving M^r. Pitt no hope even of a temporary delay, in giving
up the Presidency of the Council.

Lord Camden then told me, that having been desired by
Lord Shelburne to attend at S^t. James's, where His Majesty
would ask the opinions of his principal servants on the most
proper steps to be taken, he went thither, and was called
early into the Closet. His lordship frankly told His Majesty
that having been named to take his part in an Administration
formed from the body of the Whigs, he acknowledged that he
could not resist a prospect, at that moment, so flattering to
the country; but he had now to lament that from various
circumstances this pleasing scene was blown away: Lord
Camden said, that for his part he thought of retiring and
rarely meddling on political points in the House of Lords:
he added that he had been born, and educated a Whig, that
he never could act with men of different principles, and therefore, that he could only give such advice to His Majesty as
was conformable to his own opinions, and way of thinking:

namely for His Majesty to place his confidence in those men, who he firmly believed would conduct public affairs most to the king's honor, dignity and happiness; and to the satisfaction of his people. As to himself Lord Camden said, that from his retirement he should always gladly step forth, if His Majesty's just prerogative should at any time be attacked, in like manner as he should if any bad minister was attempting to infringe on the rights of the subject.

On the 1st of March at night it was reported that a sort of message had been sent to Lord North but this was contradicted the day following; though it was my opinion that it would still end in the Administration falling back into his hands; that M^r. Secretary Townshend and Lord Rawdon[1] were to be raised to the peerage was more confidently asserted.

On the 3^d of March Lord North was with His Majesty for two hours, in the evening; and it was understood by the friends of the Cavendishes, Lord Fitzwilliam[2] &c. that Lord North had so firmly laid before the king the necessity of a new Administration having the recommendation to the head of the Treasury, that his lordship came away *re infectâ* though his honorable conduct was much cried up by his old enemies, now become his new allies.

On the morning of the following day the Lord Chancellor was for a considerable time with the king: probably in consequence of this interview Lord North was again sent for in the evening. The morrow therefore, it was imagined, might produce some approaches to a Ministry: though I thought that all hopes of a satisfactory Government for the country were at an end.

[1] Francis, second Earl of Moira, and Baron Rawdon in the Irish peerage (1754–1826), was raised to the English peerage in 1783, became Lord Hastings on the death of his mother in 1808, and Marquis of Hastings in 1813. He was Governor-General of Bengal and Commander-in-Chief in India from 1813 to 1821.

[2] William, second Earl Fitzwilliam (1748–1826), inherited the fortune of the Marquis of Rockingham in 1782. He was one of the group of Whigs who joined the Pitt Ministry in 1794. His brief and unfortunate tenure of the Lord-Lieutenancy of Ireland is shortly characterized in Lord Rosebery's *Life of Pitt*, 174–184.

Late at night was brought to me as Lord Privy Seal, Lord Thurlow's patent for a conditional pension, with a clause expressing His Majesty's promise of the first vacant tellership, given at the time when he became Chancellor.

The next morning I was credibly informed, that Lord North had waited on His Majesty the day preceding, in consequence of the king's having desired him to take that time to consider the answer he would finally give to the offer which was made to him. Lord North immediately expressed, that it was impossible for him, or any of those, with whom he was now connected, to carry on the king's Government, unless they were allowed to recommend to the Treasury. His lordship then mentioned that the Duke of Portland would be the person to be submitted for His Majesty's approbation. There was no objection in His Majesty's breast to the Duke of Portland in any other situation. The king added, that he declared himself to be ready to appoint any neutral man, who was of no party; and to prove that even the alliance now formed should not stop that disposition, he was willing to see Lord North himself there again. But on that lord declining every thought of it, the king wished him a good night.

During this doubtful state of political arrangements, I met with a private injustice done to my friend Mr. Stonhewer, who received a notification of the Treasury decision, that no compensation would be given to him, in lieu of the place of historiographer, which he had held ever since the time of my grandfather, who gave it to him.

As this decision differed from what I had been allowed to say to Mr. Stonhewer, I wrote to Lord Shelburne on the suspicion of some mistake. In answer to mine which was ineffectual, I received a letter, claiming merit, that he had left Mr. Stonhewer in possession of two other places, to which I replied that the places being under patent, his lordship had no power over them.

March 8th as well as the preceding days, negociations of various kinds were on foot, on the king's part, as well as on that of the new coalition. Lord Gower saw the king very frequently, and I believe, that he was ready to take an active part, if M^r. Pitt could have been prevailed on to step forward. In the mean while, the coalition was in daily expectation that the Duke of Portland would be sent for by the king. Without being able to guess even what would be the issue of all these ministerial intrigues, I proposed to Lord Jersey and the Duchess to go down and pass a week together at Wakefield Lodge. While we were there, we received intelligence that the king had consented that the Duke of Portland should be at the head of the Treasury: but in that case, His Majesty expected that Lord Stormont to whom he understood there was no objection, should be one of the Secretaries of State. On the Saturday Lord North returned to the king with the answer of the united parties, who desired to decline the acceptance under this injunction. I know for certain that the Duke of Portland had not then seen the king.

On the 18th I returned to London and found matters almost in the same state as when we left it. On this day M^r. Coke [1] declared that he would make a motion on the Friday following on the state in which public affairs were left. At night, at Brookes's, M^r. Fox took me aside with a desire of recapitulating what had happened since I left London. He did this rather cursorily, and the only circumstance new, or worth remarking, which appeared to me, was that which gave cause for their objection to Lord Stormont as Secretary of State, exclusive of the consideration of his prior negociation [2]: it was, that he never could have been cordially under the same injunctions, as they all were, relative to the influence of the Crown. M^r. Fox acknowledged however, that without the Cabinet, his friends would have had no objection to Lord Stormont's holding either the President's office or that of Privy Seal. M^r. Fox's mind otherwise occupied did not allow

---

[1] Thomas William Coke (1752–1842), Earl of Leicester, 1806. He was a Whig, but a keen upholder of the agricultural interest, which in a practical way he did much to advance.

[2] The attempt in conjunction with Thurlow and Gower to 'patch up an Administration.' *supra*, p. 368.

him to see the impropriety of this expression towards Lord
Camden and myself, to whom he certainly wished to be
attentive and friendly.

As I was dressing the next morning M^r. Fox called on me,
acquainting me that the Duke of Portland was sent for that
morning for the first time, and was then actually with the
king.

M^r. Fox added that after a variety of arrangements and
changes of situations Lord North was now inclined to be
Secretary himself rather than to have Lord Carlisle[1] in that
post: and himself without an office at Cabinet: and that he
M^r. Fox concluded that the plan would be offered in this way
to His Majesty.

I could wish, said M^r. Fox, if you would allow me the
freedom of an old and intimate acquaintance, not under the
appearance of minister, to hear your opinion, on what we are
doing; especially as I know that many of our friends think
us wrong. I answered him frankly; 'with you, Charles,
I shall not hold myself up, as I might perhaps be justified
so to do towards another: but I will tell you plainly and
without hesitation, that I am of that number; and that I
do dislike your junction with Lord North and his friends
extremely. Yet in the present state of the country, I do not
see what better can be now substituted; as you have unfortunately put an end to the union of the Whigs, with
whom, and for whom alone, I could ever wish to be in office.'
He then proceeded to ask me what my friends who were in
office might think on the subject. But as he gave me no
authority to say any thing to them, I could only answer that

---

[1] Frederick Howard, fifth Earl of
Carlisle (1748-1825). He held various
offices in Lord North's Ministry, and
was Lord-Lieutenant of Ireland 1780-
1782. He resigned on being removed
by Lord Rockingham from the Lord-
Lieutenancy of the East Riding. He
was Lord Steward in the Ministry of
Lord Shelburne, but resigned from
dissatisfaction with the peace. In the
coalition Government he was Lord
Privy Seal. His poems and plays were
hardly dealt with by his ward, Lord
Byron, in *English Bards and Scotch
Reviewers*, and not altogether on their
merits. He appears to greater advantage as a letter writer. See his letters
in *Selwyn and his Contemporaries.*

they were at perfect liberty to speak their own minds; and by no means to be considered as biassed by mine: indeed if I was to sound them myself, it would be more than probable that they would give no decision, until they saw more of the present formation. In the course of our conversation, it appeared that M^r. Fox would gladly have seen Lord Camden retain his office; and as to mine he had a full right to dispose of it, since he knew well from myself, that I would not form a part of his new system.

On the 21st, the day following the Duke of Portland's interview, a misunderstanding took place between the leaders of the coalition, which had disunited them for a while, as hastily as it had been brought together. To me M^r. Fox wholly acquitted Lord North of any sinister design: and it required all his good temper and weight with them to reconcile the circumstance to his party. For it seems Lord North, unauthorized by them, had offered the Presidency of the Council to Lord Stormont, who accepted it at once.

On this occurrence, the Duke of Portland desired leave to acquaint the king, that they were no longer able to form such an Administration as they had proposed.

M^r. Fox gave me this account, with the addition of a circumstance, which I never heard, except from him, that his Grace had offered to undertake the formation of a respectable Ministry, without including Lord North. His Majesty answered that an Administration so composed, could not succeed: and the king, M^r. Fox observed, could not conceal his joy on the Duke of Portland's declining.

I told M^r. Fox fairly, that I was not sorry that this negociation was at an end, since it appeared to me, that the moment presented itself, by which something better might be formed: and I asked him, whether the Whigs might not now be again re-united: he replied, that he questioned the practicability of the measure; and said, that he should still endeavor to bring back the others.

At noon, the next day, however, the parties rejoined; and Lord Stormont was to be accepted in the situation offered to him by Lord North. A list of the Cabinet was immediately laid before the king, who wished now to know further of their measures and plans; a difficult point for them to enter far upon; and which, in that stage, could only be stated on general ground.

On the 22nd the formation of a *new* Administration was by many considered to be so much advanced that M^r. Coke had dropped his intended motion yesterday: I heard however, from good authority, some circumstances which made me still doubt whether it would be easily settled.

My brother the next day from S^t. James's brought me word, that it was there believed, that the formation of Ministry was entirely at an end. The Duke of Portland, as my brother said, stated to His Majesty, that if he was not fortunate enough to possess so much of his good opinion and confidence as to be allowed to speak of measures, as his minister, it would be of no effect to state them as a private man, he could not think of entering into that situation.

I have good reason for believing that the king saw M^r. Pitt directly afterwards: but nothing transpired relative to what passed.

At Lord Fitzwilliam's at night, the matter became public by the Duke of Portland relating what had passed at the audience that morning. The company was numerous, and expressed their approbation, that the duke had desired to decline giving a list of the removals, which had been intended. A determination was also taken to support M^r. Coke the next day in his motion; and the acceptance of Lord Stormont into the Cabinet was justified by this assemblage on the plea of necessity.

During these transactions I kept as much as I could with decency from attendance at Court: for I was so thoroughly disgusted with all that I saw, or heard, that I wished not to come near the scene. I went however to the levée the day following, merely that it should not be said, that I kept purposely out of the way of being consulted on the present alarming dilemma. I stopped there more than an hour afterwards, to see whether there was any wish to know my sentiments : but not being called in, I came away fully as well satisfied, as if I had been commanded to deliver them. I talked there much with M^r. Pitt, Lord Howe and others ; but I could see no indication to incline me in the least to think, that the former of these gentlemen aimed at this particular moment to take the lead in public affairs. I mentioned to M^r. Pitt that I knew he was acquainted from my son, that the ground, in my opinion, would be infinitely more advantageous for him than it had ever been before, provided he judged it to be firm and clear enough in other respects for him to engage : and I had desired my son to add, that I could acquaint him, that he would now meet with both support and assistance, which could not at a former occasion have been given to him. He was called in, which prevented me from having the opportunity of adding what I did say to others : that an Administration, to be successful and honorable, must stand both clear of M^r. Jenkinson's [1] etc. influence and of that of the Earl of Shelburne.

M^r. Coke's motion passed in the House without a division. M^r. Pitt declared that there was no Administration formed : but those who said that he knew of none forming went beyond his words.

At night, among other fabrications of the day, it was reported that I had been with the king in the morning, and was to come to the head of the Treasury. There never could be less ground for a report.

Tuesday, March 25th. The king having departed into the country the preceding evening, to return on Wednesday, the day offered nothing but conjectures on what might next be produced. Lord Gower and Lord Camden met by accident at my house, but nothing passed beyond ordinary conversation. When I was alone with Lord Camden he seemed to think that

---

[1] Charles Jenkinson, the first Earl of Liverpool (1727-1808). He held various subordinate offices between 1761 and the date of his death : he was much in the councils of the king, and the king's friends, and he figures frequently in the Rolliad. The 'etc.' may be assumed to mean the Court.

M[r]. Pitt might actually have it under consideration whether in the present difficult situation of affairs he ought not to stand forward. Lord Camden could see the ground in no better shape than before. I confessed, that I did; as the embarrassing and unsettled affairs of the country called for the best Government that could be procured, and that it was only at length in the failure of all other attempts, that M[r]. Pitt might now acquiesce, on being called upon, to do his best for the public service. Lord Camden saw the situation of M[r]. Pitt, with the eye of an honest but cautious statesman, while I viewed it with that of one too sanguine, I doubt. But the dread of the bad consequences, which I thought would turn out from this confused state of public affairs, overbiassed probably my better judgment.

Indeed if Lord Camden had seen matters in the light I did, and could have been induced to take an active part in a Ministry to be so formed, I should not have hesitated to have offered my assistance likewise: in case the Cabinet should be composed of men of our principles. I must observe that the dread of the mischief arising from the success of the coalition would have been a principal motive with me.

On Friday, March 28th, the king put off his levée but saw M[r]. Thomas Pitt [1] for some hours; but nothing transpired to the public. On the afternoon of the next day, Lord North was again sent for. The king pressed him much to undertake the Ministry. He assured His Majesty that it was not in his power; and begged leave to decline it. I made up my mind, on hearing this, to expect the Duke of Portland with the wretched coalition to be, the next day, the men fixed on who were to govern us. And if this last plan for an Administration should be dropped, the king would be driven to fall on some desperate step.

The king might have been served on the most honorable ground, if His Majesty would have given them his full confidence [2]. Now it is too late; and the coalition too strong to

---

[1] The nephew of Chatham; created Lord Camelford in 1783, died 1793.

[2] This sentence is enigmatical. It cannot refer to the coalition. Probably

allow of any besides themselves. The country is against them, as is the Court : who can then imagine, that it will be of any duration ?

March 31ᵗ. Mʳ. Pitt, after the levée, resigned the Seal of Chancellor of the Exchequer. On this being known, Lord Surrey deferred his intended motion, as the object of it was now answered by the expectation given, that another arrangement would come forward ; which was considered as looking solely towards the coalition. Some few persons, however, thought that if Lord Temple[1] was on his road to town, a negociation might be tried with his lordship, before it went finally to the coalesced party.

On the day following, Lord North was sent for again by His Majesty so late, that it was not known, when I left Brookes's at 12 o'clock.

On the 2ⁿᵈ of April while at breakfast, I received the king's commands to be at Sᵗ. James's with the Privy Seal at noon. I was the first who was called into the Closet: after some complimentary expressions, His Majesty said, that it had been his hope, that the Privy Seal would have remained fixed in my hand. On which I assured His Majesty, that in holding, or in quitting this, or any office, I had never been, nor ever should be actuated by any other consideration, than the desire of being of service to His Majesty, and to my country: with a due attention to my own honor and character ; I even added, that when I was last dismissed from this employment, I was driven to oppose an Administration, which, as I had then ventured to mention to His Majesty, were bringing on ruin to their country by pursuing the American War, instead of making peace with colonies which were still ours, and establishing it as they then could for ages

---

there is an omission : ' them ' must mean ' the Whig party,' and the Duke has failed to express his meaning.

[1] George, eldest son of George Grenville, the minister who passed the Stamp Act. He succeeded his uncle, Earl Temple, in 1799, and was created Mar-quis of Buckingham in 1784. He was at this time Lord-Lieutenant of Ireland. Cunningham writes to him : ' If you had happened to be here now you would have the Treasury laid at your feet.' Buckingham, *Memoirs of George III*, i. 174.

on the surest ground. I had at that time presumed to state
to His Majesty that the attempt of subjugating the colonies,
though backed by a great foreign force, was as vain as it afterwards proved : and I would wish to be allowed to prognosticate that the present coalition would neither give steadiness
to the measures of his Government, nor satisfaction to the
nation.

I said that I honored many of the individuals who composed
it, and who were to be his servants; but their union appeared
to me to be so disgraceful to themselves, and so little calculated
by the use we see them make of their experience to . . . . . .

Here abruptly ends the Diary, which I quit with some
concern; as I well know how much more exact it was, and
deserving of confidence, than the best of memories can
pretend to.

We here have just seen the various political struggles for
power; which have at length terminated in the Coalition
Administration [1]. Though it was formed of men differing
much in political principles, yet the preponderance was so
great on the side of M[r]. Fox, that had they been trusted with
the king's confidence, I am satisfied that they would soon
have shewn themselves to the public, as more deserving their
favor. And no person questioned the talents of most of those,
who filled the principal offices of Government.

The Duke of Portland became First Lord of the Treasury,
with Lord John Cavendish, the Chancellor of the Exchequer ;
Lord North and M[r]. Fox were appointed Secretaries of State.
Lord Keppel returned to the head of the Admiralty, Lord
Stormont was declared President of the Council ; and the
Earl of Carlisle had the Privy Seal given to .him. But the
Great Seal was put into commission ; and so remained for
some time.

The principal attention of the House of Commons was
called to the corrupt and restless system of government
which had prevailed in India for years back, but was now too

---

[1] The struggle lasted from February   when the king resolved to give way.
24, when Shelburne resigned, to April 1,

alarming to be deferred. Though every one felt the necessity of great and effectual corrections; yet the means of remedy were differently viewed, and occasioned much contention, even where good intention was to be found. It was asserted by ministers, that the situation of the Company was almost desperate; and that unless the Bill passed, which had been brought in by the chairman, Sr Henry Fletcher, the Company would become bankrupt. This business, with that of the loan, which was not thought to have been made on very advantageous terms by the new Treasury, took up the greatest part of the session; though it must not be passed over, that the Quakers, in a petition to the House of Commons, laid a foundation for an abolition of the slave trade, which after many fruitless attempts to put an end to the abominable traffic, stands at this moment still among the crying sins of the nation. Besides these, it must not be forgotten that M^r. Pitt brought in a Bill for the reform of Parliament, on the specific plan of adding 100 members to the counties, and by abolishing about as many from the Burgage Tenure rights, and the places become insignificant: though warmly supported by M^r. Fox the motion was overruled, by 293 to 149. A specific proposition will always struggle to disadvantage.

The Parliament which had been prorogued about the end of July 1783, was convened for the 11th of November following. In a week from that time M^r. Fox introduced the Bill he had prepared, with a view of correcting the abuses under which the Government of India laboured: and with the intention of furnishing the most effective means to restore to some order the deranged state of the finances of that country, which was now become so considerable a portion of the British Empire. If parts of M^r. Fox's plan were harsh and alarming to many from its very boldness, they were likewise so to many, on the apprehension that the Bill granted powers, which hereafter might contend with the influence of the Crown itself. These were the great objections, for few would venture to deny that M^r. Fox's plan bore the stamp of the great and able statesman who had introduced it: when it was allowed by all, that the Government in India required no common measure of correction.   But the Bill on another ground will always be remembered, as having in its progress brought on the overthrow of one Administration, of which I have already said so much ; and of the firm establishment of another, whose ill-judged measures had not long after nearly driven us into a war with Russia our natural ally ; and did afterwards actually plunge the nation into a war with France which I shall always execrate as unnecessary [1], and of which I cannot speak with patience, because I shall ever be convinced that the distresses of Europe now derive their source from the mistaken counsels of the Ministry which governed England at the time.

[1] Grafton seems always to have felt a great horror of war: but here he expresses the policy of the Whig party, which throughout our long struggle with revolutionary and imperial France was generally mistaken and not unfrequently unpatriotic.   That ' it is plain that war with France was the deliberate choice of the English Ministry' is stated by Lord Russell, *Life of Fox*, ii. 308, and was no doubt an article of faith with the Whigs and with the Whig historians, who worked their historical materials (to use the words of Sir George Trevelyan) ' according to the good old Whig processes.'   Mr. Lecky, *History of England*, vi. 131, and Lord Rosebery, *Life of Pitt*, 128, have sufficiently exploded these fallacies.

CHAPTER XIV

FARMING, hunting and other country amusements, together with attention to the concerns of a large family, had employed the greatest part of my time since the prorogation, and I received at Euston the letters which I subjoin, as being on public matters. The two first are from my very old and excellent friend M^r. Hopkins.

MY DEAR LORD,

It is impossible for me to refuse the application made to me, to trouble your Grace with the following.

M^r. Pitt sent to me, desiring he might see me this evening, and accordingly called here. His conversation was upon the business which engrosses all conversation, and upon which I sent you two successive notes [1].

He (M^r. Pitt) wished most anxiously and earnestly to know your sentiments; he did not know how to write himself, but begged me to do so: he said things were drawing to a crisis,— matters would run very near in the House; and the consequence perhaps would be such, as to make it much desired to have your Grace's assistance and advice in what here-after might follow, as well as upon this Bill.

His visit was so long, and he pressed me so much to write, that I did not know how to deny; and yet I am almost afraid you will think me too forward in so doing; assuring you at the same time, that I have not presumed to give any opinion, and have been merely passive in the business.

[1] This letter is dated the 14th of December. The India Bill had been taken up to the Lords by Fox on the 9th. The interview between the king and Temple, at which the royal influence was engaged against the Bill, took place on the 11th. The Bill was thrown out on the 17th. The urgent message sent in this letter by Pitt to Grafton suggests, what Lord Stanhope denies, that Pitt was aware of the scheme of Thurlow and Temple to obtain the use of the king's name for the rejection of the Bill. Stanhope, *Life of Pitt*, i. 155.

It is supposed that there will be a division to-morrow upon a motion for some papers : but that the question upon the 2ᵈ reading of the Bill will not come on till Wednesday.

As I shall be uneasy till I hear from you, in giving me a line (though you shall not reply to the particular subject) you will infinitely oblige

My dear lord, &c.

R. HOPKINS [1].

BRUTON STREET,
Sunday—10 o'clock. *Decᵣ*. 14, 1783.

MY DEAR LORD,

I return your Grace a thousand thanks for the honor of your letter, which reached me about seven o'clock this evening. I communicated the substance of it, as you desired, to the gentleman in question, whom I met with at the House of Lords.—He seemed and expressed himself much concerned at your wish of retirement.—At the moment, I stumbled upon the son of the peer you speak of in your letter, who knowing (not from me) that you had been wrote to, asked me whether I had heard any thing from you, or to know your sentiments, or something to that effect. I did not mention any thing to him, but judged (and I hope I have not done amiss) that there could be no harm in repeating to the noble lord the purport of your letter. I need not write what he said ; because I am confident you will hear from him. I prefaced to him, that I had no authority for telling what your Grace had expressed ; but that I took upon me on public considerations to do so.

The papers will tell you all that passed yesterday : the Prince of Wales divided with Administration in the minority[2]. The three remaining counsel were heard to-day, and by mutual consent, the debate has adjourned till to-morrow : and the House broke up before nine o'clock. The proposition came from Ministry ; so that it is looked upon as letting the thing down easily, and the Bill is regarded as given up.

A very large assembly is met this evening at Mʳ. Fox's : we shall know the result to-morrow; when some warm motion is expected in the Commons. Lord Euston, who came to town yesterday, and who meant to set out for your house to-morrow, will stay over the day here, and will carry you an account of what further may be produced. These are strange and serious times.—Though I rejoice that the Bill is thrown out, I am not yet ready to say, that the overthrow of the Ministry at this moment is a desireable event.

I am told, that his Grace of Bridgewater (who voted against the Administration) complains much of a friend, for having misrepresented to him the Bill while it was pending in our House, and in which his

---

[1] Hopkins was M.P. for the Duke's borough of Thetford.

[2] This was on a motion for adjourn-ment, on the 15th, when ministers were in a minority of 8.

members voted in support of it. I will trouble you no further, than to beg my best respects to the Duchess and to subscribe myself, &c.

R. HOPKINS.

BRUTON STREET,
    Decr. 16, 1783.

Two days after I received the following from M^r. Fox :—

S^t. JAMES'S PLACE,
18th Decr. 1783.

MY DEAR LORD,

I lose no time in acquainting you, that we have just received our dismission, and that a dissolution will undoubtedly take place immediately. I take it for granted, that you will like to have the earliest information of this event; and will you permit me, on the score of old friendship, just to suggest to you, that it is worth while to enquire into the means by which our successors have come in; and the ground on which they stand, before any honest man gives them his countenance.

I am very sincerely, my dear lord, &c.

Yours ever,
C. J. FOX.

The day following brought me a letter from M^r. Pitt in these words :—

MY LORD,

I lose no time in troubling your Grace with the information, that His Majesty has proceeded to change the Administration, and has been pleased to impose on me the burden of the Treasury. I know not whether I may presume to hope that your Grace can be induced to give the new arrangement the credit and advantage of your assistance, as a Cabinet Minister. If your Grace's mind is not decided against it, and should upon consideration of all the circumstances, be disposed to afford so essential a mark of your countenance and support, I have the king's commands to propose to your Grace the situation of Lord Privy Seal, as imagining that it would be that which would be most agreeable to your Grace.

I trust, I need not express how truly I feel the value of your Grace's approbation and concurrence on such an occasion. I flatter myself, that your Grace will allow me to request your presence, on those grounds, if you can make it convenient to you; and if you will have the goodness of indulging me with an opportunity of stating to you more fully the present situation. At all events, I shall be proud to be honored with your Grace's commands, and happy in any opportunity you will allow me of obeying them to the utmost in my power, in any arrangement that is formed. I have been the more encouraged to trouble your Grace on this occasion from the very flattering expressions of your Grace's sentiments, with

C c

which I was honored through M^r. Hopkins; of which I beg to express the full sense which I entertain.

I have the honor to be, &c.

W. PITT.

BERKLY SQ., Friday night, Decr. 19th, 1783.

The letter from Genl. Conway, of which I give you the subsequent copy, came to me on the same day :—

LONDON, 19th Dec^r., 1783.

MY DEAR LORD,

His Majesty having changed his Administration, though I can at present only tell your Grace that he last night at 12 sent for the seals from Lord North and M^r. Fox, I think it my duty to give your Grace this early information, as the dissolution of Parliament is looked upon by all as a thing certain. I should have written a little sooner this morning, but that I wished to have been able to speak with absolute certainty on this head.

In regard to myself, I have only to say, that I have the most sincere sense of your Grace's goodness, in having honored me with so flattering a mark of your friendship, and good opinion, as the choice you have made in recommending me to the borough of Bury, and that I hope you will consider your own convenience and inclination in your future disposal of it : holding myself ready to obey your summons, if you have any commands for me on the present occasion.

I should not omit to inform your Grace that I am going to beg His Majesty's permission to resign my present post of Commander in Chief, for reasons which I flatter myself you will not disapprove ; and on which I should have been happy to have consulted you, if the time had permitted.   I am, my dear lord, &c.

H. S. CONWAY.

To M^r. Pitt's letter I returned directly the answer which I transcribe :—

EUSTON, Decr. 20th, 1783.
4 o'clock p.m.

SIR,

In duty to His Majesty, and in obedience to your wishes of seeing me in London, I can do no less than set out to-morrow for London, where I hope to arrive early on Monday morning.

My acceptance of His Majesty's most gracious offer must depend on that stating of the present situation which you are desirous I should have from you.   I have the honor, &c.

GRAFTON.

R^t. Honble. W^m. Pitt.

---

[1] Grafton brought Conway into Parliament for Thetford in 1761 and 1768, and for Bury in 1774 and 1780. Conway retired in 1784.

I arrived in town on the 22^d, where I saw and conversed with many of my friends, on that and the following day, as well as with M^r. Pitt, who was extremely zealous that I should take a part in his new formation. But contrary to his wishes, I could see nothing to encourage me to come forward, where even Lord Camden declined to lend his name to the system. On the 24th I set out to return to Euston, and after seeing M^r. Pitt again, at his particular desire, early on that morning, I parted from him in perfect good humour, but without the least profession of support from me. His object in desiring this last visit, was that he might have the hopes of the assistance of my friends in Parliament: to this application I only replied, that they were at perfect liberty to follow such conduct, as their own inclinations pointed to them to be the best.

As I passed by M^r. Hopkins's door from Berkley Square I stopt to acquaint him with what I had just said to M^r. Pitt. During the course of the day, M^r. Pitt called himself on M^r. Hopkins, strongly pressing his point, that he would return to office, which M^r. Hopkins declined upon the ground that, being the only one of my friends who came into office, he should not so much shew my disposition to support, as his own eagerness for a lucrative employment; and that the world would say, that he was disregarding what those did, to whom he was bound by so many repeated obligations.

M^r. Hopkins wrote me word, that if I had desired him to accept, he should have done it; but, being left to his own choice, he had acted according to his best judgment.

At Court this day, M^r. Fox told the new minister, that he might consent to adjourn till the 8th of Jan^{ry}.

In a letter from Genl. Conway, dated on the 4th of Jan^{ry}. from Park Place, after expressing his desire of subscribing for the relief of the poor at Christmas, he has the words which follow :—

I concur most sincerely with your Grace in lamenting the miserable condition of our public affairs, and the distracted state of our councils. They have been long tending, I think, to that dangerous state of violence

C c 2

and cabal, rendered much more imminently so by the enormous load of our debt, our loss of territory, and many other symptoms of decay. I, at the same time, see the means of redress as very hopeless indeed : particularly from the ambition and impracticability of individuals, who are somehow grown to be necessary parts of systems ; not so much personally so without doubt, as because they are made so by those who suppose them so. Perhaps your Grace, and I might think the country would do as well if all of them, at least, if some were withdrawn ; for in truth when politicians grow to a certain size, there is not room for them all.—Weighed intrinsically, I should be clear of opinion there was : and that the abilities of all are not a bit too much for the exigencies of the hour : but being of such incongruous and incompatible natures, they can unite in no plan ; and that, I doubt, is an evil without a remedy. We do not so much want them, as we want that they should not disturb one another, and suffer some Administration to be permanent. But as none of them, I believe, will, if they can help it, some solid power and support seems necessary,—as we cannot prevent the will,—to prevent the power of disturbing it. And this, I fairly confess to your Grace, has made me, through many strong objections, incline of late to the concurrence with the late Administration, whose formation I could not approve, and not till other combinations had seemed impracticable ; which I doubt have daily grown more so.

A system of Administration (and one having flaws too in it) forced upon His Majesty, I much dislike ; but a system against the bent of the House of Commons, and supported only by the Crown, I take it to be impracticable. I should be happy indeed, if with the aid of your Grace, and such as are more able than myself, I could contribute my mite to soften the asperities of the times, or to promote in the midst of them measures essentially salutary to our poor, almost sinking country : but I thoroughly feel my want of weight and ability for such great things, though I should never be discouraged from the attempt should others more able see the least opening for them.

You will not be displeased, if I insert another entire letter from the same worthy friend.

LONDON, 19th Jan'ry., 1784.

MY DEAR LORD,

I feel desirous to write a few words to your Grace, though it is by no means in my power to do it so clearly, or satisfactorily as I could wish in so interesting a moment as the present : particularly on a point your Grace will naturally be so curious about, as the dissolution of the Parliament. Your Grace will have seen in the publick papers and votes the different steps taken in Parliament to ward off that desperate and dangerous measure : they are thought by many to be such as must be effectual, from the difficulty of evading, or counteracting them; as well as from the promise apparently given in His Majesty's answer to our address. But the determined silence, since observed by the ministers on that head, and the refusal of any explanation on the wording it, which left a loop-hole to evade the promise, have introduced a doubt on that question, which some little manœuvres about boroughs have tended to encrease, and as the language and present appearances at Court seem to speak a resolution in the Ministry to go on, the minds of men remain suspended between the belief of two things unknown before, at least since the Revolution: either of an Administration going on with business, in a time of difficulty, with a decided majority in the House of Commons against them, or the dissolution of a Parliament in the midst of a session, and with much important business depending. In this situation of things, I dare draw no conclusion, and leave it to your Grace's better judgment. The votes past have been strong—the resolution of the Court is so too— and there are, as usual, many recriminations, on the inconvenience and mischiefs likely to ensue. I confess, that I think the line stretched to the utmost on both sides. It was hoped, the strength on the side of Parliament would have been decisive, at least, for some new settlement; but that seems to lessen; and the late admission of my friend the Duke of Richmond into the Cabinet, who had before declared against it, certainly appears much otherwise. Lord Shelburne is come to town rather unexpectedly: but I have not heard yet, for what purpose. This is the present state of things, by no means a pleasant one for the public, or for individuals; especially those who have no ends to serve. The City have addressed, as you will have seen, against the late Ministry; and to-morrow there is a meeting advertized at a strange out of the way place in London for the same purpose in the county, which will probably be a mobbing business, being, I understand, in the purlieus of S^t. Giles.

Friday is appointed for M^r. Pitt's East India Bill, which will probably be the term of decision for future measures.

I hope your Grace has been so good as to have my little commission executed relative to the charity, and am, my dear lord, with the greatest truth and respect, your Grace's most faithful and

Obedient servant,
H. S. CONWAY.

I believe that there never was a more upright character than that acknowledged by all to be in Genl. Conway; nor could even his military ambition, though tempted by the possession of the first post in our army, cause him to swerve from what he might conceive to be the strict line of rectitude. Neither he, nor Lord Camden, though a much

respected friend of M[r]. Pitt, were to become a part of the
new formation ; so that I had little temptation to join in it
myself.

From the time of M[r]. Pitt's Ministry commencing, that
gentleman was perpetually pressing Lord Camden to accept
of the Presidency of the Council, from which Lord Gower
would readily remove to the Privy Seal.   At length his lordship so far yielded, as to say to M[r]. Pitt, that if I could be
prevailed upon to come into the Cabinet, at the same time,
it would put an end to the difficulties he had felt on the
subject.   On this declaration, M[r]. Pitt set heartily to work :
but on his finding perhaps more impediments in his project,
in immediately producing the arrangement for two openings,
Lord Camden said, that he would assent to coming into
office, provided that I would declare to M[r]. Pitt my readiness
to come into the Cabinet, whenever such an office could be
opened, which I thought I could execute with credit to
myself, and advantage to the public.   To this I readily
assented, and had in June 1784 my interview in Downing
Street with M[r]. Pitt ; when every thing passed to the expectations of us all ; it being particularly stipulated, that Lord
Camden might be assured, that no time should be lost, in
finding a suitable entry for me into the Cabinet ; and that, on
my part, such a one was to be accepted by myself.

Soon after this business was rightly understood Lord
Camden passed over to Ireland, on a visit to his amiable and
excellent daughter, at Mount Stewart.   From thence I received a letter from him, dated on the 13th of August 1784.

MY DEAR LORD,

The letter you honored me with, though it bears date the 31st of July,
did not reach me till yesterday, the 12th of this month, having been, it
seems, missent to E—— such is the carelessness of our Post office. Here
it found me removed from all the scurrilous and frantic sedition of Dublin,
which, as far as I can learn, does not extend beyond the limits of that
metropolis. For the two subjects that have inflamed that city do not
much affect the country at large ; viz., the loss of the protecting duties,
and that restraint of the Press, which in truth does not more than check
the license of the newspapers, and the circulation of hand bills, by obliging

the printers of both to put their names to the publication [1]. The first bears hard upon the woollen manufacture, which is principally carried on in Dublin: the other affects only the publishers of newspapers who are the reproach and nuisance of both the kingdoms. This might easily be corrected by the law; the other requires some consideration, and might possibly be so modelled as to satisfy both countries. But there is one question that seems to have taken possession of the whole kingdom, and that is the reform of Parliament, about which they seem very much in earnest. For who does wish so much for that reformation at home, cannot with much consistence refuse it to Ireland: and yet their corrupt Parliament is the only means we have left to preserve the union between the two countries [2]. But that argument will not bear the light; and no means ought, in my opinion, to be adopted, that is too scandalous to be avowed.

I foresaw when we were compelled to grant independence to Ireland, the mischief of the concession; and that sooner or later a civil war would be the consequence; a consequence ruinous to England; but fatal to Ireland: for she at all events must be enslaved either to England or France. This people are intoxicated with their good fortune, and wish to quarrel with England to prove their independence. Big with their own importance and proud of their volunteers they are a match, as they imagine, for the whole world. But as Galba describes the Romans 'nec totam servitutem pati possunt, nec totam libertatem.' This misfortune would never have happened, if our Government had not been tyrannical and oppressive. As to the D. of Rutland, who has been so cruelly and publicly insulted in Dublin, the resentment, though expressed against him, is in truth against England; for he has not been long enough in Ireland, either to be loved or hated, and has done nothing that can personally be imputed to him: and therefore any other person would have been as curtly treated as he has been. So much for Irish politics. The country, Dublin excepted, is very quiet, the reviews have been repeated, and the spirit of volunteering is not so brisk as it was. The gentlemen grow tired of the expense, and if both countries are in good humor with each other, this army would soon moulder away and expire.

I am, my dear lord, very happy among my children, notwithstanding the cold and wetness of the season. How the weather has been in England, I don't know, but here I have never yet ventured to change my winter cloaths or go abroad without a great coat. We are settled at present in a temporary house, built up in a hurry to hold the family till

---

[1] For an account of the agitation in Ireland on the subject of protective duties, see Lecky, *Hist. of England*, iv. 353. Foster, the Chancellor of the Exchequer, carried the Press Law, 23 & 24 Geo. III. c. 28.

[2] 'Corrupt Parliament' must mean 'the corruption of Parliament,' and Camden clearly thinks that the corruption of the Irish Parliament alone made its independence compatible with the union.

the great house is erected; it is not half finished, and we live in rubbish and among workmen: so the place is all alive: nor do I dislike this scrambling and shifting; though we are obliged to breakfast, dine, and sup in the same room. My apartment is a snug cabin upon the shore of a vast arm of the sea, and commanding a very fine and extensive prospect. The seat when finished will be a very noble one, but the plantations tho' large are yet but young. The great defect of this country is want of wood: in other respects it would not yield to England except in climate, being so much farther to the north, as it is both pleasant and fruitful. Here I forget all politics, and would to God I might be permitted to dwell in the same obscurity when I return to England; but that it seems must not be, and therefore I shall shorten my stay here though unwillingly, and come back by the middle of next month. I shall be very happy to spend a day with your Grace before I get home, but that will depend upon the place where I embark. If I go to Holyhead, Wakefield will be directly in my way. If I come through Scotland it lies too wide of the road. I expect my son here in a few days, who gives me hopes of prevailing upon Lord Euston to be his companion. Farewell! my dear lord, I am tolerably well, and so is the rest of the family here, who all command me to present their compliments to your Grace. I am, my dear lord, with the highest respect and perfect attachment,

Your Grace's, &c.

August 13th, 1784,   CAMDEN.
MOUNT STEWART.

If your Grace should honor me with a line you will be pleased to direct to me at N. T. Ardes by Port Patrick.

Lord Camden not long after his return became once more Lord President of the Council, and I was consequently ready to fulfil my engagements to him and to M^r. Pitt: but my accession to a seat at the Cabinet was frustrated as well by objections of my own, to hold the seal of the Home Department, as from scruples of delicacy, which made me stipulate that nothing should be attempted to place me, where Lord Camden desired I should be, except with the perfect good will of L^d. Carmarthen, an honorable nobleman, to whom I had personal obligations, on account of the earnest part he had taken, in my cause, in that curious transaction in the beginning of the winter 1780 in the House of Lords [1].

---

[1] In November, 1780, the Duke of Grafton and Lord Pomfret were sum- moned to appear in their places, on account of a challenge sent by Lord

At Newmarket I received a letter from Lord Camden acquainting me what was passing concerning the means of gratifying him in the desire he had of having me as his colleague in office.

MY DEAR LORD,

I will make no apology for not writing sooner, because I am sure your Grace will suppose, as is true, that I had met with nothing worth communicating. M^r. Pitt went to Brighthelmstone the day after I passed through London; and I had no opportunity of seeing him till last night. After the first compliments, I was put in mind of my promise; and M^r. P. told me, he had mentioned to Lord G. his wish that he would consent to exchange his office for the Privy Seal, and believed he should find no difficulty in obtaining that compliance; that he had not yet found an opportunity of sounding L^d. C. as it was not easy for him to make such a proposal as might tempt him to retire from his present situation, but that it was upon his mind and your Grace as well as myself might be assured, the very moment any vacancy in the Cabinet could be procured that your Grace would condescend to accept, it should be done. I told him, that I was not quite satisfied with a general promise, the performance of which might be delayed to an indefinite time: as it was of the last importance to myself, to have a certainty of your Grace's assistance, and that though your Grace had signified to him, that you would be willing to wait, and did by no means press to have an opening made immediately for yourself, I could not be quite at ease, unless I saw a certainty of your Grace's being joined with me in a reasonable space of time. I must do M^r. Pitt the justice to say, he expressed as earnest a desire as myself to a close and intimate political conjunction with your Grace, and saw chiefly the great utility of giving the Cabinet so clear a Whig complexion, as our accession would make it. I then proposed to him, to feel L^d. C.'s pulse upon the subject, adding, that if his lordship testified a willingness to accommodate himself to this arrangement, that I did believe it would satisfy your Grace, and I should then have no difficulty in taking my part immediately: and I did suppose, that if he represented to his lordship, that upon his compliance, he might have both of us, but otherwise could obtain neither, his lordship might see how very proper it was not to stand in the way of such a proposal. M^r. Pitt promised me to take that step the first opportunity. I must not forget to inform your Grace, that he said he could with more facility dispose of the other

Pomfret to the Duke. The House passed a resolution commending the conduct of Grafton, and sent Lord Pomfret to the Tower, whence he was released with censures after a few days, on his making due expressions of submission and regret (*Lords Journals,* vol. xxxvi. p. 188).

Secretary; to which I answered that your Grace had expressed so strong an aversion to that department, that I did not believe that you could be prevailed upon to accept it [1]. I have now given your Grace the substance of what passed in the fewest words: and so the matter stands at present, waiting till some further progress is made, with which your Grace shall be acquainted, as soon as it happens. . . . I am, my dear lord, with the firmest attachment, your Grace's, &c.

CAMDEN.

Sep[r]. 29th, 1784,
    ADMIRALTY.

The latter part of the letter being on private concerns I have omitted it.

I cannot give you so clear an account of this transaction, as by the letters of Lord Camden, which are indeed the only means I could resort to, myself; where I had any doubt on what had passed. The next letter came to me about a fortnight afterwards, and is here copied :—

MY DEAR LORD,

You may be assured that nothing has happened, since I had the honor of writing to your Grace, worth the trouble of a letter, nor should I now have written, but that I am to set out to-morrow for Wales, where I shall probably be detained a fortnight; and it is not fit your Grace should remain all that time in ignorance of what is going forward. I have not seen M[r]. Pitt since my last, owing to my absence from London, and his frequent journies to Brighthelmstone, where he went again yesterday: and there he proposes opening his purposes to Lord C. by letter, as conceiving that a better way than first to break it by a personal conference. He has no doubt that he shall be able to prevail, *with the entire satisfaction of Lord C.*, for he understands that neither your Grace nor myself will in any other way consent to his removal: and that M[r]. Pitt might be perfectly apprized of your Grace's sentiments in that particular, I read that part of your letter to my son, in order to let M[r]. Pitt know that Lord C.'s free consent and willingness were indispensable to this arrangement. And indeed he is under such obligations to his lordship, that he is bound by every tie of honor and gratitude to leave the measure to his option and good pleasure: so that your Grace may be assured there can be no impediment to your Grace's acceptance from that quarter. If that difficulty is removed, I should hardly allow your Grace's plea of disability, or fear to undertake so arduous an employment, to have the weight of an unsurmountable

---

[1] Lord Carmarthen was Foreign Secretary, and Lord Sydney (T. Townshend) was Home Secretary.

objection.   If that was sufficient in your Grace, who are now in the very vigour of your age and the ripeness of your understanding to warrant a refusal, what can it be said to me, who am in the last stage of life, where both mind and body are in a state of decline, and are every day tending downwards towards total incapacity. In reality, such is my backwardness to embarking in business, that nothing but the comfort of your Grace's support and co-operation could have prevailed upon me to alter my determined purpose (for so it was till I was over-ruled) for final retirement.   And, I am afraid, if I know my own feelings, I should perhaps be pleased at my heart, and almost thank your Grace, if you should, by withdrawing yourself, give me an honest excuse for breaking off.   But indeed, my dear lord, there is a great difference between us ; and the disadvantage in the comparison is all on my side.

It were very much to be wished that the Privy Seal might return to your Grace, and Lord Gower shifted to some great Court office : but his lordship it seems is too fond of the Cabinet to quit that situation : and yet I heard lately, from L^d. Sydney, that he was afflicted with a frightful and alarming disorder in his eyes, so as to become incapable of either reading or writing. He described it as a very serious malady. If it should continue, or grow worse, he must, whether he will or no, bid adieu to all business. I am again asked whether your Grace is so absolutely determined against the post of the Home Secretary. I answered, as I did before, it was my opinion you was, though it was said that office was now relieved from the single responsibility of India matters by the establishment of the Board of Controul [1]. As I have not seen M^r. P., all that has passed between us has been conveyed by my son. I hear no news : such is the barrenness of the present times ; and the newspapers themselves are dry, and can hardly find scandal enough to fill the pages. I have read the Dean of St. Asaph's trial, and confess I can see nothing libellous in the paper ; and am besides more displeased with Judge Buller's behavior [2], than I was formerly with Lord Mansfield's conduct. Something ought to be done to settle this dispute : otherwise the controul of the Press will be taken out of the hands of the juries in England, and surrendered up to the judges.   I am, my dear lord, &c.

Octr. 13th, 1784.   CAMDEN.

In a subsequent letter of Novr. 1st, Lord Camden, speaking of the right he had, after what had passed between us—to call upon me for my assistance, if a fair opening could be made in the Cabinet to receive us both—tells me that he had seen M^r. Pitt, who shewed him that this could not at

[1] The Board of Control was established by Pitt's India Bill of 1784.
[2] *infra*, p. 898.

present be accomplished : for though Lord Carmarthen has consented in the handsomest terms to accommodate to this arrangement, yet he refuses to accept of any other employment, by which it is evident, that this consent, when stripped, he says, of its courtly cloathing, is no better than a discontented refusal ; and cannot be accepted by me, M^r. Pitt, or by L^d. Camden. To which I perfectly agreed with his lordship, as well as in that door being now shut.

The letter continues in these words :—

And now, my dear lord, what part does it become me to take ? I don't ask your advice, because I have taken my part already, and have agreed to come in, but I will state my own difficulties, and the true reason that prevailed upon me at last to accept. I am more averse than ever to plunge again into business in the last stage of my life. I do not like the Cabinet as composed : the times are full of difficulty, and the Court not much inclined to persons of our description. Add to this my own aversion to business, now almost constitutional, from a habit of indolence, and above all, the want of your Grace's support—the only circumstance that made me enter into this engagement—after I had over and over again given a positive denial. These you must allow were weighty considerations ; and yet, though I was fairly released by M^r. Pitt's failing to make that opening he had engaged to make, and your Grace's postponing your acceptance till the end of the session, yet, when I considered that M^r. Pitt would be cruelly disappointed, and perhaps in some sort disgraced upon my refusal, after he had engaged Lord Gower to exchange his office, and that I was pressed in the strongest manner by all my friends, and more particularly by your Grace, who was pleased to think my coming forward would be useful to the public, and help to establish the Administration, I took a resolution to vanquish my own reluctance, and to sacrifice my own ease to the wishes of other men. But I do by no means relinquish my claim on your Grace : for your co-operation is absolutely necessary to me ; and I shall never be happy in my situation till your Grace makes a part of it.

I now transcribe what relates to public affairs in another letter from the same noble and learned lord.

Novr. 29, 1784.

MY DEAR LORD,

As I have remained in the country ever since I had the honor of receiving your Grace's last letter, during all which time I have not seen M^r. Pitt, nor had any communication with the ministers, I did not think it necessary to trouble you with an answer till I was certain of my own appointment, which is now to take place on Wednesday. Lord G. for certain reasons, which I don't know, nor think it worth while to enquire, thought it convenient to wait till last week, before he made the exchange for the Privy Seal: and I am now called upon to fill up the vacancy. I go to it with a heavy heart, being separated from your Grace, with whom I had intended to have closed my political life—iterum mersus servilibus undis—at a time of life when I ought to have retired to a monastery; but as the die is cast I will go to the drudgery, without any more complaining, and do my best. As I have lost all ambition, and am happily not infected with avarice, and as my children are all reasonably provided for, according to their rank and station, I can have no temptation to do wrong, and therefore though in my present situation, where I don't ask the employment, but am solicited to accept it, I might, after the fashion of the world put some price upon myself, I am determined neither to ask nor to accept any favor or emolument whatever for this sacrifice of my own ease.   I have employed myself of late in examining with some attention the proceedings of the Court of King's Bench in the libel cause of the Dean of S^t. Asaph, thinking it probable it might have been brought by writ of error into our House: but they have taken care to prevent that review, by arresting the judgment, and so the great question between the judge and jury in this important business is to go no further; tho' it is now strengthened by a solemn decision of the Court which never happened before [1].

This determination in my poor opinion strikes directly at the liberty of the Press, and yet is likely to pass *sub silentio*. The newspapers are modest upon the subject, because M^r. Erskine is not to be commended by one party, or Lord M. run down by the other. Thus your Grace sees that public spirit is smothered by party politics.

The accession of Lord Camden to M^r. Pitt's Cabinet made me very friendly to it: and indeed it could not well be otherwise, after the assurance I had given, that I should be ready to take my part whenever a fair opening could be made for me. I continued with the same disposition, until the determination the Ministry had taken up of going to war with

---

[1] In the Dean of St. Asaph's case the jury found a verdict of 'publishing only,' in spite of the direction of Buller J., who tried the case, that the question of libel, or no libel, was not for them. Erskine moved for a new trial on the ground that the judge had misdirected the jury on this point. The King's Bench decided against him; but he was successful in moving in arrest of judgement, for the prosecution could show nothing criminal in the alleged libel (Campbell's *Lives of the Chancellors*, vol. vi. 414-418. 21 State Trials, 847).

Russia, had compelled me to differ with the minister on so
important a measure, and to give up all thoughts of entering
now into his Ministry.

Soon after Lord Camden was fully re-established in his
office, M^r. Pitt took up with much earnestness the object of
a reform in Parliament.   The time suited the attempt; and
the minds of men were more prepared to receive a temperate
reform than I am afraid they have ever been since.   Every
man can see the corruptions, though they endeavour to blind
themselves on the consequences of the sooner or later ruin,
which they unavoidably will produce.   I have ever been
a favorer and friend to the measure, and I cannot but
be surprized to find so few persons, who are in a constitutional light aware of their danger.

In 1782 it was voted by the House of Commons, that the
influence of the Crown was too great, and ought to be
diminished.   If that position was allowed by all thinking
persons to be well founded at the time it was so declared;
the increase of that same influence in the last twenty-five
years has become incalculable.   It is pleasing on such occasions to know the sentiments of eminent men.   I shall trans-
scribe, therefore, a letter I received from Lord Camden on
this subject.

MY DEAR LORD,

I find myself under a necessity of troubling your Grace at M^r. Pitt's
request upon a question which I have always thought of the highest
importance to the constitution : I mean the reform of Parliament.   And
if your Grace thinks upon the subject as I do, you will lend your aid and
the support of it, by imparting your wishes to such of your friends as are
likely to pay attention to your opinion.   M^r. Pitt is not assured how
M^r. Hopkins stands inclined to this measure; but is very anxious to
obtain his concurrence, unless he is really and conscientiously averse
to it.   At least he wishes, and would think that he may not unreasonably
hope, that he would give his vote for bringing in the Bill.

When I have said this, I have said all that becomes me to say on this
occasion, adding only, that M^r. Pitt's character as well as his Administration is in some danger of being shaken, if his motion is defeated by
a considerable majority.   I do confess myself to be warmly interested in
the event upon every consideration : and that perhaps is the best apology

I can make your Grace, for giving you this trouble, leaving it entirely to your own wisdom to judge how far it would be fitting or agreeable to your Grace to communicate your wishes to Mʳ. Hopkins.   I am, &c.

CAMDEN.

March 19, 1785,
    CAMDEN PLACE.

The general idea of the plan is to purchase out the small boroughs by the consent of the electors, and to add to the present number of the county representations.   But this addition only to take place gradually, as the said boroughs are extinguished by a voluntary disfranchisement [1].

Soon after this I got into a bad state of health, and was at one time quite unfit for public business.   However I was tolerably well at the time of the armament against Russia, which appeared to me impolitic and big with many pernicious consequences [2].   Mʳ. Pitt hearing from Lord Camden that such were my sentiments, he must perceive that with my opinion I could never wish or even submit to execute the duties attending the office of Secretary.   He desired to discuss the situation in which we stood with Russia over fully with me: and for that purpose Mʳ. Pitt would honor me with a visit.   He appeared to be very desirous to bring me over to his opinion on this threatened project.   We went into the whole matter, with much earnestness; but we differed entirely, though friendlily, on every point of the measure. I cannot pretend, at this distance of time, to bring to my recollection the different arguments made use of by each of us.   I can only say that neither gained any ground in convincing his friend, and that I was obliged at parting to say that Mʳ. Pitt must be sensible, that being unfortunately of an opinion so different, I could no longer be expected to take a part in the Administration.

I must here observe that a few weeks after this, Mʳ. Pitt, unwilling to meet the disapprobation of the nation, who were throughout clamorous against a rupture with Russia, was

---

[1] Pitt's Reform Bill was introduced on April 18, 1785, but was rejected by 248 to 174.

[2] For an account of the Russian affair, see Lecky, iv. 290 *et seq.*   The Ministry was more seriously shaken than Mr. Lecky seems to indicate. See Lord Rosebery's *Pitt*, 106, 108.

persuaded to abandon the measure entirely. However this change of dispositions towards Russia, though agreeable to my sentiments, did not renew in me the least desire of taking a seat in the Cabinet : and probably was a little wished for by M\(^r\). Pitt and most of his friends who now saw Lord Camden easy in his situation, without having me there as a colleague. After this I saw my excellent friend less frequently, tho' always with the same affectionate frankness as ever. His health was much declining also, and when he was confined at last quite to his house, he sent through his amiable eldest daughter his desire of seeing me. It was the last time I enjoyed that satisfaction, for I must so call it, as I found him quite placid and resigned : his conversation turned soon to religious subjects, which from the little time I was allowed to remain with him, could be treated but superficially. He enjoyed beyond belief the satisfaction of having seen the rights of juries, on matters of libel, clearly ascertained in his lifetime, and it is to his exertions, seconded by those of M\(^r\). Cha\(^s\). Fox, that we owe that essential decision which restored the law of libels to what Lord Camden had always held to be the true law of the land [1]. In one word, his heart was as good as his head ; and there never lived a more worthy man ; and the share of friendship with which he favored me I shall ever consider as one of the proudest circumstances of my life.

This memoir, which from want of further documents I can now no longer continue with the same precision and satisfaction to myself, will probably be more valued by my relations and friends than by other readers, therefore I feel less scruple when I have introduced genuine letters which though not directly called for, yet serve to ascertain the amiable character of those to whom I have been particularly attached : and when written in the natural and easy stile of Lord Camden's, they will have this effect beyond every other means. I shall only add this apology for making such use of them, that every line appears to me to open the good-

---

[1] 32 Geo. III. c. 60. For Camden's speech see *Parl. Hist.* xxiv. 1405.

ness of heart of the writer: and thus close my narrative with the following, to me, most interesting letters.

MY DEAR LORD,

After thanking you again for your kindness in shutting your door against me—the cause being more friendly than any hospitable admission at any other time—I must at the same time testify my concern to understand that this town is so prejudicial to your health as to disable your Grace from living in it constantly. I have myself the strongest aversion to it, and wish myself released every day from that business that confines me to it; nor can I long continue a public man. The infirmities of age make it impossible: and yet, so long as I continue to think of politicks (for I shall still think, when I have left off acting) I shall be happy to think I have the honor of holding the same opinion with your Grace upon all public subjects. We differ on the present measure. It is unfortunate that we are tongue-tied at present, and the Opposition at liberty to suppose any case for us they please. The measure I see is unpopular. We are too poor to risk the *possibility* of a war: though the intention is to procure a long and advantageous peace. I can say no more upon the subject.

I hope, however, I may be indulged in seeing your Grace when you return to London. In the mean time your Grace will believe me when I subscribe myself with perfect attachment, your most obliged and faithful servant,

CAMDEN.

Ap. 14, 1791,
    HILL STREET.

Nov. 15, 1793.

MY DEAR LORD,

Your kind attention to an old friend in sending him a parcel of game, gives him an opportunity of thanking your Grace at the same time for your constant and repeated orders to M^r. Heath for venison. I do assure your Grace that nothing can be so grateful to me as these remembrances from your Grace, as they remind me of the business we were jointly employed in, and the time we spent together in my better days. I am now with age and sickness so reduced and enfeebled, that, in my own opinion, I shall never recover sufficient strength for active business, or to sit again at the head of the Council Board. That is the worst side of my condition. On the other hand, I am certainly advancing in strength, though by very slow degrees. My head is as clear, and my understanding as good as it ever was; and D^r. Warren says that I have not an unsound part about me, so that it is possible that I may spend the few years I have to live comfortably enough. To give your Grace so circumstantial an account of my health would require some apology, if I had not been encouraged to believe your Grace had some interest in it,

D d

by the kind notice you have taken of me. I can't conclude without congratulating your Grace upon the excellent character, I think I may call it *Fame*, that Lord Euston acquired at Brighton: that by his discipline and personal endeavors he has raised his regiment to a reputation equal to the best of the regulars; that this has not been effected by the rigour of odious severity, but on the contrary he has contrived to win the love of his soldiers, without any faulty indulgence, and commands their obedience, as effectually as if they were over-awed by fear. I say nothing of his *private* popularity; your Grace knows his temper and disposition too well to require any information on that head.

I beg leave to assure your Grace that no part of this description is flattery. What I have said and even more was universally acknowledged by every person upon the spot; and no one gave a stronger testimony of concurring with the public opinion than His Royal Highness.

I have the honor, my dear lord duke, to be with real attachment and regard, your Grace's most

Obliged friend and servant,

CAMDEN PLACE.   CAMDEN.

MY DEAR LORD DUKE,

I trouble you for no other purpose but to thank you for your kind letter, and the rather as Bayham told me your Grace wished to know if I had received it. I rejoice to find that your health is so perfectly restored, and I take for granted D^r. Halifax is not so frequent a visitor as he used to be. A circumstance in your Grace's letter respecting spectacles, gives me an opportunity of observing that you are not in truth a day older by the use of them, and I would recommend my own success from the early use of them for your Grace's imitation. I took to them the moment I found that I was obliged to move my writing to a greater distance for reading and when I was many years younger than your Grace. The consequence has been that to this very moment I have been able to read by candle light as many hours as I can by daylight, without the least pain or inconvenience; and my sight though shorter is as strong as when I was 20 years of age. With respect to my own health, I am more restored than I ever expected to be, and if I can combat this winter, perhaps may recover so much strength as to pass the remainder of my days with chearfulness: but I do not believe it possible ever for me to return to business, and I think your Grace will never see me again at the head of the Council Board. It is high time for me to become a private man and retire. But whatever may be my future condition, whether in or out of office I shall remain with the same respect and attachment

Your Grace's most faithful friend and servant,

Decr. 7th, 1793,   CAMDEN [1].

CAMDEN PLACE.

[1] Camden died on April 13, 1794, being then in his eighty-second year.

'A NOBLE DUKE'

TAKEN ON THE STEYNE AT BRIGHTON

To face p. 403

LETTERS

C. J. Fox to the Duke of Grafton

My dear Lord,

I received yesterday your letter and wish very much for an opportunity of talking over with you the strange state of things. I must go to London the tenth of next month and shall not return to this country till the end of the month, by which time I may possibly be able to tell you something more than I now know of the sentiments of some of my friends.

I am very glad to hear that you are in health and not sorry that you are out of patience, for I am sure that is the state in which every man who loves the country ought to be. It does not appear by the Gazette whether or not the proposition in the French Declaration of a mixed garrison was adopted by Lord Hood, but the whole of the business, especially Lord Hood's two proclamations, is the most audaciously insulting to this country (after what was repeatedly said in Parliament last Session) that I believe any minister ever ventured [1].

Some persons think that the misfortunes in Flanders will induce the minister to think seriously of peace, but I am not of that opinion. The declarations and exertions of men like your Grace will I think have considerable influence upon public opinion, but whether even public opinion itself will be strong enough to control the Closet and Cabinet united, in the present very peculiar state of things is a matter upon which I have some doubt. But I am sure you, no more than myself, are one of those who think doubtfulness with respect to success any excuse for not doing one's duty, and surely it is a most important one to put an end to this most horrible war, and to stem the torrent of Toryism which threatens to overwhelm the constitution.

I conclude by your letter that you do not come to the first Newmarket Meeting which I am sorry for because I propose to be there for a day or two, and should have possibly an opportunity of some conversation with you.   I am etc.

THETFORD, 19 *Sept*. [1793 ?].   C. J. Fox.

[1] On August 27, 1793, the people of Toulon admitted Lord Hood's fleet, and, shortly afterwards, a Spanish squadron, to protect the town against the Republican forces. The proclamations of Lord Hood, in which he ac- cepted the charge of the city on behalf of the French monarchy, were considered by Fox to be a departure from the declared intention of our Government not to meddle with the internal politics of France.

MY DEAR LORD,

I shall be obliged to you if you would order the venison to be sent for me to Mackay, Oilman, Piccadilly.

I do not think of going to Norfolk this year till the second week in October when if your Grace is at Euston I will certainly pay my respects to you, or if not in my way back.

I will certainly get Porson's Orestes as well as his Hecuba, and indeed this is the sort of reading I now take most delight in, politicks are too bad to be thought of with patience, and I confess I see no remedy ; and so, why should one not consider one's own ease, and do nothing ? However if any plan can be struck out that holds out any rational prospect of restoring substance and energy to the constitution of the country, or of saving us from the certain ruin which the continuance of the present expense must bring with it, I shall always be ready to give my assistance. But while what we used to call the *exploded* principles of tyranny seem acquiring even a sort of popularity, and no countenance is given in any one part of the world to sentiments of moderation, liberty, and justice ; I own I completely despair, and feel myself quite excuseable in giving more attention to Euripides than to either House of Parliament.

I am very truly, my dear lord,

Yours ever,

C. J. Fox.

ST. ANNE'S HILL,
Friday,
[*Aug.* 1798].

MY DEAR LORD,

I am much obliged to you for your letter and I will write a line to your keeper about the venison.

I did not think it likely that you should have family papers that could be useful to me, or I should have taken the liberty of applying to you ; indeed if you have any of Lord Arlington's they would probably relate to a period earlier than that I have in hand, though as I touch a good deal upon Charles the Second's reign in my introduction, I should be glad to see them [1].

As to the work, very very little progress is made in it, and I make this hot weather an excuse to myself for being lazier every day. I am very far from being so conversant in Mr. Locke's works as you suppose me, but with that particular one which you mention I am very well acquainted, and think of it as you do. However, I will get the new publication of it as well as the Catholick Apology which you mention. When I say that I am not much versed in Locke, you will not I hope, suppose that it is from want of respect to him ; but the truth is that of all studies,

[1] Fox was collecting materials for his history of the reign of James II.   The first Duke of Grafton married the daughter and heiress of Lord Arlington.

Metaphysicks have always been the least agreeable to me, and I think they are still less so to me now than when I was young.

As to politicks the indifference about the expedition appears a deadly symptom, but I think it is a piece with many others. Perhaps it is owing to my strong presupposition that the public in this country is dead to every right feeling, that I interpret everything I see and hear the same way—that is—as a proof of my hypothesis and consequently as a justification of my conduct in retiring.

If I go to Norfolk at all this year it will certainly not be till after you are settled at Euston, and I will in that case certainly not fail in paying my respects to you.

There is a very good wheat harvest here, and a very bad crop of barley.

Yours ever,

C. J. Fox.

St. Anne's Hill,
   18 *Aug.*, 1800.

INDEX

THE END

E e